ISBN 13: ISBN: 978-1-942500-41-4
ISBN 10: 1-942500-41-4

The Guild Chronicles
Witches & Warlocks
The Hunter's Sight

J.M. DeMarco

J.M. De Marco

For
Michele Ambrosino
My Inspiration, My Guide,
My Grandfather.
You'll always be in My Heart!

Contents

(1) **Not Your Average Teenager**

(2) **The Vision**

(3) **Old Friends**

(4) **New Foes**

(5) **The Hunter's**

(6) **A History Lesson**

(7) **Trapped Like Rats**

(8) **Alec & Amber's Tale**

(9) **Disturbing News**

(10) **Brett & Lindsey**

(11) **Lunch at Logan's**

(12) **Through the Mist**

(13) **The Darkling Within**

(14) **The Origins of the Seer**

(15) **The Secret Library**

(16) **The Head of the Snake**

(17) **Foresight's**

(18) **The Forest**

(19) **Crystal Falls**

(20) **The Rings of Solace**

(21) **Truth & Consequence**

(22) **Hindsight's**

(23) **A Fury Unleashed**

(24) **Moving Mountains**

(25) **The Hunter's Sight**

(26) **The Riders of Arcaine**

(27) **A Spy Revealed**

Chapter 1
Not Your Average Teenager

Angelica

If we were to take the inhabitants of planet Earth and split them into categories, we would have two totally separate worlds. The Mortal, non-magical world, and the underground societies that make up the magical realm.

Hi Everyone! My name is Angelica Elizabeth Everhardtht, and I fall into the magical world category. On August 1st, I will officially be sixteen years old; the most important birthday for someone like me. It's the age where I'll finally be considered an adult amongst my peers. Now before I get to far ahead of myself. I think a little explanation is in order.

As you may have guessed already I'm not your typical teenage girl. I'm a Witch, but I'm not your typical Witch either. I'm what my people would call a Darkling Witch, which just means I am the strongest and most dangerous of my kind. In fact, I'm the only Darkling alive today. Darklings tend to not survive to reach their teen years. Most of them are killed, some kill themselves, and others just flat out disappeared. In my society Darklings are feared above all creatures, our powers are uncontrollable. Even to the Darklings themselves. That is why by law no Darkling can exist.

So, you may be wondering how I'm alive to be telling you this story? There is a simple answer to that question. My powers are being suppressed, but we'll talk about that a little bit later.

My society classifies its people into distinct categories; we're all born with a special ability. We could be Enchanters, Masons, Nurturers, Combatants, Seekers, Prophesiers, or Sorceress. Those are just a few of the categories that we can fall into. It's impossible to name all the diverse groups. We would be here forever if I tried to name them all. The truth is that they're is so many of us out there that I'm betting there are abilities that have yet to be discovered.

Right now, you're probably thinking that I'm totally insane. This is the Technological Era, how is it possible that there could be Witches walking the planet undetected? Well here's all you need to know, magic has been around for a long time, even in the earliest of civilizations. Magic helped create strong empires, and it also brought about the end of some too. Magic has had a major impact on your mortal society. Just look at some of the famous people that have stood out in your history books. Edward Tech or more commonly known as Blackbeard was said to have used black magic during his life. Well he most certainty did, he was a Sorceress Warlock (One of the nastiest of his kind!). Joan of Arc and Gandhi could get people to follow them because they were Enchanters. An Enchanter can make you do anything! Some of the Presidents of the United States were half Mortals, half Warlocks, whether they knew it or not is a different story. Some Half-Bloods never discover their true identities. I won't go into too much detail about Half-Bloods. That is a long story best saved for another time. But between you and me Half-Bloods are looked down upon in our society. Only the pure of blood can succeed in this world.

Anyway, we have this sort of mutated gene, that allows us to do stuff that is extraordinary (It's like that movie series X-Men, with that Hugh Jackman. He's one of my favorite actors.). The gene travels through the family line. It's very rare for a Mortal to be born to a magical family, likewise for a Witch to be born to a Mortal family, but nothing is ever impossible.

My people are called the Weir, and were separated into two distinct groups. Weirlind (Witches and Warlocks), and Weirling (Wizards). Now together both groups form what we call the Weir Guild, a Guild is our government. The Weir Guild has two separate ruling bodies, which I'll discuss shortly. We were the first Guild to ever form, and soon after us, other groups formed Guilds as well. Right now, there are four major Guilds, the two Weir, Vampire, and Werewolf. (No, I'm not joking, we all really do exist!) The Guilds can be compared to a pyramid. The Weir Guild on top, with the others "slightly" below us. I say that because everyone in the magical realm knows that there is no competing with the Weir Guild. The once powerful Vampire and Werewolf Guilds no longer exist. Their societies have shrunk back into the darkness.

Now you might be wondering what we look like. To tell you the truth I look just like you do. I'm about 5 feet 8 inches tall, skinny with light skin, long brown hair, and emerald green eyes. Hollywood does a poor job representing us, for instance in that really old movie The Wizard of Oz. We are not hideous looking with green skin, pointy noses and dressed up in funny clothing, and we don't have rosy cheeks, or have sparkly dresses either. We could be 80 years old and still look like we're twenty. That's because were immortal. We don't age fast like you Mortals do. We don't fly around on broomsticks either; all we have to do is snap our fingers and we can go wherever we want. We don't have cats as pets. Most of my kind hates them because the feline communities have an extra sense that allows them to see who we really are. (I hate it when the stray cats in my town hiss at me!)

We have been hiding amongst the Mortal communities for centuries, without drawing any attention to ourselves. You may be wondering why you can't spot us? Well first off, we don't advertise ourselves by wearing funny clothing (Well, some of us don't). My style of clothing would be a pair of jeans, sneakers, t-shirts and on special occasions a dress, simple and straightforward. Of course, I love to shop, and clothing is one of my favorite items to buy. (You Mortals are awesome when it comes to making trendy clothes. The Weir, not so much. We're still stuck in the old days were tunics and robes of pure gold are acceptable.) If you ever saw me on the street you would never know what I am. We're masters at blending in, and we've had years of experience hiding from curious eyes. The closest we've ever come to being discovered was during the Salem Witch Trials, but then you Mortals went totally insane and started accusing anyone who was even remotely different. The trials showed us that we had to be more careful around Mortals. Now we have eyes and ears all around the world. If anybody gets wind of a possible discovery, it's put to rest immediately before things get out of hand. However, I'm one of the few that believe that the real reason why you can't see us is this. Mortals are close-minded, you can't handle change well either. When something new and different comes along you immediately think that it is evil. It's not that you don't want to believe magic exists. It just your simple minds not willing to grasp that concept. I think its fair reasoning. Compared to the majority of my people that think you're just plain stupid.

As you can tell. I'm a very honest person. So, I won't lie to you. There are some bad Weir out there, but the majority of our people are peace loving. Mortals who see us as a source of money making have given us a bad reputation. Now the term Witch has a huge stereotype on it. Perhaps the worst stereotype you could make about us is to think that we use wands. It's those kinds of thoughts that will get you turned into a toad for sure. It's not so much thinking that we use wands. It's confusing us with are magical cousins that could be dangerous to your health.

Wizards have to use wands. Witches and Warlocks use hand magic, which is the purest form of magic there is. Wizards can only channel their powers through their wands. We don't need silly sticks to make our powers work. They also like to make fools of themselves by wearing pointy hats, and robes. Wizards are easy to spot if you know what to look for, most Magicians are Wizards; Houdini was a good example of one.

Both sides hate being compared to the other. You would not believe the uproar that occurred in the Weir community when the Harry Potter books and movies were being released. There are still arguments going on today about them.

The bottom line is. That we're two socially separate groups of magical people, even though technically most of us are related by bloodline. I mentioned before that both groups fall under the Weir Guild. There are only two shared Guilds. Ours, and Werewolves share theirs with the Shifters.

Both Weir races have been fighting for centuries, both sides trying to prove who is the more dominant race. Neither side is willing to back down from the other, and there have been massive amounts of casualties on both sides. Our constant fighting has had a profound effect on the weather; thunderstorms are 90% of the time caused by our ongoing conflicts. If you'd like a more gruesome example of our fighting with one another. Look at your World Wars, both sides were known for controlling Mortals and forcing them to fight. Some of us joined in the fighting. One Warlock can take out more enemies than a Sherman tank.

We have a bloody history that has been marked with controversy and violence, and it is my belief that the conflict will continue until both sides learn to get along. As of right now both societies operate as two separate ruling bodies, but there are many who want one large Guild. In my opinion the only way that will ever happen is if one group takes the other one over.

I'm sorry that I probably just bored you half to death with the history of magic but prepare to be bored even further when I discuss my families' origins. My family has turned out some of the strongest Witches and Warlocks of the past two millenniums. The Everhardtht's are one of the most powerful magical families in the world. We are an ancient family that dates back to the early 1700s. Originating in England. We were part of the earliest group of magical settlers to come to the New World in search of a new life.

In those days, it was hard being what we are, always on the run from those who wanted you dead. Luckily my great grandparents had each other. Lucifer and Marigold Everhardtht were gifted Combatants. They arrived in the New World in 1704 and were able to live freely in the new land for many years. Until it was decided by the newly formed Council of Weir that they were guilty of crimes of war. Even though no solid evidence was produced to convict them. They were sentenced to death in 1740, and the only way to kill us is to use magic. (Just for the record throwing a bucket of water on us can't kill us; we don't melt! Seriously, who ever came up with that idea!)? To this day, there is still no evidence to prove that they were guilty. My family suspects that the Council was afraid of them, and had them disposed of.

Anyway, before they died they had a daughter, my grandmother Greta Everhardtht. She lived with a Mortal family until she was old enough to survive on her own. Once the council discovered who she was they led a hunt against her. She was on the run for decades. She joined the Colonists, and the Union Army, pretending to be a man to escape the Council; in all she was on the run from 1751 to 1865.

Finally, the Council had abused its power to such a point were both societies of Weir rose to overthrow them. That event became known as the War of Council, a five-year blood bath starting in 1866 and ending in 1870. Unfortunately, Mortals got caught in the crossfire, numerous lives were lost, a total of 2,000 Weir and Mortals combined. Thanks to a little mind magic. Mortals have forgotten those times. Grandma was a crucial leader in the War of Council. Without her the Council may have won. Nevertheless in 1870, victory was finally achieved, and two new governing bodies were formed. The Covenant of Wizards and the Council of Hemlock.

Grandma eventually became one of the twelve members on the Council. It's their responsibility to set forth and enforce the laws of our kind. Grandma represents all Combatants in the world; the other groups represented are Enchanters, Prophesiers, Seekers, Sorceress, Scribers, Masons, Guardians, Healers, Cryptics, and Under-Fates. The other groups are too small to have a representative. A rule that is slowly fading. You see both governments were only supposed to have 12 representatives, but rules were broken, and the Weirling Government added three extra representatives. In my world, three extra leaders are a big advantage. Wizard representatives are responsible for the Weirling that live in their country. These smaller bodies of power are called Covenants.

Grandma is a Combatant Witch. One of the most famous Combatant Witches of all time. She won't tell me how old she actually is, but if my math is correct she has over 280 plus years of experience. It's her experience, and reputation that spared my life. Just like the Darkling's before me. I was meant to die. However, because I was born an Everhardtht, and being Greta's granddaughter, the Council gave her the chance to try and save me. She cast a powerful curse on me. One that would keep my true Darkling abilities locked away. As a result of the curse I have numerous side effects that have my family worried about my long-term health. But Grandma always tells me that this curse is only temporary. So, for as long as I can remember she has been training me to learn how to harness and control my powers.

Sometimes I get over zealous and want to do more than I'm ready for, but she's always holding me back. She'll never let me extend my powers to see just how far they will go. Every time I do she'll just say that I need to learn how to walk before I can run. It drives me insane but if I want to learn at all I must follow her rules. I don't mean to sound ungrateful. She saved my life, and I'll always be in debt to her, but I just so badly want to be my own person. I want to be the Witch I was born as, not this broken shell that I am now.

To add to my problems. I'm not only a Darkling Witch, but also my special gift is being a Seer. I can see images in the past and the present. Grandma says that it is a really rare gift, and that no Witch or Warlock in the world possess it besides me. There is no way to train for my ability. I just have to bare my visions when they occur.

Grandma was also the one that made me go to a local mortal school. She says that learning about Mortals is good training to becoming a knowledgeable Witch. Not that I mind, going to school is the only time I get to be normal, hanging out with my best friends Brett & Lindsey. I can always count on them to make me feel better when I'm down about stuff going on in the magical world. Of course, I can't tell them what I am. That would be breaking one of the most ancient laws set by the Council. I'm not that popular in school, but I am a straight A student. (Though I must confess that I use magic to get through my classes, but we'll keep that secret between us if you know what's good for you!). Sometimes it's rough leading a double life. My friends get curious about my home life every now and then, and I hate having to lie. I wish I could tell them, but I'm afraid they'll treat me differently. Telling them will also put their lives at risk, and I would never do anything to hurt them.

Getting back to my family, My Dad, Rowan Everhardtht is what we call a Nurturer. He's good with healing charms and spells. He can also talk to nature (animals, trees, stuff like that). Nurturer's are rare, and powerful. Can you even imagine what it would be like to control nature? I wish I could trade gifts with him, but he says mine is more special than his. He's kind and gentle hearted, always there for me if I need someone to talk to, but don't let that fool you. He's a brutal fighter when it comes to defending his family. With the forces of nature at his disposal you don't want to get on his bad side.

My mom Gwen is an Enchanter. People are attracted to her charms, and she can manipulate almost anyone to bend to her will (Like making me do chores the mortal way, without magic!). Finally, there's Merrin my 8year-old baby sister. She's a Combatant Witch like Grandma. She is what you would naturally expect from a baby sister, loud and obnoxious, always sneaking into my room. Sometimes I could just ring her neck, but I love her nonetheless (Just don't tell her that!).

Well that's my family in a nutshell. We all live in a small town near the Canadian/Minnesota border called Crystal Falls. Don't bother looking on a map, you won't find us! Crystal Falls is a magically protected community. There are dozens of magical communities like ours all around the world. The communities are different from one another, but they all have one thing in common. They're all hidden from the Mortal world.

My family has accumulated numerous amounts of wealth over the years. We founded Crystal Falls. So naturally we own quite a few buildings and shops in town. I get a lot of things for free, so it has its advantages, but it also has its disadvantages. You see I like to compare my family to Hermits. They never leave our hilltop manor. In fact, I don't think they have ever left our house to come down to the town. All interactions between the Mortals in town and my family go through my sister and myself. So, it's natural that the townspeople think my family is kind of weird. My families' absence from the town life is one of the reasons I'm not so popular in school. I'm the girl who lives in the house that is surrounded by a gigantic forest. I'm the girl with the wealthy, weird family that no one has ever seen.

We live like this for several reasons though, the first one being that we are what we are, and second, the falls themselves have their own magical qualities. There are crystals in the river, and each one of those crystals can heal any wound and rejuvenate anybody. Should they fall into the hands of a Mortal who knows what effects they would have. Not that anyone would ever come this far up anyway. The forest is infested with wolves and other creatures that report directly to my Dad.

I have lived in Crystal Falls my entire life. I've never seen anything outside of its protective borders. I can't say that I've never yearned to see the great big world out there. I mean that's all I've ever wanted to do since I was six, but my family says that it's too dangerous in the outside world. The town is literally protected by magical borders that not only keep trouble out, but they also keep us in. The Mortals living in Crystal Falls don't even know of the magical borders. Not like it would matter if they did; no one leaves Crystal Falls. If you're born here, you die here. That's what Grandma says all the time.

The Falls has a population of about 375 and everyone knows each other just like in any other small town. We have only one road leading in and out, no major brand name stores or restaurants. Just simple small-town U.S.A kinds of shops. The town only has one school and it plays host to grades K thru 12, Crystal Falls Community Preparatory School is the local hot spot for all the teens in town. You can tell it's a small town when the local hot spot for kids is the school campus. There is no college. Once you graduate school you go to work in one of the town's many stores. (Not much of a life to look forward to.) If it weren't for Brett and Lindsey, life would be miserable for me here.

Sometimes I wish I could just fly away and leave my life behind. I want to travel the world. I've always wanted to visit places like New York City or California. Seeing some of the beautiful landmarks that make this country so wonderful. Most of my dreams are about me living and viewing exotic places. Thank heavens for T.V. I love to watch movies if you haven't already guessed. Without television, I'd probably go mad in my house. Maybe I should just count myself lucky. I'm alive, and I get to live forever. I get to have whatever I want with the snap of my fingers. I guess I'm just being selfish though because I want more. Why can't I have both worlds? Is it selfish of someone like me to want to have more than what I already have?

What I didn't know though was that my life was about to change, but it was going to change in ways that I never expected. My eyes were going to be opened for the first time, and I was finally going to see the world. I was going to see all the wonder and glory that this planet has to offer, but I was also going to see its dangers and horrors. My views on my town, society and world are going to be forever changed. Innocently enough it will all start with a vision. A vision that was going to either be the best thing that ever happen to me or the worst. My name is A.E. Everhardtht, the Darkling Seer, and this is where my story begins…

Chapter 2
The Vision

Angelica
(June 30)

I've been having these visions since I was six years old, which is the age when young Witches begin to mature. When I first started receiving them, they would really frighten me. I remember waking up in the middle of the night. Mom would always be at my side telling me that everything was all right. I never understood what they meant back then, but as I have grown older I've learned more and more about my visions. For instance, sometimes I would see things that happened in the past, and they directly related to something I was currently doing. They always occur when my body is totally relaxed. So, all of them happen when I'm asleep. Once, I fell asleep in my English class, and apparently nobody could wake me. The school ended up calling the hospital. All I could remember from that day was my Grandma stopping the ambulance before it left the school. I can't recall the vision at all, or what happened after she got me out of the ambulance. When I asked her about it later, she quickly brushed the subject aside. I asked my classmates about it afterwards. They had no idea what I was talking about.

Anyway, this vision started just like any other one that I've ever had. As soon as my head hit the pillow tonight, I felt the usual tugging sensation in my head. The best way I can describe it is that it almost feels like someone has lassoed my brain, and started pulling it away from my body. What happens next is the part that always scared me. I go through this spinning vortex. I can't see anything around me, and there is nothing I can hold onto to keep myself from free falling. All I can do is close my eyes and listen to the thousands of voices ringing out all around me. I never could understand what they were trying to say, all those disembodied voices talking at once. I later realized it was like a VCR or a DVD player. If you hit Fast Forward, you skip through all the scenes that you don't want to see. My vision was fast-forwarding through thousands of moments in time to get to the one it was going to show me.

The trip tonight was shorter than usual, which normally means that whatever I was about to see happened recently. When I opened my eyes, I had to shake the dizzy spell off before I could see anything. Finally, when the room stopped spinning. I realized that I was in a large circular hall, and I wasn't alone. Dozens of eyes were glaring down in my direction. It was a bit unsettling at first, even though I knew they couldn't really see me. Which is a good thing, because whatever clothes I'm wearing at the time are the clothes that come with me during the vision. So, I'm standing here barefooted in my polka-dotted pajama pants and my tank top shirt. My visions are very lifelike. I can touch things, smell, and taste anything I wanted. Like right now I wished I had worn my slippers to bed. The floor was ice cold on my bare feet.

My Witches Sense told me that the people in this room were all Weirling. It was a mixed group of males, and females. Some were young, some were old, and then there were some that looked really old. All their eyes were fixated on another Wizard who was standing in the center of the room not too far from where I stood. He was a short man dressed in robes of green. On the back of his cloak was a jewel-encrusted shamrock with two wands crisscrossed below it. The shamrock was the centerpiece and the number eight was embedded in the center of it. His short orange hair was gelled downed to the sides; it was thinning in several spots, and his sideburns had visible signs of graying. His face was worn and haggard looking, but his green eyes seem to fill him with life. This was definitely an experienced Wizard. He appeared to me like a man who possessed a lot of knowledge, but also one who has seen a lot of heartache as well. I can tell those things just by looking at a person. It's one of the gifts that come from being a Seer.

Everyone sat frozen in time. It was like waiting for someone to press the play button; I sighed, I hate my visions. I'm not what you would call a patient person. I liked my visions to happen quickly, so I can get them over with and get back to my life. Worst of all, I seemed to have caught a vision already in progress. I hate these kinds, because now I had to try and figure out what was going on.

While I waited, I took a glance around the room. It was simply a marvelous sight. It was circular with a huge domed ceiling. There were dozens of arches, and columns all around the room. It was all white marble craftsmanship. Definitely not made by any Weir in this century. Wizard architects in this generation don't have the time or the experience in dealing with this kind of craftsmanship. This work was simply brilliant. Stain-Glass windows were on every wall. They depicted scenes of great importance in Weirling history. There were platforms surrounding me on all sides. Behind each platform sat a different Wizard. Even the chairs they sat in were works of art.

Grandma taught me a little bit about Weirling history. They split themselves into Covenants. There are currently fifteen of them. They were only supposed to have twelve representatives just like the Council of Hemlock, but in typical Wizard fashion they broke that rule. Each Covenant must be represented in Wizard politics. Each house would set forth a member that will represent them in the meetings. Each platform had a different banner that separated them from the others, for example the platform that sat empty had a green banner. It bore the same symbols that were on the Wizards robes. Obviously, the man standing next to me represented that house. The number eight represents the order in which his Covenant was established. The smaller the number, the older the Covenant is, and the more power it could wield in politics.

As I stood admiring the room, a thought occurred to me. I must be inside the Sanctuary, the legendary, impenetrable meeting place for the members of the Weirling government. This was a once in a lifetime opportunity. Nobody outside of the Covenant heads is allowed inside this room. Upon further investigation, I noticed that there were no doors. Either they had to teleport inside or there is a secret entrance that is magically hidden to keep them safe from their enemies. The Sanctuary is believed to be located somewhere in Great Britain, but Grandma believes that it could appear anywhere it wanted too. That's what makes it so impenetrable.

"Ignatius Clearwater of the 8th Covenant." Said a deep voice that almost made me jump out of my skin. Finally, someone had pressed play. The man who spoke sat in front of Ignatius Clearwater. His platform, and chair were noticeably larger than the rest. He was an older gentleman with shoulder length snow-white hair. He was dressed in robes of black and white. His banner had the symbol of a Golden Eagle; the number 15 was grasped in its talons. His face clearly showed signs of age, but just like Ignatius. His eyes illuminated his face. They were golden brown, and he looked as if he was staring right through Ignatius. I remembered Gran telling me that the Covenant with the Golden Eagle was the United States, one of the larger covenants. This man must be Hiram Garratty, the famous Wizard that's 400 years old. Garratty is famous for leading the assault on the original Council. Grandma said he was almost invincible on the battlefield. Being the largest Covenant meant that he is the elected leader of all the decision making that occurs between the Covenants.

"You have asked to speak before the Covenants today to set forth a counter-argument to the proposal set by the 4th Covenant earlier in the meeting?" Garratty asked.

"That is correct Master Garratty." Replied Ignatius. His accent was hard to understand. It was an Irish brogue. Obviously, he must represent the Weirling of Ireland.

"Then proceed, Master Clearwater." Garratty waved his hand in a sign of approval. He sat back in his chair and waited.

"As many of you know. I have been a pacifist where the possibility of a Weir War has been concerned. It is no secret that I'm a great advocate of peace between the Weir people and have done my best to spread that word onto others. I have argued every proposal that has been set forth that would declare a full-fledged Weir War, and I will do the same with this one. The 4th Covenant has once again proposed a plan that will bring us to the brink of a war. We cannot have that. If the Weir go to war, there will be massive bloodshed that will wipe out generations of people. The War of Council will look like a picnic compared to a Weir War. Not to mention the damage we would cause to the Mortal population." By looking at the bored faces of the other Covenant members it was clear that they had heard this discussion before.

"Excuse me Master Clearwater." Came a booming voice. Looking up I saw a man in black and red robes stand up. This must be the leader of the 4th Covenant. His banner had a fiery red dragon blowing flames from its mouth. Underneath the dragon there were words written in a language unknown to me. Then underneath the words the number four was inside the shape of the British Island. He must be the Covenant leader of Great Britain. "I'm sorry fellow Covenant leaders, but I've heard enough of this already." This man radiated dark energy. Definitely not someone you wanted to pick a fight with. He was tall and heavily muscled. His long black hair was pulled into a ponytail, and his piercing red eyes were fierce looking. His goatee stuck out like a cone on his chin. It made him look very funny, but you probably didn't want to tell him that.

"Proceed Master Valdorn." Said Garratty with a little irritation.

"Thank you Master Garratty." He said, nodding to the man, and then he turned his cold eyes onto Clearwater. If looks could kill, then Ignatius would be dead. "We've heard this a dozen times before. So, allow me to save us all the trouble of hearing it once again. Ignatius is more than likely going to propose that we get all goody-goody with our Weirlind cousins. A handshake, hugs, kisses, and all the rest of that bloody nonsense that he preaches. Let me remind you that they have no intentions of ever coming to terms with us. So why should we come to terms with them?" He said. Valdorn was very animated. He used his entire body to demonstrate his point. His booming voice echoed in the room; grabbing everyone's attention. Judging by their body reactions, most of the other Wizards feared him. There were only a few who did not waver under his stare. Garratty and Clearwater were two of them.

"My brothers and sisters. Jacoby Valdorn and his Covenant have traditionally been war hungry mongrels. In the past two months they have produced six plans for war. Their ancestors before them have always been prone to controlling others by force and fear, Mortal and Weir alike. However, in the end they do not care who they have to step over to get what they want." Ignatius said, his voice rising.

"We are visionaries! We see things as they apply to today, and what we see is the Weirlind thinking they are better than us. We are not born with extraordinary gifts, while their kind are born to numerous talents. All we can do is cast charms and spells through wands, while they can use hand magic. That doesn't mean were inferior to them though. We out number them in population, and I can guarantee that we can beat them in a battle." Valdorn shouted back.

"You are murderers! Who are proposing a plan that will get us all annihilated. We can't change who we are; we were born this way for a reason. There is no need to start a bloody war over who is the strongest. That is child's play!" Ignatius face was getting redder as he got madder.

"Preposterous! My plan is a full proof scheme that will allow us to strike a major blow into the hearts of the Weirlind. All we must do is strike a blow in the Council. Something that will get them out of their Hemlock stronghold. I say we target the only member that refuses to live outside the borders of Hemlock." My heart wrenched in my stomach, for I knew whom he was talking about.

"Are you mad? You're talking about Greta Everhardtht. The woman who we can credit to the main downfall of the Council of Weir. She is the strongest Combatant Witch alive today, who can destroy you before you could put your wand up to defend yourself." Ignatius said. There was a sense of pride in his voice. There was no doubt that this man knew my Grandmother somehow. I tried to read his mind. Another ability of a Seer. But for some reason I couldn't get through to him. I wonder if there was a spell on this room that prohibited the use of magic.

"Greta is not the Witch she used to be. She has grown soft over the years. She's been held up in that town for decades, and probably hasn't fought in years. She's rusty and weak." Valdorn said. I was really starting to get angry with this man. Gran was not weak. She could obliterate you in a second, and I was willing to bet my whole allowance on it (All five bucks of it!).

"Do you not realize what you are dealing with? Crystal Falls is supposedly located in a cold mountainous region of Minnesota. A state that has little magical activity to begin with. None of us have ever had to deal with those types of conditions. We would be on foreign ground with no means of navigation. Remember that town is said to be nearly impossible to find, and even if we do discover its location, it is just as much of a stronghold as Hemlock. More than likely there will be traps, spells, and enchantments that will alert them to our arrival. On top of all of that, we are more than sure that she controls the Mortals of that town. We would be vastly outnumbered." Ignatius said. I was gaining respect for him. He is trying to protect my family, but he knew an awful lot about my town. He was right about one thing though. There are several ways for us to know if danger was coming. (Not telling you of course! Got to have some secrets don't I!) I don't know where the whole controlling of the Mortal things came from though.

"We will find a way through the barriers. We're not completely incompetent. And what harm can Mortals do to us?" Replied Valdorn. "Besides, now is the perfect time. The summer brings cleaner weather, better for an assault."

"Let's say we do get through, what happens then? We must face off with the strongest family of Weirlind in the past millennium. They're all extremely powerful. Greta's granddaughter is a Darkling! Do you want to face off with that?" Came another heavily accented voice. A tall, dark skinned Wizard stood up. I didn't know who looked bigger, him or Valdorn. His muscles rivaled Valdorn's. He was dressed in robes of light brown. His banner held a pyramid with an eye in the center. Two sphinxes were flanking it on both sides. The sphinxes each held the number one in their mouths. The 1st Covenant was Egypt. That is where the first Weir society was located. Magic was born there. "How many people are you willing to sacrifice Jacoby?" I was happy that another person was against this plan. Being the 1st Covenant gave this man a lot of pull in the outcome of potential plans.

"Master Kahne, that is why they have to be the target. We need to hit the strongest..." when Ignatius cut him off I thought Valdorn would blast him on the spot. By the look on his face I could tell he was thinking about it.

"Jacoby does not care whether we succeed in this plan anyway. Even if we lose the Council will declare war, and that is exactly what he wants." He said pointing a finger at him accusingly. Valdorn's eyes were murderous at this point. "I have no intentions of sending any of my Covenant members to a suicide mission." He added.

"I believe I was speaking to Master Kahne, Ignatius. For someone who's supposedly so concerned for his people. He doesn't give them much of a say in decision making from what I've heard." Valdorn said with a sneer. It was Ignatius turn to glare daggers at him.

"Excuse me gentleman. As much as I hate to break up another argument between the two of you. I can't help but wonder what plan Ignatius would like to present to us." Came a sweet female voice. A beautiful Wizard stood up. She had long flowing blonde hair, and breathtakingly blue eyes. She didn't need to use hand gestures to get the groups attention. Everyone was gazing upon her beauty, and she was clearly enjoying every moment of it. "As much as I disagree with Master Valdorn and everything that comes from that big mouth of his. I for one don't feel like standing around waiting to be attacked." Her robes were a brilliant shade of blue and silver. Her symbol was a dazzling gray owl that was shrouded in mist. What made her robes more interesting was the fact that the owl disappeared, and reappeared at times. The number seven glittered in and out as well.

"My dear Heather Nockthowel. I have a simple plan. It's time we call a meeting between the leading groups and work this out." Ignatius said gently.

Heather just laughed. A beautiful sound that was almost as enchanting as her voice. I hate it when Witches use enchantments to attract others to them. It was obvious that Heather Nockthowel had tons of experience in that field. "Ignatius, the Council will never agree to meet with us. First, we outnumber them. Second, they will not allow us to enter Hemlock, and we in turn will never allow them in the Sanctuary. So where do you plan to hold this meeting?" She asked.

"A meeting will give them an opportunity to slaughter us all at once. Take out their biggest threats in one full sweep. The dealings wouldn't be fair anyway. I say we fight! It is the motto of my Covenant to attack before being attacked, and I will stand by that till the death." Shouted Valdorn. That must be what the unknown words on his banner meant.

"Jacoby you're an even bigger fool if you think we can simply overpower the Weirlind. Let's make no mistake here. The Council will not hesitate to act if they get wind of any planned attack. They have brilliant spies stationed all around the world. Do not think yourselves invincible. Every one of us is being watched. So how do you think we can get away with this full proof plan of yours?" It was hard to tell whose side she was on. She seemed to me like the kind of person that hated everyone. "I will not go up against the Everhardtht's. It is a fool's mission, and like I've already said you are the king fool." Heather said. On those words the entire hall erupted into shouts and chaos. Ignatius and Jacoby were the loudest amongst them.

"Everyone calm down and be seated!" Hiram Garratty announced. The fighting ceased immediately. "I have listened to your comments and have come to a decision." Everyone seemed to be drawn to him. He had a strong presence that no one would challenge. "We will not put this plan to a vote. It is one of our ancient laws that we do not declare war unless we are provoked. I will not be the first person to break that law. From now on I want no further talk of a proposed attack on the Weirlind." I breathed a sigh of relief as he said those words. Valdorn looked furious. I could tell he wanted to argue, but he would not challenge Garratty. "If any Covenant attacks the Weirlind. The leader will be held responsible and then stripped of his or her title!" he said glaring at the Wizards around him. He held Valdorn's gaze especially longer. Jacoby squirmed under his gaze. He was afraid of Garratty; I didn't have to read his mind to see that. "Now, on to another issue. I have been tracking the activity of both of your Covenants. Jacoby, Ignatius." He looked at Jacoby, and then at Ignatius. Both men wouldn't meet his glare. "It seems that there has been a lot of activity going on in both. I don't know what is going on, but I want it to stop now! I know of the bad blood between your countries, and I know of your history together, and your relationships to Greta Everhardtht. I can't help but wonder if there isn't a bigger picture that we're not seeing here." I guessed that there might have been some kind of relationship between Ignatius, and my grandmother, but I didn't expect there to be one with Jacoby as well. Neither one of them answered.

"Let us continue this meeting, and a change of subject is in order." Garratty said. With those words my vision started to become blurry, and the rest of the meeting was becoming muffled. Normally I couldn't wait for a vision to end, but I didn't want this one to stop yet. There were still so many unanswered questions. I wanted to know more about this planned attack. I also wanted to know what Clearwater and Valdorn were up to. My vision had other ideas though. Soon the room disappeared, and I was once again falling through time.

Expecting to wake up in my room. I instead arrived in an alleyway that was nestled between two buildings. It was dark, cold and drizzly. Sounds of nearby cars could be heard from the street, and I could hear a pair of voices arguing from a window above. Wondering why I was here. I began to make my way out of the alley. The fact that this place was giving me the creeps and I'm a little claustrophobic, so this was not a place for me. Then there was a loud *SNAP* behind me, and a man appeared from out of nowhere. His sudden appearance scared me, and I backed away. Forgetting that whoever he was, he couldn't see me. When he stepped into the light. I recognized the orange hair, and green eyes of Ignatius Clearwater. He looked though as if he'd aged incredibly. His robes were worn, and there appeared to be fresh blood on them. I didn't see any visible wounds. So, the blood was not his. His hair was disheveled, and there were bags under his eyes from lack of sleep. If I were to take a guess. This vision was taking place at least a week after the meeting.

Here I could read his mind. Proving my theory to be right, Ignatius' brain was working double overtime. Ever since the meeting he's feared that Jacoby Valdorn would disobey direct orders and attack anyway. He had to warn my grandma, for old times' sake. He wasn't going to let anybody stop him. Not even his traitorous Covenant members.

My curiosity was getting the best of me. If I pressed in a little further. I would be able to see into Ignatius's past. See where he and my grandmother came to meet. Before I could do anything though, a familiar booming voice called from the shadows. "Where do you think you are going Ignatius?" We both turned to find the tall and muscular leader Jacoby Valdorn. He looked even scarier up close and personal. His long black cloak blew in the wind. In his right hand stood an ancient looking walking scepter; on the top of it stood a red stone that illuminated the dark alley. The scepter was a powerful weapon that had caused much chaos (I can sense emotions, and memories inside of magical objects as well). Ignatius clearly did not like the scepter either; he cast a nervous glance at it.

"You should have never gotten this far?" Valdorn shook his head with a frown. "It so hard to find good help in that Covenant of yours."

"How did you find me?" Ignatius asked backing away.

"Not hard to place a tracking *Zeft* on an unsuspecting Wizard. You would think by now you'd be more cautious around the people you work with." Jacoby said with a laugh. *Zeft's*, are Wizard stones that have numerous magical properties. Valdorn held up the scepter, which glowed slightly, and a small object flew off Ignatius robes toward Valdorn. He held it in his hand and sneered. "It's amazing how the smallest of things can serve the greatest of purposes." His eyes glittered as he placed the small stone in his robes. "The *Zeft* was just an extra precaution. It doesn't take magic to know where you are going. These days just about everyone in your Covenant knows your day-today whereabouts. I hear you been having some loyalty issues."

"You've poisoned them against me. Whispering false promises in their ears, clouding their judgment." Ignatius said with contempt in his voice.

"Did it break your wee heart to have to kill those men?" Jacoby mocked. "By the looks of your robes you did a brilliant job at it." Jacoby smiled. "You've always been a killer Ignatius. It's a shame you've grown so soft."

"Why are you here? What do you want?" Ignatius asked.

"To stop you from making the biggest mistake of your miserable little life." Jacoby replied.

"You wouldn't defy direct orders from Garratty." Ignatius said.

"Old Garratty will come around. Think about it. I send in a secret force to attack the Everhardtht's. They attack back in defense, undoubtedly killing them all. The Council will declare war. They attack us, and in return the Covenants think were being attacked, and declare war as well." Valdorn was still going to attack my family, and even if we defended ourselves, we would cause a conflict with the Weirling. Anger was boiling inside of me. Literally, it felt like something was bursting at my seems trying to get out. If this wasn't a vision I would have disintegrated him on the spot. "Besides, Garratty has been in control for far too long. It's time for someone new to step in. If he doesn't see it my way, then he'll just be another target to eliminate."

"You're a disgrace to the title Wizard. You will never get the other members to join your cause." Ignatius said. He placed his hand in his pocket, more than likely feeling for his wand. A fight was about to break out, and I feared for Clearwater's chances.

"Maybe I can't, but Heather Nockthowel might be able to. After all they all go putty in her hands." You do too, I thought. I hated that smug look on his face. There was no doubt in my mind that Heather Nockthowel would be able to convince the other leaders to join up with Valdorn.

"Heather will never join up with the likes of you!" Ignatius said.

"You'd be surprised. I can be pretty persuasive myself." He said with a smug look on his face. "Of course, I wouldn't mind having Heather all to myself." He said with a sneer.

"She'll never join!"

Valdorn smiled, "So the tough Irishman has a soft spot for the young Miss Nockthowel as well. She's a little out of your league." I listened in on Ignatius's thoughts. The only feelings he had for Heather, were that of a father's. I wondered how old Ignatius was, and for that matter, how old Valdorn and Nockthowel were. These were things I could figure out quickly if I had the time to explore their minds.

"If she doesn't she'll die like the rest of you! Nobody is going to stop me, and I'll be damned if I let you get in my way. I know you are in debt to Greta Everhardtht, and that you've been in love with her for decades." My head was really starting to hurt. Ignatius was in love with my grandmother. (Eww!) This whole situation was starting to become a big headache. It was one big explosion after another.

Ignatius was literally shaking with fury. He paced around like a caged animal. Then he smiled to himself. "You and I both know Jacoby that I'm not the only one in love with someone I can't have." Valdorn's smile disappeared. I noticed that his Scepter grew brighter the tighter he gripped it.

Ignatius pulled out his wand and pointed it directly at Valdorn. He didn't even flinch. "I've been looking for a reason to hex you Valdorn. Just try me!" he shouted.

"C'mon Ignatius. You and I both know that you don't want to fight me. Not after all that we've been through together. It could be like old times again. Join me, and we can reunite the old team once again. Just like in the good old days." Valdorn said. Ignatius hesitated. I went to read his mind, but whatever he was thinking about was quickly erased from thought.

"The good old days are gone, and you are long gone my friend." He said simply, raising his wand for battle.

For a moment Valdorn looked hurt. There was sadness in his eyes. "Goodbye Ignatius. Your predecessor will be easier to deal with." Valdorn slammed his scepter on the ground, and sparks flew at Ignatius. Quickly Ignatius put up a shield to block them. He shouted a charm and sent a bright orange spell back at him. Valdorn smashed his scepter down again and produced a shield of his own. Ignatius was quick, I'll give him that, with several flicks of his wand the windows in the alley shattered. The shards took aim at Valdorn who produced his wand. He spun a complete 360 and sent the glass flying in all different directions. They scattered all over the alley. Smashing everything in sight. I ducked, but one of the shards sliced into my wrist and drew blood. This was one of the reasons I was so scared of my visions. Sometimes they were too life-like. With all the commotion going on it was hard to believe that there was no one coming to investigate.

Valdorn produced a red rope from the tip of his wand that shot out at lightning speed. Before Ignatius could defend himself, the rope rung around his wand hand and scorched him. He dropped his wand and clutched his burnt arm. Valdorn got up and pointed his scepter at Ignatius. Out of the stone came a fiery red dragon, complete with teeth and glowing yellow eyes. Completely defenseless, there was nothing Ignatius could do. I saw the fear and defeat in his eyes as the dragon hit his midsection, nearly cutting him in half. It was the most frightening thing I ever saw. Ignatius Clearwater fell almost in slow motion. He landed on the alley floor and moved no more. His chest, smoking where the dragon had connected. The smell of burnt flesh made me want to throw up.

Jacoby Valdorn stood over his fallen Covenant member. "Goodbye my old friend." That's when the scene disappeared, and I woke up screaming my head off.

Chapter 3
Old Friends

Angelica
(12:00 Midnight-July 1)

I've had some really bad visions before, but the one I just witnessed was by far the worst. I watched a man get murdered by some raving, power hungry Wizard. Who wanted to do the same thing to my family. The image of Ignatius Clearwater's broken body will be forever imprinted in my mind. The thought of it made me sick.

I woke up in a pool of sweat (Absolutely Disgusting!) screaming my head off. Mom was sitting on the bed next to me, applying a damp cloth to my forehead. My shirt was drenched. It was the most uncomfortable feeling ever. I wanted to take it off, but when I went to sit up I realized that my body was so sore that it hurt when I moved my arms. I literally felt like I was just hit by a freight train.

My bedroom is in the west wing of the manor. I take immense pride in how well I take care of it, but looking around it now. It appeared that a tornado had hit. It was dark and cold in the room. I glanced over and saw that my window was shattered. It was still the middle of the night, and it was always colder at night on the hilltop where we lived. The ceiling light was on the floor in a broken heap. Glass shards were sticking out of places all over the room. My furniture was upturned. Pictures were all over the place, and I noticed that everything was wet. I tried to sit up again and survey the rest of the damage in the room, but a sharp pain ran through my body. Tears welled up in my eyes. I've never felt this kind of pain before. Mom gently pushed me back down.

"Mom, what happened?" was the first thing I managed to say. Then remembering my vision. "We're in trouble. One of Grandma's old friends is…" it was all I could muster. I was out of breath, and it was hard for me to say anything.

"You're not going anywhere just yet. So just sit back and relax." She said calmly, her voice was soothing.

"Mom please, my vision…" I managed to choke out before she placed her hand on my forehead. Instantly I felt a great rush of warmth flow through my body. I wasn't covered in sweat anymore. My bed and pajamas were now dry. Mom was using her powers to try and get me to relax, but I couldn't just lie down and do nothing. All I could think about was the lifeless body of Ignatius Clearwater on the back-alley floor of some city.

Mom kept her hand pressed against my forehead. My eyes were getting heavy. My mind was getting cloudy, and all I could think about now was resting for a while.

A part of me wanted to sleep, but the other half was shouting to be heard. I had important news that needed to be shared with my family. I couldn't sleep now. I tried to think up some counter charms that Grandma had been teaching me. Some charms didn't need to be spoken out loud, some could be cast just by thought. Mom began whispering something that I could barely make out, and before I knew it. I shut my eyes, and fell into the quietest sleep.

****

Gwen

I had to smile as Angie's head finally relaxed against her pillow. She always put up a fight when it came to going to bed. Even when she was younger she would refuse to go to sleep without a little coaxing. It has become increasingly harder as she's gotten older to get her to do something that she doesn't want to do. I had to resort to an Enchanter's Trance to finally get her to settle down. At least now when she wakes up she'll have a calm, and clear mind. I gently pushed her long brown hair out of her eyes and tucked her back into bed. Tears came to my eyes as I watched her sleep. She was sleeping peacefully now, but just moments before she was in a much different state.

Angelica started having these infernal visions when she was only six years old. Back then she would never remember the things she saw, and the visions would just come and go without so much as a hiccup. In the last few years though her visions started becoming more violent. When her mind was stuck in that state, her body would go through all types of fits. Almost all the time the fits would cause freak storms to occur anywhere her body was. I blamed all of this on that spell that was binding her powers; her Darkling powers. A Witch should never be restrained. I was afraid that the Darkling in Angelica was fighting to break free. If that were to happen nothing would ever be the same again.

I glanced around her room. It was a disaster. All her things were broken and scattered all around. It wasn't the first time that she caused damage during her fits. An Enchanter's Trance relaxes the body and takes away all pain that is being felt. It gave me the time to clean up the damage she caused and remove the memory of it from her mind. Angelica of course doesn't know that this has been happening.

The scene I walked into moments before frightened me. The fit was worse than anything she's had before. It was like a miniature hurricane. Everything was swirling around the room, and there in the center of it all was Angie. Twitching and screaming in her bed, eyes lit up like a Jack O' Lantern. It was a truly a horrifying experience. As soon as the storm calmed I ran to her side to tend to her wounds. She had a nasty cut on her arm that needed bandaging. Before I could do anything though she woke up.

I don't ever want to have to tell her the truth. I know it sounds selfish. I feel bad not telling her what was going on when she had her visions. I keep reminding myself that it is for her own good. One day it'll be worth it.

I snapped my fingers and instantly the room rearranged itself back to the way it was. Sitting on the side of Angie's bed. I just stared at my beautiful little girl. She had grown so much over the past two years. In fact, she had grown into a miniature version of myself. Long brown hair that was forever a mess, and emerald green eyes that twinkled. All I'd ever wanted for her was to find the soul mate that she would spend eternity with. Someone who would protect her and keep her happy. That kind of life was extremely hard for someone like Angie. She is so strong for her age, and her powers just take over her sometimes. These visions didn't help matters. She gets so uncontrollable that she becomes a danger to herself and everyone around her. I've always debated with myself whether binding her magic was a good idea. But then I remembered. I've seen Darkling's before; their powers are just too strong. It would overwhelm and kill them. I didn't want that to happen to Angie.

One of these days her powers were just going to burst out. All I could hope for was that Greta could train her before that happens. Which didn't settle my worries at all. Greta has become more and more hesitant with Angie's powers lately. She's afraid that Angie may not be able to control her true Darkling abilities. I was afraid of that too, but I was more afraid of what the spell was doing to her now. It was seriously affecting her health.

Surveying the gash on her arm it appeared that it was caused by broken glass. Sure enough, the shard was embedded in the wound. I summoned a quick charm that healed it instantly. What was once a nasty gash, was now clean smooth skin. Almost like it was never there. This wasn't the first injury that occurred during one of her visions and I'm sure it won't be the last.

The door to the room creaked open and Greta appeared in the doorway. "How is she doing?"

"Resting at last." I replied.

"Good." She paused. "Is it done?"

"Yes. She won't remember the pain or the damage she caused."

"It is for the best. I have a bad feeling about this one. Did she happen to say anything?"

"She said something about an old friend of yours." I replied.

"To vague. Bring her down to the den, and we'll handle this as a family. Rowan is already downstairs." She closed the door and left me in silence again.

I'll admit that I was curious as to what she saw. Experience has taught me that the stronger the storm she caused the worse the vision was. Some of her visions we had to wipe completely from her mind because they were so horrifying. I hoped this wasn't another one of those, but I knew deep down that it would be.

****

Angelica

It was the most relaxing sleep that I've had in a long time. I didn't even dream, which was weird because I always dream. My eyes were still very heavy when I opened them to a dimly lit room. I was still in my pajamas. Only now I was on the den couch. This was the room I'd always go to if I wanted to be alone. It's big and spacious with a huge roaring fireplace. The den always reminded me of one of those log cabins that they show on the travel channel.

This was also the room where we had family meetings. Sure enough, Mom was sitting opposite me on the second couch. She smiled when she saw that I was awake. She really is beautiful. I was always embarrassed when she would compare my looks with hers. She was lean with long legs. Her hair was curly brown like mine, and her eyes were also a shade of emerald green. I love when she tells me stories of when she was younger. She attracted the attention of many Warlocks when she was single (Enchanters never have problems getting dates.). Yet she chose my Dad, the Nurturer who spent all his time with animals. Despite the sixty years' difference between them. Something just clicked when they first met, and they fell madly in love. It took dad another ten years to finally get the nerve to propose to her though, and that was only because Grandma had pushed him into it. Grandma was all the consent they needed to get married, and she agreed to their union. Mom never talks about her family. It's like a giant sore spot, and all I could gather is that they didn't approve of her marriage to Dad.

He was leaning on the mantelpiece staring into the fire, which seemed to dance as he watched it. He was an averaged size man with sandy brown hair that was parted to the right. Mom said she fell for his eyes first. They were forest green, and she said it complemented his wild Nurturer abilities. His competitive nature was something that she says also attracted her to him. When it comes to games and sports, he hates to lose. Once I nearly had him beat in a game of chess, and he used a mouse to distract me. He didn't appear like much on the outside, but looks could be deceiving. Dad uses everything to his advantage. Sometimes he even gets the trees to fight for him. He was wearing one of his famous turtleneck sweaters that he even wore in ninety-degree weather.

Behind me Grandma was looking out the window, stargazing as usual. She would tell me that the stars held stories that no person could ever tell. She was of medium weight and height with spiky white hair and golden-brown eyes. She didn't appear to be over 280 years old, but once again looks can be deceiving. Grandma is the most dangerous Combatant in the world. I've never seen her fight before, but every now and then she would tell me stories about her younger years. She said her enemies use to fall all over themselves when they saw her approaching. My absolute favorite story was when she met my Grandpa during the War of Council. He died when Dad was around my age. His death is another story that's never talked about.

My family has a lot of secrets, and it bothers me sometimes that I'm not allowed to hear about them.

"Finally, A whole hour you knocked her out for Gwen with that trance of yours." Grandma said.

"It needs to be powerful. She resists all my other charms. I have to put some extra juice behind it." Mom replied with a smile.

Noticing the absence of my sister. I asked, "Where's Merrin?"

"Still sleeping." Mom replied.

"That girl could sleep through anything!" Grandma said. She left the window and came to sit down next to Mom. "So, my little one. What did we see this time?" Grandma was all business when it came to my visions.

"My vision! I can't believe I forgot!" I hated Mom's Enchanter Trances, because they made you forget your worries. I was grateful for the nice nap that I had, but my family should have known about this vision already. We had to be prepared to defend our home.

As I told them about my first vision they just sat and listened. When I finished, all was quiet in the den. Grandma seemed lost in thought. Mom was watching her for a reaction, and dad was still glaring into the fire. It was not the reaction I was expecting out of them.

Finally, Grandma sat back and said, "This is nothing to get all worried about. Do you think this is the first time Wizards have proposed plans to assault this town? They have been trying for years. They will never discover this town's location. What I'm more interested in is that you my dear granddaughter saw the inside of the Sanctuary. Do you know how many Weirlind would kill to catch a glimpse of that place? What was it like? Do you know where it's located? Anything you can tell me about it will be an advantage in the Council's favor." There was a hunger in her eyes. She was dying to know more about the Sanctuary.

"It's marvelous. And no, I don't know where it is located, but you don't understand. They've been discussing this during many of their Covenant meetings." I said desperately. I was annoyed that she was taking this so calmly.

"So what? Like I said before. They have been discussing this topic for years. Wizard Law prevents the unlawful attack against a neutral party unless said party commits an act of war. Besides, Hiram Garratty would never allow such a thing to happen under his command. Nobody is stupid enough to go against him." She said with a laugh.

"Garratty said that if anyone defied him they would be stripped of their titles." I said.

"You see! There is nothing to worry about." Grandma said. "Now back to the Sanctuary…"

"But this Jacoby Valdorn…"

"Oh Bah. I should have known it was him. Don't worry. Valdorn is stupid, but he won't go against Garratty." Grandma said.

"He's already gone against him. This other Wizard. Ignatius Clearwater stood up to him."

Grandma smiled, "Old Ignatius and I are friends from another generation." She said. "We fought in the War of Council together. I saved his life once, and he's been trying to repay that debt for many years." She smiled. So that's the connection between Grandma, and Ignatius. They were war buddies. But something was still bothering me. Were they more than just friends?

"Someone said that he was in love with you. Is that true?" I asked.

I was totally expecting her to deny it. She simply smiled. "He was madly in love with me, but I was in love with your grandfather. They were the best of friends, and they respected each other. Ignatius was the best man after all." She said.

I didn't want to tell her what happened after the meeting. Grandma was too smart though. She knew immediately that I wasn't telling her something. "Angelica what happened?"

"I had a second vision. This one happened maybe a week after the meeting. Ignatius knew somehow that Valdorn was going to go against Garratty. He was coming to warn us, but Valdorn followed him. It was a terrible fight. That's how I got this cut." I said pointing to my arm. That's when I noticed that the cut was no longer there. I glanced at mom, she smiled at me. She must have healed it when I was sleeping.

"Angelica what happened?" Grandma's tone was serious.

"Valdorn killed him." The room was silent except for the crackling of the fire. Dad was still focused on the flames, which were now burning brightly.

"That despicable coward!" Grandma began pacing around the room. When she gets mad she paces, and when she paces something normally breaks. Sure enough, the lamp on the table shattered.

"Greta honestly. Why do you have to break things?" Mom said fixing the lamp.

Grandma ignored her. "I'll make him pay old friend. I promise." She said through gritted teeth.

"How do we know that what Angelica saw was true or not?" Mom asked. Mom was always the skeptic. Mom hated my visions perhaps more than I did. She always needed proof before she believed in my visions.

"Have any of her visions been wrong before!" Grandma yelled. She took a deep breath and sat back down. "Tell me everything that happened. Do not leave out any detail."

"Valdorn is going to attack us secretly behind the Covenant leaders backs. He didn't have a lot of support from many of the others, but he said that he would take out anyone who tried to stop him. Including Garratty." I said.

"He must have some kind of support if he's willing to go this far." Grandma said.

"There is no way he could possibly attack us here. First off, he'll never be able to find us, and secondly doesn't Garratty monitor all Wizard activity in the world." Mom said.

"Sure, he monitors all Wizards in the world, but he is still just one man. The one problem Garratty has always had was dealing with those who work outside of Covenant rules. I bet you Valdorn is planning on using Wizards that are not part of any Covenant. Then he would be in the clear if they got caught or captured. I said he was stupid, but in reality, he is a clever Wizard. He never gets his hands dirty. He always lets others do the work for him. He would never have the guts to come here and face me in person." Grandma said. "It was a bold move of him to take out a member of the Covenant's."

I recalled from my vision that Valdorn had members of Ignatius' Covenant attack him first. "I think he killed him as a last resort. He tried to have members of Ignatius' own Covenant take him out first, but that didn't work."

"That sounds more like him. Only getting involved when it was truly necessary."

"Do you know him?" Mom asked.

"We have a long history. I knew him from the war. He was on the good side then, but he was always a loose cannon." It was hard to picture Valdorn as a good guy. The man I saw tonight was just pure evil. I had the feeling there was more to his story.

"Tell me more about how Ignatius died. Did he put up a fight?"

"He fought bravely. It was one of his spells that did this to my arm." I said pointing to my now healed cut. "Valdorn knew where Ignatius was going. One of his Covenant members placed a tracking *Zeft* on him. I think the others who tried to stop him, he killed. Valdorn had this scepter thing though."

Grandma closed her eyes. "Do not say anymore. I can imagine what happened after that." I guess Grandma knew about Jacoby's scepter. "Ignatius was one of the few friends that I still conversed with on a regular basis. The last time we spoke he sounded troubled. He said he was having problems within his Covenant. I offered to help, but he turned me down. Stubborn fool! I should have helped him anyway. I feel like I just lost a part of me that I will never get back." I saw a small tear escape her eye. A rare sign of emotion from her. "Don't worry old friend. He will pay for his crimes." She said firmly. "Valdorn found that Dragon Scepter after the war. He took it from one of the dead council members." She said. "I don't know how old it is or where it came from, but he became obsessed with its power."

"I bet I could have figured out where it came from. I should have looked harder during my vision." I said.

"It's better that you didn't. That thing is worse than the man wielding it." Dad finally walked away from the fire, which died down to normal level immediately. "I don't like it. I feel a great disturbance in the natural order of things. Something bad is going to happen soon." Dad was having what he calls Fire Sights. Images and feelings appear to him in the flames. "What I find more unnerving is that this hasn't been reported yet."

"His death won't be announced until it suits Jacoby's purposes!" Grandma shouted. "If he wants a fight then that is what he will get." Grandma said.

"They will never get through our barriers. It won't come to a conflict." Mom said. She despised violence.

"I don't know honey. My Fire Sight wasn't clear. The disturbance of balance I felt was close by. Something bad is coming our way. I couldn't tell what it was though. It was all foggy, and there was this weird red light." Dad said.

"I think we are putting too much stock into these visions. The Wizards haven't reported anything on Ignatius's death yet. So as far as we know this could be all speculation." Said Mom.

"It can't hurt to be prepared. Like mother said, Angelica's visions have never been wrong in the past." Dad replied.

"I still don't believe it." Mom replied. Sometimes I wished she wasn't so stubborn.

"It's not so much the fight. It's the principal behind it. He killed Ignatius! He must pay for his crime!" Grandma said looking at my mom. "We'll need everyone's help. Including Merrin's, and yours Angelica."

Mom shook her head and stood up, "They will not be fighting any battle." She said.

"We have no choice in the matter, and I will have no petty arguments over it Gwen. I am the matriarch of this family, and if I say we fight, then we fight!" Grandma said. Not one to back down Mom appeared to want to argue some more, but Dad gave her a firm look, and she said no more. She turned and walked away from him.

I didn't want there to be turmoil between us when we needed to be united as a family. I wanted them to know that I was ready to defend my home. As soon as I stood up to tell them. My body went totally rigid, and I felt my legs give way underneath me. The room faded away as I fell to the floor. I felt the familiar tug in my mind, signaling another vision. I felt myself being lifted into the air. When I looked down on the scene below me. I saw that Dad had caught me just before I hit the ground. Mom had called my name and rushed to my side. Grandma hovered over them. The next thing I knew. I was flying out the window, and into the chilly night air. I was flying! It was the most incredible feeling in the world. I could literally see everything for miles. I've never had a vision like this before. Never had I had two visions in the same day either. So, I was excited yet nervous to see what was coming next.

Chapter 4
New Foes

Angelica
(3:00 A.M.-July 1)

Let me tell you something. Flying is awesome. This beats the spinning vortex by a long shot. I loved the feeling of the cool night breeze as it flowed through my hair. I smelt the wonderful scent of pine as I soared over the treetops. I saw every inch of my small town as I flew over it.

Even though I've never experienced a vision like this before. I guessed that I was about to see something that was happening right now.

I realized that I was on course for the Weir Wall that surrounded my town. Mortals can't see the barrier, but to my family and me, it was a great orange dome. I passed right through it with ease. If I were to do that in non-vision form, I'd probably get blasted out of my shoes.

I landed just beyond the bridge that marked the entrance to the town. Taggerts Bridge wasn't very big, but you needed to cross it if you wanted to get into Crystal Falls. Mountains and forests that you won't find on any map, surrounded the town. Crystal River flows directly down from the hilltops and goes right under Taggerts Bridge. The current is strong enough to take a fully-grown man far downstream, and I don't know for certain just where the river ends.

At least I finally get to see the other side of the Weir Wall, and I must say, I was a little disappointed. There was nothing but a long winding road that went on for miles. A part of me wished I could explore further beyond the town while I had the opportunity.

As I looked around. My Witches Sense told me that something was wrong. It was eerily quiet. Nothing was moving or making sounds, which was weird, because usually you could still hear crickets chirping at this hour. Then out of nowhere a dense amount of fog began rolling in. It was spooky how it just appeared. It was so thick that I couldn't see anything through it. Not even the light from the Weir Wall was enough to illuminate it. It was starting to give me the willies. This was no ordinary fog.

A bright red light appeared in the fog. Immediately I thought back to Jacoby Valdorn and his scepter. It grew brighter as it moved closer to where I stood. As it came closer I realized that it wasn't Valdorn, unless he was in disguise. A small girl emerged from the fog. The red light was coming from her; it was gleaming off her, like an aura. She had to be around Merrin's age. She had black hair with red highlights that was pushed behind her ears. Probably to keep it from covering her eyes that were a stunning shade of red. She was dressed in ankle length black leg-ins, a denim skirt, and a matching jacket that was buttoned to the top. She is by far the most adorable looking girl that I've ever seen. She looked like a Mortal, but whoever heard of a Mortal having an aura. She couldn't be magical either. There were spells all over the surrounding area that kept anyone from ever getting up here.

She stopped just before the bridge. I had a strange feeling that she could see the great domed barrier that enclosed the town, but like her presence here, that was impossible. Only the people who placed the Weir Wall could see it. My magic was used in its creation. That's why I could see it.

I was so focused on her that I didn't notice the second figure emerging from the fog. I wasn't aware of the presence until it spoke.

"You all right sis?" It was a soft-spoken male voice that had a distinct British tone to it. I spun around to find myself face to chest with an extremely handsome boy. I caught my breath, and felt my heart beat a little faster. To say he was tall was an understatement. I had to look up at him to get a better look at his face. He couldn't be much older than myself, but his face held the look of someone who was timeless. He was in decent shape. Muscles clearly showed underneath his denim jacket. He looked like he just walked off a movie set in Hollywood.

Suddenly, I was very self-conscious of myself standing here in my pajamas, hair in a tangle and barefooted. I knew he couldn't see me, but a tiny part of me wished that he could.

What on Earth is wrong with me? Why did I notice everything about him? His thick shoulders, the curve of his smile, his eyes that matched his sisters. His hair was short and black with the same red highlights, and he cast the same red aura. I couldn't keep my eyes off him, and it was starting to bother me. No guy had ever affected me this way.

I shook my head. I had to clear my mind, because something about these two, screamed trouble. I had to find out who they were, and the only way to do that was to read their minds.

After concentrating for a while I realized that I couldn't read either of their minds. It wasn't like inside the Sanctuary when I couldn't use my magic at all. Here I felt myself knocking at their minds door, but they were locked. They must have some strong defenses to keep a mind reader like myself out. I knew now that they weren't Mortal, but how could they have gotten up here?

"Are you sure about this Alec? Were in Everhardtht territory now." The little girl had the same accent. That's when it clicked in. Their accents! They were from Britain just like Jacoby Valdorn. These two must be the ones he sent to do his dirty work for him.

I looked back at the girl. She was watching her brother carefully. They had to be here on Jacoby's orders. How else could they know we live here? I was starting to get real worried now, because they had to possess some strong magical abilities to have gotten this far. They got through all our blockades without the slightest of scratches. Were these two unregistered Wizards? I couldn't tell. My usually reliable Witches Sense wasn't helping me here. Something about them was throwing my magic off balance. I knew that if they were Weir, the Weir Wall would stop them for sure.

The boy walked over to his sister. Gosh he was tall; he had to be at least 6 feet 4. His sister looked like a Dwarf compared to him (Then again. I looked like a Dwarf compared to him!). He smiled at her; a smile that made my heart melt. Pushing a strand of hair that fell over her eyes back behind her ear. He said, "I know this is the closest we've ever been to magic of this intensity. As long as we stick together we'll be fine." He had such compassion in his voice, it was clear from the way he looked at her that he cared about her dearly. "I promised that I'd protect you, and that's a promise that I'll never break." His words seemed to fill her with confidence. She smiled an equally adorable smile back at him.

Oh boy, I'm in trouble! These two have my mind in complete disarray.

He glanced at the dome barrier, and this time I was sure that he could see it. "It was rather easy getting to this place. I was expecting a bit more of a challenge. Not that it matters. It's time Weir everywhere realize that they're other races out there beside themselves. We're going to teach them that lesson the hard way." He said. His words were so soft, and his accent made him seem more mysterious. "We could destroy them all without even breaking a sweat." He had such confidence in his tone. That I was starting to believe him, which I was ashamed of because nothing was stronger than a Darkling Witch.

"You sure we can trust these Weirlind. They have proven to be easily corrupted, and Greta Everhardtht is no stranger to corruption." She talked like she knew Grandma personally. Which was impossible seeing the 200-year age difference.

"Don't forget why we're here. Why we had to change course? I have no love loss for Greta Everhardtht after what she has done to our race. One day she will answer for her crimes, but for now she is going to be a strong cog in the she fore coming war. Don't you think it's about time and her family came out of hiding?" If my Grandma had done something bad against another race, I'm sure whatever it was, was well deserved.

"Well are we just going to stand here talking about it. It's bloody cold up here?" The girl said. "You ready?"

"I was born ready." He said, making her giggle. What they did next was both incredible, and horribly scary. They raised their hands in unison to the shield. I felt a great amount of power radiating off them; more power then I'd ever felt before. The shield seemed to be drawn to them. I realized that they were sucking the shields energy through their fingertips. I watched as the bright orange glow of the Weir Wall flickered, as their red glow grew brighter. I thought for sure that they were going to suck it all up. However, they only took enough to create a small gap in the barrier where they could walk across the bridge.

I felt my mind begin to tug again. No! I didn't want to leave yet. I wanted to know who these two were, and what they were doing here. Again, my mind had other plans for me. I followed them through the opening that closed behind us, and then I was soaring back through the town, and over the trees to our hilltop manor. I flew through the window. Thankfully it was still opened, because that would have been a huge mess for the window and my face. My parents had moved my unconscious body to the couch, and they were leaning over me.

My vision was over. So many different things were going on inside my head, that I didn't know what to feel first. Fear, disappointment, and a giddy feeling that I had no idea where it was coming from.

Mom was leaning over me, and Dad was cradling me in his arms, both looked extremely worried. Grandma was waiting behind them.

"How are you feeling Angie?" Dad's voice was greatly stressed. I felt his wild energy flowing through me.

"What happened?" I asked.

Dad glanced at mom. "Nothing sweetheart. You just fell, really hard." Mom replied.

"Your all looking at me funny." I said.

"Well you do look pretty funny looking." Dad said. I smiled, in spite of the fact that I knew they weren't telling me something.

Grandma was getting impatient. She was the first to ask about the vision. "What did you see? Was it about what you saw earlier? Is it about Ignatius?"

"No! We have a bigger problem! I think Jacoby Valdorn's minions are here." I said, standing up.

"What are you talking about? I would have felt any new presence arriving in town." Grandma said.

"That's impossible honey. Nobody can reach this town." Mom said soothingly. "Your vision has to be wrong."

"No Mom, It's not wrong!" I shouted. I was tired of her not believing me. I got up and walked away from her, but my legs were a bit wobbly and I almost lost my balance. I rubbed them to get the blood flowing again. "I saw these two young…" I hesitated, because I had no idea how to describe them. "I don't know what they are exactly, but I've never seen anybody do what they just did."

"Sweetie, how could they have gotten past our barriers?" Mom asked.

"I don't know, Mom. They just appeared out of the fog like in some horror movie." I said.

"Fog? Was there a red light as well?" Dad asked.

"Yeah. It was coming from them. It's like an aura." Grandma's face paled immediately upon me saying that.

"That's what I saw in my Fire Sight." Said Dad.

"I still don't understand how they could have gotten here. How old were they?" Mom asked.

"I couldn't tell for sure. My magic was all out of sorts around them. I couldn't read them like I normally could with people." I said.

"If this vision is true, and that is a big if, because none of us have felt any disturbance in the Wall or in the town. Then what possible harm could two young kids be?" asked Mom. I was starting to get really frustrated with her.

"They sucked the damn wall into their bodies! Is that dangerous enough for you?" I asked. Dad glanced at Grandma who looked extremely worried.

"There is no need for that kind of language young lady." Mom said.

"Stop it Gwen!" Grandma said nastily.

"Excuse me?" Mom looked like she was ready to hex her.

"I said Shut it! I need to think. Magic absorption. It's not possible. They've been extinct for years. We eradicated them." She mumbled other things that I couldn't make out. "What did they look like?" she asked nervously. "Don't leave out a single detail."

There was a sense of urgency in her voice. Her usual calm exterior was becoming unhinged. "They…had strange red eyes. Like those contacts actors use. In fact, they looked like they could be actors from The Twilight Saga. Highlights of red were in their hair." So far it was a lousy description of them. I should have done them a little bit more justice. (What could I say though? That I thought that the girl was adorably cute, and her brother was amazingly handsome. That would have gone over well!) The look in Grandma's eyes frightened me. For the first time, I saw fear in them. It was as if her worst fears had been confirmed.

Curiosity got the best of me. I slipped into her mind, and for once she didn't stop me from entering.

I was on an open stretch of field. A hundred of the strongest Combatants were at my side. Victory was a sure thing. I looked to the Combatant on my right. His name was Horatio Thatcher. I nodded to him, and he returned the gesture. He signaled others close by. Together we moved as one. Quietly closing in on our targets. They were hiding out in the abandoned town Bent Faulke. The former residents, all of them Weir were all murdered by those evil creatures. We were now inches from the spot where we would launch the attack. When a panicked scream broke the silence. One of the Warlocks closest to me had been knocked off his feet. I watched in horror as he was dragged into the town by some invisible force. Suddenly an eerie red light filled the open space. The town had come to life. It was almost as if someone had just flipped the on switch. Immediately I cursed to myself. They felt us coming, and had waited until we couldn't retreat anymore to surprise us with their own attack. "Hold your ground!" I shouted, but panic spread amongst the group. Spells were being fired into the town at the invisible enemy. Next thing I knew there was a sudden roar from the town. I heard them before I saw them. They were charging at our line. We were severely out numbered. Dozens of spells were being shot at them, but they simply swiped them aside. I sent a Disfigurement Charm at the creature approaching me. With the speed of lightning he sent it right back at me. What the hell were these things! I dodged, and quickly sent an Eruption Charm at the ground. The force of the blast sent the creature flying backwards, and out of sight. I quickly shouted to the others to do the same as I had. To my horror, some of the creatures had breached our line. There were screams coming from the clashing Weir. I barely had time to register what was happening when a blast knocked me off my feet. I landed so awkwardly on my leg that I heard a sickening cracking sound. Horatio had hit the ground right where I was standing with a spell. I didn't see the oncoming creature, and if it weren't for him. I probably would have died. "We have to get out of here!" he shouted. The Combatant's closest to us formed a barrier long enough for us to make our escape. I didn't want to leave the battlefield, but I knew we were facing some unknown horror, and we didn't stand a chance against them.

Grandma forced me out of her mind. I thought she was going to yell at me for sure, but she just sat there. She was furious by my intrusion into her memories. I was forbidden to read the minds of any family member. Breaking that rule normally led to severe punishment. The creatures I saw in Grandma's memories looked nothing like the siblings I saw tonight. "Red aura, magic absorption. They're stronger when they are young." Dad said. An understanding seemed to pass between him and Grandma. Only Mom and I were confused. "It's impossible, but what else could they be?"

"Did they say anything? Tell me everything!" Grandma asked.

"They're siblings. They were saying something about showing the Weir that there are other races out there. They also said that you did something to their race." According to Grandma's memory, she had led a failed attack against them. If she was afraid of them, we all should be afraid of them.

"They're coming for revenge. They must be taken out before they get anywhere near us. They could be on their way up here as we speak. I need to heighten the defenses around the house." Grandma said.

"Wait! You're going to kill them?" Mom said quickly.

"You don't understand Gwen. You weren't born yet, and I was just a kid, but my Mom knows them all too well. They're extremely powerful." Dad said.

"I will not be a part of any plan to kill two children!" Mom said. This time the look in her eyes told me she wasn't backing down like before. Grandma looked like she was on the verge of an eruption.

"Hang on a minute!" I said. "What are they exactly?"

"Devilish creatures that fool you with their words and looks. I can't believe Jacoby would ever stoop so low. Killing Ignatius, and now associating himself with that spawn of a race." Grandma said. She got up and headed over to the door.

"Mother you will not do this alone!" Dad shouted.

"What do you propose then?" she retorted. "I will not let them near any of you. I know how to kill them. So, I alone will take care of this."

"We handle this the way we handle everything, as a family. I can have eyes all over the town in seconds. Let's wait and see what my animals report back." He said.

"I will not play a waiting game Rowan. Not with these creatures. We don't have time to wait for your animals." Grandma said.

"We have not felt any disturbance in the town yet. Obviously, they would have been here already if they just wanted us dead. Remember what Angelica said? Jacoby Valdorn just wants us to attack so it would be on us if a conflict breaks out."

"They're not part of any Covenant!" Grandma shouted.

"How do we know that? As far as we know they could be a part of Valdorn's Covenant! You think he would have sent them if they weren't?" Grandma still made her way to the door. "You had this sick obsession with them before, and if they're back? I'm not going to let that happen again."

"I won't put this family in danger…" She began to argue.

"Mom you may be the Matriarch of this family. But I have an oath to keep to Dad, and I'm not about to break it!" With those words, Grandma froze in her tracks. She looked defeated for the first time. She left the room without another word.

I had a thousand questions that I wanted to ask. I was hoping Dad would shed some light on what was going on.

"Dad what's happening? What are these creatures?"

"I'm sure it's nothing, dear. It's probably just your Grandma over reacting again. Don't worry about these things, we will handle it." Mom said simply. "I want you to get some sleep. It's been a long night. Things will seem brighter in the morning."

"But..." she gave me a firm look that meant the discussion was closed. I looked at Dad for support, but none came. She tried to stroke my hair, but I was so mad that I flinched from her hand. "One-day you guys will stop lying to me!" Then I stalked out of the room. I liked to have the last word when I was angry.

I knew from the look on their faces that I had surprised them with my words, but I was so mad that I didn't care. I was so tired and fed up with the lies. Grandma knew Jacoby Valdorn, and she knew who our visitors were as well. What had happened all those years ago? What oath had Dad made to grandpa? Most of all why was everyone so keen on keeping me in the dark?

I walked back to my bedroom. As I entered the room I glanced around. Something was nagging at the corner of my mind that I couldn't quite place. I shook my head and laid down in my bed. I didn't know why I was trying, because I knew that I wasn't going to get any more sleep tonight. I was wide-awake, my head was swimming with all the night's events. Worst of all, the image that my mind had decided to settle on was the one thing that aggravated me the most about tonight. I couldn't get Alec and his sister out of my head.

Chapter 5
The Hunter's

Angelica
(6:30 A.M.- July 1)

It was 6:30 when I finally decided to give up trying to get back to sleep. I got up thinking that breakfast might help settle my mind. Last night was perhaps the weirdest ever. I had two visions in a three-hour time span, that has never happened before. I also learned that there is another way to have visions. I guess when you see things in the past you go through the spinning vortex. Then when you see things that are in the present, you go into what I now call; ghost form.

I didn't know which one of my visions unnerved me the most. In one I stood by helplessly as an innocent man was murdered. In the third, I watched my hometown be invaded by two of the most fascinating people that I've ever laid eyes on. Apparently, they had been enemies of the Weir a long time ago.

Today was going to be a beautiful Tuesday morning, I could tell just by looking out my window. The sun was just beginning to rise above the trees; casting a bright orange glow as it did. I opened the window to a fresh cool breeze. Summer time was the best up here on the mountainside, but it was also the most unpredictable. Sometimes it was cold, and snowy, and other times it could be hot, and sticky. Either way, the sunrise was one of the things that I loved the most about Crystal Falls. When you have little else to do, you learn to appreciate the little things in life. It's the tiny things that make Crystal Falls special.

I jumped into the shower for a quick wash, hoping the water would wash away my troubles. I was still really upset that my parents didn't trust me enough to tell me something important. After all, I saw the visions. I think I should have the right to know what was going on. Mom's Enchanter Trance may have temporarily made me forget what happened in my room, but it was all too clear now. My room was a disaster site, and I felt like I had just gone three rounds with the world's greatest boxer. Something was happening with my unconscious body while I had these visions. I came to the conclusion last night, that if my parents weren't going to tell me what was going on, then I'm going to have to figure it out for myself.

There were other things that I was sure they weren't telling me as well. For instance, they won't tell me what happened to my Grandfather, or why Mom never talks about her family, or better yet why they won't leave this house? The secrets were beginning to pile up on one another.

I'm not a baby anymore, I'm turning sixteen in a month. That meant I was going to be an adult in Witch years. Maybe then my parents would trust me with more information. I pondered the possibilities of life as an adult while I dried myself off. I knew leaving town wasn't an option, my parents would never allow it, but it couldn't hurt to dream. For some reason though the thought of leaving this place put a damper on my spirits. It's the only place in the world that I know, and I truly feel safe here. Well, that was until last night.

I especially didn't want to leave now, seeing as things were finally starting to get interesting around here. My thoughts returned once more to that boy, and his sister. Why did they affect me the way they did? I couldn't use any of my Seer magic on them. I also went completely gaga when I laid eyes on him, which was unlike me. Maybe it was because none of the boys in town ever really interested me. The only boy I ever talk to is Brett, but he's my best friend. I sighed. So much for forgetting about last night.

I stood in front of my dresser, trying to convince myself that I wasn't going crazy. I decided that a simple pair of jeans and a t-shirt would be suitable enough for today. So, with a quick wave I had on my most comfortable pair of pants, and a short sleeve t-shirt (I bet some of you wish you could do that, it'd save you a lot of time and hassle.).

I didn't bother throwing on shoes or socks, because I always walk around the house barefoot. As for my hair, not even magic could tame my stubborn locks. So, a simple knot would have to do to keep it in place.

I quickly made my way out of the west wing. Into the second-floor corridor, and down the grand staircase that led to the 1st floor (You literally need a map to get around my house, its huge! I'm not gloating though. Okay, maybe just a little.). My house was built in the 1980s when Grandma first moved here with Mom, and Dad. It was specifically placed on the hill for privacy. The forest is the only thing separating us from the Mortals in town, and no one has ever dared to enter it. The old manor holds a lot of secrets. Hidden rooms, and passageways led to parts of the house that you can't see from the outside. Of course, I probably wasn't supposed to know where these rooms were, but let's just say I have a thing for mysteries and breaking the rules. Our kitchen was to the right of the spacious living room, through a set of double wooden doors.

Mom and Grandma were already there when I arrived. Grandma was sitting at the bar counter sipping her famous peppermint tea, which she says is the perfect cure for a troubled soul. Mom was making her own tea. She preferred spearmint, which she takes to help cure severe headaches. I hated the stuff, I've tried so many varieties of tea, and I still haven't found one that I like. Most of them just made me want to throw up. I was told that each Witch has her own preference for tea, and I would just have to discover mine along the way.

They were apparently not talking. Their backs were turned from one another, and you could cut the tension in the room with a knife. I hated it when they fought. It happens a lot between Enchanters, and Combatants. Enchanters could talk their way out of a conflict, while a Combatant preferred to fight their way out of one. Enchanters accuse them of being jealous of their beauty. Likewise, a Combatant would argue that their supreme fighting skills spark an Enchanters jealousy. They have been fighting for centuries. Grandma was always arguing with the Enchanter on the Council. She even called her a pre-Madonna once.

"Good morning Angie?" Mom said as I sat down at the table.

"Morning." I said softly. I still haven't decided if I was going to stay mad at them for lying to me. So, I just gave them both the silent treatment.

A short stack of pancakes, a side of sausage, and an ice-cold orange juice was my choice for today. All I have to do is think of it and the dish will appear right in front of me. Another perk of being a Witch is that you never have to cook. If you have the ingredients in the house, you're good to go. If you didn't have the products, then they would have to come from the nearest convenient location. Seeing milk disappear off a store shelf or out of a refrigerator could turn into an ugly mess.

"Where's Dad?" I asked, noticing that he wasn't around. He was usually up at the crack of dawn.

Grandma gave Mom a look that could kill. "Your father took Merrin into town this morning." I gagged on my orange juice and spit it out. "Same reaction I had." Grandma said.

"He went into town! You guys never go into town!" If anybody saw him they'd probably arrest him for kidnapping Merrin. "Why would he pick now of all times to go down there. Especially with possible enemies that want to kill us."

"I said the same thing Angelica, but your father and especially your mother are thick headed." Grandma said.

"He is just doing a quick patrol, honey. His animals reported back that the town was all quiet last night, just the sheriff was moving about. He wanted to go down and check for himself. Don't worry. Your father is a very capable Warlock and he can take care of himself."

"I know Rowan is a capable Warlock! He's my son!" Grandma shouted.

"And he's my husband!" Mom shouted back.

"You do not know these creatures like I do Gwen. If anything happens to him. So help me I…"

"Stop it! Just stop it!" I shouted. Both stopped and stared at me. There was a look of concern on both of their faces. I looked down at my fists. I had slammed them down on the marble so hard that I cracked it. Funny thing was, I couldn't remember doing it. This is one of my many unfortunate side effects. Sometimes when I get angry, I do things without realizing it. I quickly repaired the crack.

"They're not going to be anybody's anything if something happens." I said. "How could Dad take that kind of a risk?"

"Merrin doesn't know about are visitors yet. She wanted to go down early, and your father wasn't going to let her go down alone. So, he decided to go with her." Mom said.

"Not telling her is another mistake." Grandma retorted.

"I do not want to frighten her, and besides we don't even know if there's any danger yet. We haven't heard a peep out of these supposed villains yet."

"Fool." Grandma muttered.

I knew they were about to go non-stop with each other. This was just round one, and I didn't feel like sticking around for the next. With my appetite suddenly gone, I finished my juice, and left the room without even looking at them. I wanted them to know that I was angry, but I doubt that they even paid me the slightest attention. We should be united as a family in times like this, not yelling at each other like they're doing. Dad and Merrin were taking huge risks by going into town. I was ashamed to admit it, but I was also a little jealous that Merrin was down there, and not me.

I went outside to the porch. The wood was damp with morning dew, and it felt cool under my feet. I dried one of the benches with a quick Drying spell, and sat down, placing my feet up on the railing. It was beautiful out. The sun was now above the trees, and you could hear birds chirping. The forest surrounding the manor possessed its own magical qualities, that's what made it so mysterious. There was only one roadway that led up to the manor, but it's dark and poorly lit. There is only two ways to use it. One is by taking a car, and the second is by teleporting back and forth. Only Weir can teleport, and you'd have to be a fool to drive on the road. Dad enchanted the forest so that no one but us could step foot or wheel in it.

I should have brought my I-Pod out with me, music would take my mind off worrying about Dad and Merrin. I was just about to use a Summoning Spell to retrieve my I-Pod, when I felt that tug in my mind again. Another vision! I've never had this many in such a short amount of time before.

It seems I've been saying that a lot lately. What was happening to me? I didn't fight it though. I was glad that I was getting to see what was going on.

This was another ghost form vision. As I hovered over my house, I looked down at the porch to see myself sleeping happily on the bench. It was kind of weird watching myself sleep. I wondered if I would be able to see what was happening to my body while I had a vision.
Right now, nothing appeared to be wrong.

I didn't hover for long. Soon I was soaring back over the treetops. I was heading towards the town again.

It was deserted, which was normal at this time of the morning. Eight o'clock is when most of the shops open for business. It's also the time when people start moving about. There were only two figures walking down Main Street. I recognized them immediately to be Dad and Merrin. My sister is a smaller version of myself. The only trait that we didn't share was our hair color. Her hair is such a light shade of brown that she could probably pass for a blonde. I've always been a little jealous that she can keep her hair in perfect condition. Even now when she has it pulled back into a tight ponytail, there wasn't a single hair out of place.

I landed on the street just behind them. I'm going to have to start wearing shoes, I thought. I carefully watched where I stepped as I followed my dad and sister. "Remind me again just why you had to take me to town today?" Merrin asked.

"Is it so wrong for a father to want to take his daughter out somewhere?" he responded.

"I'm not saying it's wrong, but you like never come to town. It's not even collection day." Collection day is at the end of each week. Where either Merrin or myself go around to the shopkeepers to collect the rent.

"Your Grandmother was the one who came up with the rule that we should never go into town. I always thought that it would make us look foolish, but there is no arguing with your Grandmother."

"How did you use to collect the rent before Angelica and I were born?"

"The shopkeepers would place the rent in our mailbox at the edge of the forest."

"I'm glad Grandmother doesn't keep us locked up there as well."

"Before we decided to have you two, your mother and I made a pact that we would let our children be as normal as possible and your grandmother agreed."

"I'm happy for that, but it's still weird that you just decided today to come to town. People are going to think you kidnapped me or something."

"Come on. Do I really look like a bad guy?"

"Dad, you're as stiff as a board, and you keep looking around like someone is going to pop out and attack us." It was very hard to get anything by Merrin. Which is why I didn't understand why they didn't tell her what was going on. Sooner or later she was going to catch on that something was wrong.

"Anybody ever tell you that you're too observant?" Dad said. "I guess I'm a little nervous. I haven't walked these streets in a long time." He still glanced around every now and then when Merrin wasn't looking. I couldn't help but glance around myself. I was expecting our visitors to attack at any moment, but Main Street was quiet.

"So where are we heading?" Dad asked.

"To get breakfast at the Java Café." Merrin replied.

"The Java Café is one of the shops that we own, right?"

Merrin sighed. "Yes father. We own all the shops."

Dad did his best imitation of her voice. "Then lead the way oh fearless leader."

Merrin giggled. "You better not embarrass me." Merrin led Dad to the shop right on the corner of Main Street. Dad stepped in front and held the door open for Merrin. He bowed to her as she walked by. "My lady."

Merrin giggled again. "You're so goofy."

They entered the café too the jingle of a bell. I entered behind them before the door closed.

"Merrin dear! How are you doing on this fine morning?" Exclaimed the woman behind the baking counter. Then she noticed my Dad.

"Hi Ms. Monti. I'd like you to meet my father." Merrin said back. Valerie Monti was the proprietor of the Java Café. She's a short and plump woman with rosy red cheeks and freckles all over her nose. She is Crystal Falls version of Mrs. Santa Claus. Literally, she plays the role every year. Right now, her cheeks flushed a deeper shade of red.

"Oh… Mr. Everhardtht. We don't normally see you down here sir. Is anything wrong?" I felt bad for her. Ms. Monti is the sweetest person in town, and she makes even sweeter pastries. I'd be nervous too if my boss showed up unannounced.

"Nothing is wrong my dear. I just thought today I'd take my daughter out for a walk." Dad smiled and held out his hand. "I must say that I've heard a lot about you, and your pastries from my daughters."

Ms. Monti blushed as she shook my Dad's hand. He certainly knew how to turn on the charm. "Well…I do my best." She replied. "Can I get you both something?"

Merrin looked at the mountain of goodies in the glass case. Ms. Monti hand bakes all her food every day. "I'll have a strawberry Danish, and a small lemon ice tea." She said.

"Excellent choice. And for you Mr. Everhardtht?"

"I will take one of these cinnamon twists to go. I have to actually run some errands this morning." He said.

Merrin looked at Dad suspiciously. "I knew you had some reason for coming down here today."

"I just have to take care of a few things. You stay here. Then when I get back we'll go for that walk."

Merrin wasn't convinced. Ms. Monti watched them nervously as she got the food. "Here you go dear." She said handing Merrin a plate and a glass. Dad got a small brown bag.

"Here you go Ms. Monti." Merrin said handing her a ten-dollar bill. We always paid for our snacks here. Even though we could probably get it for free.

"It's on the house dear." Ms. Monti said nervously.

"Nonsense." Dad said handing her the money. "Keep the change for yourself."

"Your too kind Sir." She said taking the money.

The bell jingled again, and a big man in a brown uniform stepped into the café. "Good morning Sheriff Hansen." Ms. Monti said.

"Mornin' Val." He replied. Kyle Hansen is my best friend Lindsey's Dad. He's a tall man, with short brown hair, and a goatee. His deep brown eyes always seemed to be analyzing you when you'd talk to him. He's been single ever since he broke up with Lindsey's mom Grace. Since the breakup he's been devoted to his job. He's the local sheriff, and he's one of the nicest guys that you'd ever meet. But he takes his job very seriously. Right now, he was all business.

"I saw Merrin enter with this man. Is everything alright?" he asked. I noticed that his hand was on his gun. This was just great. Dad goes to town, and the sheriff shoots him.

"This man is Merrin's father Sheriff." Ms. Monti said.

"Oh crud. I am so sorry Mr. Everhardtht. I've just never seen you before, so I thought that Merrin might be in trouble."

"You were just doing your job sheriff." Dad said holding out his hand. "Rowan Everhardtht."

"Kyle Hansen." He said shaking his hand.

"Hansen. Would that be the same as Lindsey Hansen?" Dad asked.

"Our daughters are best friends." He replied.

Dad grinned. "Thank you for watching out for my daughter."

"Anytime."

"Merrin, I'll be back in a little bit." Dad said. Merrin looked like she rather be anywhere but here.

"I told you that you looked too suspicious." She replied.

Dad smiled. "Nice to meet you Sheriff, Ms. Monti." The bell jingled again, and he walked out.

Merrin went to sit at the table farthest to the back. Sheriff Hansen looked at Ms. Monti with an expression of relief. "I feel like such a knucklehead." He whispered.

"How do you think I feel? When I found out who he was, I thought I did something wrong."

Said Ms. Monti. She glanced at Merrin to see if she was listening, but she was busy opening her book that she took with her. It didn't matter anyway, I knew she was listening. You can't have a secret conversation with a Witch around. "I wonder why the girls don't talk about him."

"Don't know. He seems nice enough."

"It's nice ones you have to watch out for. You don't think he hurts them, do you?" she asked. We were used to these kinds of conversations about our family.

"I don't speculate Val, but the girls show no signs of abuse." The sheriff replied.

"It can't be good that he's in town. Do you remember ever seeing him down here?"

"Not that I can remember." He replied. "It's probably nothing."

"I hope so." She said. "Anyway. I guess you want a large cup of coffee, light with milk, two sugars and a small glazed cruller."

"You know me too well Val." He winked.

"You've only been ordering the same thing for the past five years." She said rolling her eyes.

"What can I say? Your coffee and crullers are too hard to resist." He replied.

Sheriff Hansen glanced at Merrin again. From reading his thoughts I knew that he was concerned about my Dad being in town as well.

Ms. Monti handed him a dish with his cruller, and a cup of coffee.

"Thanks Val." He said giving her four bucks.

He made his way over to his usual spot by the window. He sat down and began to read his newspaper. Can you imagine doing the same thing over and over again every day of the week for five years? Talk about a rut. He really needs to find another woman. I made a mental note to talk to Lindsey about that later.

So far this was turning out to be a very boring vision. What was so important that I had to see my sister and the sheriff eat and read?

A few silent minutes passed by. I was beginning to think this vision was a total dud. That's when the door opened again. My heart dropped into my stomach when I saw who was standing in the doorway. The girl from the night before had stepped into the café. Her aura wasn't as bright as last night, but it was still clearly visible.

The sheriff looked over his newspaper and smiled at her. "Well Miss Davenport. I see you found the local hot spot."

"Hi Sheriff." She said sweetly.

"Sleep well last night?" he asked. He put his paper down and gave his full attention to her. He couldn't look away from her. It wasn't just me they affected. The sheriff seemed bewitched by her charms as well.

"Thanks to you. I don't know what we would have done if you hadn't driven by last night." She replied.

"My pleasure. I was just doing my civic duty. We don't get visitors here often. I was surprise to see you walking up Main Street that late at night." He said. He shouted to Ms. Monti who had gone to the backroom. "Val! You get this little lady anything she wants. It's on me."

The girl blushed slightly. "Thanks."

"Well I don't think I've ever seen you in town before." Ms. Monti said.

"Her brother brought her in last night." The sheriff said, and then he mouthed the word "Orphans"

Ms. Monti face soften instantly. "Well don't you worry honey. Anything you want, it's yours. On the house of course." She nodded toward the sheriff who frowned. They were both prepared to fall head over heels for this girl and they didn't even know her.

"Thanks for being so generous." She said softly. "Do you mind if I have it to go?"

"Of course, dear." Ms. Monti replied.

I guess this was why they didn't come straight to our house last night. The Sheriff caught them on Main Street. Mom did say that Dad's animals only saw the sheriff out last night.

"I detect a strong accent in you dear. Where are you from?" I could tell from Ms. Monti's thoughts, that the young girl fascinated her, and she wanted to know more about her.

"Painswick." She said. "It's a small town deep in the heart of the Cotswold's in Gloucestershire England." She added.

"You're a long way from home. Why did you leave?" Ms. Monti asked.

"My brother and I were raised by foster parents. When they passed. There seemed to be no point in staying there." She said. There was hurt in her voice, which caught me off guard. She sounded so sincere. "My brother is my legal guardian and we were able to use the little money that they left us to get plane tickets to the U.S. We got on the first plane leaving. It was going to Minnesota. How we managed to get this far north on foot is still a mystery to me." That was absolute rubbish! This part of Minnesota didn't exist to the outside world. They had to know that the town was here.

"If you don't mind me asking. What happen to your biological parents?" Ms. Monti asked.

The girl paused. She seemed to be contemplating what to say. "We never knew them. They left my brother on the doorstep of my foster parent's home and they did the same with me a few years later. The letter they left for the Davenport's said that they worked for the government. I don't know whether it was true or not, but the Davenport's seemed to believe it." I didn't know whether I believed the girl's story or not. She made it sound so believable though, and I couldn't help being glued to her every word.

Merrin's mind was soaring at this point. She noticed the girl's aura when she walked through the door, and she immediately thought she was a Witch like her. I wished Dad would hurry back. I had a bad feeling about this.

Ms. Monti handed the girl two large bags of goodies, and a container filled with ice tea.

"Thanks, but I can't possibly carry all of this." The girl said.

"I'll help." Merrin said. She packed up her book and went to help the girl.

NO! NO! NO! Merrin what are you thinking? Can't you tell something is wrong with this girl?

"Thank you." She smiled in such a way that made me think she deliberately set this situation up.

"Miss. Davenport, this is Miss. Merrin Everhardtht." Said the sheriff.

"Nice to meet you." Merrin said shaking the girls hand. When magical people make contact with one another, there is usually an exchange of power that takes place. I could tell by the look in Merrin's eyes that she just felt that exchange.

"Amber Davenport." The girl said with a smile.

"Merrin is just the young lady who can show you around town. She knows everything about it." The sheriff said.

"I'll be glad to show you around!" Merrin said excitedly. "My family owns most of the town." Merrin was trying hard to impress this girl as well.

"Sounds cool. I have to drop these off first though." Amber said.

"Okay." Merrin grabbed the container from the counter. "Ms. Monti could you tell my Dad where I went."

"Of course dear. You have a wonderful day. It was nice to meet you Amber. I hope to be seeing more of you around here." Ms. Monti said.

"Thanks." Amber took the bags.

"Tell your brother that I would like to have a word with him." The sheriff said.

"I will sheriff, and thanks again."

Both girls stepped outside the shop. I followed behind them.

This was bad! Merrin didn't realize what kind of danger she was in. Once outside, and clear of the shop, Merrin rounded on Amber and said. "Are you a Witch like me?"

Amber smiled. "Not exactly a Witch, but yes I'm kind of like you."

"I knew it!" she jumped up and down with excitement.

Amber giggled at Merrin's enthusiasm. "It's not that big of a deal."

"Are you kidding? I don't know anyone magical besides my family." She said. "How old are you?"

"I'm twelve years old." Amber replied. "And you?"

"I'm eight. So, if you're not a Witch, then what are you?"

"Blimey, No. I'm not allowed to talk about it in public, but my brother will gladly tell you if you want to hang out for a bit." Amber said.

Merrin agreed immediately. I stood frozen on the spot as both girls made their way north. I tried to follow Merrin, but I couldn't move. Panic started to set in as I struggled. I had to follow my sister! I needed to make sure she was okay!

The vision was no longer following the girls. I looked around franticly for the reason I was stuck here. That's when I noticed Dad sneaking up the street behind me. He was teleporting from one place of cover to the next. He was clearly following Merrin and Amber. Once he passed me, I unfroze. I was following him now.

I felt a little better knowing that Dad was close to Merrin. He wouldn't let anything happen to her. He kept just enough distance from them where he wouldn't get noticed.

We followed them all the way to Grace Hansen's Bed and Breakfast. Lindsay's Mom is the proprietor of the B & B, and that was where she stayed during the week. Her parents, though divorced were still on speaking terms. I was now worried that all the Hansen's could be in trouble, if Amber, and her brother were up to no good.

Dad stood on the corner and watched as both girls walked up to room 2D and stepped inside. Amber closed the door behind them. For the briefest of moments, I could have sworn that she smiled directly at Dad. He apparently saw it to, and he was now hesitantly debating on his next move. If he was being baited into a trap, like he thought he was. Then it was a darn good one. Using his daughter as bait. Knowing that he would follow her no matter what. He cursed himself silently. He never should have left her alone. There was no time to get reinforcements. Merrin was in danger now.

He knew he was in trouble, but he walked toward the building nonetheless.

I felt so totally helpless. They already had my sister, and now they were luring my Dad into a trap. I followed as he walked up to the door. He used magic to open it. He stepped over the threshold, and into the dimly lit bedroom. I on the other hand stood frozen again just outside of the door. Talking, and laughing could be heard from the other room. He slowly made his way to the door and peered through the small opening.

He was going to use an Explosion Charm on the door. But nothing happened. Dad looked at his hand in confusion. "Damn Hunter's." he mumbled.

"How nice of you to visit." Said a familiar soft voice. Dad turned around as a tall figure emerged from the corner of the room. The door slammed shut, and I was once again airborne.

Chapter 6
A History Lesson

Angelica
(8:00 A.M.- July 1)

I woke up face down on the floor of the porch. My clothes were drenched and once again I felt like I had been in a terrible fight. I tried to get to my feet, but as soon as I moved, a sharp pain ran up my legs and spine. I let out a small squeal as I fell back down to the floor. I used the railing to get to my feet. It wasn't easy, but I managed to support myself. Through watery eyes I surveyed my surroundings. The bench that I was sitting on was snapped in half right down the center. The memory of my destroyed room returned to me once more. I repaired the bench with a wave of my hand. Instantly I felt light headed and nauseous.

I must shake this off. Grandma and Mom need to know what I just saw. I ran to the door, which wasn't the smartest of ideas, because I barely moved a foot before my legs gave way. I grimaced, as I forced myself back up again. I limped the rest of the way through the house and into the kitchen, where I hit the floor for the fourth time.

"Angie!" Mom shouted. She ran over to me. "What happened sweetheart?"

"Vision." I squeezed out through gasps of air.

"Let's get her to the couch." Grandma came around the counter and grabbed one arm while Mom held onto the other. Together they easily managed to get me into the living room. I felt a great amount of relief flowing through my body. Mom's soothing Enchanter magic and Grandma's strong Combatant magic combined was allowing my aching body to heal. By the time they got me to the couch, I know longer felt any pain, and my clothes were dry once more.

"What did you see Angelica?" Grandma asked, sitting down beside me. Mom sat down on the other side and rested her hand on my shoulder. I flinched from her touch.

"No! No Enchanter Trance. I know you've been wiping my memories and taking away my pain, but I don't want to forget. I just want to know what's happening to me?" I cried. It was bold of me to make an accusation that I wasn't a hundred percent sure of.

Mom looked taken back at first. Then she said. "Alright. No Enchanter Trance. Angie, I just…"

"We can talk about that at another time. Angelica what did you see?" Grandma asked.

"You promise?" I asked.

Mom and grandma looked at each other. "We promise." They said together.

Quickly I described everything that I saw in the vision. When I finished, Mom looked completely bewildered and Grandma looked like her worst fears had just come true. "The Hunter's have them?" she asked.

She called them Hunter's. I recalled Dad saying the same thing. Grandma immediately realized her mistake and tried to change the subject. "We have to act fast! Gwen use your link and try and contact him."

"Wait! What link?" I asked confused.

Mom closed her eyes and concentrated. A frown appeared on her face. "I can't reach him. It's like the line has been disconnected." Mom said in a panicked voice.

"I was afraid of that." Grandma replied. "We have to take immediate action!"

"Hold on!" I jumped up. My legs were feeling great now. "You just called them Hunter's, Dad said the same thing. What is this about a link? I want to know what is going on here!" I shouted.

Grandma looked at Mom for support. "She has the right to know. We can't keep this from her any longer." Mom said. Then she cupped her face in her hands. "I should have believed you." She mumbled.

"It's not your fault Gwen. You don't know them as well as I do." Grandma replied.

"What are they?" I repeated.

Grandma sighed. "You have to understand Angelica, I didn't want to tell you about these creatures. Or even your visions for that matter because I was afraid for your safety."

"I know Grandma, but I can handle it."

"I know you can. You're a tough one. You get that from me." My face reddened at the compliment. "Sit down darling." I sat down gingerly. "First, with your visions. I don't know what is happening. I believe it to be another one of the side effects of the spell I placed on you. You're causing these miniature storms every time you have a vision. I don't know how to stop them. We've been wiping your memories instead, so you wouldn't be afraid. As for an Empathy Link. It is a connection that a Weir can share with another Weir. Your mother has one with your father. They can always communicate with one another no matter the distance. It comes in handy if one or the other is in danger, like right now. As I feared though, the connection is broken at the moment."

Wow. That was a mouthful. For years I wished that they would be more straightforward with me. I guess I finally got my wish. How could they keep such a secret like that from me? I was shocked and hurt by their deceit, but I decided that I'd be angry with them about keeping my vision problems a secret later. Something else that grandma had said was bothering me more. "If the link is broken. Then doesn't that mean that the bearer is…" I couldn't bring myself to say the word dead.

"That doesn't mean that the worst has happened. Let me give you a quick history lesson and try not to interrupt me. We have a limited time frame." She said, and I nodded.

"In 1920, they were known as The Vampiric. Afterwards we simply called them Hunter's. It was dark times Angelica. It would later be called the Decade of Decimation or the Hunter Craze. You see before that. The Vampire Guild was getting out of control in America. The Royal Family couldn't do anything to stop them. In the south there were numerous newborn wars. People were disappearing. Mortals were starting to get suspicious. Then in Austin, Texas some Mortals pleaded to these four women who they considered to be Witches. Absolute rubbish! They called themselves the Elemental Ark. Later, we discovered the correct term for them.
Gypsies."

"Gypsies? You mean like the women who read your palm and tell fortunes?"

"You watch way too much television. That's another stupid Mortal stereotype. Truthfully, I don't know what they are exactly. They're not Weir and they're not Mortal either. They're something in between. They're filthy Half-Bloods if you ask me." She sounded disgusted at the thought of them.

"If they're Half-Bloods, then they have to possess Weir blood?" I asked.

"No. There was something primeval about them. They weren't from our time-period, that was for sure. All we could discover about them was that they had a certain knack for controlling the elements." She paused, then continued. "Anyway, the Gypsies agreed to help the Mortals. For a price of course. They used these abilities to create a new type of creature. A creature that would be designed just like a Vampire. There was one male, and one female, and they had all the abilities of a Vampire. Only ten times stronger. Incredibly powerful, fast, and irresistible to look away from, and just like a Vampire, they were immortal. They were given another ability though. One that would allow them to track a Vampire with deadly accuracy. From what I gathered, all they needed was one scent and they would find you in a matter of minutes, no matter the distance."

"When they were set loose, the South was decimated with Vampire carnage. Unfortunately, they didn't stop there. The Gypsies enjoyed the power that the Hunter's gave them. They set them loose into other territories and they began destroying the clans there as well. It was total chaos. The Vampires were caught so off guard that they couldn't stop them. Once they get a hold of you, they suck the magic out."

"I thought Vampires didn't possess any magic?" I asked.

"Vampire powers like speed, strength, and immortality is in its own way their form of magic." She replied. "Once they lose that ability, they cease to exist. Literally turning to dust."

"I saw how they sucked the magic from the shield, but how can they take it from a living thing." I imagined myself being sucked dry like a juice box. I shivered at the thought.

"I've seen it happen to many people. Good, strong people turned to dust in a matter of seconds. Trust me when I say it is a nasty sight." She replied.

"How could two creatures possibly cause that much destruction? And what does this have to do with you?"

"Their unrivaled strength, and the fact that they soon began to develop minds of their own, because up to that point, the Gypsies were controlling them. There was some sort of falling out and they broke away from their creators. Shortly after that, they began to reproduce their numbers. Soon, there were dozens of them." Now I know I don't pay attention in Health class, but I was sure that was physically impossible.

"How can that happen? Two people can't...well you know? Have that many babies in that short amount of time."

"Don't ask me how it was happening. It was so unnatural. They were spawning at such an expedite rate. They grow rapidly as well, not in age but in physical appearance." That would explain the extremely large physique of Alec. It was weird to think that he could possibly be younger then he looked. "They had such large numbers that they formed their own army. That's when things got worse. They caught on to other scents, Werewolves, Shifters, and Weir. Soon they were decimating all populations, and there was nothing that any of us could do to stop them."

"So, for the first time in history. The Royal Family of Vampires met with the Council of Hemlock. We formed a fragile alliance. We agreed that we had to take out these creatures by any means necessary. We planned our assault. I was placed in charge of a hundred Combatants as you already saw in my memories last night. We converged on the small town of Bent Faulke, Oklahoma, it was once a magical town where Weirlind lived. That was until the Hunter's arrived and murdered the entire population. It was a brutal confrontation, we were totally unprepared and outnumbered. Our enemies surprised us. I broke my leg in the battle because I lost my concentration. We had to abandon the fight." She paused and closed her eyes.

I tried to imagine what it was like for a commander to leave his or her troops on the battlefield to die, but I knew she had no choice. "Grandma you would have died. If that man didn't stop the Hunter. You could have been killed."

"Horatio, myself and five others were the only survivors. Five people out of a hundred. That night still haunts my dreams." She said. "I was determined after that battle to avenge my fallen Combatants. The Vampires launched their own attack on the town, but they were met with the same fate. We tried numerous different tactics, but they all failed. The Hunter's just barricaded themselves within the town."

"What about the other Guilds like the Werewolves and Wizards? Did they help?" I asked.

Grandma laughed. "The Werewolf population was spread too thin as it was back then. Besides, those ruddy dogs were too scared stiff to help, and the Weirling were faring no better than the rest of us." she said. "They tried launching an aerial attack, it failed within minutes."

"What did you do?" I asked.

"We went back to the drawing board. For the second time in history, Weirlind and Weirling working together. We tried to learn all that we could about them. We went back to the first place where they appeared. That's when we discovered the location of the Gypsies. Who better to ask then the people who created them in the first place."

"Myself, and several other Warlocks and Wizards formed a group. It wasn't easy finding them, they guarded their secrets with their lives. We tried to form an alliance with them, which was a lengthy process that never truly succeeded. They were hesitant at first, but eventually we came to an agreement." She said.

"What were the Gypsies like?" I asked.

"Like I said before. There was something ancient about them. I just couldn't place them in any time-period." She said. "Anyway, they told us that the only way to kill the Hunter's was with the magic that created them, their magic. They felt it was their natural right to kill them. We didn't argue, as long as they were destroyed. So, we watched the town on this huge water orb, I must admit that it was quite impressive magic. Up until that point I thought they were nothing more than Hags." Hags are extremely old women who obsess over money. They're not magical, but they sell magical items.

"They started chanting an incantation, and before we knew it, this huge red explosion set the town up in flames. It was an unbelievable sight. Mortals said that they saw it from miles away. Bent Faulke was reduced to nothing but ash."

"Mortals saw it?" I asked.

"There was no way an explosion like that couldn't be spotted. All the magic that kept the town hidden went up in flames with it. The fire department ruled it an out of control forest fire. After all, they didn't know that a town was there, and nothing was left to rule it otherwise."

"What happened after that?"

"All seven of us paid a price for the incantation to create the red flame, and it was a good thing that we did, because we hadn't seen the last of the Hunter's. Over the years we had numerous confrontations with them, but as time went on they became few and far between. The last one was back in 2000, when a small group was killed just outside of London. After that, it's been quiet. No Hunter's and no Gypsies. We thought we had seen the last of them." She said.

"What price did you have to pay?" I asked.

"Nothing of importance. We never saw them again afterwards." Grandma said.

"This is why you think the ones in town are after you?" Mom asked. That was the first thing she said throughout the entire conversation.

"I believe that is the reason. What worries me is that these two have gone under the radar for so many years. Jacoby probably had a hand in that. What's worse is that these two seemed to have evolved from the normal attack and kill strategies of old. The way they used your sister to lure your father is uncannily smart. It is a strategy I would have used." Grandma said. "I can't believe Jacoby would stoop this low. First Ignatius, then sending Hunter's to attack us."

"He's an evil man." I said, remembering Jacoby standing over the dead body of Ignatius.

"He was one of us. One of the seven. He despised the Hunter's just as much as I did, as we all did. He gave up…" Grandma paused.

"But…" Grandma knew Jacoby well after the War of Council. I wondered what he gave up to the Gypsies.

"I told you. He was a good guy back then."

"What happened to him?" I asked.

Grandma hesitated. She seemed to be lost in thought. For a split second, I debated on whether to read her mind again. Testing my luck twice with grandma wasn't wise though.

"I don't know." She said finally. I knew there was more to this story, but this was a good start. She is finally starting to open up to me. "All you need to know is that these creatures are killers."

I tried picturing the girl Amber as an experienced killer, taking down a fully-grown Vampire. "I just can't…"

"I know! They're very deceiving. They draw you in immediately with their charm. That's how they were able to kill so many of us without so much as a fight. It is that feature that we have to avoid when we face them." Grandma stood up. "You both have to listen carefully, because we have wasted much time. Just like a Vampire can't live without blood. A Hunter cannot live without magic.

That is how we will catch them. Angelica, you will play a crucial role."

Mom who finally seemed to snap back to reality stood up. "No way! I know what you're thinking, and you are not using Angie as bait!"

"Gwen will you please let me finish! Angelica will provide the distraction. They will not be able to resist a Darkling's magic. Gwen, you will be the blockade. Your Enchanters charms hopefully will counteract their abilities long enough for me to recite the incantation and burn them."

It was a well thought out plan. Grandma is a great battle strategist. It's one of the perks of being a Combatant. "I'll be right back. You might want to change into a proper attire." She said looking at me, and then vanished.

My thoughts immediately jumped to Dad and Merrin. After what Grandma just said, I couldn't even imagine what was happening to them right now. I turned to Mom. "Mom what if something bad has happened to them? What if they are already dead..."

"Don't think like that. They're alive, I can feel it in my bones." A tear escaped her eye. "I should have listened. I just wanted so badly for this to be a false alarm." She said. She stood up and put on her game face. "You're going to have to be strong, and you're going to have to do things that you've never done before." She said.

I knew what she meant. "Mom I don't think I can kill them or watch them be killed for that matter."

She smiled at me. "I know you wouldn't hurt a fly. Your Grandmother will be doing all the action. I want you to stay back as much as possible. Be prepared for anything though. If something goes wrong, you find your sister and get out. Do you understand?" She placed her hands firmly on my shoulders. I nodded. Looking down I noticed that she had changed my clothes. I was wearing a fresh set of jeans, an undershirt, a warm sweater, socks, and combat boots. My hair was no longer a mess but, was pulled back into a ponytail.

Grandma popped back downstairs. She was now dressed for action with a long cloak on over her shoulders. "Are you two ready?" she asked.

"As ready as we'll ever be." Mom replied.

"To not attract attention, we'll arrive behind the old car garage across the street from the B & B." I took Grandma's hand with my right, and Mom's with my left. Together we vanished from the room.

Teleportation is a quick and refreshing way to travel, wind blowing in your face as you disappeared from one place and arrive at another. It was easier to do if you were alone. When you're in a group you can't let go of the connection or lose sight of where you're going. If one person loses sight, the whole group could end up somewhere completely different. The first time I tried teleporting with Merrin. We wound up in a Chimney rather than our intended target, Chimnay Street.

We arrived behind J.T.'S Car Garage just across the street from the B & B. J.T Daley, the town's only mechanic loves to blast his music when he works. It was easy to arrive unnoticed and unheard. It's amazing the difference one hour can make in this town. Like clockwork every day, the town comes to life at eight. Before the streets were empty, now people were out and about. Ms. Nordstrom was walking Avalanche her Siberian Husky, and my archrival Kelly Jackson was doing her annual morning jog. I shook my head in disgust. Kelly Jackson liked to stay in shape, and she made fun of all those who in her mind were overweight.

Grandma peered up and down the block. When Kelly finally rounded the corner, she turned to us. "Ready? Stay behind me. I'll take the front door. Gwen, you take the left window, and Angelica you take the right."

I looked at the B & B. Then back at Mom and Grandma. They were both ready. But was I?

Chapter 7
Trapped Like Rats

Angelica
(9:00 A.M.- July 1)

Grandma and Mom were going in no matter what. They needed me, the plan involved all three of us and it would fall apart if I chickened out here. I took a deep breath and concentrated on room 2D. Merrin and Dad were in there. As I thought of all the horrible things that could be happening to them, I started to get angry. I would not let them down. I would kill those Hunter's if harm had come to my family.

"Once inside we stick to each other like glue. Understand?" Mom nodded. All I managed was a grunt. She sounded really far away to me. I was too preoccupied. All I could think about was getting in that room.

"Stay close to me Angie. We'll be fine." Mom said, but I could barely hear her.

"Let's go!" Grandma shouted as we all took off for the room.

It felt exhilarating to be doing something. I was going to be a part of a huge fight. As I ran, I felt a hunger awaken in me. I wanted this fight! I needed this fight! Mom broke left, and I broke right, heading straight for the window. Grandma demonstrated why she is a feared Combatant. She sent a blue sphere up into the air, and then did a spin kick, sending it through the door with a huge bang. I sent a powerful Thunder Ball towards my window. The black sphere crashed into the window with such impact that part of the wall shattered with it. We probably just alerted the Hunter's with our displays of magic, but I didn't care. I wanted them to know that I was here.

I did a front flip through what was left of the window as Mom came crashing through hers. Grandma followed through the door. As soon as I entered the dark empty room, I felt exhausted. How did I get here? The last thing I remembered was being outside the B & B.

I had little time to think before Grandma said. "Together!" We stood in a Combatant formation, with our backs to one another. We faced different directions to ward off any sneak attacks.

"Angie, where did you learn that charm?" Mom asked in a concerned voice.

"What charm?" I asked.

"The one that you used to take out half the wall." Mom exclaimed. I glanced at the half-destroyed wall. I literally couldn't remember anything that happened in the last few minutes. After I had gotten angry, I must have had one of my blackouts again. It was the only explanation I could think of.

"Now is not the time for questions." Grandma said in a hushed voice. As we moved into the room. A shiver went up my spine as I looked around. I've been in Lindsey's room before, it has always given me a sense of warmth. This room was the complete opposite. The beds were made, the lights were off, and there wasn't even the slightest of sounds. This scene screamed. TRAP!

Sure enough, a noise sounded behind us. We all turned to see the door and windows repair themselves by some invisible force. "You know you Everhardtht's sure know how to make an entrance." Amber appeared from the corner of the room. How were they able to hide in plain sight like that?

On instinct, I sent a curse at her, but nothing happened. Apparently, Grandma and Mom had done the same thing and had similar results. Amber just smiled sweetly at us. Grandma took a step towards her, but Amber held up her hand. Grandma froze on the spot. It didn't take long to realize that I couldn't move as well. I looked at

Mom. She seemed to be struggling as well. It was like Amber had just taken control of my body. "That will prevent you from making any rash moves." She said with a smile. The way she circled us, reminded me of the National Geographic Channel where a predator stalks its prey.

"Do you like this little spell of ours? I hope you don't mind, but we took a page out of your book." She said sweetly. "You see, with the magic we took from your Weir Wall last night. We created our own little wall, but unlike yours that keeps magic out. Ours doesn't allow any magic within this room. As you can already tell though, I can still control your magic. You won't be going anywhere for quite a while." It was different seeing her up close and personal. She really was quite intimidating. Her aura, like her eyes were a stunning shade of blood red. There was a hunger behind that intense stare, and she seemed to be staring right at me.

She approached me. "Stay away from her!" Grandma shouted.

Amber just smiled at me. I stared back. It was all I could do not to melt at her glance. She was just so adorable! "You are simply brilliant. Yet quite strange. The creature I felt approaching this room, that blasted through that wall. Is not the one that I feel standing before me now? It's almost as if you're two persons in one." I didn't understand what she meant. How could I be two separate people? Amber reached out like she was about to touch me.

"Don't touch her!" Mom shouted. Amber blinked as though she was coming out of a trance. She put her hand down and backed away. She still gazed at me though, and it was starting to unnerve me.

"What do you want, fowl creature? Where is my son and granddaughter?" Grandma said through gritted teeth. Amber was still preoccupied with me. I was starting to lose all focus under her stare. All I could think about was how pretty she is.

"Do not ignore me!" Grandma shouted.

Amber finally looked away. I was instantly able to think clearly. "Two things. One, hold your tongue! I am after all only twelve years old. Two, you are to do exactly what we tell you to do, and no one gets hurt." She might be twelve years old, but I've never seen anyone stare Grandma down like that.

"What if we don't?" Grandma retorted back.

Amber smiled at her. She raised her hand again, but this time she raised it towards me at a distance. Instantly something took hold of my body.

I tried to scream, but my voice was choked off. It felt like the life was being squeezed out of me. I fell to my knees. Mom screamed at her to stop, but she continued to smile at Grandma. I was glowing a bright orange.

"Alright stop!" Grandma shouted.
Immediately the glow vanished, and air flew back into my lungs. I collapsed to the floor. My breathing was labored, and when I coughed, I tasted blood in my mouth. "Leave my family out of this! It's me you want."

"This involves all of you. Not everything revolves around you, Greta Everhardtht!" Amber said plainly. "Let that be a reminder that we can kill you in a heartbeat. I don't even need to touch you. You're very lucky I stopped. Her magic is quite addicting. I don't think I'll be able to stop a second time. Do you really want your family to pay for your stubbornness?" Grandma stared daggers at her.

"What do you want?" Mom asked. I felt her eyes on me as I slowly got to my feet. My body seized up once more as Amber took hold of my magic.

"I'm going to let go of you and you're going to walk right through that door over there.
Any sudden movements and we'll start the entire process all over again."

As soon as we were free. Mom came to my side. "Are you all right?" she asked. Instantly, I felt Amber take hold of me once more.

"I don't believe I told you to ask her any questions." She said. "If you can't do this simple task then I'll move you myself. Trust me, it'll be more painful that way."

"I'm fine." I said.

"Good. Now that you know that she is okay. Let's start again. Shall we?" Amber let go of us once more.

"Move." Amber said from behind. Grandma was in the lead. Mom in the middle, and I brought up the rear. I felt Amber's strong gaze on my back. It was unsettling. We went through the door, which I knew led to the living room area. The lights were on in here. There were two couches facing each other, and four matching chairs. Dad and Merrin were sitting on the couch facing the door. Behind them stood the tall figure of Amber's brother Alec. He had one hand on Dad's shoulder and the other on Merrin's. Both sat rigid on the couch. When Alec let go their bodies relaxed.

"Honey." Mom said rushing to hug them. She froze before she could get to them.

"You really have trouble following orders, don't you?" Amber asked.

"I'm fine Gwen." Dad said. "Merrin is too." I knew something was wrong though. Mom apparently did too. Dad and Merrin both looked a bit shaken up.

Alec smiled. "We took a spot of magic from them, but not enough to cause permanent damage. We did a little negotiating as well. No worries though."

"You touched them! I'll…" Grandma began to approach him, but she froze instantly. Amber shook her head as she walked into the room.

"You'll do what?" Alec asked mockingly. "We're in control here Witch. Not you. You'll do well remembering that."

"She's a nasty one." Amber told her brother. She let go of her hold on Grandma, and Alec approached her.

He smiled charmingly. "She's Greta Everhardtht. I really didn't expect anything less from her."

"I'm losing my patience with you creatures. I don't need my powers to kill you!" With uncanny speed, she reached into her robe and pulled out a small vile. Before anyone could react, she threw the green liquid into Alec's face. He swore and fell backwards. Grandma turned toward Amber, but she wasn't quick enough. Amber kicked the vile out of her hand and delivered another to her chest. Then she shoved her so hard that she flew across the room, slamming against the wall. Grandma got up quickly but let out a scream and fell to her knees.

"Don't touch him! Don't you ever hurt him again!" Amber shouted. She wasn't the sweet little girl that I had seen in the visions anymore. She just took out the world's strongest Combatant with only a few blows. She has the strength of Mark Henry, the professional wrestler. Her red aura filled the entire room now.

"No, stop!" Dad shouted. He got to his feet and attempted to grab Amber, but without even looking at him, she swiped her hand through the air. Dad flew backwards over the couch, landing hard on the floor. Mom attempted to do the same, but she met the same fate. She fell back against the wall.

I didn't know what to do. Grandma was on the floor twitching in pain. Mom and Dad didn't even get close to her, and she stopped them. I leapt at her anyway, knowing I was going to get stopped. Sure enough, I froze midleap. Amber moved her hand upwards. I crashed into the ceiling. Then she waved her hand down. There was nothing I could do as I hit the floor with bone shattering force. I didn't know what hurt worse. My face or my back.

"Amber please stop!" Merrin shouted. Even though she made no attempt to get at her. Amber swiped her hand again. Merrin was knocked off her feet and she flew backwards over the couch.

"Amber!" Alec had gotten back up. His hand was over his right eye. "Let her go. I'm fine." He said softly.

Amber hesitated, but she let go when Alec placed a hand on her shoulder. Grandma let out several choked coughs, spitting blood out onto the floor. Amber retreated to the wall, breathing heavily.

Mom came to my side to see if I was all right, but I shrugged her off and got up myself. I was embarrassed that she kept coming to check on me.

Alec bent down and picked up the vile. The green liquid had burnt a hole in the rug where it had fallen. It also had a pungent rotten eggs smell. He removed his hand from his eye and I did a quick intake of breath. I was sure I was about to throw up. His eye was swollen shut. The skin around it was puffy with a nasty shade of green. Several parts appeared to be dead black. He looked at the vile then back at Grandma. She was slowly getting back to her feet. "Mullein?" he said. "You think I'm an evil spirit Greta?" He laughed as he approached her. I was afraid he was going to hurt her. At that moment, I stepped in front of Grandma. It was probably the most foolish thing to do, but I wasn't going to let her get hurt again. It worked though, because he hesitated and took a step back. He wouldn't even look at me.

Grandma didn't answer him. Instead she gently pushed me aside and stared coldly back. Curiously I asked her, "What's Mullein?"

"It's a Witches herb believed to cleanse of evil spirits." Mom said. Her voice was as shaky as mine. Dad was helping Merrin back up off the floor.

"Nasty stuff. Gives quite the burning sensation. Enough of it can kill a normal person." Alec said. "But I'm not normal, am I?" he asked. His hand glowed. The remaining contents of the vile disappeared. He then put a hand over his eye and it glowed bright red. When he removed it. His eye was back to normal. He tossed the empty vile back to Grandma. She looked at him with rage filled eyes.

"I guess I should have suspected you'd try something like that, seeing as you can no longer use the spell you had planned for us." He said. "Anything else hidden in that robe of yours?" he asked. He raised his hand and a small navy-blue stone flew from the inside of her robes. Grandma made a lunge for it, but missed. Alec inspected it, turning it over in his hands. "A Zeft. These kinds are really rare." He looked impressed. His hand glowed again. The stone turned a shade of brown. It looked like a normal rock now. Navy blue Zeft's were used to shock everything within a mile's radius. Grandma must have taken the vile and the stone when she went back to her room to get her robe. It was just like her to have a quick backup plan. It almost got her killed though.

Grandma was about to say something that was more than likely going to get her into more trouble. When Dad interrupted, "Mom stop! For your Granddaughters sake, please." He was a little wobbly on his feet after hitting the floor so hard.

"You should listen to your son, Greta." Alec added. "We only want to talk."

"I don't associate myself with Hunter's." Grandma said. "And how dare you use my first name like we're old friends!" Grandma stepped in front of me this time.

Alec shook his head. "I guess we're going to have to do this the hard way." In an instant, she was swept off the floor. She hung in mid-air for a moment, her body as stiff as a board. She was thrown onto the nearby chair. Ropes came from out of nowhere to tie her up. "Sit down everyone!"

Not wanting to be forced to sit like Grandma. I sat down immediately. Mom sat down next to Merrin on the couch. She put an arm around her. Merrin didn't look so good. I could tell that she was scared more than anyone. Dad sat down next to me.

"You're all trapped here! Trapped like rats! Until we decide to let you go!" Alec shouted. I noticed that his aura got brighter when he shouted.

"Alright, let's calm down!" Dad said. "Look, I know my mother can be stubborn at times, but if you just tell us what you want than maybe we can avoid more conflict. You two obviously went through a lot of trouble to get us here."

Alec stopped. He was breathing heavily. He closed his eyes and backed away. He cursed out loud. "My apologies." He sat down in a chair and let out a long breath.

Grandma broke the silence. Her voice was hoarse. "I don't get it. You're not like the Hunter's I've confronted in the past. I thought you creatures just killed on sight, but you two are cunning and smart. You plan your attacks out."

"Believe me it's taking all my will power not to attack you. Your magic is intoxicating. Some more than others." He didn't look at me when he spoke, but I knew he was referring to my powers being the hardest to resist. "It appears my sister is doing a better job at this then myself." He said.

"Barely, I wanted to kill her right then and there when she threw that liquid on you." Amber said glaring at Grandma. I'm never going to look at her the same again. She took out all of us without even breaking a sweat.

"You're right though. We're not like the Hunter's of old." Alec said. "Let me introduce myself. My name is Alec Davenport. This is my sister Amber." He said. "We're Pure Blood Hunter's? The last two of our kind." He added sadly.

"We killed thousands of you. I thought there were none of you left. How did you stay hidden for so long?" Grandma asked.

"Well for one thing. We weren't alive for what you people call the Decade of Decimation. Our parents were smart enough to avoid any major conflicts. They were top soldiers for the Creators, the original Hunter Pair. When I was born, they realized that it would be safer to keep their distance. They left me on the porch of a Mortal family. Then they did the same with Amber a few years later." He said.

"Mortals just decided to take you in? Knowing what you were?" Grandma asked.

"They knew right from the get go what we were. Our parents left them a note explaining it to them."

"And they still took you in?" she asked.

"Not everybody has a cruel heart Greta. Not all Mortals are bad." He replied.

"Please." Grandma said with a laugh. If it was one thing Grandma hated more than Half-Bloods, it was Mortals. "They are nothing more than an inferior race to us."

"You really are closed-minded, aren't you?" Alec asked.

Grandma was thinking of some nasty things that she wanted to do to Alec. She was also looking for ways to get out of the situation we were in. It took me a second to realize that I was reading Grandma's thoughts. That was impossible though. I quickly scanned the room, reaching out to everyone's mind except Alec and Amber's. Their minds weren't open to me, like during my vision.

"Wait. I thought you said we couldn't use any magic in this room?" I blurted out.

"That would be correct." Alec replied without looking at me.

I know it was probably hard for him to be this close to my magic, but it irritated me so much that he wouldn't look at me. "The least you could do is face me when I talk!" I shouted. Everyone stared at me. Alec turned his stunning red eyes on me. For a moment, I was at a loss for words. There was such a vastness to them that I felt myself getting lost in his gaze. "How come I can see everyone's thoughts then?" Merrin looked at me, her face turned red. Grandma immediately cleared her mind.

Amber looked at her brother. It was one of those I can't believe she doesn't know looks. "You're a Seer, correct?" She asked.

"Yeah." As if that explained everything.

"Well there's your answer." Amber replied. "A Seer can never stop seeing. It's impossible."

"I don't understand." It was infuriating how much I didn't know about my gift.

"The Art of Seeing is not your typical form of magic." I still didn't understand what she meant. I could tell it irritated her that I didn't know. "It's magic of the mind, not the body. Unlike your other powers that come from being a Weir. Seeing can't be turned on and off. It can only be controlled by the Seer." Amber said.

"I still don't get it." I said. If that was true. Then why couldn't I read the minds of the Wizards inside the Sanctuary?

"Seer's are a very rare breed. It's surprising that you even have the ability at all. It is not a gift that Weir are blest with." Alec said.

"How could you possibly know that? I'm sure there have been dozens of Weir before Angelica with this ability." Snapped Grandma.

"Because I'm one myself. That's how!" Alec snapped back. "You know you make me laugh Greta. You're trying so very hard to keep your mind clear, but the truth is. You can't hide anything from a Seer. If I wanted too, I could dig deep within your mind, find out everything about you. All those dark little secrets that you've tried so very hard to forget. I could unmake you within a second. However, who would want to be inside that dark mind of yours?" I watched Grandma's reaction. For years she has forbidden me to read her mind. She would set harsh punishments on me if I tried. Now I knew why.

"You're really a Seer?" I asked.

"All Hunter's are blest with the curse of sight. It is a gift that the Elemental Ark gave to us when the Creators were born. Therefore, it is only a gift that a Hunter should possess. You would've had to been cursed by a Gypsy to have the gift bestowed upon you. Which leads me to wonder how you gained it in the first place." He looked at me intently, as if I knew the answer. I was just as curious as he was. I just heard about Gypsies this morning, and what did he mean that I had to be cursed by one to have gained my gift?

"What exactly is a Gypsy?" I asked.

"We are straying off topic here! I believe we were discussing why you two have invaded my town?" Grandma said sharply. I looked at her. She deliberately wasn't looking back at me. Which led me to believe that she was lying about something again. Here I thought we were making progress in that department. I wondered if she had told me the truth this morning.

"She knows how you got that gift. She's not going to tell you though. You should read her mind and take it for yourself. Go on, she can't stop you." Alec said. His voice was so alluring that for a moment I debated on doing it.

"I believe I asked you a question." I said. Ignoring his paralyzing glare.

He smiled. "I'll answer that question for you at another time. You should be honored though. The art of seeing is a great responsibility. To know ones deepest, darkest secrets is a great burden." He looked directly at Grandma when he said that. Grandma stared back, unwilling to back down from his glare.

"Why can't I read your mind's?" I asked.

Again, he frowned. "Don't they teach you anything about what you are? I would think that a Weir who had your gift would learn everything about it. I'm surprised your government is not using you against its enemies." I went red in the face. "A Seer can't see into another Seer's mind. The only way you can read my mind is if I allowed you access to my thoughts. Likewise, I can't enter yours without your permission. Everyone else however, is free game. Like I said before, there is no way to block a Seer."

Grandma's face went red with fury. Curiously I asked. "Grandma blocks me out sometimes."

He laughed. "The only thing she's doing is trying to make her mind completely blank. I bet on those circumstances you find emptiness. Anybody can keep their mind clear of thoughts. If you push hard enough, you'll be able to get through." He said with a smile.

"That is enough of this! I want answers now!" Grandma shouted. "Were you sent here by Jacoby Valdorn to kill us?"

Amber got up. She glowed with fury again. The ropes binding Grandma tightened. "What are you talking about? It's because of you Weir that we are in this predicament!" she shouted.

Chapter 8
Alec & Amber's Tale

Angelica
(10:00 A.M.- July 1)

After Amber's outburst. It took several minutes for her brother to calm her down again. She nearly suffocated Grandma with those ropes. Once she settled down. Alec turned to face us. "What my sister meant to say is that the Weirling are responsible for the predicament we find ourselves in. We would never work for slime like Jacoby Valdorn. However, we blame all Weir for this problem."

"That's a little harsh don't you think?" Mom asked.

"Don't talk to me about harsh. You don't know the meaning of the word." He replied. "I was telling you earlier that our parents had left us with the Davenports because they thought we would be safer there. Fredrick and Ally Davenport cared for us like we were their own. They were scholars and they taught us everything we know. They taught us all about the different Guilds and their histories. We focused on the Weir a lot."

"Impossible! There is no way that Mortals could possibly know about magic." Grandma said.

Alec smiled at her. "Oh, I beg your pardon. Did I say that the Davenport's were Mortal? I meant to say, Half-Mortal."

The room went silent for a moment, then Grandma asked. "Half-Mortal?"

"Correct. Half-Mortal, Half-Hunter." Alec replied.

"Damn you creatures! You mated with Mortals?" Grandma was absolutely revolted at the idea.

"We didn't mate with anything. The Hunters of old did. There are hundreds of Half-Blood Hunter's all over the world."

Grandma wasn't doing a wonderful job at hiding her thoughts now. She couldn't believe that after all these years, there were still Hunter's out there. She was already thinking of ways to dispose of them.

"You're never going to find them. Their Mortal half shields them from magic, so don't bother trying." Alec took immense pleasure in taunting Grandma. He was reading her thoughts like me.

"Why are you toying with us? Why didn't you just tell us that in the first place?" Mom asked.

"Because it's much more fun this way." Alec replied with a laugh. "And we absolutely love to have fun."

"The Davenport's number one rule was to enjoy life, because you never know what could happen." Amber added.

"They taught us to be prepared for anything. If we made a plan, we had to think it through thoroughly, before putting it into action. That's why we took our time capturing you. We could have simply attacked, but it was much more strategic to have you come to us, and that's exactly what happened." Alec said.

"By using my family members as bait!" Grandma shouted.

"Like I said, it was all part of the strategy. You should appreciate that."

"When we were studying you. There wasn't that much information about this place. Did you know that Crystal Falls is one of many magical towns that exist in the United States? However, it is the only one that has Mortals living in it. Don't you despise Mortals?" he asked with a smile. "That concept has always intrigued me. Now that I'm here, I intend to discover more about that." Grandma was shocked by Alec's boldness and knowledge. No one was supposed to know about the magical towns. I knew very little about them myself. They're spread out all over the world and each one of them supports their own community. Like Crystal Falls, the magical towns were meant to stay hidden from enemy eyes. Alec was clearly enjoying Grandma's reaction. "You can't hide magic from us. The Hunters of old made sure that they knew of their enemies' strongholds, no matter how well they were hidden."

Grandma was really getting angry. She started struggling to get loose from the ropes, which only tightened more. "Free me from these binds and face me one to one." She challenged.

Alec completely ignored her. "Anyway, the Davenport's also taught us how to resist magic cravings. You see unlike us, Half-Bloods don't need magic to survive. They made us go weeks without magic. They showed us that we could last lengthy periods of time without it. That constant lust for magic that plagued the Hunters of old, doesn't happen to us."

"I don't believe you." I said. Everyone stared at me again, even Alec. This time I was determined not to get lost in his eyes. "Your sister said she had trouble stopping before when she tried to take my magic. You clearly admitted to having trouble yourself. I don't think that training is working very well."

"Oh, I wasn't taking your magic. I must touch you for that. I was merely controlling it." Amber replied.

"Your correct though. We knew it was going to be a challenge facing you. We've never been this close to magic of this level before. That's why I didn't look at you before. I meant no disrespect. I was afraid I was going to lose control." He replied. For some strange reason. I felt a lot better knowing that Alec wasn't trying to disrespect me.

"The Davenport's trained us to take only what we needed, and to use that magic sparingly. That's why we didn't drain your entire shield. They also said that we should take magic from other sources, like that Zeft." He said pointing to the now ordinary looking rock. "The only time we should take it from a person was in matters of life and death, and if that someone didn't deserve their powers in the first place."

"They sound like stunning role models. How dare you think that you can determine who deserves their powers and who doesn't." Greta replied

"We adored them." Amber said softly. She squeezed her hand into a fist. The ropes tightened once more around Grandma. I wished she would stop making them mad.

"What happened to your real parents?" Mom asked.

"The Davenport's told us they were killed in a confrontation with a group of Weir, but even they weren't sure. News was always hard to come by in Painswick." He said with a smile.

For the briefest of moments Grandma looked at Alec, not with anger, but with curiosity. Something in her eyes told me that she was remembering something. I quickly entered to find out what she was thinking, but whatever it was, it was gone. I debated on pushing harder like Alec said, but I decided that now was not a good time.

"We lived happily there until a week ago. One day a group of Wizards dropped by our house. Their robes bore the insignia of the 8th Covenant." Amber said.

"No!" Grandma said immediately. I knew whom Amber was referring too, Ignatius Clearwater's Covenant. "If Ignatius knew of your existence he would have told me!"

"Mother now is not the time!" Dad said. He was concerned like I was, that Alec and Amber would lash out at her if she said something wrong.

Alec simply looked at her with disgust. "I know exactly who they were. As if the robes and the Irish accents weren't enough to give them away!"

"I think you've been in this bloody town for too long. Ignatius Clearwater hasn't had control of his Covenant for a very long time." Amber said. I immediately thought back to my vision. Ignatius had said that Jacoby was poisoning his member's minds behind his back.

Grandma was shaking her head. She didn't believe anything that they were saying. "What did they want?" asked Dad. He was hoping to draw their attention on him.

"Us." Alec said simply. "They wanted our allegiance. They said that a war was coming. A war that would pit the Weirling against the Weirlind. The outcome would change the course of the magical world forever. They wanted us to be a part of history, a chance to have our own Guild. That, and so much more they said would be possible if we joined them to fight against your kind."

"What did the Davenport's say to that?" asked Dad.

"They were brilliant scholars, of course they knew better. They knew that we would do all the heavy work. We would put a huge dent in your numbers. Then after we were exhausted or killed. The Wizards would come in and finish the job." Amber said. "They told them not bloody likely."

"How did they react to that response?" Dad asked.

"They said we had no choice. It was either join them or die." Alec replied. "They were fools though. They gave the Davenport's several minutes to think it over, allowing me and Amber the chance to run. The Davenport's said they were going to hold them off long enough for us to escape." Alec seemed to be lost in the memory. "We got to the edge of the block when we realized we couldn't abandon them. I was going to go back and help. That's when the house was shredded to bits by an explosion." There was a long silence before he continued. "No one survived."

Amber continued for him. "I was scared and angry. If it weren't for Alec, I don't know what I would've done. We've never been outside of Painswick before. We had no idea where to go. There were more of them waiting for us though, and they followed us wherever we went. Her eyes grew intense. "We stopped running and we killed them."

"What happened after that?" Dad asked.

"We wanted revenge. We decided that the best way to get back at them was to align ourselves with the people they wanted a war with. If we told the Weirlind what they were planning. Then we were positive that they would help us make them pay." She said.

"But England is filled with old school Weirlind. Those who still believe in the Council's every bloody move." Said Alec.

"As they should!" replied Grandma.

Alec snorted. "Please! Do you think everyone is under the Council's thumb? The United States holds the most radical groups of Weirlind anywhere, those who refuse to follow the status quo. Look at yourselves for instance. Who ever heard of Weirlind living amongst Mortals? We knew that in this country we would find those that would gladly help us to go up against the Weirling."

"We easily charmed our way onto an airplane. We got on the first one leaving. It was by chance that it was going to Minnesota. We figured, why not? Why should we pass up the opportunity to confront the legendary Everhardtht family?" Amber said. "We didn't realize it was going to be this easy to find you. This state has no magical activity besides your Weir Wall, which has a strong scent by the way. There was nothing stopping us from getting to you, that's not smart on your part. I'm surprised your enemies haven't found you." They had to be lying. I knew for a fact that there were enchantments placed to keep people away from this town.

"We planned on arriving quietly, not wanting to attract any attention until we met with you personally. Running into the sheriff was not part of the plan. We told him that we were orphans looking for a good place to start over. My sister seemed to charm her way into his heart. Now he wants us to stick around town for a while, adjust to life in Crystal Falls." Alec was shaking his head at his sister. She blushed.

"What can I say? I have that effect on people." She said innocently.

A sudden thought popped into my head. Grandma had mentioned earlier this morning that Hunter's appeared older than they really were. I was curious as to how old Alec and Amber really were. "If you don't mind me asking. How old are you two exactly?" I asked.

"Technically Hunter's don't age. We only grow in physical strength and appearance as time goes on. Twenty years from now I'll probably look as young as I do now. We are immortals. However, I would be eighteen in Mortal years and Amber would be twelve." He replied.

"Female Hunter's grow differently. We don't grow as quickly as males. I might never get to be Alec's size at all, but we do tend to be much faster than they are." Amber said proudly.

"This is all well and good information. I'll be sure to tell the Council when I meet with them, but we seemed to be overlooking the big picture here once again. You have yet to specify why you have breached our borders? I'm sure it is not because we are famous, and you want our autographs." Grandma replied.

"Simply put, we want an alliance." Alec said.

"An alliance?" Grandma asked in a sarcastic tone. "For what?"

"They took the only family we had away from us. We want revenge." Alec said.

"Wait a minute. You want a war?" Mom asked. She couldn't believe what she was hearing.

"You misunderstood. I never said we wanted a war. We want revenge on those responsible for the Davenport's murders." Alec replied.

"The 8th Covenant?" Dad asked.

"Exactly." Alec replied.

"Absolutely not." Said Grandma. "There is no chance I'd help you go after a friends Covenant." I looked at Grandma. She knew very well that Ignatius was dead and that a supporter of Jacoby Valdorn was probably running his Covenant.

"I understand that your angry for what has happened to you, but that was a separate incident by people who wanted to start trouble. I'm sure if you discussed this with the right officials, you could bring those responsible to justice." Mom said.

Grandma shook her head at Mom. Alec replied. "Are you daft? Talk to the right officials. Who are we supposed to talk to? The leader of the Covenant? Like we said before, Ignatius has lost all control of his Covenant. Some say that he's disappeared, I'm not surprised."

"How could you possibly know all of this?" Grandma asked.

"Davenports, scholars, taught us everything we know." Alec said sarcastically. "Do we really have to go back to that again?"

"You can't blame a whole group of people for the actions of a few." Mom said.

"The bloody hell I can't! If our actions cause a war, then so be it! This has been brewing for years! No one is innocent in this conflict. You Weir think your better than everyone else, and you step on all those who are inferior to you!" Alec said.

"That's not a fair judgment! We're not all like that." Mom pleaded.

"What's fair about any of this? Is it fair what happened to us?" he shouted. Mom couldn't give him a reply. Alec began pacing around. "I wish that I would wake up, and still be in my bed in Painswick, but that life was taken from me! They wanted us to be a part of this conflict. Well now we are! We won't stop until we have our revenge! We know what we want!"

"Do you even hear yourself?" Dad said. He had gotten up from his seat. "I'm sorry son, but getting revenge is not going to bring you peace of mind. It's not going to bring your family back!" Dad said firmly.

"Don't you dare call me son." Alec replied. Dad was no small Warlock, but even he had to look up at Alec.

"What you want, will get thousands of people killed! It will start a war that'll tear apart everything. Do you really want that?"

"It's called casualties, it happens in wars. If I recall what I learned about you correctly Rowan Everhardtht, was that you were a radical. Weren't you once a major supporter of a Weir confrontation? I believe you once said that nothing opens people's eyes more than unnecessary bloodshed." It was really starting to piss me off that a stranger knew more about my family then I did.

"That was a long time ago. I have a family to take care of now, and we will not be taking part in any hair brained scheme concocted by a child, who's pretending to make a man's decision." Said Dad. Alec didn't respond, he just smiled back at Dad. "We're leaving now."

"Your free to go." Alec responded.

The ropes binding Grandma disappeared, and she got up. She was very happy that Dad had put Alec in his place. "Well said, Rowan." She got right in Alec's face. "You and your sister can get out of our town. We no longer have any interest in you or anything you have to say."

Alec smiled back. "Who's going to make us? You?" He said sizing her up. "You can't use that spell you're thinking of. If you try, you'll only burn down the entire building. You wouldn't want to hurt innocent people, now would you?"

I got up, ready to retort back. Lindsey and her Mom lived here. If anything happened to them I would kill him myself.

"We'll be going now." Dad said. Mom grabbed Merrin's hand. I followed quickly behind them. I was anxious to get out of this room and away from Alec and his sister. There were just too many things to process at once, my head was going to explode. Grandma however was still glaring at Alec. Neither one showed signs of backing down. "Mother let's go!" Reluctantly, Grandma backed away. Alec smiled. This was far from over. I was sure of it.

****

Alec

It was quiet for a moment after the Everhardtht's had left. Amber broke the silence. "Well that went well."

I took a deep breath, that could have been disastrous. Blimey they're extremely powerful, it took all my willpower not to break. "It could have been worse. We almost killed them on several occasions." I laughed.

"What happens now? Do we heed Greta's advice and leave town?" she smiled at me. She already knew the answer to that question.

"Of course not. For now, we lay low. We got our point across. We'll let it sink in before we have another go at them. We'll divide and conquer."

Amber was silent for a while, which was never a good sign. It meant that she was debating on asking me something, and she was afraid of how I'd react. "Rowan Everhardtht certainly had big words for you? What if we are too young to be making decisions like this one?"

"To be honest, I'd been thinking about that long before Rowan ever brought it up. He did strike a nerve though, I love his boldness. I guess he forgot about the little agreement he made with us before his family arrived." I said pulling out the parchment that had his and Merrin's signatures on it.

"We have two of them, all we need is to set our terms and conditions." I said.

Amber nodded slowly. She sat down on the couch and closed her eyes. Sometimes I wondered if I put too much pressure on her. She was only twelve after all. I was forced to grow up fast for both of us, and I didn't want that for her. At times, I thought running away with her would be the best thing I could do. It would be nice to live somewhere away from all the conflicts that shrouded the world. I tucked the parchment back into my pocket and went to sit next to her. Once I put my arm around her shoulder, she cuddled close to me. "What do you think of them?"

"Well Greta is everything I expected her to be. Extremely stubborn, strong willed, a compulsive liar."

"She's powerful." I nodded.

"Alec, I read her mind. If we didn't place this wall, we'd be dead. She despises our race."

"I know. She's going to be the hardest."

"We're still going to attempt to bring her to our side?" she asked. "Maybe we should just take what we need from her and be done with it."

"You want to kill her?" I asked.

"She's never going to join our cause. You heard her, she won't attack a friends Covenant. You and I both know of the secrets she keeps, we should just take her knowledge and magic and be done with her." It was true that Greta held a lot of interesting secrets. I briefly glanced into her mind to read her thoughts, but there was a whole lot more hidden within her mind.

"She's a key member of the Council of

Hemlock. If we kill her, then we'll have to worry about them coming after us. We already have one government looking for us, we don't need another. Besides she has the Council's ear. Anything she says to them will be taken into consideration." We needed powerful allies, and there is no group more powerful than the Everhardtht family. "We keep her alive for now."

Amber sighed, "If you say so." She curled up and put her head in my lap. I smiled, back home she used to do this all the time with Fredrick. It reminded me that I was her guardian now, and I needed to be strong for her.

"I feel a little bit bad about what we did to Merrin and Rowan." She said.

"I know, but it paid off. We have both of them now." I said, patting my pocket. "Two down, and three to go."

"Gwen's the typical Enchanter." She mumbled.

"Indeed. She's quite beautiful." I said. She elbowed me in the stomach. "Hey, what was that for?"

"She's quite beautiful?" she said sarcastically.

"What? All Enchanters are stunning. That's why they're called Enchanters." She put her head back down. I couldn't see her face, but I was sure that she just rolled her eyes. "She's got a dark past though, it's been pushed to the deepest part of her mind. Her past will be how we get to her."

"That leaves only one." She said.

"Angelica is definitely complex." I said.

"You couldn't wait to meet her. Is she everything you expected?" I knew she was toying with me. Of all the Everhardtht's, Angelica was the one I really wanted to meet.

"We know her story Ambs. The only Darkling alive in the world and the only Weir to ever possess the gift of sight."

"How do you think she received that gift?"

"Her Grandmother definitely knows. You heard the questions she was asking. She doesn't know a bloody thing about her gift. They're keeping it from her for some reason. I don't think they realized what that spell has done to her."

"Alec, When I was using her as an example for Greta. I felt something evil, it was egging me on. Almost like it wanted me to take her powers. It

almost felt like she had another person inside of
her."

"I felt it too." I said. "She yelled at me to look
at her. Her eyes were a different color, they were as
black as night."

"What do you think it is?"

"I don't know, but were going to have to find
out what it is, if we want her on her side.
She's the prize Amber."

"She's kind of fit too." she said casually.

"What does that have to do with anything?" I
asked. Of course she's pretty. That fact didn't escape
me.

"Nothing." She said innocently. "What do we
do now?"

"Well if we're going to stay in Minnesota,
then some warmer clothes would be nice." I said.

She giggled. "That would be good. These
clothes are starting to wear thin."

I laughed. That was because we were wearing
the same ones for a week. Something I wouldn't
recommend doing if you didn't have magical
powers.

Chapter 9
Disturbing News

Greta
(6:00 P.M.- July 1)

It was starting to get dark when we arrived back outside the Manor. I couldn't believe that I wasted an entire day in the presence of those Hunter's. I couldn't believe the events of the past 24 hours. They were just too unreal to be true. A part of me didn't want to believe that my dear old friend Ignatius Clearwater was dead, but I knew better. Angelica's visions were always correct. They had become a curse to my family. Every time she had one, grave news always seemed to follow.

Jacoby Valdorn was causing trouble again. That man has such a strong hatred for Weirlind. It goes back as long as I can remember. It's not the first time that egotistical maniac has tried to start a war. This time however he seems to have taken things to a whole new level. He wants to make a statement at my families' expense. Well if it is a fight he wants, then a fight is what he will get, and after he is defeated once again. I'll spit on his grave for killing Ignatius.

On top of all of that, now I must deal with two adolescent magic thieves, who think they can invade my territory and demand that we join them in their own glorified schemes. I didn't believe a damn word of that story. I knew Ignatius was having problems within his Covenant, but he wouldn't tell me what they were. I knew for sure that he would have told me if he found out about the Hunter's continued existence. He was a part of the group that helped me kill them. If Ignatius lost total control of his Covenant, then it was his people who were to blame for this mess.

Those runts embarrassed me in front of my family. What a wretched spawn of a race. Now with the discovery of Half-Bloods out there, the world will be damned until I get rid of them. There's never been an enemy I feared more than them, and even though these two were just hatchlings. Their powers were not to be underestimated, I'll never underestimate them again! Something bothered me about these two. They sparked a memory from my past. Something that up until now, I had forgotten about. They were also unlike any of the Hunter's I've come across before. They were far more advanced than their ancestors.

Worst of all, they go planting ideas in Angelica's head about the true origins of her abilities. I've spent years keeping her gift a secret from her and I'll be damned if I let them surface now. If she ever discovers her true powers, it'll be the end of everything I worked so hard to achieve.

This was all for her well-being. If she only knew about the forces out there that wanted her powers. There were people who would use her for their own selfish ends. I was never going to allow that to happen.

There were moments today where she really frightened me. I must go back and strengthen that curse on her. The Darkling inside of her was appearing way too often. I must set her straight, before things go too far.

"Angelica, we need to talk." I said.

She spun on her heels. "Why should I listen to you? Because apparently, you haven't told me one truthful thing yet!" She shouted. There it was again, the change in her eyes, they were black.

"You're going to believe the words of two total strangers over your own Grandmother?" I asked.

"Two total strangers who just happen to be just like me. I know you said that my gift was rare among Weirlind. But now I find out that Weirlind aren't even supposed to possess this gift." She said. Her eyes changed back to their normal emerald green. She was starting to cry.

"It is a rare gift, a special gift." I replied. "You think it to be a curse." She cried. Darn it! She was reading my mind again. I must squash this out of her. I will not put up with this nonsense.

"After everything they just did to us, you can't possibly believe anything that comes from their mouths. They used Merrin to get to your father, all so they can lure the three of us out of hiding. Then they go and give us that long sob story of how they're the innocent ones. Yet they want to go off and start a bloody revolution."

"I didn't say I believed them. But I saw the expressions you made when they were talking about my gift. There was a moment Grandma when I wanted to push further into your mind like that boy said. Is it true that I can? Do you know more about my gift then you've been saying?" She asked.

I didn't know how to answer her. She was probably feeling betrayed, but I only did this for her own good.

"It is true, isn't it?" She sobbed.

I took a deep breath, trying to control my anger. Darn those Hunter's for what they have done. "I'm doing this for your own good Angelica. There are things you just don't understand."

"Then explain them to me! For my entire life you have been giving me that same lame excuse. Tell me the truth for once Grandma!" Suddenly lightning crackled in the clear night sky. Those black eyes were back again. They were staring at me with such hatred, but as quickly as they were there, they vanished just as fast. I had to fix that spell.

"You're still not going to tell me, are you? You're good at telling lies and keeping secrets. You've had years of practice I suspect."

I stood there too stunned to say anything. Gwen broke the silence. "Angelica Elizabeth Everhardtht! That was uncalled for, and you know it. Apologize to your Grandmother this instant."

She just stared at me for what seemed like an eternity. Her words felt like a knife through my heart. Angelica always looked up to me. Never once did she question that I didn't have her best interests at heart. I'm going to make those Hunter's pay for this! "Please mother. Like you don't know the truth."

"Angelica apologize now!" Rowan said, coming up from behind me. There was no sign of Merrin, she must have sneaked into the house.

"Fine! I'm sorry! I'm sorry for ever trusting you! If none of you want to tell me the truth, then

I'll find it out on my own!" She stalked into the house, slamming the door behind her with such force that it splintered.

"Angelica." Gwen ran in after her, repairing the door as she went inside.

If anyone could make her see sense, it was Gwen. I meanwhile, felt like I was going to explode. I shouted with so much fury that I blasted a nearby tree into flames. It felt good to let some frustration out.

"Blast it all!" I shouted.

"Mother calm down." Rowan said putting out the flames. "She didn't mean what she said."

"I know that!" I snapped. "You saw what I saw. She's not herself right now. Once she calms down, she'll be fine. You must keep her calm until I return. I'll strengthen the spell then." I said. I couldn't do it now. Not with Angelica feeling the way she does about me.

"What are you going to do?" he asked.

"I have to take care of some things." I replied. Things needed to be set right, and only I could be the one to do it. I quickly entered the manor. Rowan was right on my heels.

"Mother what are you thinking?" he asked. "You're not going after those Hunter's again."

"I can't believe I'm saying this. The Hunters are the least of my worries. We thought that Jacoby had sent them, but after this afternoon that apparently is not the case. That's the one thing they said that I believed. They don't want us dead, they want our help to get revenge. In a way, I can't blame them. Somebody tried to recruit them, and I attend to find out who that someone is!"

"Do you believe they were from Ignatius's Covenant?" Rowan asked.

"Ignatius knew nothing about this, I'm sure of it. Someone else is giving the orders." I said.

"What about the Hunter's?"

"It is going to be your job to make sure they leave." After climbing the main staircase, we turned left down the east wing hallway. At the end of the hall, there was a large mirror. As we approached it, I waved my hand and the mirror vanished, revealing another long hallway. Most of the east wing was hidden by magic. This is where my bedroom is located, and other secret rooms.

Rowan followed me into the wing. The hallway we just came from disappeared as soon as we entered, replaced by a solid wall. Hanging on it was a large picture of Salazar the Wicked, and Alexander the Great. The city of Alexandria was in the background. Alexander may have conquered almost all of Europe, but Salazar was the true mastermind behind his might.

"How do you propose I make them leave?" Rowan asked.

"Find a way, because if they're still here when I get back." I said. "Let's just say, some unpleasant things will occur."

"You're just going to let them leave?"

"Of course not. I'm still going to kill them. I'll give them a head start though." They should be lucky I'm giving them a chance at all.

"Where are you going?"

"I must go to Hemlock, but first I need to check on the spells we placed. Those Hunter's should have never gotten to this town that easily." When I asked them how they had gotten here, they said that they had smelled our Weir Wall. I placed dozens of enchantments to keep people miles from this place. They shouldn't have been able to smell a thing. Something wasn't right.

"Are you going to tell them about the Hunter's?" Rowan asked.

"Of course not! If I tell them about the Hunter's. They'll say that they were right from the beginning. They'll say I should've been living in Hemlock and not here on my own. You and I both know why they want us living in Hemlock." No one ever tells me that I'm wrong. I'm not going to let that start now, because of those brats. "The Half-Bloods must be dealt with as well. How? I don't know yet."

"Mother there is something I have to tell you." He said.

I interrupted him, I needed Rowan to know the game plan. He was in charge once I left. "Listen to me." I said, stopping and turning to face him. "You must keep Angelica away from them at all costs. She can't find out about her gift. You saw what it did to her today."

"I understand mother, but I still need…"

"What I really want, is to know how come I haven't been informed of the actions of the Weirling. We have spies all over the world. You would think I would've been informed about Ignatius's death. Or if Weirling were seen scouring the countryside looking for something. We should have been the first ones to find those Hunter's. I want to know just how exactly they found them?"

My room was the farthest door in the corridor. Once in front of it, I placed my hand on the wooden door. It swung open to admit us. My room was by far the largest bedroom in the house. The king size bed held sheets that were once used by Weirlind the likes of Henry VII. The furniture belonged to the Great Mongol Warlock Genghis Khan. The walls were filled with shelves that contained many magical artifacts. Potions, Zefts, scrolls that were taken from the library in Alexandria, a golden locket that the ancient Greeks believed the goddess Aphrodite wore. There were artifacts scattered all over the room. I've collected thousands of rare items over the ages. Most of them were worth a fortune. I'll be damned though if I let them rot away in some museum.

As soon as we arrived in the room, I knew something was different. When I left the room this morning. The clock that hung in the corner didn't have letters sticking out of the slot where the bird usually pops out. The clock dates back to the Civil War. Weir officers would pass information on the location of the Confederates to one another. There were only two of them. I had one, and the other hung in the main hall at Hemlock.

I rushed to the clock and grabbed the letters. Two of them were newspaper clippings and the other was a certified letter from Hemlock. I broke the Council's seal and read:

Greta

One of my spies picked these up yesterday. Something is going on in the Covenants. The Council is deciding on whether to call an emergency meeting to discuss future actions. You have to read these articles! I wanted to be the first to extend my sincerest of apologies. We will get to the bottom of this!

Sincerely Yours
Evangeline Medwid
Guardians

I folded the letter up and gave it to Rowan. Evangeline Medwid represented the Guardians on the Council. Her kind had a talent for spy work. They protect some of our most valuable secrets, like the locations of the magical communities of Weirlind. For her to send a message directly to me, I knew something was wrong. I unrolled the newspaper clippings. The first was a piece of the front page of the Wizard Gazette.

COVENANT LEADER FOUND DEAD

We regret to inform you this morning of the death of Ignatius Clearwater, Head of the 8th Covenant. Clearwater (260) was found in his

Northern Ireland home by fellow Covenant members. They were checking up on him after he failed to report in after an annual Covenant gathering. Wizard investigators were summoned to the scene immediately. After a thorough investigation of the house, officials stated that there were no signs of forced entry or any physical marks on the body. The Covenant leaders were informed that he died of natural causes. Clearwater has no living relatives. Funeral arrangements will be handled by his protégée and second in command; Gregor Langston. Langston is expected to be sworn in as the new head of the Covenant as soon as possible. "No one will ever fill old Ignatius shoes, but I will do my best to make him proud of me." Said Langston through bloodshot eyes. Clearwater was a veteran of the War of Council and an advocate for peace among the Weir. "It will be my honor to continue the mission that he started." declared Langston proudly.

"Bidding You Adieu"
Georgia Ravencroft
Wizard Gazette

I threw the paper down with disgust. Hearing it from Angelica the other night was hard enough, but to read it all over again, and have it confirmed made it feel a whole lot worse.

"What is it?" Rowan asked.

"They found Ignatius's body." I said softly. Rowan picked up the article and read it silently. After reading it, he asked. "Who the hell is this Langston fellow?"

"That's what I would like to know. Ignatius didn't believe in protégée's. He told me that his Covenant would elect the next leader after him by popular vote." I remembered that Angelica had told us that Valdorn had known whom Ignatius's replacement would be. "He is probably Jacoby's pawn." I said through gritted teeth. "He's probably the one causing all the trouble. They won't get away with what they've done."

"What does the other article say?" he asked.

I looked at the second clipping. It was from a newspaper that I've never heard of before; Weirling Truth.

Ignatius Clearwater:
Death By Natural Causes, or was it
Murder?

If you happened to be reading the Gazette this morning, you couldn't help but notice the lovely little front headline article by Georgia Ravencroft. Don't you find it interesting that Ignatius Clearwater, a war veteran, and a visionary for peace. Who has lived up to the age of 260. Only received a half-page's remembrance. If you could call it a remembrance at all. It's barely sixteen lines! Where is everything else? Where is his life story, everything that he has accomplished over the years? What about his role as the leader of a Covenant that has fought for peace for nearly two decades? Don't you find it a little suspicious that a man who had perfect health just suddenly died of natural causes? When was the last time you heard of anyone magical die of natural causes? Isn't it strange that they announced that his funeral would be a private one, only for his Covenant members? It makes one think that someone is trying to cover something up. My dear readers. Simply put. Our Wizarding Government doesn't care too much about his sudden death.

What could they be covering up you ask? Well I'll tell you. With significant risk to my life, I bring you a story of treachery. Before his death, Ignatius Clearwater confided in me that there were moles within his Covenant. These moles were poisoning his member's minds and turning them against him. He told me that he didn't know whom to trust anymore. Ignatius also confided with me the recent events that were taking place within the Sanctuary. A place where the original leaders forged a government that would protect all Weirling. Recently there have been several discussions by a leader. Who would like more than nothing to declare war against our Weirlind cousins. This leader is none other than the famous Jacoby Valdorn. Leader of the 4th Covenant (Great Britain).

It appears as though Valdorn has tried numerous times to pass along an order, that would declare a full out war with the Weirlind.

This is an issue that he has argued for since the founding of the Covenants. As I'm sure you all know, a war with the Weirlind will cause massive destruction. Not to mention the number of casualties that both sides would suffer. Why would one of our government officials be discussing such a plan? When he should be looking out for the safety of his people.

Ignatius said that he had fought off every proposed plan that Valdorn has put forward. The arguments between the two became common during the annual meetings. As you know, a majority vote is needed to pass an order. And according to Ignatius, the last order that Jacoby set forward caused such high tensions among the leaders, that an uneven rift was clearly beginning to form between the Covenant heads. This time Hiram Garratty had to squash the plan. He didn't even let the order go to a vote. Although none of the other Covenant leaders spoke up at the meeting to support Valdorn. Ignatius said that it was clear to him, that some were leaning towards the plan. It is also no secret that Valdorn would stoop to intimidation if necessary to get what he wants.

Garratty, Clearwater, Kahne and Valdorn are the four founding members of the Covenant of

Wizards. These four men were once comrades in arms during the War of Council. Jacoby Valdorn's beliefs. Seem to have created a gap between the once friends. During this last meeting both Clearwater and Kahne argued vigorously against him. Valdorn was visible upset with the latest failed outcome and was especially furious with Ignatius for several slandering remarks he made against his Covenant.

So, I'm asking you, as the reader. To think carefully on what I'm about to say. There has been no official statement by the 8th Covenant on Ignatius's death. All we have is that lovely little article by Georgia. No statement means we have no solid information on what actually happened. The one piece of information this author is most interested in, is the time of death? After all, I spoke with Ignatius a day after the last meeting, and although he was nervous about the state of his Covenant. He was clearly in good health. Now there is no way to prove that foul play had anything to do with Ignatius's death. However, it is this writer's belief that if Jacoby Valdorn would stoop to intimidation, then he would definitely stoop to murder.

Ms. Ravencroft is a horrible writer to be covering any story. She made several boneheaded Comments in her small piece. The first was when she said that his Covenant members were checking up on him after the meeting. This is now July the

1st. The meeting took place on the 23rd of June. Does that mean these people went a week without hearing from their leader, and only now they decided to check up on him? Ignatius was not a reclusive man. He spent much of his time with his people. Wouldn't you check on him sooner if no one saw or heard from him? Another one was that she said that the investigators found no signs of forced entry. Well of course there weren't any. If the actions were carried out by a Weir. Then they wouldn't need to force their way into the house. Thirdly, bodily scars can be hidden for a certain amount of time. I wonder what we would see on his body if we used some revealing spells.

Unfortunately, no one will get the chance to do so, because his body is being cremated. An order that was passed down by Gregor Langston. A scrawny excuse for a Wizard, who now comes to the forefront, and says he is second in command. My excellent sources told me that Ignatius never officially confirmed a second in command. Who is this so-called protégée? This and many more questions will be answered in my next piece. For now, I invite you to read more about Ignatius Clearwater. This is a true remembrance for this extraordinary man.

I know that once this news spreads, my work will not be allowed to be viewed, but don't worry. Nothing will keep me from getting the truth out.

I'll have to write my summaries while on the run, because there is no doubt that people will be coming after me.

Stay tuned to my next issue. Until then I wish you all the best in these dark and uncertain times.

Phantom of the North

I dropped the paper and sat down on the edge of my bed. I couldn't bear to look at the remembrance yet. The articles words were echoing in my head. Apparently, Ignatius had confided in this "phantom". That bothered me more than I was willing to admit. Why didn't he come to me? I would have helped him, I would have saved him. I didn't trust this "phantom". Why didn't he or she speak up sooner? Ignatius might still be alive if they had. There were just too many unanswered questions, and it was time that I had some answers.

I know from experience, that speaking out against a government normally leads to backlash. I knew it wouldn't take long for Jacoby to find this person and silence them. I had to beat him to it. This person held more information to this story.

Rowan had just finished the article. He was looking at me.

"They sabotaged him. Jacoby and this Langston." I said.

"There may be no truth to this story."

"That article, along with Angelica's vision is enough proof for me." I responded. "Valdorn's guilty and his punishment will be death."

"What's vengeance going to accomplish?" I stared at him with an opened mouth. There was a time when Rowan would agree with me on matters such as this. "You're listening to your wife way too much, you're going soft."

"I have a family to protect." He responded.

"Which is exactly what I'm doing!"

"Answer the question mother." He said.

"Ignatius will have his vindication." I answered.

"Would Ignatius really want that?"

"I DON'T CARE! HE WAS FAMILY!" I shouted. "And nobody gets away with hurting my family." I stood up, more determined than ever to get my answers. I snapped my fingers. Instantly I had on a fresher set of clothes. I tucked the Weirling Truth article into my pocket.

"What do you expect to achieve by going to Hemlock?" he asked.

"An emergency meeting WILL be called. It's long overdue that we discuss this Weir conflict."

"Do you think there really will be a war?" he asked.

"That boy was right about one thing. This has been brewing for a long time. It's time Weirling learned their place in our society." I said. "Remember what I told you. Those Hunter's better be gone by the time I get back."

"Before you leave. You have to…" I vanished from the room before he could finish.

Chapter 10
Brett & Lindsey

Alec
(8:00 A.M.- July 4th)

Wednesday and Thursday seemed to fly by in an instant. It's been two whole days since we first made contact with the Everhardtht's. Ever since then Amber and myself had been second guessing our next move. We made it here without a hitch. We flawlessly lured them into our trap, but now they know what to expect from us. Our next move would have to be just as cunning as our first.

Amber and I haven't left the room since then. I think she's starting to get a little cranky with me. We have gone over a dozen different plans, but not one of them seemed right to me. Amber complained that I was being too much of a perfectionist. She wanted to take a risk and try one of our plans. I liked taking risks myself, but not if it meant she could get hurt in the process. I couldn't afford to be reckless with her life. I needed to protect her. She was still sleeping peacefully in the bed next to me. I meanwhile, have been up for the past hour thinking things over in my head.

Yesterday our planning was interrupted by several nosey visits from both Grace Hansen and

Sheriff Hansen, they were going to be a problem. They had it in their heads that we should live here in Crystal Falls. The sheriff came by to suggest that I get a job at his station, answering the telephone. I respectfully told him that I'd think about it, even though I have no intentions of ever saying yes. I felt a little bad for the guy. I found out from reading his thoughts, that he saw very little action in this town. Most of the time he was bored at work, and there was nobody there to keep him company. He also came over to drop off brand new sets of clothes for us. It was perfect timing too, because the ones we were currently wearing were starting to break down. After a while not even magic can repair some things. Grace had come by to check on us. She wanted to make sure that we were comfortable. She lingered forever, asking us if we needed anything. It was bloody annoying. They're nice people and their hearts are in the right place, but they were distractions that we didn't need.

I decided to get up and take a bath. It felt good to bathe again on an everyday basis. While we were on the run we barely had time to eat, never mind bathe. Cleaning yourself with magic works brilliantly, but nothing beats the real thing.

Twenty minutes later I was clean. I threw on a pair of black jeans and a long sleeve dress shirt. The workman's boots that I've been wearing were still in good condition. I put them on. These clothes must have cost Sheriff Hanson a bomb. I made a mental note to repay him some way. When I arrived back in the bedroom, Amber was up and dressed.

"I thought you missed taking a bath?" I asked.

She smiled. "I did. However, using magic is much simpler." She waved her hand, and a bit of orange magic floated above her.

I frowned at her. "Remember what the Davenports said about using magic sparingly?"

"Don't lecture me. It's not like I used all the magic I have." She said, sticking her tongue out at me.

"All I'm saying is that we're pretending to be Mortals. That means getting cleaned like Mortals do. That shouldn't be hard for us." I said, sitting down next to her on the bed. The Davenports raised us the Mortal way. They taught us not to always rely on magic. "We have to use the magic we take wisely."

She rolled her eyes at me and asked; "So do we have a plan for today? Or are you going to nitpick at every little detail again?"

"I'm just being cautious."

"Alec there is a difference between being cautious and being paranoid. We must take a chance. Nothing is ever going to run smoothly. I know you're worried about me, but as long as we're in this together, nothing bad is going to happen. We've made a few mistakes. So far, they haven't turned out that bad. I mean look at these brilliant clothes the sheriff gave us." She said, standing up and showing off her fresh look.

I sighed. "I guess running into the sheriff wasn't that big of a mistake. He and Grace have treated us well. I never expected that we get room and board for free." I said. "That's not the mistake I'm thinking about though."

"Alec, we can't change what happened. We were both scared, and we made mistakes."

"We had a plan though, even before the Davenport's were killed. I should have stuck to those plans."

"Nothing bad happened. We're both still here, and we're following through with that plan. We had a hiccup along the way. Who bloody cares?" Amber said.

I looked at her. "You're sure I'm not putting too much pressure on you?"

"I'll be fine Alec. Didn't you see the way I handled the Everhardtht's?" she asked.

I smiled. "Yes. You took out all five of them by yourself but remember they couldn't use magic."

"A mere technicality. I could have done it even if they did have their powers." She said proudly.

I laughed at her. "Alright. I guess I underestimated my baby sister."

"You think?" she said sarcastically.

"Don't get smart."

She smiled. "What are we going to do?"

I thought about it for a moment. One thing was for sure, we had to get out of this room. The longer we stayed in here, the more stir-crazy we were bound to get. "Well the first thing..." Someone knocked on the front door. "Blast! It must be the Sheriff or Grace again."

"I'll go inside. Maybe if I'm not in the room they won't stay long." One of the advantages of being a Hunter is that people are naturally attracted to us, because of our beauty. Mortals are more susceptible to our charms then magical folk. It comes in handy when I'm trying to impress a pretty girl, but in this case, when were trying not to draw attention to ourselves, it becomes a curse. "Try not to be too much of a Prince Charming." Amber said as she left the room.

I shook my head as she left. It's not like I can flip a bloody switch and stop being handsome. She's worse than me when it comes to attracting people. The sheriff is absolutely enthralled with her.

When I opened the front door. The person standing in front of me wasn't whom I was expecting. A girl probably around sixteen was smiling back at me. Caught off guard for a moment, all I managed to say was; "Hi."

"Hi." She said still smiling. She was of fare height, with shoulder length blonde hair, that she pushed back behind her ears, dark blue eyes, and her skin was tanned. She looked very familiar to me. Almost like I've met her before, and her dark blue eyes reminded me of someone.

Realizing that I was staring at her. I cleared my throat and asked. "May I help you?" "I'm really sorry to bother you, I know you just moved in and all. Mom told me not to come over right away, but I just wanted to introduce myself." She talked fast, like she was nervous. "I'm Lindsey Hansen." She said holding out her hand.

"Hansen? As in Sheriff and Grace Hansen?" I asked. When I went to shake her hand, I received a jolt. Suddenly, all I could see or hear was Lindsey. Everything else around me became a blur. Usually I never prided into Mortals minds unless I had to, but I had no control over this. I wanted to let go of her hand, but it was almost as if I lost my will power to move. There was something strange about Lindsey. She had no magical scent, but there was something off about her. The moment we shook hands, a telepathic connection opened between us. I could hear her thoughts. Most of them were about me.

"My mom is Grace, and my dad's the Sheriff. Their divorced, but they still have a good relationship with each other." She said.

I realized at that moment that her dark blue eyes were exactly like her father's. However, there was still something familiar about her. I felt like I've known her my entire life, but that's crazy. I've only just met her today. Realizing that we were still holding hands, she finally let go. The connection cut off immediately after she let go of my hand. "Sorry." She said blushing.

"That's fine." I said smiling. She stood there awkwardly for a moment. She was waiting for something. It took me a second to realize I hadn't introduced myself.

"I'm Alec Davenport." I said.

"I was beginning to think you didn't have a name." She replied.

"Sorry about that. I'm not usually this daft." I said. "Did you need something?"

"Yah. I was wondering since you're new to the town and all. I thought that maybe you would like me to give you a tour?" She asked awkwardly. At least I wasn't the only one uncomfortable with this conversation. "I'm meeting my friends later, we're going to get lunch. Would you like to come?"

Absolutely not. Something about this girl was strange. I just couldn't put my finger on it. "Sure, that would be great." Wait a minute, why did I just say that?

"Cool" she said, smiling again. "Are you ready now? Or do you still need to get ready?"

I was still shocked that I said yes to her, when I clearly wanted to say no. Why did I do that? I'm usually much more forceful. Now I would look like a total heel if I said no now. I guess I'm taking a tour today. It wasn't exactly what I had planned, but I guess it would have to do. "I just have to tell my sister where I'm going."

"Okay, I'll wait for you."

I opened the door behind me and stepped back inside. That's when Amber's voice made me jump. "Who was it?"

"Amber you gave me a freight." I said. What was wrong with me today? First, I can't say no to a girl. Then my baby sister scares me.

"Alec, you look like you've just seen a ghost. Who was it?" she asked.

"Lindsey Hansen, the sheriff's daughter." I replied. Then I got an idea. "Listen, I want you to follow me and her around today." I said.

"Alec we're supposed to be working on the Everhardtht's. Not going out on dates. Weren't we just discussing about making mistakes?" she asked.

"First off, it's not a date. Secondly, I wanted to say no to her."

"Then why didn't you?"

"I don't know. I just sort of blurted it out."

"Is it possible that you just like her?" she asked.
"Look. She is rather fit. I'll admit to that, but that does not explain the telepathic connection we just had with each other."

"Wait a minute. You mean you read her mind?"

I shook my head. "I didn't do anything. When I shook her hand, I heard her immediate thoughts. That's never happened with any Mortal I've met before. I had no control over myself. I couldn't even let go of her hand. I just stood there staring at her like a bleeding bum. She had to let go." I said.

"That doesn't make any sense Alec. Are you sure you weren't trying to read her mind?" She asked.

"I'm sure Ambs."

"Was she able to read your thoughts?"

"If she felt what I did, she gave no indication of it." I said.

Amber looked concerned. "This isn't good Alec."

"I know, but that's not the worst of it. Amber, she has no magical scent. She's a Mortal."

"How is that possible?" she asked. "Could she be lying about who she is?"

"No. She has her father's eyes, and her mother's hair and skin tone. Even if she was in disguise, I would have sensed the magic." I said.

"The sheriff and Grace didn't have a scent either." Amber said. "They're all Mortals."

"I know." I ran a hand through my hair.

"Alec. There's something else you're not telling me."

I looked at her. "I can't shake this feeling that I've seen her before."

"Maybe the Hansen's have been to Painswick."

I frowned at her. "Amber you know as well as I do that nobody ever visited our town."

"It's just a suggestion." She said. "Do you think the Everhardtht's know about her?"

"Possibly." I responded. I hadn't thought about that until now. This could be a plot by Greta.

"She could be working for them."

"Well if she is an enemy, it's best to keep her close, and find out all we can about her." I said. "I need you to follow us and stay in constant contact with me. Stay close enough to us where you can see and hear her. Tell me if you feel something strange about her like I do." "Alright. I'll leave a few seconds after you do." She said. "Where are you going?"

"On a tour of the town. Then she's meeting a few friends for lunch."

"Alec. Are you sure this is worth it. We could be wasting time."

"It won't be a waste, trust me." Lindsey had to be supernatural. I was now determined to figure out who, and what she is?

She was waiting for me when I stepped back outside. "Ready?" she asked. "Does your sister want to come?"

"Amber's more of a shy type." I said. I gave her a charming smile. She blushed.

"Shy!" Amber's voice shouted in my head. Seer's can communicate telepathically with each other. Amber and I also have access to each other's thoughts. That's how come we both know how the other is feeling.

"I'd like to meet her." Lindsey said.

I didn't want Amber anywhere near her. "Sure! Maybe later." Bloody Hell! I can't say no to this girl! That was the second time that I wanted to, but couldn't.

"I hope she doesn't ask to kill us! Because if she does, then were totally screwed." I smiled and took a deep breath. This was going to be a long morning.

Sure enough, we spent the entire morning touring the town. Lindsey showed me every single nook and cranny. For a small town, there definitely were a lot of places to see. Lindsey explained everything to me in detail, and I was glued to her every word, no matter how ridiculously boring they were.

"Alec. Usually this kind of stuff would bore me, but the way she's telling it, I can't get enough." Amber said. She had been quiet for most of the tour. She had told me earlier that Lindsey's words were mesmerizing her. I was glad that it wasn't just me she was affecting.

"I see what you mean about her being familiar. I feel like I know her too. Maybe I should try reading her mind."

"It's worth a shot." I hadn't thought about trying that. As Amber tried to read Lindsey's mind.

I tried to keep up with the story she was telling me about one of the shops on Main Street.

"You know you're really full of beans." I said smiling.

"Full of what?" she asked.

I laughed. "Sorry, pardon my slang. I meant that you're full of energy."

Her cheeks flushed red. "I guess I was rambling a bit. My friends tell me I do that all the time." She said. "Are you hungry? I'm meeting them at the diner."

"After that tour, I can go for a drink, I'm parched." I said.

"I love your accent." She said with a giggle. "We're going to Logan's Deep-Fried Diner."

"Deep-Fried?" I asked.

"Oh, they don't fry everything. That's just the name of the diner." She said.

"Alec, I can't read her mind!" Amber shouted at me.

"What do you mean?" I asked.

"I mean that her mind is closed to me!"

"That could only mean that she's a Seer. How the bloody hell is that possible? She's a Mortal." I've been close to Lindsey for the past few hours and I still haven't detected a scent on her.

"Is it possible that Mortals can possess our gift as well?" Amber asked.

"I don't know. The Davenport's said that the art of Seeing was a Hunter thing only. Maybe they were wrong. Let's see if I have any luck." I doubled checked to see if I could read her mind, but it was closed to me as well. This girl was starting to unnerve me. Seer's could enter everyone's mind except another Seer's. If she is indeed a Mortal. Then somewhere in her life, she would have had to been cursed by a Gypsy. They were the only ones who could bestow this gift. I didn't understand any of this. Angelica and Lindsey were both sixteen. Gypsies have been gone for centuries. It was impossible for either one to ever have encountered one.

The Diner was on a side street just off the Main roadway. It was small and quaint, like every other building in this town. The smells coming from the diner brought back memories of when Amber and I were little. The Davenports always made us home cooked meals, and it always tasted great.

I followed Lindsey as she approached a boy of about the same age as herself. He was standing in front of the diner. He smiled happily at her. His face darkened when he realized that I was with her.

Oh Brilliant! That's just what I needed now. A jealous boy thinking that I'm trying to cozy up to his girl. He was tall and lean like myself, he clearly worked out. His hair, which was light brown, was combed back with a super amount of hair gel. He was sizing me up with those lime green eyes. He was tall, but not as tall as me.

Lindsey gave him a hug when we approached. Then she stood back to introduce me. "Alec this is one of my best friends, Brett Ramsey. Brett, this is Alec Davenport. He just moved into town a few nights ago. He's staying at the B & B."

Brett held his hand out. I extended mine and we shook hands firmly. "Pleasure to meet you Brett."

"Likewise, Davenport. Strange accent you have there. You're not from around these parts?" He asked.

"I guess the accent gives me away. My sister and I are from England." I replied.

Brett whistled. "You're a long way from home. If you don't mind me asking. Why are you here in Crystal Falls?"

I did mind him asking! *"Calm down Alec! Just answer his question!"* Amber yelled.

"Amber I can handle myself!" I yelled back.

"Are you sure, because you two look like a couple of bloody bulls during mating season."

"Oh, Shut it!"

"It's a long story." I said to Brett.

"One that I want to hear as well." Lindsey said smiling at me. Now Brett's mind I could read. He clearly didn't like me, I was the new guy invading his turf. "C'mon I'm hungry. Let's go get a table." Lindsey led the way into the diner. At the hostess desk, a friendly face smiled back at us when we walked in.

"Well what a surprise! Miss. Hansen and Mr. Ramsey coming to eat at my restaurant." Said the hostess. Her gentle smile reminded me of Ally Davenport. Once again, old feelings flooded back into my mind. I quickly cleared them away. I knew Amber could see my thoughts, and I didn't want her to get upset.

"Who's this scrapping young fellow with you?" The hostess asked. She smiled brightly at me.

"Violet this is Alec Davenport. Alec this is Violet Krenshaw. She and her husband run the diner." Said Lindsey.

"It's a pleasure to meet you Mam." I said.

"Ahhh! This must be the young Englishman that the sheriff was talking about." Said Violet.

I frowned. Laying low in this town was going to be harder than I thought. "I guess news travels fast around here."

"You'll get used to it honey." She said winking at me. "Table for three darlings?" she asked.

"Four, Violet." Lindsey replied.

"I should have known the third Musketeer would be coming." Violet said. "Follow me."

Violet showed us to a table near the corner of the room. Several sets of eyes followed us to the table. I knew they were all looking directly at me. I guess everyone wanted to get a glimpse at the new guy in town. *"You're a star Alec."* Amber said sarcastically.

"Didn't I tell you to shut it?" I said back.

Violet spent at least 10 minutes at our table trying to get me to tell her my story. The sheriff had already told her, but she wanted to hear it for herself.

I figured, why not tell them all at once, and be done with it.

I shared with them the same story that we told the sheriff. Most of it is the truth. Every time Violet Krenshaw asked a question. I replied with a No Mam or Yes Mam. "You're so respectful dear. If only I can get my husband to talk to me like that." She said shaking her head. After I finished the story, Violet and Lindsey both had tears in their eyes. Brett wasn't balling. I don't think he bought a word of the story. I was going to have to watch myself with him. "Oh dear. That is such a sad tale. It was very brave of you to leave the place you grew up in."

"I had to take care of my sister. She would have been placed in a foster home if I didn't take guardianship of her." I said. The whole foster home story was for added effect.

"Well dear. If you need anything, don't hesitate to ask me or my husband Logan. When he is finished cooking, I'll introduce you to him." She said.

"Thank you Mam." I replied.

Violet sighed. "Maybe some of your manners will rub off on him." She said walking away.

"You're planning to stay in town Alec, right?" Lindsey asked. She was using her napkin to wipe the tears from her eyes.

"For a while I suppose." I replied.

"Of all the places in the United States to choose from. Why did you decide to come to our sleepy little town?" Brett asked curiously. My Hunter charms weren't working on him as well as it was everyone else.

"Like I said before. We hopped on the first plane leaving, it was going to Minnesota." I replied.

"Which airport did you arrive in?" he asked.

Brett was starting to annoy me. I was about to answer him, when a waitress came over to our table. "Hi, Welcome to Logan's Deep- Fried Diner." Said the waitress. She was strikingly familiar as well, with her light brown hair and lime green eyes. I took a guess that she was probably about eighteen years old.

"We know the name of the restaurant, you don't need to tell us that." Brett said. I was surprised to hear the clear irritation in his tone. "I don't believe I was talking to you, runt." The waitress replied. Blimey! Brett had that coming, but I thought waitresses were supposed to be nice to the customers. Maybe it's a custom in American restaurants to talk to each other like that.

I looked at the waitress, then at Brett, then back at the waitress again. Same hair, same eyes, they had to be brother and sister. That explained the animosity. She looked at me and smiled. "My name is Blair, and I'm going to be your server this afternoon." She said sweetly. "Your name is?"

"Alec, it's nice to meet you." I said smiling back at her, which made her blush. Lindsey didn't look very happy at the attention Blair was giving me. Brett didn't like the attention I was getting from both of them. What do you want from me? It wasn't like I had asked for any of their attentions.

"Aren't waitresses supposed to take orders?" Brett asked.

Blair gave her brother another dirty look. "Don't mind my brother. He was kidnapped at birth and raised by gorilla's. Can I get you something to drink?" she asked.

"I'll have…" Brett began to say before his sister cut him off.

"Alec, what would you like?" She said looking at me.

"Do you have hot tea here?" I asked. I haven't had a good cup of tea in a long time.

"Of course." She said brightly. Brett opened his mouth again to give his order, but Blair cut him off again. "Lindsey?"

"I'll have an ice tea Blair."

Blair turned to leave. "Hey! You didn't take my order!" Brett shouted.

"Yeah I know. An orange juice with extra pulp." She said in a mocking voice.

"You know I hate pulp!" Brett stared at his sister loathingly. He squeezed the knife he was holding in his hand.

"Brett the knife! You're going to cut yourself." Lindsey exclaimed.

Brett slammed it down. "I hate her! I keep praying that she'll move out of the house one day, or at least get abducted by aliens." He said.

"Honestly you two should get along." Lindsey said.

"You're lucky Linds, you're an only child. Do you have a brother or sister, Davenport?" Brett asked.

"A sister." I replied.

"Does she ever get under your skin?"

"Well." I began. *"Be very careful with your words Alec. I'll get back at you later."* Amber warned. "She can be annoying at times, but I still love her." I said.

Blair brought the drinks to the table. My tea wasn't as good as what I was used to back in England, but it was tea nonetheless. Lindsey said that we would wait for her other friend before we placed our orders. I looked through the menu, consciously aware of Blair Ramsey's eyes watching me from the counter. Besides peeking glances at me, Lindsey kept glancing at the door. It had occurred to me that she hadn't mentioned the name of the friend that was joining us for breakfast.

Curiously I asked; "Lindsey, what's the name of the friend we're waiting for?"

"Oh, I'm sorry." She said, her face turning red again. "We call her Ange, but her whole name is Angelica. You'll definitely like her." Lindsey said.

At the mention of the name, my head perked up. How many people could possibly have the name Angelica?

"Blimey Alec! She just appeared out of nowhere. Can you believe our luck!" Amber shouted.

I smiled as I heard the front door of the diner open. Maybe this day wasn't going to be so bad after all.

Chapter 11
Lunch at Logan's

Alec
(11:15 A.M.- July 4ᵗʰ)

This couldn't have worked out any better, I couldn't believe my luck. Lindsey Hansen and Brett Ramsey are best friends with Angelica Everhardtht!

A plan was already beginning to form in my head. *"Alec, are you sure you want to take a chance like this with her? She has control of her magic now."*

"Don't worry Ambs. The Mortals don't know of the Everhardtht's true nature. She won't make a scene here. Not in front of everyone." I replied. We had originally thought that the townspeople knew that the Everhardtht's were Weir, but since arriving here, that has been proven false.

The potency of her magic was brilliant. Even if Amber hadn't warned me, I would have been able to sense her presence.

"Alec this is my BFF, Angelica Everhardtht." Lindsey said. She got up and gave her a big hug.

I looked up at her and gave her my most charming smile. "It's a pleasure to meet you Angelica." I gripped the seat cushion. Her magic is intoxicating.

"It's nice to meet you." She smiled back. I could tell that it was a forced smile. She wasn't expecting to see me here. The feeling was mutual, because I wasn't expecting her to show up either. I thought Greta would have her entire family on lockdown.

"Amber, keep an eye out for any of the other Everhardtht's. She can't possibly be here alone."

"Blimey Alec. I was so caught up with the Hansen girl, that I forgot that this could be a trap. This confirms that they're in this together."

"All this confirms is that they are friends. If this is a trap, then we'll know soon enough. In the meantime, this is the perfect opportunity Amber. We could use Brett and Lindsey to get to Angelica."

"Be careful Alec." Amber warned. I could tell by her thoughts that she was worried that this could be a set up. Angelica was clearly shocked at my being here though. I'm almost positive that this isn't a trap, whether Angelica knew of her friend's strange abilities remained to be seen.

"I heard that there were visitors in town." Angelica said.

"How did you find out?" Lindsey asked.

"From your dad." She replied.

"Oh, that explains it." Lindsey said shaking her head.

"You'll have to get used to the fact that there are no secrets in this town. If you have any dirty laundry, everybody will know it soon enough." Brett said.

"Dirty Laundry?" What the bloody hell did that mean? Why would anybody in this town want to know about my dirty clothes?

Lindsey giggled. "He doesn't mean your actual clothes. It means that the whole town will know your secrets, if you have any." Blimey, and American's think we're hard to understand. "It's like that in small towns, everyone knows your business." Lindsey said.

"Are you two going to sit down so we can order our food?" Brett asked.

"Brett's a little cranky today." Lindsey said.

"I'm not cranky, I'm just hungry." Brett said defensively.

"Sure, Brett." Lindsey said, sitting down next to him.

"Ange, you can sit next to Alec." Lindsey said. Angelica eyed me. She clearly didn't want to sit down next to me. I wasn't too thrilled about it myself. The closer she got to me, the more likely I would be tempted to take her magic. When she finally did, she stayed closer to the edge of the booth. I gripped the seat so hard that I probably tore a hole in it.

"You'll have to excuse Brett. He likes two things, sports and food." Lindsey said giving him a playful shove.

"Nothing wrong with that." Brett smiled and pushed her back. It was clear that he liked her. "Hey waitress! We're ready to order." Brett shouted at his sister.

Lindsey sighed.

"Are you two still fighting?" Angelica asked.

"They're always fighting. I don't think I've ever seen them not arguing when they're together." Lindsey replied.

"It's her fault. She always starts the problems." Brett said defensively.

"You guys should try and get along. You are brother and sister after all." Lindsey said. "Why should I get along with her?" he asked.

"Because you might actually like it."

"Fat chance."

Lindsey shook her head, then looked at me. "I bet Alec and his sister get along fine together."

"Remember what I said before." Amber warned.

"I wasn't going to say a thing." I replied. *"Any sign of the other Everhardtht's."*

"Nothing yet." She replied. It seems that I was right about this not being a trap. It was surprising though that Angelica was out by herself.

"Amber's all I got. I wouldn't know what to do if she wasn't there to constantly nag me." I said.

"I don't nag."

"Told you." Lindsey said to Brett.

Blair made her way back over to the table to take our orders. She was still staring at me, it was starting to get a bit uncomfortable. "Hi Angelica. How ya been?"

"Fine Blair, and you?" replied Angelica. Blair started to talk to Angelica about her recent trip to the nail salon, when Brett interrupted. "Excuse me. Are you going to take our orders anytime soon?"

Blair gave him the nastiest of looks. She took out her pad and pen and began taking our orders. She spent the longest on mine. She kept asking me if I wanted any side dishes with my pancakes. I politely declined all of them. Blair purposely took her brothers order last. When we all finished, she took the menus and went to place our order.

"Ange, how come your dad came into town the other day? Dad told me he almost drew his gun on him." Lindsey asked.

"He said he had a few errands to run." Angelica replied.

"He clearly had everyone shocked."

"He shocked me as well." Angelica replied.

"I wish I could have met him. I'm dying to see what he looks like." Lindsey said.

Angelica laughed. "He looks like a normal person Linds." I smiled to myself. Normal wasn't a word I would use to describe Rowan Everhardtht.

"Angelica's family founded the town, they also own all of it." Lindsey said to me.

"Really?" I faked my impression. "I guess that would make you quite wealthy?"

Angelica glared at me. "I guess you can say that, but I don't like to flaunt my money around in everyone's faces." She said with a smile. I must give her credit. She's doing an excellent job hiding her clear annoyance of me.

I decided to see how far I could go with her. "How come you don't know what her dad looks like?" I watched her expressions as Lindsey and Brett explained how her family never comes to town. "That's rather odd, don't you think?"

"I tell them that every day. My grandmother runs the household though, and she's rather old fashioned." Angelica continued to smile at me. If I was getting under her skin, it wasn't showing.

"Be careful Alec." Amber warned.

"We try not to talk too much about our families when we go out together. When you live in a small town though, sometimes there's not much else to talk about." Lindsey said.

After that, the conversation switched to the latest movie news. I learned that Angelica and Lindsey are quite the movie buffs. Then they started talking about recent town gossip, the name Kelly kept coming up repeatedly.

"Chick talk." Brett said shaking his head, then he looked at me. "Davenport, are you into any sports?"

"As a matter of fact Ramsey, I am."

"I know you British are crazy about soccer. I don't find it that great of a sport." He said.

"Football is a national pastime in England. I do happen to like your American version of the game though." I know a lot about sports. The Davenport's made sure we learned everything we could about Mortal games. They said it would help us blend in better. They were right about that. They were right about almost everything.

Since we were in Minnesota. I was willing to bet that Brett's favorite team was the Vikings. I surprised him when I started to recite everything I could recall about the teams' history. After that he seemed to drop his guard a little. His cold demeanor began to melt away. I had to admit that the conversation was a good distraction for me. Angelica's magic was just a fingertip away, and Lindsey's voice was simply mesmerizing.

"Brett's in his glory. He's got someone to talk sports to." Lindsey said.

Once the food arrived, all conversation died down a bit. Lindsey was still chattering on though. Most of what she was saying was rubbish, but I listened to it all. When everyone finished, Blair came back over to the table. "Mom just called. She wants to know if you dropped those letters off at the post office?" she asked Brett.

"Not yet." He said.

"Those letters are important. You better deliver them. I bet you haven't dropped off the package to Mrs. Sareolla yet either."

"Who do you think you are? Mom? I'll deliver them when I'm ready. As you can see I'm out with my friends."

"Mom specifically told me that you had to take care of all those things before you did anything for yourself. I guess I'll just have to call her." She said, reaching for her cell-phone.

"Alright I'll go!" Brett said. Blair left the bill on the table and walked away with a smile on her face. Glancing briefly in her mind. I realized that she did it, so Brett would leave. So that she could talk to me without him listening.

Brett swore under his breath. The things he was currently thinking about his sister, almost made me laugh out loud. Lindsey elbowed him in the ribs. It was almost like she knew what he was thinking, which made me wonder if she is indeed a Seer.

"What? She did that purposely to embarrass me." Brett said.

"I know, but it's not nice to say that kind of stuff about your sister." She replied.

"I didn't say anything." Brett replied.

"It was written all over your face."

"What are you, some kind of mind reader now?"

"Don't be foolish Brett." She replied. "I know you too well by now."

Brett frowned. "She's not my sister, she's more like the spawn of King Kong."

Lindsey elbowed him again. "She does look a little ape like, don't you think Davenport?" Brett asked, loud enough for Blair to overhear. Lindsey elbowed him again, but it was clear that he was enjoying every bit of it. Brett took out his wallet and left the money for his meal on the bill.

"See you later Ange." He said getting up. "I'll call you later."

"I'll walk with you Brett." Lindsey said getting up. He was clearly enthused about that. "I'm paying for your meal Alec, since you're my guest." She said.

"Thank you. You really don't need to." I said.

"I insist." She replied with a smile. I really wasn't going to argue any further, seeing as I didn't bring any American money with me. In fact, I didn't have any money at all. So far, Amber and I have gotten everything for free. That wasn't going to last forever though. I needed to get my hands on some money soon.

"I owe you one." I said smiling at her. She turned a bright shade of red.

"You can repay me, by agreeing to accompany me to the Fourth of July Picnic." Bloody Hell! I had totally forgotten that today was the fourth. With everything that was going on recently, it had slipped my mind. The thought of being around Lindsey any further was daunting.

"I would love too." I said.

Lindsey smiled brightly. Brett frowned, and Angelica gave me a dirty look.

"I'll come by around five. I still want to meet your sister." She said.

"Come by whenever you want." I replied. I wanted to bang my head on the table. Why couldn't I say no to her?

"Sounds like a date. Well…not a real date, but…you know it sounds like a plan." She said awkwardly. "Ange, you're going to be there, right?" She said turning her attention to Angelica.

"I'll try." She replied.

"You better be there. I'll call you later though."

"Okay." Lindsey led Brett out of the restaurant.

"I think she likes you." Amber said. *"She could have said it was a date and you would have agreed anyway."*

"You try saying no to her then." I replied.

"No thanks. I'd rather keep my distance. Her voice had me in a trance before."

As soon as they left the diner. Angelica got up and sat down across from me at the table. Well, here we go, I thought. "You're targeting my friends now?" she said with a sneer.

"I'm doing nothing of the sort." I said innocently.

"I'm sure. First you sought out my family. Now you're going after my friends." She said.

"First of all, I didn't seek them out. It was your friend Lindsey, who sought me out." I said.

"I don't care! Just stay away from them!"

I sat back and crossed my arms over my chest. "I don't think so. I think Lindsey and I would be great friends. It won't take long to get Brett on my side as well. He was starting to warm up to me when I started discussing sports."

"You rehearsed those lines. No one could possibly know all those facts about one team." She said.

"No one could know that much possible nonsense about movies either." I retorted. "You are such a hypocrite. But just for the record, I did have training in that area of Mortal culture." I said that just to get a rise out of her. I wanted to show her just how smart and cunning I could be.

"I'm warning you! If you don't stay away from them."

"What? What will you do if I don't stay away?"

"I'm a Darkling. You don't want to make me angry." She said through gritted teeth. For the briefest of moments, her eyes changed to a shade of black. The lights in the diner flickered. I glanced around curiously.

"Don't worry everybody. It's the old wiring in this place. Enjoy your meals." Said Violet Krenshaw from the front.

I turned back to Angelica. Her eyes were back to their normal shade of emerald again. She seemed to be a little shaken as well. Now I knew what Amber meant when she said that Angelica was two people in one.

"You should listen to me more often." She said.

I snickered at Angelica. "Some Darkling."

She was about to comment, when another female voice broke the conversation. "Well if it isn't Angela Everhard." The voice belonged to another teenage girl about the same age as Angelica. It was a shrill voice. It sounded fake and forced. She had bleached blonde hair and blue eyes. Her body was lean and well-toned. I could tell just by looking at her, that she ran a lot. She was staring at me like everyone else had today. Her eyes clearly said. "Who's the new guy?"

"It's ANNE-GEL-ICA EVER-HEARTH." She pronounced each syllable slowly for her.

"Whatever." The girl said without even looking at her. She was one of those girls, that have the I'm better than you mentality. "You going to introduce me to your friend?" She said batting her eyelashes.

"He's not my friend." Angelica said.

"That's your loss then." She replied. Angelica and this girl clearly hate each other.

"The name is Alec Davenport." I said holding out my hand and giving her a charming smile. "You'll have to excuse Angelica. I guess she's having a bad morning."

"I would be too if I had hair like that."
She said with a smile. "My name is Kelly Jackson."
Ah! This must be the Kelly the girls were discussing
earlier.

"Pleasure to meet you Miss. Jackson." I made
a mental note in my head about Kelly. Anybody
who didn't get along with Angelica could come in
handy at some point.

I knew how to handle people like Kelly.
Smile, compliment them, and make them think that
they're the center of attention.

"You're new in town, right?" she asked.

"That's right." I said.

"I thought so. I know everybody in town. We
should hang out sometime. I'm much better
company than what you have now." She said.

"That'd be brilliant." I said.

"Can I call you then?" Kelly asked.

"I don't have a phone, but I'm staying
over at the B & B. You can find me there."

"I'll be sure too." She winked at me and
walked over to the counter to place her order. Blair

was giving her nasty looks as she took her order. Angelica swore some beastly things under her breath.

"Looks like your turning some heads today, brother." Amber said.

"This is starting to get bloody ridiculous." I replied. Normally I liked the attention I would receive from girls, but here in Crystal Falls, I was on a mission.

"Where were we?" I asked Angelica.

"Listen to me very carefully Hunter. You'll stay away from my friends and family, if you know what's good for you?" Angelica said. "Now as much as I would like to stay here and chat with you, I have to be getting home."

"We are far from done here." I replied. By the time I'm done with your family Angelica, you'll all be under my control.

"No. I think we're done." She got up to leave. I noticed that she magically produced the money in her hand.

"Don't you think it is a bit reckless to produce money out of thin air? Especially in a diner full of Mortals." I said a little loudly. Nobody overheard, but it was enough to make Angelica look around nervously. She sat back down.

"Are you crazy? Keep your voice down." She said.

"I was always curious as to how your family was able to live amongst Mortals. But you guys have everyone totally fooled. How does it feel to live a lie every day?" I asked.

"Blast you. My town, my family, my friends, my life is none of your business." She said angrily.

I was having fun torturing her. *"Try not to push her too far Alec."* Amber warned.

"And I know how to use my abilities." She said.

"Are you sure? Because apparently you know nothing about being a Seer." I replied.

She flushed bright red. "That's none of your business."

I laughed. "Is that your comeback for everything?"

"Listen here, at least my magic is pure. You have to steal yours." She said. Pointing her finger at me.

"She's got spunk. I'll give her that." Amber said.

"Is this something you really want to get into right now?" I asked. Angelica looked around the diner. The couples in the booths across from us were watching our exchange.

"Your right, we're far from through here. We'll finish this conversation outside." She said.

"Lead the way." I said getting up. Angelica pushed by me and walked towards the counter. I smiled as I followed her.

"You're enjoying this banter with her way too much brother."

"What? I needed a way to keep her here." I said back.

"You better come up with a plan quickly." She warned.

At the hostess counter, Violet Krenshaw was standing with a bald man with a thick mustache. "It looked like you two were having quite the volatile conversation." Violet was asking Angelica as she processed the bill.

"It was…" Angelica began.

"A friendly debate about American movies." I interrupted. Angelica gave me a sideways glance.

"Well that explains the heat." Said the man. "Angelica here knows more about movies than anybody in town." He smiled, then he turned to face Violet. "I told you there was nothing to worry about, it was just a friendly conversation."

"Well it sure didn't look like one." Violet said, handing Angelica her receipt. "We don't want to set bad examples Miss. Everhardtht."

"It's like Alec said. We were just having an enthusiastic conversation." Angelica said.

"Drop it Violet." Said the man. He smiled at me and held out his hand. "The name's Logan Krenshaw. You can call me Logan. My wife hasn't shut up about you since you walked in. I wanted to let you finish your meal before I introduced myself." He said. "I heard of your situation. If you need anything young man, don't hesitate to ask."

"Thank you, Mr. Krenshaw." There wasn't very much else I could say to him. Just like everyone we've met so far, he was a nice person, who was willing to fall on his face for us. Like I said before, it's all a part of the Hunter charm.

"No need for Mister. Logan is just fine." He said with a smile.

Violet made a face at him. "Don't listen to a thing he says. You have great manners Alec. I don't want my husband or anyone else rubbing bad ones off on you." She said, giving Angelica a stern look.

Logan frowned at his wife. "My wife is all bark, but no bite." Logan said winking at me. "Have a good day you two."

I followed Angelica out of the diner. For a while. We didn't say anything to one another.

I scoped my mind out for Amber. She was close by, hanging out in the shadows of one of the trees. Once we were out of earshot of anyone, Angelica rounded on me.

"How dare you invade my town? Then use my family and friends like they were nothing more than pieces on a chessboard. You've barely been here for a week and already they're siding with you, over me." I wondered if she was referring to Violet Krenshaw's reaction a couple minutes ago.

"I guess I'm just a charming fellow." I said.

"You're a slimy sneak. You're using that darn magic of yours to confuse people. Their minds become all foggy. All they can think about is you." I smiled. She talked liked she knew from experience what was happening.

"Why? Am I getting to you too?" she blushed bright red.

"Because of your actions in there, the whole town is going to be talking about us now." She said angrily.

"That was your bloody fault." I repeated. "You were the one that was getting all hot under the collar."

Angelica literally dragged me into a gap between the diner and another store. She was angry now. I was consciously aware of our proximity to each other. Her magic was just a fingertip away.

"Who do you think you are, that you can just drag people around?" I asked.

"I'm a Darkling Witch! Nothing is stronger than me!" she shouted. Her eyes had changed again. The presence in front of me now, was not the one from moments before.

I didn't back down. "You like calling yourself a Darkling, but I doubt you even know what that means. Because if you knew what Darkling's were really like, then you would know that you're nothing like them."

The ground beneath us began to shake. Maybe I had gone a little too far. "What are you talking about?" Angelica's voice was deeper now.

Cracks began to form underneath us. I'm in trouble now, I thought. "Just look at yourself. Don't you feel what's happening?"

Suddenly, the shaking stopped. Her eyes returned to their normal shade, and she fell into me. It took all my willpower not to take her magic. I felt it egging me on, almost as if her magic wanted to be taken, to be set free.

Angelica caught her breath and quickly regained her composure. She pushed away from me. "You're right. I know nothing about being a Darkling, because of this stupid spell my Grandmother placed on me."

"The one that's restricting your powers?" I asked.

She nodded. She didn't even seem surprised when I mentioned I knew about the spell binding her. When the Davenport's told us that Angelica was the only living Darkling. I wondered why The Council of Hemlock allowed her to live. Then they told us it was because she was being controlled by a spell. I couldn't help but feel bad for her. Nobody should be bound by magic. What good was a tame Darkling. Especially one that loses control on a regular basis.

"You want to know the truth about me? I'm a horrible Darkling. A horrible Seer. I'm just a horrible Witch." There was genuine hurt in her voice. That's when it hit me. I knew how I was going to get her.

"What if I trained you to be a Seer?" I asked.

She looked at me curiously. "Why would you want to do that?" she asked.

"Because ever since I first heard about you. I was enthralled over the fact that you were a living Darkling. I thought it was a travesty that a Witch like you was being controlled. However, there is still hope for you. I can teach you a bit of magic as well, and about the Darklings that came before you." I said.

"You know nothing of magic. All you can do is steal it." She replied.

"I won't deny that. But the magic I do take, I can still use." I said.

She held my gaze for a while. "What's in it for you?" she asked.

I smiled. I had her right where I wanted her. "You'll owe me a favor." I said, reaching into my pocket. I pulled out another piece of parchment and a pen.

"What's this?" she asked.

"It's called a Binding Pen. The ink inside of it is magic. Once you sign your name to this parchment, it becomes a binding agreement. I'll sign my name. Promising to you, that I will teach you everything you need to know about being a Seer. I will also show you whatever bit of magic I can." I said, signing my name to the parchment.

She looked at me suspiciously. "What will I owe you?"

I shrugged. "Like I said. A favor to be cashed in at my choosing." I handed her the pen. "Do we have a deal?" I asked.

She took the pen. I held the parchment up, so she could see it. I could tell she was fighting a battle within herself. If she wanted to learn about her ability, as much as I thought she did, then she would sign.

Sure enough, she did.

"You have your deal?" she said angrily.
"So how do we do this?"

I placed the pen and parchment back in my
pocket. "First things first. We need to discover what
spell is binding your magic, specifically? We don't
want any ghastly things occurring during our
lessons."

"And how are we supposed to do that?" she
asked.

"Not we. You." I said pointing to her. "It's
your family. Figure it out. Until we find out what it
is, we proceed no further." I valued my health. I
couldn't have her going all crazy on me like she did
before. If she hurt herself, then she would be of no
use to me.

"Fine." She said in a huff. Then she vanished.

Once she left. I breathed a sigh of relief. I
can't believe that worked.

Amber appeared at my side immediately.
"What was that about?"

I smiled. "Three down. Two to go."

Chapter 12
Through the Mist

Angelica
(5:00 A.M.- July 5th)

I couldn't relax no matter how hard I tried. I kept reliving yesterday repeatedly in my mind. I still couldn't believe that I signed that blasted piece of paper. What was I thinking? This was just like the movie Ghost Rider with Nicolas Cage. Now I was in a binding agreement with Alec.

Alec! I've never met such an infuriating person before in my life. He's so egotistical, so cocky, so full of himself, so adorably handsome! It's enough to make you want to throw up. I allowed him to get under my skin, and it's probably going to cost me my soul.

I kept thinking that I could've handled the situation a million different ways. I should have had him agree to stay away from my friends and family. I could have made him leave town. There were so many different things that I could've done, and I just didn't, I failed.

I was just so upset that I lost control in front of him, not once, but twice. I was weak and vulnerable, and he took advantage of that. He preyed on my desire to know more about my gift, I was blinded by it. Now I'm stuck with no visible way out. I keep thinking about that favor I now owe him. What's he going to make me do? Probably something that involves his quest for revenge, I'm sure of it!

I had been lying on my bed, staring at my ceiling for what seemed like an eternity. Every few minutes I would glance at my clock. Hoping that somehow, magically, time would have sped up. It was only 5:00 in the morning.

I think I was dreading having to tell my parents the most. They didn't even know that I snuck out of the house yesterday. I haven't spoken to anybody since Tuesday. I thought for sure that Grandma would have come to try to speak with me. I haven't heard a peep out of her for days, that was never a good sign. Mom placed strict no leaving the house rules on Merrin and me. When Lindsey called me though and had asked if I could meet them for lunch, I said yes instantly. The Hunter's hadn't shown themselves either since we met. I thought that maybe they had heeded Grandma's warning and left town. I decided that taking the risk was worth it. Boy was I wrong! What a stupid decision!

When I hang out with Brett and Lindsey. It's almost like I'm normal for a little while, and I can forget about all this magical nonsense. That's one of the reasons why I left the house to go meet them. The other reason was because I wanted to defy my family. They were all lying to me. Sneaking out of the house was the best way I could think of to get back at them.

Alec ruined everything though. The minute I saw him sitting in the diner with my best friends, I wanted to hex him into oblivion. If he had hurt them, I just might have. I didn't believe Alec at first when he said that he didn't know they were my friends. When Lindsey called me last night though, she confirmed that she was the one to invite him out. Now that he knew about them, they were in danger. Lindsey is completely enthralled with him, she said so on the phone with me. She had gone with him to the Fourth of July picnic and had a fun time. She said he was a complete gentleman. I wanted to go myself. Brett even asked me if I would go with him. He was going to ask Lindsey, but he never got the chance. I told him no though, I couldn't risk sneaking out twice.

I tried to downplay Alec as much as possible. I didn't want to tell Lindsey flat out to stay away from him, in case she got mad or suspicious with me. How could you downplay someone who was as physically perfect as Alec? I could always make Lindsey stay away from him if I wanted too. I didn't want to use magic on her. It's a law not to use magic on Mortals unless it was a life or death situation. This was that kind of situation though! One thing was for certain, I had to keep Lindsey away from Alec.

I sighed, there was no point wishing for time to speed up. Grandma told me stories of Weir who tried to fool around with time. It only brought them despair. I got up and got dressed. Alec's words were still echoing inside my head. He had said that I should find out more about the spell that was binding my power. If I didn't, he wouldn't teach me about being a Seer. I knew nothing about the spell. Grandma never told me what it was called. In fact, we never spoke of it unless my blackouts occurred.

Mom and Dad knew about it, but they weren't going to tell me. That made me so mad!

The cracking of glass startled me. My mirror had cracked down the center. Not again! I repaired it quickly as tears welled up inside me. Forget them, I told them the other night that if they weren't going to tell me what was going on than I would do it myself, and that's exactly what I intended to do!

I wiped away my tears. No more feeling sorry for myself. I would show them all that I'm capable of handling my own problems. I'm not even going to tell them about the agreement I made with Alec. I will handle him and the agreement on my own.

I knew what I was going to do, confront Alec and show him that he wasn't going to push me around. If he wanted my help, then he's going to have to assist me in figuring out my predicament. Of course, I knew this was a stupid idea. Alec could most certainly push me around if he wanted to, but I was hoping that I could bluff just enough to get away with it.

This plan also involved sneaking out of the house again, an art that I've perfected over the years. I use this illusion spell, that casts an almost perfect replica of myself. That way if my parents come looking, they'll see me in my room. Of course, it's just an illusion. If you try to touch it, the spell will shatter immediately. That's why I magically seal my door and window from the inside. That way no one but me can get into my room. Locking myself in my room is so common, that my parents never suspect anything.

After casting the illusion. I magically sealed the door and window, so they could only be opened by my voice. I quickly threw on a pair of shoes and a sweat jacket, then I teleported from my room.

I landed just in front of the B & B. It was quiet, and the wind made the empty streets feel absolutely deserted. I began pacing outside of the building, debating on whether this was a good idea or not. That's when the door to 2D opened and Alec stepped out. He looked as handsome as ever in his turtleneck shirt, and blue jeans. His red aura wasn't there anymore. I had noticed that yesterday. I guess he could turn it on and off at will.

"I thought I felt your presence out here." He said.

I marched right up to him. "We need to talk." I said.

"I gather you found about the spell then." He asked.

"No, I haven't."

"Then we have nothing to discuss." He replied.

"Oh yes we do." I said pushing past him as I entered the room. It probably was a stupid move coming in here again, where I couldn't use my magic. I wanted to show him that I wasn't afraid though.

"No worries then. Just invite yourself in, it's only five in the morning." He said. As I looked around, I noticed that his sister wasn't in the room.

"Where's Amber?"

"That's none of your bloody business." He replied.

"My town, my business." I replied firmly.

Alec smirked. "Someone's found her voice. She went out. Where I don't know. What do you have to tell me?"

"You have my signature on that parchment. You have my support whenever you want. But if you want my help, then you're going to have to contribute some yourself."

"Oh really."

"Yes, really! I don't know a darn thing about this spell because my family chooses not to tell me anything. That means you're going to have to help me figure this out." I said, pointing at him.

"I must say, you surprise me Everhardtht." He said.

"I'm just full of surprises." I retorted sarcastically.

He smiled. "Alright, I'll help you. What do you want me to do?"

I can't believe that worked, he was agreeing to help. I couldn't mess this up now and show any weakness. "Tell me about the Darklings that came before me. You said you would. Maybe if I knew more about being a Darkling, then I could figure out what kind of spell this is." I held my breath as he toyed with my idea.

"That sounds fair." I exhaled on the inside. "Sit down."

"Oh no! Not here! You control too much inside this room. These are my terms, we'll go somewhere that's on my turf." I said firmly.

Alec laughed a ridiculously adorable laugh that almost threw me off. "I like this side of you. You have fire, that'll come in handy." I didn't like the sound of that. "So where do you want to go?"

"There's a park on the edge of the mountain. We'll go there."

"A park? Isn't that your father's domain?" he asked.

"Not this park, Dad promised it to Merrin and me as a place where we can go and be alone."

"You believe him?"

"He always keeps his promises." I said.

"But he does lie. You said that before." Alec prodded. He's good at playing with my emotions, I won't let him get to me though.

"In a way, I don't blame them, they're just trying to protect me."

Alec smirked. "Whatever you say." I walked passed him, and out the front door. I heard him close it behind him.

"The park's quite a walk from here." I said.

"You know, I'm not a fan of walking." He replied.

"That wasn't the case yesterday when you walked the entire town with Lindsey." Alec exhaled slowly.

"What? Am I getting under your skin now?" I smiled at him. I didn't intend on that being a shot at him, but I think I may have hit a nerve.

He laughed again. "I'll give you that one."

"Like I said, I'm just full of surprises."

"What I meant to say is that I'd much rather use a different form of transportation." He replied.

"I can teleport us there." I suggested. It was easier then walking.

"No." he said all too quickly. "No teleporting."

I smiled at him. "You're afraid of teleporting?"

"I'm not afraid of anything." He said defensively. "Hunter's just prefer a different mode of transportation."

"Like what?" I asked.

"Mist." He said flatly.

"Excuse me? How will mist be of any help to us?" I asked.

"It's starts off as mist, then it changes to fog. You walk into it in one place and reappear in another." He said.

I recalled my vision of the night they arrived in town. When both appeared out of nowhere, there was an intense amount of fog that night. "That's how you appeared out of thin air." I said to myself.

"How do you know that?" he asked. Then it dawned on him. "You had a vision of us arriving, didn't you?" I smiled. I finally knew something he didn't. I liked being able to throw him off his game. This is going more smoothly then I intended.

My moment didn't last long because I got to thinking about what they said to us about arriving in America. "I bet you lied to us when you said you came by airplane."

It was his turn to smile. "Of course, we lied. Why go through all the hassle to travel the mortal way? When the mist can take us anywhere we want. We left straight from England and arrived in Minnesota."

I shook my head. "Is any part of your story true?" I asked.

"Most of it. Of course, some things were exaggerated for effect." He replied.

"Like that orphan garbage you keep telling everyone."

"Doesn't it just make you want to weep." He asked with a smirk.

"More like throw up." I needed to regain this situation. "Enough of this. How do we travel by this mist?" I asked. "Is it safe?"

"If you follow all my instructions. First, you're going to have to think of the place you want to go before we enter. I can't make it form unless you have a good mental image of the place." He said.

"Okay." That was simple enough. I've spent enough alone time in that park to know it's every detail.

"Secondly, the mist can be an extremely frightening experience for a first timer. When walking through, it will get thicker as you move, and it'll turn into fog. You'll hear all kinds of noises, but whatever you do, don't stop. It's just the fog trying to play tricks on you." He said.

"What happens if you stop?" I asked.

"You get lost." He said simply.

"Has anyone ever gotten lost before?"

"Where do you think all the sounds are coming from, the lost. Hunters of old used the mist to trap enemies, saving them for dessert later." Well that did wonders for my mind. I pictured myself lost forever in a swirling cloud of fog.

He stepped out onto the street and held out his hand. "Take my hand."

I hesitated. For a moment, I thought it was a trick to take my magic. He wants me alive though. "Don't worry. I can resist your magic." He said.

"You keep telling yourself that, I think your still struggling." I replied. When I locked hands with him, I heard his intake of breath. I knew I was right about him struggling to resist my magic. I smiled, knowing that I could take him by surprise. Now I just hoped I could get through this fog.

Alec's grip was firm. The way he held my hand reassured me that it was going to be all right. Holding hands probably meant that if I got lost, he would get lost as well.

"Think of the place clearly." He said. I concentrated, and before long it wasn't hard to picture the park in my mind. It held a special place in my heart. "Start walking." This would really get the town buzzing if someone saw us walking hand in hand. Thankfully, it was early in the morning. As we walked, it started to get misty. It felt cool as it hit my face.

"Won't people see us?" I asked.

"Mortals see only what they want to see. In this case, all they'll see is a dense amount of fog." He replied.

Slowly the mist changed to a thick fog. It was so dense that I could no longer see the road or the surrounding buildings. It was just a wall of thick white all around me. It gave off an eerie sense of foreboding. I felt like I shouldn't be here right now. "Keep walking." Alec said. His voice sounded so far away. I turned to look at him, but he wasn't there anymore. Instantly, I began to panic. What if I let go without realizing I did! It had only been a couple of seconds, I couldn't have lost him! If I just go back, I might be able to find him. It was then I felt a reassuring squeeze of my hand. Alec was still here! He was still holding my hand. I just couldn't see him.

Suddenly, noises started coming from all around me, they were loud and frightening. They sounded so close that I began looking in every direction, expecting something to pop out at any second. I felt like I was five years old again, being afraid of the monsters that lurked in the darkness. I closed my eyes and kept on walking. If my eyes were closed, it didn't seem so scary anymore.

The voices were getting louder, some were shouting for help, others were crying. I just wanted them all to be quiet.

"We're here." Alec said.

As quickly as it came, the fog disappeared as we stepped out into a sunny clearing. Alec was next to me again. I was gripping his hand so hard, that I was surprised he didn't complain. "That felt like forever." I said. "I'm never doing that again."

"It was only a few seconds." He replied. He seemed satisfied that the fog had unnerved me.

"No way! It felt like forever." I said.

"It always feels longer if you're afraid."

"I wasn't afraid." I said, regaining my composure. I let go of his hand and walked about.

"It's okay, Amber wasn't keen on it at first as well. The more times you successfully navigate it, the less scary it becomes." He said.

I remembered all the noises and voices I heard while in the fog. The thought of all those lost souls brought me chills. "All those lost people. Can they be found again?"

"I don't know. The Davenport's just taught us how to navigate the mist. We never talked about those lost within it." He replied.

"That's a horrible fate." I replied

"I try not to think about it." He really was cruel, I thought. "Wow, this place is brilliant." He said.

The trip through the mist made me forget why we were hear. I wanted answers.

Chapter 13
The Darkling Within

Angelica
(6:00 A.M.-July 5th)

The sun was just beginning to rise over the treetops of the great pines that surround the park, it cast a beautiful orange glow. The grass here is a luscious shade of emerald green, with not one brown patch to be seen; the morning dew twinkled in the early sunlight. I absolutely love this place. Dad had given it to Merrin and me as a Christmas gift. It is our secret place where we can go and be alone with our thoughts.

Alec began walking around, admiring the scenery. "This place is natural, untouched, everything working in perfect harmony. Nature at its purest." He said. "How come I don't remember passing by this place with Lindsey?"

"Because only Merrin and I can get to this place. There is no entrance to the park from the town. It's a secret." I replied.

"And you're sharing this with me?" Alec asked. I didn't trust him at all, and I felt bad for spoiling this secret spot, but this was the only place I could think of. This was my haven, nothing could get me here. "No one will bother us here."

"What about your sister?"

"We're not allowed to leave the house. She won't be bothering us." I replied.

"Rebellious as well." He said, staring at me with his stunning red eyes.

I wasn't going to get lost in his eyes today. I'm the one in control. "Enough nonsense. I brought you here, so you can tell me about Darklings." I said.

"One moment." He held up a finger. "Amber's coming."

"Wait, what? I thought you said that she went out?" I asked.

"She did. Technically though, no matter where Amber and I go, we're always together." He said, pointing to his head.

Then it dawned on me. "She's reading your mind."

"Something like that." He smiled that

cocky smile of his, as the fog rolled into the park, shrouding everything in its path. The only thing I could see was a familiar red glow. When the fog disappeared, Amber stood waiting. "I brought breakfast!" she exclaimed. She was carrying a large bag from the Java Café, and a large container of juice. "Marvelous, this place is great!" she said.

"Amber's become quite addicted to the pastries at the Java Café." Alec said.

"What can I say? They're delicious." She said, smiling at me. I couldn't help smiling back at her. She seemed so perfectly innocent. It was amazing just how much she looked like her brother. Today she had her black and red hair pulled into pigtails.

"Why red?" I blurted out. "You have red highlights, red eyes, and a red aura."

"Honestly, I have no idea, and they're not highlights, it's our actual hair. I guess the Gypsies had a thing for red." Alec replied. "Shall we sit?"

I conjured up a table for us to sit down on. Alec laid out all the goodies that Amber undoubtedly charmed out of Ms. Monti. In one quick motion, she took the pastry she wanted, and ran to a tree. She climbed up it in a flash, and perched herself on one of the branches.

"Wow." I said. "You're really fast."

"Don't encourage her." Alec said, rolling his eyes. "She's showing off." She stuck her tongue out at him.

"That was like Robert Pattinson fast." I said.

"Blimey, You're into that whole Vampire love story fluff?" Alec said, making a face.

"It's not fluff, it's classic literature." I said defensively.

"Sure it is." He said rolling his eyes.

I was about to retort back, when I remembered why we were here. I shook my head. I had gone off topic again. "Listen, we didn't come here to argue about books. Are you going to tell me about Darklings or not?"

"Alright." He said defensively. "You're extremely pushy, you know that?" I just stared him down. "What do you know about Darklings, you have to know something?" He asked.

Quite frankly, I didn't know that much. "All I know is that they were extremely powerful. The law states that no Darkling can live because they can't control their powers. But because I'm an

Everhardtht, I'm allowed to live, as long as this spell was placed on me." I replied. "Powerful is not the word I would use to describe the Darklings that came before you. I would use words like; dangerous, uncontrollable, deadly, and pure evil." A shiver went down my spine. "For a Darkling to be born, it takes a union of two extremely powerful Weir. Seeing as your entire family is incredibly powerful, it's no wonder that you were born a Darkling. Now, there was only a handful of them to ever reach maturity. You see a Darkling, like most Weir, don't gain their full strength until they reach adulthood." I shifted uncomfortably on the bench. My sixteenth birthday was less than a month away. I would be an adult by then.

"If full powers aren't gained until adulthood, then how do they know I was born a Darkling at all?" I asked.

"Your eyes." Amber said. I looked up at her. "Darklings have pure black eyes."

"But my eyes are green."

"Not yesterday, when you were having that…" Alec began.

"Blackout." I said. A sick thought just occurred to me. "Your saying my eyes change color."

"When you're having these blackouts as you call them? Yes."

I was too stunned to say anything for a moment. "I still don't understand. If my eyes are supposed to be black, then why do they change back and forth to green?"

Alec looked at Amber. A silent conversation seemed to pass between them. I wished that I could read their minds. "Amber and I have a theory. We've both felt two very different Angelica's."

"Excuse me? I think your English is off. What is that supposed to mean?" I asked.

"Hear me out. Yesterday, in the alley, and the other day when you came crashing in through the wall. We've felt a different Angelica than the one that is sitting here right now."

My head was really starting to hurt. It was so bad that I started to laugh. "Okay, you've lost me here."

Alec sighed. "How can I put this? All magical folk have a distinct scent. As Hunter's, we were created with an extra powerful sense of smell, that allows us to track down those scents from miles away. Now, while your family, and every other magical person that we've confronted, had one scent, you have two."

"Why would I have two?" I asked.

"We're going on a hunch. But we think that when your Grandmother placed this spell on you, it created two people in one." Alec said. "Wait a minute. Are you trying to say that there's two of me?" I asked. This was not what I expected. This was just plain weird.

"That's exactly what I'm trying to say." He replied.

I shook my head in disbelief. "How is it possible that there could be two of me? I'm just Angelica, that's all."

"Look at it this way. There's Angelica, the girl who is sitting in front of me right now. Whose magic is very powerful, and incredibly addicting, that it's hard for me to resist." Alec closed his eyes and exhaled. "Then there's Darkling Angelica. Who've I felt only once, whose powers are unlimited and dangerous. She is quite maniacal"

"Think of it as two different personalities. When your calm and happy your one person. When you're mad, your Darkling side comes out." Amber said.

The more they explained, the more things started to make sense; all those times when I blacked out and did something I couldn't remember doing. Could this be the explanation? "I can't believe it, but it actually makes sense. There are times where I do things without even realizing it." I said.

"I bet those times are when your mad." Amber said.

"Yeah, I can't recall them afterwards."

"Because it's a different you." She replied.

"This is a lot to absorb. It changes everything." I said, rubbing my temples. Then another thought occurred to me. "When I have my visions, my families been saying that I've been causing storms. Is that…"

"Your Darkling side, trying to get free." Alec said with a smile. "That's bloody crazy. Angelica, I think that your two sides are fighting with one another. Your Darkling part is trying to fight this magic bound side of you." He said looking at me. "That's brilliant!"

"That's not brilliant!" I shouted. "What happens if my Darkling side breaks free?"

"Who knows? Untold destruction maybe?" He replied. Alec seemed to be thrilled with this revelation.

My heart dropped into my stomach. "You said that only a handful of Darkling's made it too maturity?"

"Yeah, the earlier Darklings like Hekcuba Dredda. She was a novice priestess who caused Mount Vesuvius to erupt in 79AD, destroying the city of Pompeii along with herself. Then there was Tornac the Groundshaker. He was a Shaman who caused one of the largest earthquakes ever, that buried the city of El Dorado. Simon Von Lark created a massive whirlpool in the Indian Ocean that sunk the city of Atlantis. Or more recently, Alphonse Landry, who created the black plague that wiped out half of Europe. Or…"

"Okay stop!" I cried. With every Darkling he mentioned, my heart beat a little faster. Now, it felt like it was going to burst out of my chest. Darklings were monsters. Was I destined to end up just like them?

"Your Council got smarter though. They forbade the existence of Darklings because they are that dangerous. That's why they are killed as newborns, before they become adults."

"I said enough!" I shouted. All that bravado that I had showed earlier was slowly beginning to crumble.

"Sorry if that sounds harsh. You're the one who wanted this information." Alec said.

I looked at him. Was he deliberately trying to get me mad? "Your trying to get a rise out of me." I said.

"I won't deny that." He said simply.

I calmed myself. I wouldn't let Alec get the best of me, not here. "It's fine, I guess I should have expected something as bad as this." I replied. "It's a good thing that Grandma placed this spell on me then?"

"For now." He said ominously, making me feel worse. He is so infuriating. Of course, he was right though. If both my sides were fighting with one another, it was only a matter a time before one took out the other. As far as I was concerned, I wanted this Angelica to win; the one sitting here right now.

"What do we do?" I asked.

"We?" he asked.

"Yes, we!" I replied. "How do I stop my fighting halves?"

"Who says that's a terrible thing? Maybe we should let the Darkling out." He said.

For a moment, I was nervous that he wasn't going to help me. I decided that I would use this newfound information to my advantage. "Because you don't want an uncontrollable Darkling. You want someone who you can control. Someone who can help you in this quest for revenge." I replied. I had a hunch that that was the stipulation that Alec would evoke. I was hoping that he would want me controllable and not a monster.

"Hmm, so maybe a balance of both your halves. Of course, this is all-just speculation. Until we identify the spell placed on you, we have nothing." He said. Alec got up from the table and began pacing. He was muttering under his breath.

Amber giggled from the tree. "Don't worry. He does this a lot when he's thinking."

"Alright, this is what we're going to do. It is important that we identify the spell. However, in the meantime, I promised you that I would teach you about your gift of Sight." He said.

"Yeah?"

"So maybe, if I train you well enough, so that your gift of Sight becomes more powerful. Then maybe that will appease your Darkling side for the time being."

"You think that'll work?" I asked.

"It might, after all, every Darkling had one thing in common."

"And that was?"

"They wanted power." He replied. "Your Darkling side probably thinks your weak. If we give you a bit more power…" he waved his hand at me.

"It might make her happy and keep her at bay for a while." I replied.

"What do you say?" he asked.

I thought about it for a minute. I had already agreed to his wretched deal, so what harm could it be to try and keep my other half appeased for a while. Maybe some good could come out of this mess yet.

"Do we have an accord?" he asked again.

"A what?"

He sighed. "A deal?"

"Deal." I said. Then I decided to test my luck further. I knew that if he wanted my support, he would agree. "But you must add it to our agreement, that you will do whatever it takes to help me keep my Darkling side at bay." I added.

He thought about it for a moment. Then he pulled out the pen and parchment from yesterday. He added the stipulation, then showed me for confirmation. "Done." I nodded. "What time is it?"

I took out my phone. "It's almost 9:00, why?"

"Because if you're going to learn about being a Seer, then you're going to have to learn of its origins." He said.

Amber moaned from the tree. "This morning just got longer."

Chapter 14
The Origins of the Seer

Angelica
(8:55 A.M.-July 5th)

"You know, you should be down here telling parts of this story, instead of making me do all the work." Alec said to his sister.

"It's much more fun letting you do all the work." She replied.

I smiled as Alec and Amber fought with each other. The way they argued, reminds me so much of Merrin and myself. When they were finished, Alec came over and sat back down on the bench. He took a piece of crumb cake and popped it into his mouth. He washed it down with a little juice.

"Let's start at the beginning, shall we." He said. "Now we don't know for certain who the original holders of the knowledge of Sight were. What we do know, is that somewhere in history, the Elemental Ark stole that knowledge."

"How do you know it was stolen?" I asked.

"Gypsies can control the elements, Fire, Water, Earth, and Air. Now, reading minds doesn't really fit in with the rest of their abilities, they have nothing to do with one another. The Davenport's believed that the Gypsies conned the information from somewhere. They're experts at making deals."

I laughed. "They sound like they're from Avatar the Last Airbender." Alec stared at me like I had spoken a different language. "It's a cartoon on…Never mind. Do you think they're still around?" I asked.

"No one knows for sure. They disappeared after they made that bargain with the Weir." "The other day you said that I had to have been cursed by a Gypsy to have gain this ability."

"I know, that is rather strange." He was looking at me like I was a puzzle that needed solving. I could feel my heart beat faster as he stared.

"What happened afterwards?" I asked.

"Let's go back just a bit. Around the end of the Mortal American Civil War, the Vampire race had reached its peak in population. America was the land of opportunity, and Vampires were taking full advantage of it. There were these groups in the south that wanted to form their own armies. They began changing Mortals, people were disappearing so mysteriously, that they were attracting too much attention." Alec's story was very similar to what Grandma had told me. Maybe she was telling me some of the truth.

"Some Mortals, thinking that the Gypsies were Witches, asked them for help?" I asked.

Alec paused for a moment. "You've heard this story before?"

"My Grandmother told me her side of the story. It's very similar to what you're telling me."

"Shocking. Shall I continue, or do you want to?" he asked sarcastically.

"Keep going." I wanted to see just how much of the truth she was telling me.

"Okay, The Elemental Ark agreed to help the Mortals, providing they pay a hefty sum. Which they did."

"I'm going to assume that Gypsies are immortal, right?" I asked.

"That would be correct." Alec seemed to be annoyed at my constant interruptions. I smiled to myself. "Now, after that, the Elemental Ark created us. Well, not us, the Creators."

"Wait a minute, the Gypsies created the first Hunter pair. Wouldn't that make them the creators and the Hunter's the creations?"

"It's a wee bit confusing. I'll explain it momentarily." He replied. "After that..."

"Yeah, I know." I said, remembering the story "The Hunter Craze, your ancestors went on a murdering spree."

Alec frowned. "The Creators were only supposed to target the Vampires of the South. Specifically, the ones starting the newborn wars. The Elemental Ark however had different plans. They decided to see if the Creators powers worked on other races, which of course they did. That's when the Hunter Craze began."

He was trying to make it sound like The Hunters were the innocent ones. "It doesn't matter if the Gypsies set the Creators loose. They still murdered thousands of innocent lives." I replied.

"There's no denying that. After all, they were created to kill." He said.

"Grandma said that there was some kind of falling out?" I asked.

"Yeah, the Ark didn't like that The Creators were becoming close with one another."

"What do you mean?"

"They were becoming close romantically." He explained. "That was not allowed."

"Why?"

"The Creators weren't supposed to have feelings. The Ark felt that that made them weak. If they were developing feelings for one another, then they would start developing feelings for their prey."

"What happened?"

"The Ark ordered them to kill one another. They refused, and eventually broke free."

"How does Bent Faulke play into this?" I asked.

"That was where the Creators were going to start a new."

"What about the Weirlind that lived there?"

"They tried to talk to them, but they wouldn't listen. They attacked, The Creators defended themselves."

I shook my head. "It still doesn't justify killing an entire town."

"You have your opinion, I have mine." He replied. "Anyway, The Creators knew that there be retribution for their actions against the other races, and their defiance of the Ark. They decided to build up their forces. Hunter's grow so rapidly that it was easy for them to have many children in a brief time span." That concept was still weird to me. Having that many babies in that short amount of time defied nature. Then again, the presence of Magical people in the world defied nature.

"You probably know what happens next." He said.

"Yeah, the Gypsies sold them out." I said.

Alec nodded. "The Immortal Flame, payback for their defiance." He smiled though. "The Creators were smart though. They knew that their time was eventually coming to an end, but it wouldn't be the end of our new-found race. They sent some of their children out into the world, hoping they could get away and start their own groups."

"Your parents were among the ones to get away?" I asked.

He nodded. "What the Creators didn't plan on, was the Ark giving away their knowledge of the Immortal Flame. Your grandmother and her group must have given them an offer they couldn't refuse." He said. I recalled Grandma saying that they each had to give something to them in return. I wonder what she gave up? I wonder what Jacoby Valdorn had to give up?

"What kind of deal did they make?" I asked.

"I don't know." He said. "The price had to have been very steep. Gypsies are very secretive about the knowledge they possess. They wouldn't have given it up lightly."

It was silent for a few moments. Alec and I were both lost in thought, when Amber broke the silence. "There you go, that's the Origins of Sight." She said. "Riveting story as always Alec." Amber said with a smile.

"Nice of you to finally speak up." He said.

"My pleasure." She replied.

"Are you going to teach me now?" I asked.

Alec looked at me and smirked. "Somebody's eager. I should make you wait. Since you interrupted me a bunch of times and ruined my story."

"Aww, maybe if you weren't so boring, I wouldn't have had to interrupt." Amber giggled. "No better time like the present to start learning. If your teaching takes as long as your stories, I could be in for a long summer." Alec smirked. Maybe I was enjoying getting under his skin a little too much. The quicker he taught me though, the faster I would learn how to control my gift. Then hopefully, I'd be strong enough to control my Darkling half.

"Fine then." He said. I sat up a little straighter. I'll admit that I'm a little excited.

"There are three forms of Sight. One of them is called Foresight, that's the ability to see things that are currently happening. Have you had any of those before?"

"Just one. The night you two arrived was my first Foresight." I said. I wouldn't tell them about the second one, where I saw Amber lure my sister and dad to the B & B. I had to have some secrets for myself.

"She had a vision of us that night?" Amber asked.

"It seems like our arrival didn't go exactly as we planned. We knew you were a Seer. We just didn't know how much you knew about your gift.

As I mentioned before, it's a gift that only Hunters are supposed to have. Nobody seemed to know how far progressed you were,
we had to take a chance."

"Sorry to spoil your arrival" I said.

He shrugged. "Anyway, Foresights come in Astral Form, that means that the soul detaches itself from the body." He said.

"Wait, your telling me that the ghost form of me was my soul?" I asked.

"That's one way to put it. I like Astral Form better, and yes that is your soul that detaches."

"That's cool."

"It's one of the easiest forms of Seeing." He said. "The second form is called Hindsight, that's the ability to see things that have past."

"I've had plenty of those." I think, who knows how many visions that Mom and Grandma wiped from my mind. Most of the visions I do remember though, were Hindsight's. "I hate that stupid spinning vortex."

Amber giggled. "Spinning Vortex?"

"That vortex as you say, is really a timeline." Alec said.

"I gathered that much." I said.

"Hindsights are Amber's specialty. When it comes time for you to learn them, she'll be doing the honors. Why don't you tell her a little bit about them Amber? My voice is starting to get hoarse."

"Oh, you poor thing." Amber rolled her eyes at her brother. "There's not much to tell. Like Foresights, your soul does all the traveling. Only now you're going back in time to see things that have already past. There really quite enjoyable once you get use to them." She said. "They've never been enjoyable for me." I mumbled.

"You must have had some terrible Hindsights." She said. The memory of the last one still haunted me. Ignatius's death still replayed repeatedly in my dreams. Alec and Amber were both looking at me expectantly. They may be teaching me about being a Seer, but I wasn't ready to tell them about some of the visions I've had.

"Why do we receive visions? Is there any reason behind them?" I asked, hoping to change the subject.

"The Davenport's said that most of the time the visions that we receive have a direct effect on what we're doing at that moment. However, there are times when we receive visions at random. Sometimes they don't have any direct effect on us, we just get them. It comes with the territory." Alec said.

"What's the third way to have a vision?" I asked.

"That would be Farsights, or seeing things that will happen in the future. We don't know much about them. Amber and I have never experienced one, but from what the Davenport's could gather, they're very similar to Forsights." I wondered what it would be like to know the future.

"Why don't we have a demonstration."

"What kind of demonstration?" I asked. "You mean like a vision?"

Amber looked at Alec like she couldn't believe I had just said that. "Angelica, you do know that you can have a vision anytime that you want, right?" Alec asked.

"I thought that they only happened when they came to you." They both looked aghast. My cheeks flushed three shades of red. I've must have sounded completely stupid to them.

"Blimey we have our work cut out for us." Alec said.

"It's not my fault." I said defensively.

"It's your grandmothers fault." He replied.

"Listen! I'm not on the best of speaking terms with my grandmother at the moment, but for this deal to work out, you will not insult my family!" My grandmother is no saint. My family have their fair share of issues, but they were still my family.

"Whatever you say." He replied defensively.

"How am I going to do this demonstration?" I asked.

"We'll do something simple. Like…" he thought for a second. "Like seeing what your sister is doing right now." He said.

"She's probably doing what she's always doing." I said.

"Well how would you know unless you look?" he asked.

"How?" I asked.

"You're going to use Foresight. Relax your body, pretend your meditating out here by yourself with nobody around." I closed my eyes and focused. I imagined myself all alone in the park like I always am. "Just picture your sister in your mind and it'll happen before you know it." Alec's voice sounded miles away again. It was eerily similar to our trip in the fog. I focused only on my sister. I kept repeating her name repeatedly in my head. Soon I felt that familiar tug in the back of my mind. I felt my soul tug away from my body. It was different from last time though, because my vision was blurry for some reason. I was still flying up over the trees and towards my house. As soon as it came into view, the vision became even more clouded. I struggled to keep the house in view as I hovered outside the bedroom window of my sister. I was barely able to make out her small form as she sat on her bed all by herself. It was all I managed before I lost grip of the vision and sailed back towards my body in the park.

When I arrived back in my body. I quickly looked-for Alec to tell him what happened, but the sight that I saw, froze me on the spot. The bench we were sitting on was now a bunch of splinters. Amber was on the ground coughing and patting down flames off her shirt. The branch she was on moments before laid in an ashen heap not far from her. Alec was on the other side of the clearing, and he was sopping wet from head to toe. Curiously enough, this time I was as dry as can be. "Oh no. It happened again?" I asked.

"You weren't kidding. You were only gone a minute and you manage to cause quite the storm, complete with wind, lightning, and rain. You blew Alec right off his feet, and that lightning bolt almost fried me." Amber said. "Your Darkling side means business."

"I'm so sorry. I didn't mean for this to happen." I said, feeling like a total failure.

"What do you have to be sorry for? You didn't cause the storm." Amber said.

"Technically she did." Alec replied.

"You're not helping Alec." Amber replied.

"I saw Merrin. She was sitting in her bedroom by herself, but everything was blurry." I said.

"That was because it was your first time inducing a vision. They'll get clearer with practice. I'll keep teaching you Foresights and Amber will do the same with Hindsights." He said. "With a little luck, and our supreme teaching skills. You'll be an expert in no time, and that Darkling may stop rearing her head. If that doesn't work, we can always invite her out for tea."

I rolled my eyes. "Okay." I glanced at my phone, it was almost noon. I was testing my luck being out too long. "I should be getting home. When do you want to meet for these lessons?"

"The sooner the better." Alec replied. I couldn't agree with him more. "Remember what I said. Unless we can find out about the spell, then this is all just speculation. I'm almost positive that we're correct, but it would be nice to know for sure."

"Okay." I said. "I trust you can find your way out of my park." I cleaned up the mess I made with a wave of my hand. "If you value your health, you'll keep its location a secret." Then I teleported.

******

Alec

As soon as Angelica left, I used some of the magic I had left to dry off from my run in with Darkling Angelica. That was one mean storm.

"You know, I think that version of Angelica is feistier than the Darkling side."
I laughed. "Both sides of her are powerful. We need her in balance though, can you imagine what she would be like then?"

"You think our theory is correct?"

"Like I said, I'm almost positive we're correct." The thought of having a trained Darkling on my side was too good to pass up. Once she was trained, she'd be unstoppable, we'll be unstoppable. Our enemies beware.

Chapter 15
The Secret Library

Alec
(7:00 A.M.-July 6ᵗʰ)

"Alec can you please stop pacing, you're driving me crazy." Amber said from the couch.

"I can't help it. I hate waiting."

"You have to give her some time, she's not as fast as us." She replied.

"I know that, but I still hate waiting." I replied. Not for nothing, we told Angelica what we thought was happening to her, and we told her about the Origins of Sight. The least she could do was figure out the bloody name of the curse on her.

"Why don't you go do something constructive." She said.

"What do you propose I do?"

"Why don't you invite Lindsey over? She seems to know how to distract us." Amber replied.

"Not bleeding likely. Don't even get me started on that one." I resumed my pacing of the room.

After we got back from our meeting with Angelica. The rest of the day past by without anything of interest happening. Unless you count Lindsey showing up, wanting to meet Amber. It was driving me mad that I couldn't figure out what was up with her. I even pondered the possibility that maybe I like her. She really is quite fit like Amber said. Then again, my sister feels the same compulsion to her. So that couldn't be it. Something was off with Lindsey Hansen, and it was really infuriating me that I couldn't figure out what it was.

She spent the whole afternoon talking...and talking...and talking. I didn't think it was possible for someone to talk non-stop about total nonsense for hours at a time. No matter what she said, we couldn't help being glued to her every word. She talked about movies, and celebrity gossip. She wanted to know what it was like growing up in England? Did we do the same things as American teenagers? At some point the conversation switched to Angelica's family. How she thought it was strange that they never came down to the town. How she always wanted to visit Angelica's home.

Besides the parts about Angelica's family. The rest of the conversation was just bloody nonsense. Still, I sat there like a bum.

"Have a pastry Alec." Amber said.

"That's another thing. If we keep eating these pastries, we're going to become lethargic." Every day since we've arrived here, Amber has gone to the Java to pick up pastries.

"Oh please." She rolled her eyes. "You know just as well as I do that we burn calories fast. It's impossible for us to become lethargic.
Besides, you like them just as much as I do."

I moaned, sitting down on the couch next to her. I took a bite of a jelly donut. I hated it when she was right. I haven't met this Ms. Monti yet, but her cooking was out of this world. "I should have at least asked Lindsey for her telephone number." I said.

"Why do you want Lindsey's telephone number for?" Amber asked.

"Not Lindsey's number, Angelica's." I said.

"Oh, you have to be more specific Alec."

I threw my hands in the air. "This is ridiculous."

She rolled her eyes at me again. "You know, calling her cell phone will just make her more brassed off at us. We'd have to tell her where we got her number from."

"Amber, I'm not the one initiating conversation with Lindsey." I said.

"I know that, but Angelica doesn't seem to know about her friends' peculiarities. Besides that, even if we wanted to call, it wouldn't matter because we don't have phones." Amber said. We were so used to communicating telepathically our entire lives, that phones weren't a necessity. If we used the room phone, it would cost money. I know Grace Hansen had said that it was free, but I still didn't want to take advantage of her hospitality.

We sat there for a couple of minutes eating our pastries and trying to figure out what we were going to do, when there was a knock at the door. "Maybe that's Lindsey again." Amber said with a smile.

"Bloody Hell, I can't do that again." I went to go answer the door. When I opened it, it wasn't Lindsey, but Angelica, waiting outside.

"I figured it out." She said pushing past me.

"Again, just invite yourself in." I said. She ignored me and sat down on the edge of my bed.

"After I got home yesterday, I was determined to get answers from my grandmother. Much to my surprise, she wasn't even there. She left town."

"That would explain why she hasn't come down here to exterminate us." I said. Amber and I had been wondering why Greta hadn't come down to have another go at us yet.

"I thought you could smell magical scents?" Angelica asked.

"That's right." I replied.

"Then how come you didn't know she left?"

I laughed, this is another thing that infuriated me about this place. "I can track your scents up until the forest line. Once I get there, my nose is bombarded by a thousand different magical scents. Your father did an excellent job concealing your location."

"Oh." She replied.

"I can ask the same question, you live in the same house." I replied.

"Just because we live in the same house doesn't mean we see each other all the time."

"How big is your bloody house?" I asked. She was about to reply when I interrupted. "Never mind. You said you figured it out, you're talking about the spell?"

"Right, sorry. After I found out she left, I started thinking. The spell is definitely an uncommon one. It's probably not the kind of spell that you can memorize, meaning it would have had to come from a book."

"A spell-book?" I asked.

"That's what I thought. The answer we seek could be in my family's library. I went to check before I came over here, but I couldn't find anything." She said.

"Greta's smart. She wouldn't keep that kind of knowledge just lying around.
Information like that will be well hidden. Where is this family library?"

"A few blocks from here." She said.

"The one in town?" I thought that a family library would be in their own house. "The Mortals here can use the library?"

"They could, but not many do. The library's closed most of the time. Mrs. Sareolla, the librarian only opens it twice a week. There's a section of the library that's always closed off, that's the section my family uses. I thought that maybe that gigantic sniffer of yours might pick something up that I couldn't." She said.

"Oh, please go Alec. It'll give me a break from your constant pacing." Amber said.

"Oh, Shut It." I replied. "Sure."

"Let's go then." She said impatiently. I followed her out the door.

"So how are we getting there?" I asked. I remembered passing by the library a few days ago with Lindsey. "I could get us there by mist."

"Absolutely not! I'm never doing that again."

"Then I guess we're walking." I said.

"We're going to teleport." She replied with a grin. "I traveled your way yesterday, today you'll travel mine. Unless your too scared of course."

I gritted my teeth. Teleporting wasn't my favorite thing in the world. I've tried it before with zero luck. Being a Hunter allowed me different modes of transportation. "I'm not afraid of anything." I replied. "Isn't teleporting in broad daylight suspicious though, what if someone sees?"

"Nobody gets up in this town until eight, it's like clockwork every day." She replied. That was something I noted as peculiar about this town as well. Only a few of the shopkeepers were up and about early. Everyone else didn't show themselves until after eight o'clock. I found that rather strange.

Angelica walked to the edge of the sidewalk and held out her hand. She smiled again. "We could walk."

I took hold of her hand. I was starting to get used to being close to her. The magic was still intoxicating though. I closed my eyes. "One…two…three." The street disappeared, and I felt the wind rush out of me as we teleported. Let's just say it felt like my brain was being scrambled into mush. We landed on the street just outside the library. Angelica landed on her feet, I landed on my face. Angelica giggled as I brushed myself off. "Not so graceful after all."

"Very funny." I looked up at the library. It was small and modern. It didn't appear to be anything special from the outside. "Is it opened today?"

"No, but I can get in whenever I want. Follow me." I could tell that Angelica liked being in charge of the situation. I'll just let her keep thinking that she is. She walked up to the front door and waved her hand. I heard the clicking of the lock as the door swung open to admit us. Once inside she waved her hand again, and the lights flickered to life. I followed her as we passed dozens of shelves loaded with books. We stopped at another door. She placed her hand on it, the door glowed briefly. Then swung open. The room we entered was dark as well. She again waved her hand and the room came to life.

"Brilliant, this place didn't look that big from the outside." I said.

Angelica shrugged. "Looks can be deceiving."

To say the room was big was an understatement, it was huge. There was a great big circular wooden table in the center, with matching chairs. The floor was made from hard cherry wood and hanging in the center of the ceiling just above the table hung a big crystal chandelier. "This is your section of the library, I presume?" I asked.

"This is it." She said. I began looking at all the books on the shelves. "These two cases our mine." She said pointing to the nearest bookcases.

"Two whole bookcases just for you." I said scanning the shelves. There had to be thousands of books on the shelves. "Blimey you're a bookworm."

"I am not." She said. "It's just for when I'm bored."

"You must get bored a lot then." I scanned the titles of the books. "I see you have all the Harry Potter books." I said looking at the seven novels.

"Now don't tell me you haven't read those books either." She asked.

"You're kidding, I grew up in England." I said with a smile.

"Sometimes I wish I was in her world instead of mine." Angelica said with a sigh.

"Rowling's words are magic, there is no doubt about that." I said turning to face her. "You said you couldn't find anything here?" I asked.

"Just look around, what's missing?" she asked.

I looked around the room. There were tons of books, but they were all mortal books. You would think that a Weirlind family library would have more interesting stuff inside it.

"Where are all the spell-books? By looking at this room you'd never know that a family of Weirlind kept books here." Angelica said. "I know my family is secretive, but you'd think that there be at least one book in here that talked about magic."

I closed my eyes and concentrated for a moment. "What are you doing?"

"Using my gigantic sniffer to search for a scent of magic." I replied. So far, all I've smelt in this room is the spell on the door.

"Your telling me that spell-books have a scent?"

"All magic has a scent." I said scanning the shelves more closely. I stood in front of the wall facing opposite the door. There were only two bookcases on this wall, and they were both placed directly in the center. "The magic is faint here, but I can still smell it." I looked at the bindings of the books on these shelves. They were all older books, and there was a coating of dust on most of them.

"I never look at those cases. There all old boring novels like Shakespeare." Angelica said.

"A perfect place to hide a secret door." I said. I breathed in deeply, there was magic on these shelves.

"Sounds like something out of a Scooby Doo cartoon." Angelica said, coming over to the cases. "I wonder if one of the books is a key."

I raised my eyebrows at her. She smiled and blushed with embarrassment. "I watch a lot of T.V."

"You think."

"There is nothing wrong with Scooby Doo."

"Shall we split up and search for clues then." I said with a smile.

Her mouth hung opened for a moment, then she punched me in the shoulder. "You take that case, and I'll take this one."

As I was scanning the books. I noticed writing etched into the wood of the shelves. "Jinkies."

"Stop making fun of me." She said.

"No, I'm serious Angelica, look." I said, pointing to the writing.

"Mine too!" she said excitedly.

She cleared off the dust with a spell. I coughed as most of it hit me in the face. She giggled again at my expense. I cleaned my face and looked at the shelves. Sure enough, there was writing on all the shelves.

"You've never noticed this before?"

"Like I said, I only come in here when I'm bored, and I never look at these shelves." She replied.

"Start at the beginning, what does it say?" I asked.

With Great Knowledge,
Comes a Great Mind

With a Great Mind,
One Gains Great Power

With Great Power,
One Achieves Great Riches

But Seekers Beware!

Great Riches Will Not
Bring Great Happiness

Beyond This Room Lies
Great Power and Knowledge

For Those Keen Enough to Seek It"

"Now this is getting interesting." I said.

"What does it mean though?" Angelica asked.

"It's a warning." I replied. "There has to be a secret room beyond these bookcases that can only be accessed by someone with an intelligent mind. I guess it's up to me then."

"Very funny, how do we open it though?" she asked.

I looked at the bindings of the books again, most of them were of English poetry. The titles were familiar to me because the Davenport's made us read all the old novels. Then I came across a book that I've never heard of before. Seekers Wanted by G. Hart. "I wonder." I pulled the book out and no sooner than I touched it. A voice echoed in the room. It was the voice of Greta Everhardtht.

"No knowledge comes to thee, unless you answer my riddles three."

"Great! I'm terrible at riddles. Leave it to grandma to come up with something like this." Angelica said.

"To understand a riddle, you must understand the person giving it." I said.

"What starts with a T, ends with a T, and has T in it? Thirty Seconds or you fail."

"A time limit? Perfect." I mumbled. "Now, does she mean the letter T, or the drink?"

"Know the person giving the riddle." Angelica mumbled. "Grandma loves to drink tea brewed from a teapot. Starts with a T, ends with a T, and has tea in it. Is it a Teapot!" she shouted.

"Correct. Riddle Two. What always runs but never walks, often murmurs, never talks, has a bed but never sleeps, has a mouth but never eats?"

Angelica's excitement from answering the first question vanished upon hearing the second. I thought for a second, then said. "It's a River."

"How do you know?"

"A river is always running. It has a river bed, and a river mouth." I said. "I happen to be good at riddles."

"Show off." She said. "Is it a River?"

"Correct. Final Riddle. At night, they come without being fetched. By day they are lost without being stolen. What are they?"

Angelica smiled. "Just like grandma to use a riddle about her favorite activity. She likes to stargaze. Is the answer the Star's?" she asked.

"Correct."

"I thought you said you were terrible with riddles?" I asked.

"Like you said, you have to know the riddle giver." She responded. "What now?" Angelica asked. As soon as she said that, the bookcases began to separate from each other, revealing an archway barred by a gate. I breathed in deeply. The magic behind this gate was stronger. When I placed my hand on it, a scorching pain shot through my hand. I examined the gate closely. It was made entirely of Black Onyx, which was toxic for super natural's. There was a keyhole, which meant that we could only open it with a key.

"This isn't a normal keyhole." I said examining it. "It's shaped like a prism."

"I hoped she left it in this room somewhere." Angelica said. She began searching the room more thoroughly then before. She pulled out books, looked under the table, and the chairs and even tapped the walls for hollow places.

I sat down in a chair. Would Greta be stupid enough to leave the key in the room? I didn't think there was much of a chance of that. Then I just happened to glance up at the chandelier. "That's where the key is." I said.

"Where?" Angelica asked. I pointed up to the chandelier.

"But there all diamond shaped." Angelica said. Looking up at the chandelier.

"Look closer." I said. "It has to be there."

Angelica got up on top of the table. She hovered in the air as she searched each one of the crystals. A few minutes passed, when she finally shouted. "I got it!" She came down, and showed me the prism shaped crystal. It was dented and cracked in several spots.

She smiled and hurried back over to the gate. When she pressed the crystal into the hole it glowed bright orange. The gate clicked open. We both glanced at each other before stepping into the darkness. As soon as we entered the room, torches that lined the walls lit up instantly.

"Now this is more like it." I said. This room was old and dusty. It reeked with a combination of old book smell and magic. The walls, floor, and ceiling were all stone, like a dungeon in a castle. There had to be at least fifty bookcases all around the room. Thousands of books were stacked on the shelves.

"Look at these books." She said admiring them all. "I can't believe this has always been here."

"Nobody's been in here for a while." I said. There was dust, and cobwebs everywhere. I was admiring the books myself. What I would give for the chance to read them. The Davenports would have done anything to get their hands on a collection such as this. The secrets that could be learned here were unimaginable.

"Look at these?" Angelica said.

"What?" I asked, coming over next to her.

"Spell-Books. There are thirteen volumes of each. *Spellbound*, and *Spellbind* by Merlin the Great." She said.

"That is remarkable, a complete set of twenty-six." The great Sorcerer Merlin wrote twenty-six volumes of magical spells that he had accumulated over his lifetime. Some of these books were rare now, having a complete copy of the set was extremely rare.

Angelica took a volume of *Spellbound* off the shelf. As soon as I saw the cover, my heart skipped a beat. "That's no copy. That is the original volume written by Merlin himself." I said. I glanced at the other covers. Sure enough, they were all originals.

"How can you tell?" Angelica asked.

"Look at the covers, Merlin's seal is on them." Merlin's insignia was a blue pointy hat. "These books were believed to be lost when King Arthur fell."

Angelica cradled the book, like she was carrying something fragile. "Arthur was a Combatant, wasn't he?" She asked.

"A great one. His best friend Lancelot and his wife Guinevere betrayed him. That allowed the Sorcerer Mordred to kill him." I replied.

"The spell has to be in one of these books." She said, sitting down and going through the pages.

While she looked through the books, I walked around the room. Admiring the works that I saw on the shelves. Some of them were originals like Merlin's spell-books. *The Art of Levitation* by

Leonardo da Vinci, he was a Mason. *Animalia: Magical Creatures* by Charles Darwin, perhaps one of the greatest Nurturers of all time. *The Netherworld* by Edgar Allan Poe, he was an Under-Fate. Poe had a strong connection to the spiritual world. *Zefts: Magical Stones* by Kerstin Keyes. She wasn't as well-known as da Vinci, but she was a gifted Mason.

The more I looked around at the volumes of history, the more I wanted to read them. The knowledge that I would gain just by reading these books would be unbelievable. I didn't want to appear too eager in front of Angelica though. I kept moving along the shelves until I came across a book that caught my eye. It looked to be quite old. I carefully removed it. It was quite heavy. The cover was made of a material that I've never seen before. The picture on the front looked to be a giant tree. The words were faded greatly, but I could make out the word *Hlaetisk*. It was a word I'd never heard of before. Before I could open it up, Angelica called me over. "Hey look at this. I think I found something." I swore under my breath and quickly put the book back on the shelf, determined to come back and read it.

"What did you find?" I asked.

She was looking over the book *Spellbind Vol. 3*. The page read;

Binding of a Witch The Darkling Spell/
Valor's Curse

It followed with an ancient spell.

"What language is this?" Angelica asked.

"Arthurian." I replied. "Merlin wrote all of his spells in that tongue."

"Isn't Arthurian a forgotten language?"

"It's extinct to all but a few scholars. The Davenport's spoke it fluently." I said.

"Of course, they did." She replied.

Fortunately, they taught me a little bit. I scanned the page. "This is the part we need. Listen to this; *Named after Syren Valor. This curse is meant to bind a Darkling Witch within her own body. As a colleague and a friend of mine. I warned Syren that it wasn't a clever idea. I never fully tested this spell to perfection. I wasn't sure it would work. Besides, Darkling Witches were never meant to be kept alive. Unwilling to listen to me. Syren was sure that this spell could bind his daughter's powerful magic. Using the blood of a Nymph and the heart of a Unicorn, Syren cast the spell. At first it seemed to work, but over time his daughter's magic broke free. Killing Syren, his wife and his daughter. I pass on a warning to all those wanting to use this spell. As you know, a spell is only as powerful as the person casting it. No matter how strong you think you are, there is no way to bind a Witches power forever, especially a Darkling Witch. This spell will work temporarily, but eventually the magical binds will wear thin, causing the magic to explode out in force. Once the spell is applied. The same ingredients used to cast it, can only remove it. The ingredients needed are rare and are not easy to come by. Beware! This spell maybe permanent. However, it is my belief, that if the Darkling can be trained properly while under the spell, then the results may not be as devastating."*

"That means I need the heart of a Unicorn, and blood from a Nymph if I want to get rid of the spell totally." Angelica said.

"Bloody Hell." I said running a hand through my hair. "Rare is an understatement. Nobody has seen Nymphs or Unicorns in centuries, they're both believed to be extinct."

"Grandma had to have come by these ingredients somewhere recently." Angelica said.

"Who knows where, or even when." I replied. I read the page further. "Look at this; *As I observed the young lady, I noticed several side effects of the spell. She would have random outbursts of magic depending on her mood. Outbursts that she could not recall. Upon experiencing these outbursts, I can only describe them as a multi personality dysfunction."* I looked at Angelica. "Multi Personality, two people in one. I wonder if your grandmother read Merlin's words before she cast this spell."

"This spell can't be removed without the ingredients, I'm stuck with it?"

"Merlin said, that he thought training would be a good solution. Angelica, what I said was correct. If I can train you to become a powerful Seer, that may buy us some time."

She looked at me. There was a fire in her eyes. "Fine. I'm ready." She said with confidence.

Chapter 16
The Head of the Snake

Angelica
(2:00 P.M.-July 6th)

I didn't realize that I had spent most of the morning in the library with Alec. I knew it was a bad idea allowing him access to the library. Those books had to be old and filled with tons of secrets. I saw Alec's reaction when he walked around the room. He was like a little kid in a candy shop.

Lately, I had no idea what I was doing. I gave him access to the library and my secret park. I signed a binding agreement, and I kept sneaking out of the house and going to meet him. Worst of all, I wasn't talking to my parents. I was basically lying to them. This wasn't me, I'm losing control. I wanted answers so badly that I resorted to un-Angelica like behavior.

Then if I wasn't feeling guilty and overwhelmed, I was angry and pissed. How could my parents not tell me about the Darkling Spell? Why would grandma place a spell on me knowing it would cause a dual personality effect? These are just a few of the questions rolling around in my head.

I told Alec that I needed time to rest and that we could start training tomorrow. I knew he wasn't happy about leaving, but I had to get him out of there. Alec used the mist to go back to the B & B. Now, I know what you're thinking. I just showed him my library, now he'll be able to get back in again. I'm not stupid though, you see there's an enchantment on that room that prevents it from looking the same way twice. The furniture changes every time I visit. The chandelier will always be made from those crystals and the bookcases will always be there, but it will never be arranged in the same order. I also knew that he could probably find the room again on scent alone. When I locked the gate with the crystal prism, instead of placing it back in the chandelier. I placed it in my pocket. That way if Alec did manage to get back into the room, he wouldn't be able to open the door without the key. Hunter's weren't the only ones who could be sneaky. I smiled, rather pleased at myself.

Now, I laid on my bed alone again. My mind exhausted from the onslaught of the past day's events. Sleep came quickly, but as usual, it didn't last long. A trio of Hindsight's disturbed my rest.

After falling through the stupid timeline. I landed in a large underground room. I could tell that I was underground just by the feeling the room gave off. It was cold, damp, dimly lit, and gave off this strange earthy smell. The room was circular with large stone columns holding up the ceiling. I had the feeling, that if you were to remove those columns, the ceiling would cave in. I imagined myself under a pile of dirt and rocks. I shuddered at the thought. Being buried alive was not a way I wanted to go. Aligning the walls were metal cells. This place reminded me of a king's dungeon. It took me a moment to realize I wasn't alone in the room. Three men stood in the center. Torches that were magicked to levitate around them, illuminated their faces. One of them, a tall man with thick shoulders, long jet-black hair, and an ice cream cone goatee was none other than Jacoby Valdorn. He stood there with his red and black robes, with the scepter in his right hand. That thing scared me more than he did.

A shorter man stood next to him. His round belly made his robes of green look two sizes too big for him. He had short-cropped hair, that had a huge balding spot, dark beady eyes, that looked like they were going to pop out of his sockets, and an orange beard that didn't mesh well with his baby-like face. A third man, with long mullet-like hair, and bushy sideburns stood facing them. When I say bushy. I mean it looks like he has two furry animals on his cheeks. His green robes were tattered and weathered. It appeared that he hadn't slept or cleaned in weeks. He had an I-just-rolled-around-in-mud smell to him. His head was bowed to Jacoby. Out of the three men, it was clear that Jacoby was in charge here.

The vision unfroze, startling me as usual. "Mr. Rheal Cromier. There better be a good explanation as to why you return here alone and empty handed." Jacoby said in that deep voice of his.

"Begging your forgiveness Master Valdorn. I did exactly as I was instructed to. I led my team to Gloucestershire England, just like Master Langston said. We found the house that you wanted, the one with the two special children." Rheal had a thick Irish accent. He was slurring his words badly, probably because he's nervous. It wasn't helping me understand him any better though. "We discovered that the parents were the same creatures as the children."

Jacoby glared at the small man next to him. "Why was I not told about this sooner?"

The smaller man just bowed his head in embarrassment. Jacoby glared at Rheal. "They are called Hunter's by the way, not creatures." He said. Instantly, I knew that they were talking about Alec and Amber. This confirmed their story of being attacked by Wizards. Jacoby Valdorn was behind the attack on The Davenport's.

"And! What happened?" Valdorn shouted impatiently.

Rheal and the smaller man jumped. "I sent three of my men inside to confront them, while myself and three others covered from the outside. Moments later, we saw the two children run out of the house. We followed them. That's when a fire erupted from the house. In a matter of seconds those red flames swallowed it up. My men and the older Hunters were inside."

"You're telling me, that two Hunter's, two possible allies are now dead because your men couldn't control the Immortal Flame. A power that you shouldn't have had knowledge of in the first place!" Valdorn shouted, glaring again at the smaller man. The men shrank further under the eyes of Jacoby. "Did the fire spread?" Valdorn asked.

"It just burnt the house, then extinguished itself." Rheal said.

"What happened to the children?"

"We followed them for days. We even had the young girl in our grasps. When the brother found us, and..." Rheal hesitated, like he was remembering the event. I didn't need to read his mind to imagine what happened. "Well he wasn't happy. He killed my other three men. After that they just vanished."

"Vanished, into thin air?" Valdorn said.

"I searched all over the place Masters. They just weren't there anymore." Rheal said. There was a plea for mercy in his voice.

"Let me get this straight." Valdorn turned away from Rheal. "There were four Hunter's, two of them you killed. The original two that you were sent out to get, you've lost. In the process of all that, you managed to get your entire team, excluding yourself killed, is that all right?"

"Yes, Master Valdorn." Rheal said quietly. He was shaking uncontrollably.

"Mr. Cromier, how long have you been serving the 8th Covenant?" Valdorn asked.

"Ten years Master Valdorn." Rheal said proudly.

Valdorn turned and stared at Rheal with malice in his eyes. I knew what was coming. "Well I regret to inform you that your services are no longer required." With lightning quick speed, Valdorn swung his scepter at the man. Rheal had only seconds to scream before the red dragon smashed through his chest. I let out a small squeal as Rheal Cromier fell to the floor.

Valdorn turned his attention to the small man. "I'm disappointed Gregor. I thought you could handle this job, but at every turn, you prove your incompetence. I will kill you, just like I did Ignatius! Just like I did that pathetic excuse for a Wizard!" He said pointing to the lifeless body of Rheal. This man Jacoby was yelling at, must be the predecessor he was talking about.

"I can Jacoby. Really, I can. If you just give me the chance to explain. I..." Gregor began. His voice was so small and timid compared to Jacoby's.

"You gave away the secret of the Immortal Flame!" Jacoby shouted. "I knew giving that knowledge to you was a mistake!"

"I thought..." Gregor began.

"You were not placed in charged to think! You were put in this position to follow orders! You have now failed to follow those orders! Now you must pay a price!" he said. I thought for sure Jacoby would use his scepter again. Apparently so did Gregor because he begged for forgiveness.

"Please Jacoby, give me another chance." He begged.

"The knowledge of the Immortal Flame is too much for you to handle." Jacoby said, approaching Gregor with his wand drawn. "Amneio." Jacoby said, pointing the wand at Gregor's head.

Immediately Gregor let out an earsplitting scream and fell to his knees. From the wand tip, I watched as Jacoby pulled a silvery like strand from Gregor's head. He just took a memory from him.

Jacoby leaned over the panting Langston. Gregor's beady eyes stared blankly ahead. "Find me those children, they can't just vanish. They must be in England somewhere. Do not fail me!"

"I won't Jacoby." Gregor squeaked.

Valdorn vanished from the room, as the scene dissolved, and I went traveling ahead in time. The room I found myself in now, wasn't any better than the one I had left. It was hot and dimly lit, but I could see the coffins on the pedestals all around the room. I was in a funeral home. Even when I was little, caskets scared me. They symbolized an ending, a conclusion to life that no one should have to go through. I stared around at the creepy coffins. I nearly jumped out of my skin when I saw one was opened, with a body inside. It was Ignatius Clearwater's body. He looked perfectly preserved, just as I remembered him from my vision.

I jumped again when the door opened, and the lights flickered on. Three men walked in the room, they were in a heated discussion.

"Master Langston wants this body

cremated now. I don't make the rules, I just follow them." Said a tall lanky man with an Irish accent. All three men had the same accent, and robes of green. Which meant that they were all probably from the 8th Covenant.

"All I be sayin Liam is that we could have done this in the mornin. Nobody is going to be gettin to him in here." Said the younger man. He looked to be only nineteen. He was clearly the youngest of the three.

"Look here Colin. I don't want to be gettin on the new head's bad side. Let's just finish the job and be done with it." Liam said.

"Could we do this now please?" Said the third guy, he was an older man with gray hair.

"You two move the body, while I go prep the oven." Liam said as he left the room. They were going to cremate Ignatius! Then nobody would know what had happened to him. Just the thought of Jacoby getting away with murder made me sick.

Colin and the older guy moved a cart over to Ignatius's casket and lifted it onto it. "I can't believe we have to do this Shamus. If Master Langston wants to get rid of Clearwater's body, then he should be doing it himself. Surely you object to this?" Colin said.

"Listen here boy. When you get to my age, you'll understand not to ask questions and just follow orders. That's how you stay alive and remain on the bosses' good side." Shamus replied. "Now let's move, the quicker we get rid of him, the better off we be."

"It's a shame, after all Clearwater accomplished, to be burned without any recognition." Colin said.

"Ignatius Clearwater may have been a war hero, but he had no business running a Covenant. Ireland's Weirling have suffered for centuries under his rule." Shamus replied fiercely. I got the feeling that Shamus had suffered personally from Ignatius' rule. "Things will be gettin better soon."

"But why Langston? I would've chosen a dancin monkey before him." Replied Colin.

"You and I both know Langston is just a figurehead. Jacoby Valdorn runs the show now."

"But he's not even Irish. What business does he have running Ireland?" Colin argued.

Shamus stared a hard gaze at the younger man. "If you know what's good for you, you be keepin your mouth closed. Now let's get this over with."

Just as they began to move the cart, the door to the room burst off its hinges. A black hooded figure stepped into the room. Colin reached for his wand, but the figure just swiped a hand at him. I ducked as Colin flew over me and crashed against the nearby wall. Shamus drew his wand and sent curses at the figure, which were swiped away with ease. The figure lifted Shamus off his feet. While in mid-air, I heard the sickening crack of bone, and Shamus crashed to the floor. The hooded figure had snapped his spine. On the other side of the room, Colin was getting to his feet, just as the hooded figure sent a coffin flying at him. I ducked again. Colin screamed before the coffin crashed on top of him with bone shattering force. With both men down, the hooded figure approached Ignatius's coffin. There was no doubt that this person was a Weirlind. There was something familiar about the way he or she walked with a purpose.

Standing over Ignatius, the figure pulled off its hood, and I was shocked to see my grandmother standing before me. Her eyes shined brightly as she stared at Ignatius. "Dear Ignatius. What have they done to you? It's time for a proper burial, for a real hero." She said. I still hadn't gotten over the shock of my grandmother's appearance, and the two men she just killed, one of them a mere child. The scene dissolved again, and I went forward in time once more. I was standing in the funeral home again. This time Valdorn and Langston were there. The man named Liam was talking to them.

"What happened here?" Valdorn said, waving his arms around at the room.

"I went down to prep the oven. I realized that they were takin too long. I came up here to hurry them, and I found both of em dead." Liam said.

"Ignatius's body?" Valdorn said, his eyes were closed, he knew the answer already.

"Gone, Sir." Liam said.

"Looks like quite a struggle took place up here. You didn't hear anything?" Valdorn shouted.

"The basement is sound proof Master Valdorn." Liam said. "Sir if there is anything I could…" Before he could finish, Jacoby slashed his wand across his chest. Liam coughed up blood before he collapsed. I think I'm going to throw up. How could someone just kill another person like that and have no remorse what so ever?

"I've never seen a Covenant display such a total incompetence like this one!" Jacoby said to Gregor. "Find Ignatius's body! If it falls into the wrong hands, you'll be the next body. Clean this mess up!" he said pointing to the room.

The scene changed again. This time, I was outside on a street block. The night was cool and clear. All the nearby buildings were quiet and dark, except for the funeral home directly in front of me. Lights glared from the windows. Only one person stood on the street. He had robes of green, curly hair, bushy eyebrows, and a big mustache. He was watching the funeral home. The front doors opened, and Gregor Langston approached him.

"Any news on the siblings?" Gregor asked.

"None Master Langston." The man cringed as he said "Master." Almost as if it pained him to say it to Langston.

"Keep looking Mr. Darby. We must find them and ole Ignatius. If we don't, we're as good as dead." Said Gregor Langston.

"England is Valdorn's domain. Why isn't he sending his own men out to search for them?" The man sounded quite irritated.

"Because Clarence, a man like Jacoby Valdorn never gets his hands dirty. Always lets others do the dirty work for him. That's how he's been able to get this far." Gregor said.

"What are we going to do about this?" Clarence asked, pointing to the funeral home. As soon as he said that, the home erupted in an explosion.

"Wait five minutes, then inform the authorities of a fire at the funeral home." Gregor said.

"Yes, Master Langston." Clarence said. The scene vanished once more.

*****

(6:45 A.M.-July 7th)

I didn't wake up again until the next morning. I really must have been tired to have slept straight through the afternoon and the night. When I looked around my room, I noticed that there wasn't any damage like there's been on my previous visions. It looked the same as it did when I fell asleep yesterday. I glanced over at my clock, it read 6:45. I was meeting Alec today for my first lesson. I got out of bed and stepped down onto a drenched carpet. The whole floor was a gigantic puddle. Perhaps I did have another fit last night. I used a drying spell to clean up all the water, and quickly ran to get washed and dressed.

"I'm going to learn how to control my powers. Then, you're going to stop showing your ugly face." I said to my Darkling half in the mirror. Oh Great! Now I'm talking to myself.

The visions from last night were still fresh in my mind. I had to tell someone about them. The first thought that came to my mind, was that I had to tell my parents. They would know what to make of them, especially the one of grandma. Then I thought about all the lies and secrets that I discovered these last few days. I'm still mad at them. I knew eventually I would have to tell them what's been going on, but I would do it on my time. This will give them a taste of their own medicine.

The next thought that came to my mind was Alec. I was meeting him today for Foresight lessons. Maybe telling him was my best bet, but trusting him was even harder. What am I going to do? I can't trust anyone anymore. I've never felt this alone.

*****

(8:00 A.M.-July 7th)

"You're positive about everything you saw?" Alec asked an hour later. I had just finished telling him everything I had seen in my Hindsight's. I spilled everything I could remember to him about all my visions, including the one where I first saw Jacoby Valdorn. I was going to keep it to myself, but as soon as I saw him standing underneath a tree in my park, all tall, dark, and handsome as usual, it just poured out. Poor Alec. I didn't even give him the chance to speak, but he just stood there and listened to everything I said. It felt good telling him about my visions, because he understood what it was like to have them. It felt like a huge weight was being lifted off my chest as I spoke to him. For now, I wasn't sharing this burden alone. I just hope it wasn't a huge mistake trusting him with this knowledge.

"The leader of the 8th Covenant is a man named Gregor Langston?" he asked.

I recalled the small baby-faced Wizard, who seemed out of place next to the intimidating Jacoby Valdorn. "He's a puppet Alec, and nothing more than that. Valdorn is the true mastermind."

"True, Jacoby Valdorn is calling the shots, but Gregor Langston still followed orders and sent his men to target my family. He's responsible for the Davenport's deaths. He will pay for that." He said. "I'm glad that Rheal chap is dead. I'm just sorry I didn't get the chance to kill him myself, after what he put my sister through."

"He said that he had captured Amber, but you came to the rescue. What happened?" I asked. For the first time since I've met him. Alec looked vulnerable. He wasn't the strong and intimidating Hunter. He was just a scared normal teenager. It made me wonder just how much of a bad guy he really is? Or if it was just a show he was putting on?

"Doesn't matter anymore." He replied.

"Alec, just so you know. I just relieved myself of a huge burden. If you want to do the same. I'll listen. I won't push though."

He sighed heavily. "Never mind, he's dead now." His tone indicated an end to the topic. I respected that, but I couldn't help but be a little curious. "Langston and Valdorn are the priorities right now."

"Why don't you just hunt them down? I mean, that is what you do, right? It would save us a lot of grief. More importantly, it would put an end to a despicable villain."

Alec laughed. "It doesn't work like that. I must have his scent before I can properly hunt him. Once I have a scent, I could track you down anywhere on the planet." That was a creepy concept indeed. To think, no matter where I went, Alec would always be able to find me.

"What about Valdorn and what he's done? He said that he's going to attack here. We thought originally that you guys were the attack." I said.

"Your Grandmother's retrieval of Clearwater's body was noble of her. No matter what she has done in the past, she is loyal to her friends." After I had gotten over the shock of seeing her kill those men. I realized I was happy that she did. Ignatius deserved a better ending then the one he was going to get. How could anyone work for a slime like Jacoby Valdorn?

Those men deserved to die.

"You still didn't answer my question about Valdorn." I said.

"Jacoby Valdorn." Alec said. "He's the head of this snake that has been causing problems not only for my family, but yours as well. Do you see now why men like this Valdorn must be stopped?" he asked.

"This is why you want a war?" I asked.

"This is bigger than you and me Angelica." There was such a passion in his voice, that I was riveted at his words. "This is about the future of both our kinds, the future of the world. Therefore, I need your families help." He said. "We can't do it alone."

I still wasn't completely sold on his idea, but I'll admit, that it was starting to grow on me. "At least I know that the story you told was true."

"I told you, we only dramatized certain events for effect." I nodded. "Now, it's time to learn about Foresights."

Chapter 17
Foresights

Alec
(8:25 A.M.-July 7th)

I was already in quite the nasty mood, even before I went to meet Angelica in the park. I had spent the whole night unsuccessfully trying to get back into the library. Those books were calling to me. I needed to get my hands on them. However, if I stole the magic from the door that led into the Everhardtht's section. Then they would know that I had tried to get back in there. I tried using the mist to get back into the room. I had a clear picture of it in my head, but no matter how hard I tried. I couldn't get the mist to form. It was like the bloody room never existed. Angelica must have tricked me somehow.

I was beside myself at that point. I didn't know whether to be angry or impressed that Angelica had tricked me like that. I had clearly underestimated her. To top all of that off, Amber had no luck trying to penetrate the forest that surrounded the manor. There were just too many scents in that forest.

I debated on whether making an example out of Angelica for tricking me. Then she shows up and drops more lovely news on the top of the pile. She told me of the visions she had of the Weirling and the damage they were causing. Apparently, Jacoby Valdorn was responsible for what was going on. Being from England, the Davenport's made it their business to know of the people who ran our enemies' government. They always suspected that Valdorn was a slime ball traitor, but for the most part, his Covenant in England remained quiet and out of the public spotlight. I guess we now know why. I'm going to get him, one way or the other.

I was quite agitated when Angelica explained her visions to me. How come she received the vision of Gregor Langston? Why did she get the privilege of seeing inside the Sanctuary, when Amber and myself haven't seen one thing in the past month that would help us?

I knew why suddenly, Angelica was getting visions. Seers tend to set one another off when were in close range of each other. We haven't gotten anything though, and I just couldn't understand it. What was so special about this girl, that fate was willing her to see these things?

That's how I was taught about which Seer gets to see what vision. There were things that we could see on our own, and then they're the ones that come to us. The Davenport's said, that it's left up to fate; a higher force of magic that couldn't be explained. No one really knows much about fate. Many believe that it's controlled by beings of untold power. That was rubbish though, beings like that don't exist. It's ridiculous just to think about it.

I cleared my mind for the task at hand. If I was going to teach Angelica Foresights, then I was going to do this right. It wasn't going to be easy for her, I'll make sure of it.

*****

Angelica

"Foresights, the ability to see things the way they are now." Alec said. He had taken off his jacket and tossed it on top of the bench that I conjured. It was a little chilly out, but it didn't seem to bother him. He was wearing a plain black t-shirt, that showed off his impressive physique. I couldn't help but stare at his arms, and muscles…. No! No! No! Focus Angelica! I shouted at myself.

"Last time that you tried to do this, we focused in on your sister. Seeing people is a little bit harder than seeing objects or places. For your first task, I want you to see… Crystal River." He said.

"How do I do that?" I asked. Then the suspicious side of me thought. "Why the river?"

"Because it is a place I'm sure you're familiar with. Now, using the same technique you used to see Merrin, focus on the river. See nothing else, it will come naturally." He replied.

I was still suspicious of his intentions, but I pictured Crystal River in my mind. I thought of nothing, but the river, like Alec said. I felt the usual tugging sensation. My soul lifted into the sky, but I could tell just like last time, that something was wrong already. My vision was blurry. I couldn't see anything. I felt myself flying, but not being able to see. I didn't know where I was going. This was nothing like when the visions came to me. Those were crystal clear. A few seconds past, then I felt myself falling backwards towards my body.

My eyes opened. I was panting and wet. I looked over at Alec. He was drenched from head to toe, like he had just taken a shower with his clothes on. Everything clung to him, and I could see that he had a perfect set of abs. Here I thought he couldn't look any better than he did before. Stop, I shouted at myself again.

"I guess I should have expected that." He said, shaking his head like a dog, which was adorable in a weird way.

A part of me wanted to cry. There was no way that I could do this without my stupid Darkling side coming out. "I'm so sorry."

"Stop! Stop feeling sorry for yourself. This is going to keep happening until you can harness your strength. We'll figure out a way to keep this from happening."

"How?" I asked. I was beginning to think that it's impossible. I was going to be plagued by this Darkling half for the rest of my life, I just know it.

"Leave that to me." He said. I trusted him, everything he said I couldn't help but believe. He's just so damn charming and he wasn't even trying! He looked at himself and sighed. "I guess I should asked you for a permanent drying spell before we try again." He said with a smile.

I laughed despite myself, and with a quick wave, I placed a spell on Alec and myself. So now when I caused a minor hurricane, we would both stay dry.

"Now, tell me. Did your *Yani* detach itself?" he asked.

"My what?" It sounded like he just spoke Chinese.

"*Yani*, that is what the Davenport's called the part of the soul that detaches itself from the body." He replied.

"Part of my soul? You mean that there is more than one part to a soul?" I asked.

"Well of course there is more than one part. If you're entire soul were to leave your body, you'd be nothing more than an empty shell." I suddenly had a flashback of the third Harry Potter movie, when the Dementor was sucking Harry's godfather's soul. I shuddered at the thought.

I still didn't understand what he meant about there being more than one part to a soul.
"I still don't get it."

"Many ancient cultures believed that the soul is split into many parts. The number of parts varies depending on what they believed in. A lot of them seemed to agree that there are at least five parts to the soul. The one we want to focus on, is the *Yani*. Basically, the Astral form.
The ancient Egyptians I believed called it the Ba, other cultures called it by different names, like I said it varies."

"Okay, so the *Yani* or *Ba* is like my spirit, and that is the only part that can leave my body?" I asked.

"Correct." He replied. "It is also said, that it is the part that remains behind after death."

"Like an actual ghost?" I asked. Immediately my mind thought to the T.V. show Ghost Whisperer.

"Indeed, I've never seen an actual spirit, but yes, ghosts do exist." He replied.

It's weird, but kind of cool. Normally, you don't think of your soul as an actual part of your body. Without your soul though, you wouldn't be able to exist. It was like the light of your body.

"What happened?" Alec asked.

It took me a minute to realize he was asking me about my vision. "It was blurry, and I couldn't see anything." I replied.

He shook his head. "You weren't concentrating on the river hard enough."

"I was." I said defensively.

"Harder this time! Focus your mind!" I didn't like being yelled at, but I did as I was told.

*****

(3:45 P.M.-July 7th)

As the day wore on, I was still making very little progress. The visions weren't as blurry, and once I even saw the river, but it didn't last long. Alec kept pushing me hard. It felt like I was in gym class with Mr. Hatcher, and he was pushing me to run harder or climb faster. After every attempt, I would be more out of breath then the last. Alec didn't give me any time to rest. By late afternoon, most of the surrounding area looked like a flash flood had hit it, but Alec and I stood dry.

"You're still not focused!" He said for what seemed liked the hundredth time.

"I'm trying!" I shouted back at him. This was easy for him. I was beginning to think he was pushing me hard on purpose.

"You're just concentrating on the river. That is not going to get you anywhere." He said.

"But that's what you said…"

"I said to focus on the river! That means to think about it as a living, breathing form of life. What makes the river itself? What makes it tick? Concentrate on everything you can think of. What makes it so special? Why does it exist?" He said.

I breathed deeply and closed my eyes once more. I think I understood what he meant now. I concentrated. No one knows Crystal River better than me and my family. This time, when I thought of the river. I pictured a bright sunny afternoon. The sun shining bright on the clear white water as it flowed smoothly down the stream. So clear that you could see the bottom of the sandy riverbed. It's untainted, untouched by the hands of people, not polluted like most rivers. I imagined it, as it picks up speed when heading to the falls. The way it smashes up against the rocks and the embankments. It's controlling, forceful, and majestic. Nothing could stop it as it moved. It carved its way through the surrounding landscape. Anything in its path is swooped up in its grasp.

I felt my *Yani* leave my body, and this time, I saw everything in crystal clear perfection. It was beautiful. I soared over the treetops, heading for my destination. I knew where I was going, I'd been there a hundred times.

The river came into view soon after. The sun was shining down on it. From way up here, I saw how it sparkled like diamonds. I dropped straight towards the river. It was the most thrilling sensation. When I hit the water, it was cool, crisp, and refreshing. I flowed with the river. Wait, that's not right. I was one with, the river. This is how it felt to move like water. I was commanding, and I was the master of my own fate. As I neared the falls I picked up speed, splashing around against the rocks as the falls neared. My anticipation for the drop increased and I realized I was anxious. Or at least, the river was. As I went over my *Yani* soared out and took off back towards my body. Words couldn't explain just how wonderful an experience this is. This was a proper vision.

I opened my eyes again. "I did it! Everything was so clear. I imagined myself as the river. It was amazing!" I said.

Alec smiled. "That's how you see properly. You must truly be the thing you are seeing. By doing that, you understand it in a way no one else can. If you don't do that, then nothing will ever be clear to you." He said.

After that Alec ended the lesson for the day. I was so excited that I didn't want to go home. I couldn't wait for our next lesson.

*****

(July 8th-10th)

As the week wore on, Alec and I came to the park every day to learn about Foresight's. We tried focusing on other places in town. Eventually I graduated from seeing places, to seeing other living things. Alec would have me summon an animal to the park and study everything about them. When I set them loose, I envisioned them as they moved through the forest. I strutted like a bear, pranced as a deer, scurried like a squirrel, and hopped like a rabbit. Every Foresight that I had was clear and pristine. Alec said that the more I'd practiced, the stronger the visions would become. I practiced at home every night from the safety of my room. I was proud of myself for every successful Foresight. Of course, the Darkling was still coming out, but I wasn't going to let that discourage me. I just put a shield around me and cleaned up after I was done. Nothing would break my spirit.

Everything was going well. Until I walked into my bedroom one night and found my dad waiting for me. He had a serious expression on his face, which I knew meant, he was going to give me a reaming.

"How did you get in?" I asked.

"I know my daughter. Which means I know what kind of spell she might use to keep her room blocked off from her family. Did you really think that image of yourself would fool me?" He asked. I cursed at myself. I knew that my luck would run out sooner or later. I was just hoping that it would've been much later.

"Why are you here?" I asked.

"Because this little no talking act you're pulling on your mother an me, isn't going to work forever." He said. He closed the door to my room and summoned me closer to him. I hate it when he does that. It felt like a vacuum sucking me up. "You think that we don't know that you're sneaking out every day against our wishes. Just because you have a spell on your room, doesn't mean we can't guess what you're up too. We are your parents after all. Besides that, every time you leave the borders of this house, we feel your presence depart." He said.

I bit my lip. I should have known there were wards on the house. "Now your mother thinks that you're going to see your friends. That's why she hasn't made a big deal about it, but she isn't in town every day now is she?" He asked.

"How do you…" Then I remember that dad was a Nurturer. Duh, Angelica! The animals.

"I know you're meeting that Alec boy every day." he said.

What could I do? I had no choice, but to nod my head. "Dad he's teaching me to be a Seer. He's telling me stuff that I had no clue existed…" I began.

He quieted me instantly. Tears stung my eyes, as I waited for the worst. Then he said something I never expected.

"I'm not mad." He said.

I looked up at him, shocked by what he just said. "What?" I said. I thought that I had heard him wrong.

He held my shoulders and took a shaky breath. "Listen to me Angelica. Learn everything that you can from him. He can teach you things that we never could." He said.

I stared at him. His eyes watered with emotion. At that moment, everything came pouring out of me. Everything that I was feeling, everything that I discovered, everything that I saw and did. I told him it all. It was so relieving to finally tell someone that I could trust.

He hugged me tightly after I finished. I wish I could stay like this forever, I thought. "My little girl. I'm so sorry for lying to you. We thought that it was the only way to keep you safe. There are so many people out there that want to use you for your powers. The Council, the Covenants, people who we believed to be friends. We had to protect you, but then you were getting so powerful that we didn't know what to do. Your visions, your Darkling powers, everything was coming at us too fast. We..." He couldn't continue.

It all started making sense to me. The reason that my family lied to me. The reason that Grandma chose to live outside of Hemlock. The reason why we live amongst Mortals. It's because they were keeping me safe from those who wanted me for their own selfish purposes. The same selfish purposes, that Alec was training me for.

"I'm such a fool." I choked.

"For a long time, we feared that you would never fit in properly because of your gift. I'll admit what your grandmother has denied. No other Weirlind or Weirling before you have ever possessed such a gift like yours. We didn't know how to handle it or control it. All we could do was keep as much of it from you as possible. I should have known better. You can't block magic. You were just so powerful that..." He hesitated. "This gift is what makes you so special." He said smiling at me. "I should have never lied to you about that." He said. "Can you ever forgive me?"

My eyes stung. Even though I knew this already. Hearing it come from my dad, made it all seem official.

"From now on. There will be no more secrets between us." He said. "I never want you to feel alone, because you're not. Angelica, you are no fool. Alec didn't just trick you, he got me and Merrin too."

"What?"

"We signed a similar agreement to the one you made with him."

"When?" I asked. I couldn't believe what I was hearing.

"Before you guys arrived that day. He threatened to unmake Merrin with his gift if I didn't promise to stay out of his way and agree to help him when needed. I signed. He threatened Merrin the same way." I remembered back to the day we first met the Hunter's. Dad and Merrin both appeared to be shaken up when we arrived. I clenched my fists. I thought that Jacoby Valdorn was wicked, but Alec was just as devious as he was.

"I'm going to kill him." I said breathing heavily. I was trying to control my anger because I was afraid of what would come out if I didn't.

"Don't tell him that you know." Dad said.

"Why?"

"Alec is cunning, and he knows it. From what you have told me, you've been just as smart as he's been. You've matched him move for move. You even got him to change your agreement. He may be using you Angelica, but use him back. Like I said, there are things that he can teach you that no one else can. Learn from him, use the knowledge he gives you to become stronger, but whatever you do. Don't trust them." He said. "Promise me."

"I promise." I said.

He let out a long breath. "I'm here for you if you need to talk, I'll listen. I'll see what I can uncover about this split-personality disorder. I don't know much about the spell mother put on you, but maybe it's time I did." His grip loosened on my shoulders. "As much as I don't want to. I won't tell your mother about this. She won't handle it well. It'll be between you and me." He said.

I hugged him, and he held me tightly in his arms. For the first time in a while, I wasn't alone anymore. My dad was with me.

*****

(7:30 A.M.-July 11th)

"What did you tell him?" asked Alec the next morning. I had just finished telling him about what happened with my father. I was hoping that he would slip up, but he was as calm and cool as usual. Darn him!

"He told me not to trust you." I said.

"He's right." I looked at him. Alec stared back at me. "Your father was alive during the Hunter Craze. He knows what we're capable of and he's just trying to protect you." He paused for a moment. I could tell he was debating on whether to say something. "I should have told you this before we started." For a moment, I thought he was going to tell me about the deal he forced dad and Merrin to make. "If there is one thing above all that I can teach you, it's that you should never trust us." He said.

"Why are you telling me this?" I asked. Wouldn't he want me to trust him? Isn't that what all this was about?

"I want no surprises. There will come a time when you'll probably want to kill me for something that I've done. It's inevitable that it will happen." He said. For the briefest of moments, he let his guard down again, and I saw sadness in his eyes.

"It doesn't have to be like that." I said.

"It's in our nature Angelica. Hunters were created for one purpose, that's to kill. We're not meant to have feelings, it's just a distraction." He said.

"I don't believe that Alec. Maybe Hunters of old weren't supposed to have feelings, but you told me that the Creator's fell in love with one another." I said.

"Look what feelings got them." He replied.

"It was a different time Alec. You were raised differently. The Davenport's obviously showed you love. Or else you wouldn't be so gung ho on wanting revenge. What you share with your sister, is love."

Alec shook his head. "Deny it all you want, but you can't hide it from me." I said. He may act like a tough bad guy, but deep down, I knew there was a much different Alec.

"What else did he say?" Alec said, changing the subject.

"Just not to trust you." I lied. Alec nodded. The silence between us was awkward. I decided to ask him a stupid question. "Does it bother you ever to read someone else's mind?" I was expecting him to give me a tough guy response.

"Like you're trespassing on foreign ground?" he said. I looked at him closely. That's exactly how it felt to me. "Since I've been on the run. I've only read a person's mind when there was an absolute dire need for it. Most of the time
I keep that power to myself."

"Except when you were reading my families' minds. There was a dire need for that." I said sarcastically.

He laughed. It infuriated me that I found it so charming. "What we did to your family was more of a probe. A person's mind is like a catacomb of chambers. When it came to your family, we only looked for leverage we could use.
We didn't penetrate deeply." He said.

"Is that supposed to make a difference?" I said. My temper was rising.

"Be lucky it wasn't what I did to the Wizards who were trying to catch us. You want to know how I killed them? I broke them from the inside. I penetrated deep into their minds and I shattered it. Break a person's mind and you break them, it's called unmaking." That's what he threatened to do to my dad and sister. "You still think I have good in me now?"

"Enough of this." Alec said. "Back to business." It also infuriated me how quickly he put one set of thoughts aside and moved to a completely different one. "You've successfully learned how to see places and animals. So now I think you're ready to try and see a person again." He said.

"Who?" I asked.

Chapter 18
The Forest

Angelica
(8:00 A.M.-July 11th)

Alec said that Seeing people was harder than Seeing places or animals. This was going to be a true test of whether I was in control of my Foresights or not. I didn't see any harm in finding out what my best friend was up to. In fact, I was interested to see what she was doing. I haven't seen or talked to her since the Fourth of July. I felt bad about not calling her, or answering any of her calls or texts. I've been so distracted lately. I kept telling myself, that I would call her tomorrow, but tomorrow always came and I still haven't spoken to Lindsey or Brett yet.

"Ready?" Alec asked.

"I'm ready." I said confidently.

"Just do the same thing that you've been doing with your other Foresights. Concentrate on your intended target. Be the thing you want to see."

"But how do you be somebody that's totally different from yourself?" I asked.

"You'll have to figure that out on your own. You say that she's your best friend?"

"She's like a sister to me." I replied.

"Then you should have no trouble seeing her. The stronger the connection between the Seer and the thing they want to see, the easier it is for them to find it." He said, then he stepped back and watched.

I closed my eyes and envisioned Lindsey. We've grown up together. I've known Lindsey since we were just five years old. We shared each other's secrets, well, most of them. We played, gossiped, cried, and laughed together. She was family. I pictured her in my mind. Her silky shoulder length hair. She was a natural blonde, not a fake like most girls are today. Her dark blue eyes always remind me of the ocean. She was always smiling. I don't think I can remember a time that she wasn't smiling. She has naturally tanned skin. She is a very pretty girl, but she always nitpicks herself, trying to improve. When all along she has been perfect the way she is. She is the perfect friend. She's my perfect friend.

I felt the tug and my *Yani* took flight. I was happy that everything was as clear as my previous Foresight's. I soared back over the treetops heading into town, but I noticed I was losing air too soon. I immediately thought that I had done something wrong, because the B & B was nowhere near where I was landing. I was on Forest Hill Drive, the road that leads up through the forest and to my house. I landed outside a familiar ranch. The second house closest to the tree line is Brett's home. I've been to Brett's on numerous occasions and I'm always amazed at how well his parents kept their garden. There were dozens of diverse types of flowers in the beds that surrounded the house. The roses gave off the most beautiful smells.

Lindsey and Brett were sitting on the porch. It was natural that I would find Lindsey here. She hung out with Brett just as much as she hung out with me. I knew that something was wrong immediately. Brett and Lindsey were clearly arguing with each other. They bickered with each other all the time, but this was different.

"You can't tell me Brett, that you think that nothing is wrong." Lindsey said to him.

"When it comes to Angelica and her family, you have to admit that there a bit abnormal." Brett replied. Great, they were arguing about me. The abnormal comment about my family hurt, especially coming from Brett.

"Angelica is not like them. Come on Brett, she has never not answered any of my calls or texts before." Lindsey said.

"Maybe she's punished. It's a logical answer as to why she is not answering." Punished, where did he get that idea from?

"She would have told me if she was punished. We tell each other everything." Lindsey cried.

Brett got up. "I don't know Linds. Like you said, it's only been a week. They're could be several reasons why she hasn't answered. Maybe she's sick? Maybe her phone broke? Who knows?"

Lindsey just shook her head. "No, something's not right."

"It's probably that weird family of hers." Came a shrill voice. I turned to see my least favorite person, Kelly Jackson. She was wearing her usual running gear.

"It's rude to eavesdrop on other peoples' conversations." Lindsey replied.

"I was just running by and couldn't help but over hear." Liar! She was eavesdropping. It's what she does best.

"Sure you were." Lindsey said sarcastically.

"Oh, C'mon Hansen. Don't tell me you haven't thought about the same thing before.

Her family is strange. They never come down here. When her father did come down, I saw him acting all weird, looking around all over the place, like he had something to hide." She was such a liar. I know for a fact that she wasn't anywhere near my dad that day. "They probably mistreat her, that's why her hair always looks the way it does."

"She's my best friend. She would have told me…"

"Would you tell anyone that your parents were psycho's? I think not. If she was my friend." She made a disgusted face at the thought. "I would see what was wrong." She smiled and jogged off. Ugh, she disgusted me!

"Lindsey, tell me you didn't believe a word out of that harpy's mouth?" Brett said.

"Think about it Brett, What's the one thing that Angelica never talks about? Every time we bring the subject up, she clams up." Lindsey asked. "Her family, she never talks about them. There must be a reason for that." I didn't like were this conversation was going. This was more than just random gossip about my family. My best friends were discussing if I was an abuse victim. "I'm going to find out what's wrong."

"Lindsey, I know that look, you can't go. Those woods are private property. You'll get into trouble if you get caught." Brett said. I was starting to get worried. Getting into trouble was the least that could happen. If they only knew just how dangerous the forest surrounding my house really was, then they would know never to step foot within it.

"Come with me." Lindsey asked.

"Lindsey, your dad's the sheriff. You know how much trouble I'd get in?" Brett said.

"So what? She's your friend too!" Lindsey shouted.

Brett shook his head. "Why am I even bothering trying to talk you out of this? You haven't listen to a word I said yet." Brett replied.
"Why don't you take Alec with you?"

Lindsey looked furious. "Not that again! What do you have against him?"

"What do I have against him? Well let's see. For starters, he appears out of nowhere and claims that he is an orphan looking to start over in America. He comes to Minnesota of all places, which is not exactly the most ideal place to start a new life. He claims that he walked all the way up here to one of the most out of reach places in the state. Secondly, he looks like he just walked off a movie set. He has red highlights in his hair and red eyes that you can't tell me are not creepy. Who has red eyes? He's built like a darn brick wall. He has a sister that I've never seen. Worst of all, he seems to have everyone in town under his spell. Everybody talks about him like he is some saint. Nobody is looking at him like he could be a possible threat."

"A threat? Are you kidding me? Who do you think he is? A Hitman?" Lindsey asked.

"I don't know. He's British, maybe he's MI6 or something."

"A spy, that's your brilliant theory?" She asked. Here I thought I watched too many movies. Brett's been watching too much James Bond. I got a hand it to him though, Alec wasn't fooling him.

"It's a working theory."

"It's absolute nonsense Brett. For the record, I've met Alec's sister and she is as harmless as he is." Lindsey said. Oh Lindsey, if you only knew.

"That's another thing." Brett said, pointing a finger at Lindsey. "You barely know the guy. For all we know he could be a killer. Yet you've been hanging out with him like your old buddies."

"That's what you really don't like about him? Your jealous." Lindsey said.

"Jealous? Of tall, dark, and creepy, I don't think so." Brett said. Which I knew immediately was a lie. Brett's had a crush on Lindsey since forever. He gets jealous of anybody who looks at her with interest.

"So, what if I hang out with him? So, what if I might like him? What's it to you?" That hit a nerve with Brett. I suspected that Lindsey had some feelings for Alec. She told me as much the last time we spoke. She couldn't resist his Hunter charms.

I didn't realize that Lindsey had hung out with Alec on more than one occasion. That was something I was going to have to talk to Alec about.

"I don't care who you like. It doesn't bother me one bit." Brett replied. It was Lindsey's turn to look hurt.

"Fine! This is about Angelica though. I'm going to find out what's wrong, whether you're with me or not!"

"I'm telling you it's probably nothing." Brett replied.

"It's not nothing! It's one thing if it was just Angelica not answering her phone, but we haven't seen Merrin since the day her father came to town." She stormed down the garden pathway and slammed the gate behind her. I didn't need to read her mind to know that she was really upset. About Brett not believing her, or taking her seriously, but mostly though she was worried about me. This was my entire fault. I hated myself for what I was putting her through. I should've at least called to tell her that I was all right. I had just been so caught up with what has been going on in my other life, that I hadn't had the time.

Lindsey stopped in the middle of the street. Something I wouldn't recommend doing if you lived in a city. Here in Crystal Falls, cars rarely passed by, and basically none traveled down Forest Hill Drive unless you lived on it. Lindsey turned towards the forest and the road that led into it. I didn't like the expression on her face. It was one of her famous determined looks. Once she got something in her head, there was no talking her out of it. I knew what she was going to do, and I was powerless to stop her. I cursed myself. I cursed Kelly Jackson for egging her on. Lindsey was going to get herself hurt.

She checked to see that no one was watching her. Then she ran to the forests edge. She stopped one more time, breathed heavily, and set off. I followed her. She moved at a breakneck pace along the road. As she continued, the slope began to rise, and it became darker along the road, but she kept going. I was surprised that she got this far without anything happening, but I knew it wouldn't last for long.

Then, quite suddenly. The true nature of the forest kicked in. A frigid wind blew through the air, and the trees rustled. Lindsey stopped and looked around, but nothing was there. I knew it was about to get a whole lot worse. She was probably feeling that there was someone watching her. In truth, the forest itself was watching her. Dad has eyes and ears all around. That way, if anyone were to step foot in it, without an Everhardtht's permission or without one of us accompanying them, that would mean that you were a trespasser. The forest didn't like trespassers. It was magicked to torment you until you leave, or go insane.

Lindsey closed her eyes and ran forward. The further she ran, the darker it became. There were no lights along the road. Unseen animals began to make noises. Lindsey stopped again. She was breathing heavily as she searched franticly around for the creatures responsible for the sounds. Just then, the bushes to the right of us rustled, and a large wolf stepped out onto the road. Its coat was a dark gray, and its fierce yellow eyes stared Lindsey down hungrily. It growled, barring its big teeth as it stepped closer to her.

"RUN!" I tried shouting to her. This was no ordinary wolf. The animals here were a size bigger than their normal counterparts. The wolves' purpose in this forest was to attack intruders that ventured too far. Lindsey had to leave now!

As if she heard me, Lindsey turned on her heels and ran back the way she came. She only got a short way before the wolf howled. Looking over her shoulder, she didn't see the tree uproot itself, causing her to trip and fall. She hit the pavement hard and landed on her knees. She put her hand out to stop the fall, but her chin still smacked the concrete. She tried to get back up, but gasped and fell back down clutching her knee. The wolf howled again. This time louder and closer. Lindsey shouted for help as I was pulled away. No! I can't leave her now! I had no control as I soared back towards my body.

Alec was leaning over me as my eyes opened back up. I was so mad that I blasted him backwards. He hit the ground hard.

"What the bloody hell did you do that for?" he said getting back up. He was durable, to take a shot like that and get back up.

"Sorry, I didn't mean to blast you." I said panting heavily. I need to regain focus. Lindsey needed my help.

"What did you see?" he asked.

"Lindsey, she's in the forest! No one's allowed in the forest but us. She's going to get hurt." I cried. Why didn't I just call her. Then this wouldn't be happening.

"What are you doing here then? Go and help her." Alec said. I looked at him. He seemed to be genuinely concerned for my friend. "Your Foresight lessons are over anyway. You've mastered that ability." He said. "You better hurry. I've felt what's in that forest of yours."

I couldn't believe what he just said. I'll celebrate mastering Foresight's later. Right now, my best friend needed me! Dad was probably already aware of an intruder in the forest. I had to get to him before he went after her himself. There was a chance that he knew that it was Lindsey, but I couldn't bet on the fact that he was watching through that wolf's eyes. I teleported back to my house.

I arrived on the front lawn just as the door swung opened, and dad ran out of the house. He leapt the stairs in a single jump. Mom came out onto the porch right behind him.

"Angelica, get in the house. We have an intruder in the forest." Mom said.

"I know, it's Lindsey." I said.

"What?" Dad said stopping short. "How do you know?"

"It's a long story." I said.

He looked at me and nodded. "One that you will explain to me." He replied.

"You will also explain why you're out of the house?" Mom said curtly.

I looked at dad. "Please, I must come with you. She was worried about me. That's why she went into the forest."

He stared at me for a moment. He saw the guilt in my eyes. "We'll take the car." He said, waving his hand in the air.

"Rowan, is it really necessary that you both go?" Mom asked.

"It will be fine Gwen." Dad said. I heard an approaching vehicle, dad's Ford Expedition pulled to a stop in front of us. You don't need keys to start a car if you're a Weir. We both got in, and dad took off down the road.

"Mom's going to kill me." I said after a moment of silence.

"I'll take care of it." He said. "I told her you've been spending time out in the forest lately, by yourself of course."

"Thanks dad." I said.

"You were training with Alec, right?" he asked.

"I was learning how to use Foresights on people, Lindsey in particular. Dad, Alec said that I've master them." I still couldn't believe that I had.

"That's great sweetheart. Just remember what I said about him." He said.

"I know." Not another word past between us as we continued down the road. I was worried. What if Lindsey was really hurt? I would never forgive myself. I just kept repeating that she was going to be alright. Lindsey is tough.

Dad knew exactly where Lindsey was. We pulled to a stop in the exact same spot where my vision had ended. Lindsey was huddled with her back against a tree, and her head covered between her legs

.

I leapt from the car and ran to her. "Lindsey!"

She looked up at the sound of my voice. Her eyes were red and wet from crying. "Angelica." She said with relief. I threw my arms around her, and she hugged me back. "How did you know I was here?" she asked.

"Cameras." Dad said quickly. "You're trespassing on private property. You alright, Miss. Hansen?" he asked.

She looked up at my dad timidly. "My knee hurts, I can't walk." She said. Lindsey kept glancing at the forest around us, as if she was afraid something might jump out. Dad looked at her knee. Her jeans were ripped opened from the fall and there was some blood. I also noticed that her palm and chin were bleeding as well. Dad quickly scooped her up in his arms and placed her in the back of the truck. I sat in the back with her. Lindsey put her head back on the chair and closed her eyes. She was squeezing my hand tightly, I squeezed back. Without having her notice, I allowed some of my energy to flow through her.

We were out of the forest in no time. Lindsey opened her eyes and let out a long breath. Parked in front of the Ramsey's house was the sheriff's car. Lindsey moaned. "I'm in so much trouble."

Dad pulled the car to a stop, opened the back door and picked Lindsey up. The front door to the Ramsey's house opened. Kyle Hansen ran out, followed by Ted Ramsey and Brett.

"Lindsey!" The sheriff shouted. Dad passed Lindsey into the sheriff's arms.

"She's a little banged up, but none worse for the ware." Dad said.

"Sara get the first aid kit!" Ted Ramsey shouted to his wife. He cleared the way as the sheriff carried Lindsey inside and sat her down on the couch.

"What happened?" the sheriff asked. "Brett called me and told me that you went into the forest." Lindsey glared at Brett, who shrunk away.

"That's where we found her." Dad said. Lindsey glanced at me. Her cheeks were flushed red. A silent message passed between us. This was the last place she wanted to be.

Sara Ramsey hustled into the room carrying a first aid kit. Like her son and husband, she had brown hair that was pulled into a fancy bun. "It seems like I'm always patching one of the three of you up." She said. Instantly, she went to work cleaning Lindsey's scabbed chin and hands. "How did you manage this?" she asked.

"She went into the forest." Ted said. Mr. Ramsey was short in stature, with a thick mustache.

"You what?" Sara asked.

"Lindsey, what were you thinking? You know the rules about the forest. That's trespassing, going onto Mr. Everhardtht's property." The sheriff said. "How did you manage all these cuts?"

"I fell." She replied simply. Lindsey wouldn't look at anyone.

The sheriff let out a sigh of relief. He got up, rubbed his beard, and faced my dad. "Mr. Everhardtht, I'm so sorry about this. I know the forest is your private property and that you may want to press charges. I can assure you that Lindsey will be severely punished for this."

"Nonsense, no harm no fowl." My dad said immediately. "And it's Rowan." He added. "I must say, it's finally nice to meet all of you. I've heard all about you from Angelica."

Sara Ramsey straightened her dress, and Mr. Ramsey looked extremely awkward. Brett who just noticed that my Dad was in the room, was gawking at him with his mouth opened.

Dad broke the uncomfortable silence. "I think Miss Hansen has now learned why no one is allowed in the forest." He said, looking at Lindsey sharply.

"I'm so sorry Mr. Everhardtht." Lindsey said. She was choking back tears. I felt so bad for her. None of this would have happened if I had been a better friend.

"Don't worry about it. As long as you don't go in there again, at least not by yourself." He said with a smile.

He looked at the Ramsey's. "You're in good hands now. I better be getting back home. I'm afraid I left my wife in quite the panic."

"I'll walk you out, Rowan." Ted said.

"Thank you." My dad replied, then he looked at me. "Keep me informed." He whispered to me.

As both men left the room, Brett glanced at me. "Oh, wow! That was intense." He said.

"You kids are going to drive me up the wall." Sara Ramsey said, packing up her first aid kit. I was reading her thoughts. She was extremely flustered at meeting my father for the first time.

"Lindsey, we're going to have a nice long talk with your mother about this." The sheriff said.

"I know dad." Lindsey replied.

The sheriff sighed and kissed the top of her head. "Don't do anything like that again." He said.

"I won't"

He got up. "Let me go move my squad car before the neighbors start asking questions."

As soon as all the adults left the room, Brett said. "Your dad, he's not what I expected him to be."

"What did you expect him to be, a crazy person?" I replied, and immediately regretted it.

Lindsey let out a choked cry and buried her head into my shoulder. For the first time, we were all speechless.

Chapter 19
Crystal Falls

Angelica
(10:00 A.M.-July 12th)

After the whole fiasco with Lindsey, I decided to ask my dad if it was okay if I took both her and Brett for a picnic in the forest. He wasn't thrilled about the idea, especially when he found out where I wanted to take them. After a lot of negotiating and bargaining. He finally agreed, only if he could drive us back and forth.

A day alone, with just the three of us, was long overdue. I needed to set things right. I couldn't have Lindsey getting hurt because of me. She called me last night and said that she just barely avoided grounding. Her father and mother had lectured her all night about the dangers of trespassing on other people's property. They said that she was lucky that my dad went easy on her, or that she didn't receive more serious injuries. In the end, her punishment was having to go to work with her father every day for the rest of the summer. Lindsey said she would have rather been grounded.

My dad and I picked up Brett first. We were waiting outside of the B & B for Lindsey to come out. I hoped she would soon. Brett was still awkward in front of my dad. He was sitting in the backseat, most of the time with his mouth open, gawking at my dad like he's a celebrity.

"You know Mr. Ramsey, if you open your mouth any wider, flies might land inside of it." Dad said sarcastically. Brett put his head down in embarrassment. Dad looked at me and smiled.

Finally, the front door to Lindsey's room opened, and she stepped out. I told Lindsey and Brett to wear warmer clothing, because it was going to be chilly on the mountain today.

"You ready?" I asked her, as she opened the car door.

"Yep." She said.

"I'm not." Brett mumbled. "After what you told me you saw and felt yesterday. I can't believe you want to go back in there. I always knew there was something creepy about that forest."

Dad chuckled to himself.

"I told you yesterday, I had a lot on my mind. I was probably imagining half of the things I saw." She replied. "Besides, this is the only chance I'm going to get to do this, since I'm going to be spending the rest of the summer helping dad at the station. Just kill me now."

"The forest isn't so creepy once you get used to it." I replied.

"Easy for you to say." Brett replied. Lindsey punched him in the arm.

"My dad's going to drive us back and forth anyway. That way we can avoid all the wildlife." I added.

"It's really cool of you Mr. Everhardtht for allowing me to come. Especially after yesterday." Lindsey said.

"Ah, Angelica told me why you did what you did. Maybe if I came to town more often, people wouldn't assume I was a crazy nut job." Dad replied with a smile. "I can assure you that I have never once hurt my daughters." Lindsey blushed red and averted her eyes.

"Alright then, where should we go to pick up food. The Java Café or the Diner?" I asked.

"It'll take too long to get food at the diner." Brett said. "I really don't want to see my sister either."

"Java Café it is then." I said.

As we drove to the café, Lindsey rattled on about her dad's lecture to her. She also mentioned that her knee still hurt from her fall yesterday. I hoped she didn't have any permanent damage.

Dad stopped the car in front of the café. We all decided to go in. I had a feeling it was because neither of them wanted to sit alone with my father. I was hoping that the café would be empty. I didn't see anyone from outside the window, but that wasn't the case when we stepped inside. The last person I wanted to run into was sitting at the back table. Kelly Jackson in a short skirt and a tight shirt that showed off her curves. That outfit was way too small. Who did she think she was, Daisy Duke? She had her slimy arms all over the second person I didn't want to meet today. Alec had apparently just told a joke, because Kelly was laughing that fake shriek of hers. The sight of her sitting there with her hands on Alec, made my ears turn red. It wasn't because I was jealous or anything. It was because I hated her more than anything, especially after yesterday.

"Well, if it isn't the three amigos." She said with a sneer. "Haven't seen you in a while Angela. Where ya been?" she asked.

"None of your business, and my name is not Angela." I replied through gritted teeth. It didn't take much for her to get under my skin, and she knew it.

Then she turned her attention to Lindsey. "Lindsey, I heard what happened yesterday, pretty crazy."

Lindsey turned three shades of red. "You told me to do it."

"No no no. I told you that if she was my friend, that I would help her. I didn't tell you to go crazy, and go into the forest. What did you do, walk into a tree?" Lindsey fingered the bandage on her chin.

It was amazing just how much of a vindictive liar she was. She wanted Lindsey to go into the forest yesterday. She wanted her to get in trouble. Kelly turned her attention back to me. "What did you see Hansen? Are the Everhoot's hiding something in that forest?"

"Again, that's none of your business." I replied.

Kelly smirked. "You see Alec. There are some people in this town that have no class or sense of fashion. Angela Everdoo and her side kick Lindi are two of the worst offenders." Lindsey looked like she was about to burst. I could hear her thoughts. She despised Kelly more than I did. She really hated the fact that she was so close to Alec. For his part, he looked annoyed at the fact that she was on top of him. I haven't spoken to him since yesterday's lesson. I mastered Foresight's, I knew that I would probably have to learn Hindsight's next, but I really needed this day off.

"It's nice to see you dears again!" Valerie said, coming out from the back. "I haven't seen you three together in my shop in a long time." She said with a smile. I love Valerie Monti. She was always so cheerful.

"What can I get for you, dears?" she asked.

"We're having a picnic Ms. Monti. Could you gather some things for us?" I asked.

"Of course I can. I'll be right back." She said, disappearing to the back.

"Going on a double date, Ramsey?" Kelly asked. "That must be so awkward."

I closed my eyes and tried to pretend that she wasn't there. Lindsey was having a much harder time of it. "It's not a date! You know we're just friends."

Kelly snickered, then said to Alec. "You see Lindi and Angela are both in love with Ramsey. I don't know why, he's not even that good looking?" That was a lie as well. Kelly had tried numerous times to get with Brett, but he's turned her down on every occasion.

"I'm not in love with him!" Lindsey shouted at Kelly. Her face was so red, that it looked like an apple. Brett grabbed her arm, but Lindsey flinched away from him. This was going from bad to worse. Lindsey wanted to rip Kelly's head off. Brett wanted to profess his love for Lindsey right now.

"That's right, you're in love with Alec, aren't you? I saw the way you were drooling over him the other day in the diner." Kelly said with a sneer. "I bet Alec prefers a woman though, not a little girl like you."

Lindsey had had enough. "Listen you snot-nosed brat. Not even a father could love a person like you."

Now it was Kelly's face that turned red. She got up from her chair and approached Lindsey. "What did you just say?"

Lindsey smiled right at her. She realized she had hit a nerve. "You heard me. You're a snot-nosed brat, with a face that not even a father could love." She said.

I stepped in front of Lindsey. I didn't want Kelly to do anything bad to her. "Kelly, just leave me and my friends alone."

She laughed at me. "Honey, you think that you're so special because your family has money. I may be a snot-nosed brat, but you're a spoiled rich brat." She said.

Lindsey grabbed the coffee that Kelly was drinking from the table and splashed it all over her. Kelly shrieked, and I laughed.

"You'll pay for this Hansen!" she shouted. That's when chaos broke out. Kelly attacked Lindsey. They both grabbed at each other's hair as they tumbled to the floor. Brett grabbed Kelly, while I held Lindsey back. Alec just sat at the table with a bemused expression on his face. He was no help what so ever. Kelly screamed so many swear words at us, that if we were on cable TV, they would have bleeped every other word out.

"That is enough of that!" Valerie Monti came hustling from the back and got right in Kelly's face. "I will not have that kind of language in my store. Do you hear me Miss. Jackson? You are banned from here for a week!"

"A week! What about her? She threw coffee on me!" Kelly said.

"You heard me Miss. Jackson." Valerie replied.

"Wait until I tell my aunt. She'll have words for you." Kelly warned Ms. Monti.

"You tell your aunt dear. I'll have words for her too. Now get out!" Kelly sneered. I smiled with satisfaction. That was probably the first time that Kelly Jackson had ever been dismissed from a room.

Kelly glanced at me evilly. Go ahead! Just try it and I swear I'll turn you into a bug! She stormed from the café.

"Thanks Ms. Monti." Lindsey said.

"Oh, my pleasure dears. I like you guys better than that one." She said with a smile. "You okay Lindsey dear. I can call your father if you're hurt."

"No!" She replied immediately. "Ms. Monti can you please not tell my dad what happened. If he found out that I got into a fight after yesterday, I'll be grounded to the end of the century."

"Well, if you are not hurt, it'll be our little secret. I'll go get your food." She said.

After she left, Lindsey looked at me and smiled. "I've wanted to do that for so long."

I smiled. "I always knew you had it in you."

"Remind me never to get on the bad side of you two." Brett said.

Lindsey turned to face Alec. She forgot that he was in the room, and now she was embarrassed of herself. "How can you let that she-demon touch you?"

Alec was about to reply when Ms. Monti came back out with three bags. "Mr. Davenport here was just coming by to meet me, when Miss. Jackson walked in and started smothering the poor dear. He was a complete gentleman though. I would have told her to shove off."

"Oh." Lindsey replied happily. She was glad that Alec didn't enjoy Kelly's presence. She really likes him, I thought. "I'm afraid I acted a little childish though."

"That was brilliant. I like a girl with fire, and you two definitely have fire." Lindsey beamed, Brett frowned, and I sighed. Just being your charming self as usual Alec.

"Why didn't you speak up before? Or help for that matter?" Brett asked Alec.

Alec smiled at Brett. "I didn't see you saying anything either." Alec replied. "I like to avoid the petty squabbles that you Americans are prone to."

"Are you saying that Americans are petty?" Brett responded.

"Exactly, this discussion we're having right now proves it."

Brett was about to argue some more, when Lindsey stopped him.

"Thanks for the food Ms. Monti." Lindsey shoved two of the bags in Brett's hands.

"Wow, did you pack everything in here?" Brett asked.

"Oh, I just packed a few things." She said with a smile. "That will be fifteen dollars."

"That's sounds a little cheap." I said, pulling the money from my pocket.

"There's a discount today." Ms. Monti smiled again. "Thank you." She said taking the money. "I haven't seen your sister in a while. Tell her that I miss her business."

"I will." I replied.

"Well, I better be getting back to my room." Alec said.

"Wait, why don't you come with us?" Lindsey asked.

Brett wasn't happy about that idea, and neither was I for several reasons. I wanted this picnic to be a magic free one. Yes, I know I'm going into a magical forest, but that doesn't count. Then there was that slight problem of Alec not being allowed to step foot in the forest. Who knows what kind of trouble he would cause. How do I tell Lindsey he can't come without making her get suspicious?

"I'm sure Alec has other things to do." I replied, giving him a stern look.

He smiled. "Actually, I don't. Where are you heading?" I closed my eyes in frustration.
He was enjoying watching me squirm.

"The forest." Lindsey whispered.

Alec gave me his most surprised look.

"I've only been here for a while, but from what I heard, no one goes into that forest."

"Angelica's dad is taking us." Lindsey replied.

"Really?" he said.

"Yes, and I'm afraid we're making him wait. We better be going." Brett said, heading for the door.

"I'm sure Mr. Everhardtht won't mind another passenger." You want to bet on that, I thought to myself.

"Sure, why not." Alec replied. If steam could come out of my ears, then that's what would be happening right now. The only reason he wants to go into the forest is, so he could get closer to my family.

Brett huffed. "Great!" Lindsey replied excitedly. Both her and Brett went to bring the food to the car. As soon as they walked out, I rounded on Alec.

"What do you think you're doing?" I asked.

"What?" he replied innocently.

"Don't act innocent with me. Do you think I would allow you anywhere near that forest?"

"I already told you. My sense of smell gets messed up every time I get near that forest. You have nothing to worry about."

"Doesn't matter."

"Then perhaps you would like to tell Lindsey why I can't come?" He said with a smile. I really wanted to blast him through the window. I walked passed him. Dad wasn't going to like this.

"Mr. Everhardtht. This was the extra passenger I was talking about. This is Alec Davenport." Lindsey said.

Dad smiled at Alec in such a way that I knew he wasn't happy. He was one angry Warlock. "I've heard about you Alec."

"Nice to meet you Sir." Alec replied. Holding out his hand for my dad. I watched as they exchanged a handshake, neither one of them backing down. There was an exchange of power going on. I knew for sure that my dad wouldn't allow Alec to come.

"I'd be delighted to have another passenger. Let's get going, shall we." He said. For a moment, I was shocked. Then I remembered the deal he made with him. Alec had us trapped again.

It was the weirdest car ride ever. One Warlock, one Witch, one Hunter and two Mortals. Nobody said a word but Lindsey. Who just rambled on about one thing or another. I tried to get my dad's attention, but he wasn't making eye contact. He was focused on the forest road. It was darker and creepier than usual in the forest today. We followed the road for most of the way up. Then dad branched off to the right. He pulled to a stop just at the edge of a clearing.

"Oh, wow!" Brett said.

"That's magnificent." Alec replied.

"Is that?" Lindsey asked.

"How the town got its name, Crystal Falls." I said. The only way I could explain Crystal Falls, was through a movie reference. Think of the movie Journey to the Center of the Earth, the newer one, when Brendan Frasier and his group first laid eyes on the beautiful landscape. That's what it was like now. This was the most beautiful part of the forest. The grass was a luscious green. The trees were as tall as skyscrapers. The river was perfectly clear, and the falls created an ambiance of tranquility as it fell from high above.

"Oh my gosh." Lindsey said getting out to look around.

"Why don't you guys go and get set up. I need to talk to my dad for a moment."

"Okay." Lindsey replied. She seemed to be mesmerized by her surroundings. Brett and Alec grabbed the bags and followed her.

I turned to my dad. "What are we going to do?"

"Don't worry, I won't be far." He said. "I don't think he'll cause trouble with Brett and Lindsey here, but just in case. I'll have some of my animals watching."

I nodded. I didn't think Alec would cause trouble either, but I'm still nervous. "Dad he can get back to this place, now that he saw it."

"I guess I'm going to have to change the scenery around." He smiled. That's perfect! We'll use the same trick as the library. "Be careful, especially with your friends."

"I will." Dad got back in the car and pulled away. It felt good knowing that he would be close by, even though I could handle Alec on my own.

"Why did you pick here Ange? Besides it being absolutely beautiful." Lindsey asked.

"I want to show you guys something." I replied. I led them over to the river.

"Is that?" Brett asked.

"Crystals." Alec replied.

"Not just any Crystals. They're very rare and can only be found here."

"This is amazing." Brett said.

"There so sparkly." Lindsey added.

"Guy's, it's time I'm honest with you." I said to them. "About the reason I'm so secretive about my family." Brett and Lindsey looked at each other.

"Ange, I'm sorry about yesterday." Lindsey began. I knew that she felt bad about thinking my father abused me.

"No, I have to tell you this." I took a deep breath. I rehearsed this story repeatedly with dad. I hoped it worked. "My parents are scientists. They study these crystals here." I said pointing to the river. "They discovered that not only are they rare, but they have special properties."

"Like what?" Brett asked.

"They give off energy, more powerful then solar, wind, electric and nuclear combined."

"That's incredible, they could change the world." Brett said.

"They're uncontrollable though. Untested and worth a lot of money. Should they fall into the hands of the wrong person?" I said.

"They could be turned into a weapon." Alec said.

"Yeah." I replied.

"Does the government know about them?" Brett asked.

"My grandmother works for the government." I said, it was the truth technically speaking. "They pay her quite the handsome sum to keep this place a secret. The world's not ready for these crystals. My parent's job is to test them and get them ready for use."

"That's why you don't talk about your family? Because the government doesn't want anyone to know of this place?" Lindsey asked. "I wanted to tell you guys so badly, but it would put your lives at risk if you found out." I said.

Lindsey hugged me tightly. "This is so much better than thinking you were being abused."

"That is so cool." Brett said.

"This place, and these crystals must be protected. This must stay between the four of us. No one can know of their existence. If my grandmother finds out. Who knows what she'll do?" I said, looking at Alec especially. They all nodded.

"I feel like a covert op." Lindsey said.

I smiled at my friend's enthusiasm. That went better than expected. After that, we set the picnic food up away from the falls, because soggy food wasn't very appetizing. Ms. Monti had thought of everything. There was even a blanket. She packed different varieties of pastries, everything from chocolate éclairs to vanilla cream puffs. There were ham and turkey sandwiches and bags of chips, water and soda bottles as well.

I was having the best time. We just talked for hours about the forest, our families, our dreams and plans. We laughed and joked around. Just typical, normal teenager things.

"Ange, What's the rest of your family like?" Lindsey asked.

"Mom's a bit eccentric, and my grandmother is an acquired taste." I replied. Alec who was silent throughout the entire meal, cracked a slight smile. He seemed lost in thought most of the time. I wished that I could read his mind. He excused himself politely and walked over to the river. Uh-oh, here comes trouble. I followed him.

"Don't worry, I won't drain any of them." He said without looking at me. "I must admit, you're a pretty convincing liar." He said with a smile. "We're not so very different."

"Speak for yourself. I lie because I have to, you lie because you want to." I replied.

He laughed. "They're called Crysantillium." Alec said.

I nodded. "Magical Gems with healing capabilities."

"They can do much more than that." He said. "They're vessels. So even if I was to drain them, they wouldn't be destroyed."

"So, they can be anything?" I asked.

"That would be accurate." His knowledge of magic was unbelievable. Mine was poorly lacking compared to his.

"You've master Foresight's. Amber's going to teach you Hindsight's."

"I know, I just wanted a magic free day." I replied.

He gave me a funny look. I smiled. "I know, Magical forest."

"Your dad's watching us." He said.

"I know, he's watching you mostly."

He laughed. "I can tell. There are two hawks watching from that tree across the river. A squirrel to the right of us, and a pair of raccoons to the left. For added measure, there's a gigantic brown bear just underneath those clusters of trees there."

"Can't be too careful." I said. He smiled again. "Oh, by the way. Grandma sent us this newspaper clipping about Gregor Langston. Apparently, we're not the only ones who think he's dirty."

"I'd like to see that."

"I'll get it for you."

"Thanks."

Lindsey and Brett's laughing turned my attention to them. She was laughing at something he said. He looked overjoyed to have her attention all to himself. They really were perfect together. A splash of water drew my attention back to Alec. He was still staring at the river.

"It's cold up here." He said stuffing his hands in his jacket pocket.

We went back to join Brett and Lindsey. We started talking about my birthday coming up in a few weeks. I couldn't believe that I'm going to be sixteen soon. I smiled to myself. Everything is going perfectly. I mastered a part of seeing. Brett and Lindsey are happy, and Alec was behaving himself. Nothing could ruin this moment.

Chapter 20
The Rings of Solace

Angelica
(2:00 P.M.-July 13th)

I was glad that I finally got the chance to hang out with my friends. I got to show them a little piece of my world, without totally revealing myself. The best part of yesterday's picnic? Being able to be normal for just a little while. It couldn't have gone more perfectly. Even Alec behaved himself.

Now, it was back to Seer lessons. I wanted to get started on Hindsight's right away. Alec told me that Amber would meet up with me in the same spot as always. Unfortunately, Amber wasn't really a morning person. I had to wait until the afternoon to start. I was a little nervous about having Amber teaching me instead of Alec. I had just gotten used to his presence and his teaching style.

It's like elementary school. You stay an entire year with one teacher, and when it is time to move on to the next grade, you get nervous that your new teacher is not going to like you. I didn't really know much about Amber. She only came to the park once and even than she really didn't say anything. I think Amber scared me more than Alec. The way she took us all out the first time we met was quite impressive, or I could just be nervous about practicing Hindsight's. Truth be told, I hated having them. I seem to have my worst episodes when I was experiencing them.

Dad and Mom were in the kitchen having lunch. I had no desire to have another fight with my mother. We started somewhat talking to each other again, if you counted yelling, complaining and nagging as talking. I think she is purposely trying to pick fights with me. Can you believe that?

Before I left, I managed to swipe the two articles that were sent to us by magical post. I'll give them to Amber to give to her brother.

I quietly opened and closed the front door. When I turned around. Merrin was sitting on the banister.

"Going out again?" she asked. There was an edge to her voice that I didn't like.

"Just to the forest." I lied. I been using dad's excuse a lot.

"Sure, the forest." She didn't believe me. The nerve!

"I am going there."

She smirked sarcastically at me.

I didn't like the attitude she was showing. "Look, I need to be alone. The forest is the only place I can get away from mother."

"You need to be alone!" She said, jumping off the banister. "You get to leave this house every day, and who gets stuck with mom? Me!"

Then it hit me. Once again, I had forgotten about someone. First it was not calling Brett and Lindsey and now it was Merrin. While I've been out training with Alec. Merrin has been stuck in the house with mom, that had to be rough. I sighed. "Merrin I'm sorry. I didn't realize…"

"Do you know what she has been like the last week? Every day you leave the house. Dad won't support her by making you stay. She keeps me bottled up in the house instead, while you get to go hangout with that Alec boy."

"I haven't been hanging out with Alec." I lied again. "Are you mad. They're the enemies, remember. I haven't seen them since the day we met."

"Oh, who are you trying to kid? He's been teaching you how to read minds and stuff." To

Merrin, my power was only about reading minds and invading the privacy of others. That bothers me.

"It's more than reading minds, it's more complicated than that." I said.

"I knew that's what you were doing." I silently cursed at myself. She was just speculating until now. Darn her for being so sneaky. She learned from the master, me. "I guess them being enemies means nothing to you."

"They're just teaching me how to use my powers." I said. "It's not like were friends or anything."

"You're so selfish! Just because you want to learn about your stupid gift, you'd risk our entire family."

My face heated up. How dare she say that I didn't care about our family? "You don't know anything! If you knew what our parents were keeping from us right now, you'd feel differently. If you knew what they did to me!" How dare she accuse me. She didn't know anything. "You're just upset that Amber tricked you."

Tears welled up in her eyes. I had struck a nerve. Serves her right! I should hex her for speaking out of term. Merrin stepped back from me.

It took me a moment to realize that she was scared, of me!

Wait a minute! What was I thinking? I didn't want to hex my sister.

"Oh, yes you do." A horrible voice rang out in my head. A voice that sounded like my own, except more raspy and creepy. My Darkling side, she wanted to hex my sister, not me.

"She deserves to be hexed."

"Get out of my head!" I shouted at the invisible voice.

"I wish I could, but we're stuck with one another."

I fought back against the voice. It wanted me to hurt my sister. I wouldn't do it. I was in control, not her!

Slowly, I felt my anger subside. I was in control again. I looked at my sister. She looked horrified. "There's something wrong with you." She said. "Do what you want. You always do. Just remember that mom isn't stupid. She'll catch you sooner or later." And with that, she disappeared.

I stood there out of breath. I couldn't believe what just happened. I almost attack my little sister. Well, Darkling me almost did. That was the first time I felt my other half, and I didn't like her one bit. It was one thing to have a split personality. It's another thing entirely to hear it talk to you.

I took a deep breath and regained my composure. I didn't have time to think about what just happened, and truthfully, I didn't want to. I had somewhere to be. I teleported from the yard to the park. Amber was already waiting for me.

"You're late." She was sitting underneath a tree. She had on a sweater and jeans. They looked to be brand knew. I wondered where she got them, or who she bewitched to get them from?

"You look horrible." She said.

Well that's a confidence booster. "I'm sorry, I was talking to my sister." I replied.

"How is Merrin?" Amber asked. Her eyes focused intently, it felt like she was staring right through me.

"We just had a fight." I said adverting her eyes.

"About what?"

"About me sneaking out to meet you guys." I replied.

"Oh." Amber seemed lost in thought. I wondered if she worried about my sister?

"Should we get started?" I asked. I really didn't want to think about my sister at the moment.

"Yes." She replied with a smile.

"Should I put a drying spell on us?" I asked.

Amber looked at me. The expression on her face made me feel like I said something wrong. "You know every time you placed a drying spell on Alec, you were basically feeding him."

I didn't like the way that sounded. "Feeding him?"

She shook her head. "You're feeding him your magic."

Reality just smacked me in the face again. Alec's been taking my magic, and I've basically been giving it to him! Why didn't I think to remove the drying spell afterwards? I'm so stupid!

I didn't want to get mad again. I started pacing back and forth and counting backwards in my head. I read online somewhere that counting was a good cool down exercise. "Why would you just rat your brother out like that?" I asked.

"Because, while Alec likes to use theatrics to disguise his purpose. I'm a more in your face type of girl. What you see is what you get. If you're going to train with me, you better get used to that."

Talk about being abrupt. Amber pulled less punches than Alec.

"I can see that you're getting frustrated. Relax, don't get your knickers in a twist. We don't need a Darkling episode."

"Relax! Your brother has been stealing my magic! He tricked me again!" For the second time today, I felt myself losing control. "Count backwards Angelica, 10, 9, 8, 7…" I said to myself.

Amber laughed. "From what he's told me, you have been tricking him just as much as he has you." She was referring to the library, and dad changing the scenery at Crystal Falls. "He doesn't want to admit it, but he's actually enjoying the competition."

"I bet he is."

"I mean it Angelica. We're learning from you, just as much as you are learning from us."

"What do you mean?" I asked.

"We've never been in the outside world. We've just learned from the Davenport's. This is our first authentic experience." She said. I thought about that. Alec and Amber have spent their entire lives in England, while I've spent mine here in Crystal Falls. We were alike in many ways.

There I go, feeling compassion for them again! From somewhere deep in my mind, I thought I could hear the voice again, telling me to hex her. I ignored it.

Amber was studying me with those eyes of hers. I couldn't believe just how red they really were. They looked like the eyes of a hungry Vampire, and I guess that would make sense, seeing as they were molded after them.

"His tricks are worse though. He has to stop!" I said.

She shook her head again. "You're still not getting it."

She was starting to irritate me. "Get what? Why are you making this so complicated? Just tell me what I don't understand?"

"Life is not going to be that simple. You're not going to have the time to read everybody's mind. Alec was trying to teach you a lesson." She said.

"I'm supposed to believe that?" I asked.

"Angelica, a Seer is never more vulnerable than when they are having a vision. Your *Yani* is not attached to your body. It is left vulnerable to attack."

"That's a load of garbage. Teaching me a lesson? I applied the drying spell before I had the visions." I said. The only thing Alec was teaching me was that he was a lying rat. Just when I start to trust him, another bomb is dropped.

"Okay, his logic is messed up."

"You think?"

Amber smiled for a moment. "I won't lie to you. He probably just wanted to feel your magic. He's still having a tough time resisting it, especially when your Darkling comes out. Think of this as a learning experience. Now you know, learn from your mistakes."

There was no hesitation in her eyes. She was unnervingly calm. I started to relax again. I should have suspected something. This was partially my fault. "Alec knew you be upset, but it is crucial that you learned about this. Because now, I'm going to teach you how to protect yourself from attacks while you're having a vision."

"I thought you were the Hindsight expert?" I asked.

"I am, Alec gets very few Hindsight's. I rarely get any Foresight's. Don't ask me how that work's, because I don't know. It probably varies from Seer to Seer, because you get both types of visions." Amber rubbed her hands together and stood up. She was all business like now. She seemed so much older than a girl that is twelve years old.

"I'm going to show you how to summon the Rings of Solace." She said.

"That sounds like something out of the Lord of the Rings." I said. "What are they?"

She smiled. "The Rings of Solace, basically, is a Seer's insurance policy. Only a Seer can use this magic. It benefits us greatly."

"How does it work?" I asked.

"With a simple three-word incantation. You will create three rings. The outer ring is your first line of defense. When approached, the ring will deter anyone who tries to get close to it. Most of the time this works on passing Mortals, who happen to walk along and get curious. However, if you find someone who has enough will power to fight the ring. For example, another Weir, then they could pass through the ring undeterred. Once the ring is breached, it vanishes. If that happens, the vision you're currently having will blur. That is your first warning that someone is approaching your body. The center ring will cause temporary forgetfulness, but like the first one, if you have enough will power, you can get by it. If for some reason you have not return to your body, you will receive a shock. If you feel that shock, you had better get back pronto. The inner ring is the hardest to get through, it causes massive confusion and paralysis. However, it is not impossible to get by. Your *Yani* must be back in your body, and you had better be ready to defend yourself from attack."

"What happens if you are killed while having a vision?" I asked.

"If your body is attacked and destroyed. Your *Yani* would have no vessel to return too. You would be stuck in that suspended state."

"Like a ghost?" I asked.

"I suppose so. I'm not that familiar with souls. You would have to ask an Under-Fate for more specifics. They're really good with the after-life." Amber said. "Anyway, moving on."

"Wait, one more question." I asked. "If Ghosts or Spirits do exist. Does that mean that there really are Mortals who can speak to them?" It was a stupid question, but I was thinking of Ghost Whisperer again with Jennifer Love Hewitt.

"A Medium is the product of an Under-Fate, Mortal relationship. They're not immortal like us, but they have special qualities about them." She replied. "Now enough about Spirit's. Let me show you how to summon the rings." She moved a wide distance away from me. "Clearly say the words. If you pronounce them wrong, then the rings will not form. Only Seer's can spot the rings. So that's another advantage, but a disadvantage should you be attacked by another Seer."

Amber closed her eyes and said. "*Teihnon Vespa Sahnon.*" Amber glowed for a second, as three golden rings formed around her. Each one, a fare distance apart from one another. The rings sparkled in the afternoon sun. "To remove the spell, you just reverse the incantation." Amber closed her eyes again. "*Sahnon Vespa Teihnon.*" The rings vanished just as quick as they appeared.

"Now I want you to try it." Amber said.

I closed my eyes like Amber did and said; "*Tahnun Vespa Sanon.*" I opened my eyes and saw nothing.

"You pronounced it wrong. It is not *tah*, like you pronounced, but *tay*. Also, it is not pronounced as nun, but as noon. Put it together and you get TAY-noon. The second word is the easiest to remember. The third is pronounced as SAY-noon."

I closed my eyes and tried again. "*Teihnon Vespa Sahnon.*" This time. I felt a tingling sensation in my hands. The three golden rings formed around me, I was excited to get it on my second try.

"Now I want you to have a regular Foresight like Alec showed you. While in the vision, I will attempt to cross the rings to get to you. Your job is to feel the difference and arrive back in time to stop me. Think of it as a test."

"What should I see?" I asked.

"Anything you want." She responded.

I sat down in the middle of the inner circle and thought for a moment. Who should I see? I didn't want to think about my sister, never mind see her. I decided that I would have a Foresight on my parents. I was curious to see what they were up to, when I wasn't in the house. Just like Alec taught me. I became the things I was seeing, in this case my parents. I felt my *Yani* tug away, and lift off over the trees. Man, I went over these tree's a lot. I arrived through the open living room window. Mom and Dad were arguing with each other.

"It is not right Rowan! She keeps going off to be on her own. She's isolating herself from us. That will just make her angrier and you know what happens when she gets angry!" Mom shouted.

"Gwen, she is fine. I've been keeping an eye on her and the Hunter's. She doesn't leave the forest, and they for the most part keep to themselves in the B & B." Dad said. "They wouldn't be able to get to her in the Forest anyway. I made sure of that." I was glad that Dad was still covering for me with the whole forest bit.

"It makes no difference! What about yesterday? You could have been attacked. Why have we not dealt with them like Greta said?" Mom shouted. I've never seen my mother like this. She was clearly agitated. She was pacing the room and her face was bright red.

Dad frowned. He hasn't told her about the deal that he and Merrin were forced to make. "It's complicated."

"So un-complicate it. If Greta gets back and they're still here, who knows what she'll do?" she said. "That's not even why I'm worried. Angelica is still mad at me and now Merrin is as well."

"Merrin will come around. She doesn't like being cooped up. As for Angelica, she is a big girl now. She is going to be sixteen in a few days. She'll be an adult." Dad said.

"So, what? That doesn't mean she can defy me. I'm still her mother and I know what's best for her!"

"Do we really know what's best for her?" Dad said back.

"What is that supposed to mean?" she replied.

Dad closed his eyes. "All I'm saying. Is that maybe we should trust her with a few more things." I held my breath for a moment as mom thought about what dad said.

At that moment, my vision blurred. It was like static on a T.V. Amber had crossed the first ring. I couldn't go back yet though. I've never seen my parents this mad before. I hoped it would take some time for her to breach the second ring.

"I know what you're thinking Rowan and we can't." Mom said.

"We have to Gwen. We should have a long time ago. She deserves to know the truth about who she really is." Dad said. Of course, I knew most of this story already, but Mom didn't know that.

"That thing that's inside of her is not our daughter. It is not my Angelica." Mom replied. That hurt.

"It is a risk not to tell her. I went and looked at that spell again. Do you know that it causes multiple personality disorder?" Dad asked.

"Those are her blackouts, when she gets mad."

"They've been happening more frequently recently. That spell won't hold for long. I'm surprised that it has."

"It will hold, as long as she stays happy, then we don't have to worry about them. Then when Greta returns, she'll reinforce the spell like she did the last time." Last Time? That means that

Grandma has reinforced the Darkling Curse before. Now that, I didn't know.

"She could die." Dad said.

"She won't! For years I've second-guessed allowing that curse to be placed on her. I now know that it was the right move. If we didn't place it on her, we would have lost her long ago. I won't lose my daughter, and I won't hear anything else on the matter." Mom said.

"Darn it Gwen! She's my daughter too!" That was the first time that I've ever heard my dad shout at my mom. Mom looked just as shocked as I was.

A nasty jolt went through my body. I crumpled to the floor. It felt as if someone took a knife and pierced it right through my chest. Amber had crossed the second ring. I had to get back or I would fail her test. I didn't want to leave yet though, torn between staying and going. I finally decided to go back. I could always come back later. Alec taught me that if I wanted to end a vision early. All I had to do was clear my mind again. My *Yani* took flight once more.

I opened my eyes just in time to see Amber breaching the third ring. She had a look of extreme concentration on her face. She forced her way through. The ring disappeared, and the spell broke.

She raised her hands to me. I quickly sent a stunning curse at her, but she easily blocked it. She thrust her hands out and I crashed through the soggy dirt. My pride was wounded along with my body. I failed.

"That must have been one bloody good Foresight for you to have let me get that far." She said shaking her head. She waved her arm. My body seized up. She pulled me closer to her. It was insane how she could control my magic like that. "We are going to keep practicing this until you get it right." And that is exactly what we did.

Chapter 21
Truth & Consequence

Alec
(5:00 P.M.-July 13th)

I didn't know what to do with myself while Amber was out training with Angelica. I wasn't used to being the one sitting idly by and waiting for things to be done. I was the action guy. I had to be doing something at all times or else I would drive myself crazy. That's exactly how I felt all day. I just couldn't seem to settle my mind.

I was too busy wondering what they were doing. Wondering how Angelica took the news of me stealing her magic, probably not well. I smiled at myself. I thought it was one of my cleverer ideas. Every time she placed a drying spell on me. I felt just a tiny bit of her raw power. It was quite addicting. I know it was sneaky of me, but I don't care. She'd been messing with me just as much as I was with her. I tried getting back to the falls, but just like at the library. I couldn't get the mist to form.

I was impressed with her. She had progressed very well with Foresight's. Her Darkling storms were even getting less violent with the more practice she got. That worried me a bit also. I didn't want her Darkling side to be too suppressed. I needed her to be a combination of both. I wish I knew what they were doing right now. I thought about going to check up on them, but I promised Amber that I wouldn't interfere. This was her turn to shine.

My mind was racing though. I was thinking about more Seer training techniques for Angelica. I also had an idea on how to fix her storm causing problems. It was a working idea. More of a hunch, but I was hoping it would work.

Being alone really gave me too much time to think. I thought about the Davenport's. The day they died still haunted me. Thinking about their deaths just made me think about Gregor Langston. The bloody knave responsible for their demise. Then I thought about Jacoby Valdorn, the man pulling the strings. I had to get even with them. The only way I could do that is to have powerful allies at my side. For that, I needed Angelica trained, and that just made me think about going to the park again. At least with Amber around, we would bicker with one another and that would distract me.

I started to think about why we came to Crystal Falls in the first place. Originally the goal was to start a conflict between the Weir. A conflict that would tip the balance of power in the world between the magical communities. After the Davenport's murder, it all became about getting revenge on the Weirling for what they did. Then meeting Greta Everhardtht only led to a feeling of hatred towards the Witch that killed my entire race. Now I'm training a Darkling Witch with a personality disorder in the art of Seeing. All my motives seemed to be muddled together. I was having a tough time trying to sort them all out.

Sitting on the couch, I decided to lay my head back and relax. No sense driving myself insane.

It didn't take long for me to start dozing off. There was no sense in fighting sleep. If it wanted to come, it would come. There was something strange about this sudden urge to sleep though, because I usually didn't feel tired in the middle of the day. I felt my skin start to tingle, and soon I felt the sensation throughout my entire body. I knew what this meant. It's been a long drought since my last vision. I almost forgot what it felt like.

My *Yani* didn't fly to the place it wanted to take me like Angelica's did. Mine just woke up in the place where the Foresight would take place. I opened my eyes. I was staring up at a beautiful, cloudless night sky. I felt the dampness of the grass below me. I sat up. All was still and quiet, except for the familiar sound of running water behind me. I got up and saw that I was on the bank of the River Thames. There was no mistaking this river. I was back in England, I was back home. I looked around to find the source of this vision. No one was around for miles. Then I heard approaching footsteps. A tall man wearing running sweats and a pullover sweatshirt came jogging into my line of view. He had light brown hair and a slight stubble on his face. He stopped and bent over to tie his converse shoes. However, he didn't use his hands to tie his shoes. He just twirled his finger and his shoes magically tied themselves. Getting a whiff of his scent revealed him to be a Warlock. Judging by his stature, I surmised that he's a Combatant.

"Very ingenious, Horatio." Came a familiar drawl from behind me. I turned to see another figure emerge from behind the trees. She removed her black shawl, revealing the white spiky hair of Greta Everhardtht. Her hair stood out like a sore thumb compared to her all black attire. I'm surprised I didn't catch her scent sooner. She must have just arrived. It was no excuse though, I must be careful. If I was here in person, she could have snuck up behind me.

"Your attire doesn't look any better. At least I look like a Mortal." Horatio responded.
He had a thick British accent like mine.

"If anyone looks at me. All they will see is a black shadow." Greta responded.

"Not with that hair of yours." Horatio said with a smile. Greta smiled back at him. "Is there any reason for you calling this meeting?"

"You know that I always have a reason for what I do." She responded. Horatio smiled again. "Any news in Demby?" Demby was one of the three magical communities in England, located just outside London.

Horatio's expression turned business like. "Not much. I spoke to some contacts in St. Bernard's and Eros. They have heard very little as well."

"I would expect news from St. Bernard's at least." St. Bernard's is a large magical community of Wizards in northern England. It was the home base of Jacoby Valdorn's Covenant. Eros and Demby are Weirlind communities.

"Jacoby has kept things close to the vest. I've spotted some of Evangeline's spies patrolling the area. I also have my contacts out there as well. We pick up a few things here and there."

"Like what?" Greta asked.

"Like an explosion at a funeral home in O'Doul Ireland." Horatio said, raising his eyebrows at Greta. O'Doul is a magical community of

Weirling in Ireland. Many believe it's the home base of the 8th Covenant. "You found his body, didn't you?"

Greta closed her eyes. "They were going to burn all traces of him. I had to do it."

"I didn't say there was anything wrong with it. How were you able to get into O'Doul anyway? They say it is the most secret Weirling community in Ireland."

"I figured that would be the place they take him. And no, I will not give away my secrets." Greta said. I briefly glanced into her mind. O'Doul Ireland was indeed the home of the 8th Covenant. Ignatius Clearwater confided that to her.

Horatio looked at her. "You transfigured yourself, didn't you?"

"I'm not saying a word." I glanced into her mind again. Greta had indeed transformed herself, into a bird, a raven to be exact. The spell that guarded O'Doul had a weak link that only she knew of. Ignatius had allowed it so only she could get in and out. That information was good to have. I love being able to read minds.

Horatio smiled again. "Where did you bring him?"

"Someplace where he can rest in peace. Where he will always be among friends." Greta said. I read her mind again, knowing where Ignatius' body was, would be a reliable source of leverage. What I saw was quite interesting. "How did you find out about the explosion?"

"Weirling Truth."

"Any idea who this Grey Phantom is?"

"Your guess is as good as mine. My sources tell me that Valdorn has plain clothed Wizards all over England, searching for this person. Whoever it is, has got him worried, that's for sure."

"How reliable are your sources?" Greta asked.

"I won't give you names incase we're overheard, but I've known them long enough to trust their judgment." Horatio said.

"We need to get the word out. Anybody with leads on this Phantom should come forward. The enemy of our enemy is our best friend."

Horatio nodded in agreement. "It has to be someone close to Valdorn."

"You think there is a traitor in his Covenant?"

"It's not uncommon. He's certainly thinking that way, if he has people searching in England."

"Keep your ears open." Greta said.

"I suppose this isn't the only reason why you called this meeting?" Horatio asked.

"I have news of my own. If I don't tell someone, I'm going to burst."

Great, I had a feeling what her news was going to be.

"Is everything alright?"

"No, about two weeks ago, Crystal Falls had some visitors." Greta said.

Horatio frowned. "That's impossible."

"That's what I thought. Until two adolescent Hunter's showed up."

"Impossible! We killed them all!" This guy had to be one of the Weirlind that persecuted my race.

"I thought so too. Until they showed up in my town and lured us all into a trap!"

"What happened? Did you kill them?" He asked.

"No. They used our own shield energy, to make one of their own. They trapped us in a small space and were able to block our magic."

"What? Are you sure they're Hunter's?"

"I thought it was strange too. Horatio these two are not like the ones we encountered years ago. They're not like the ones we hunted down. Those Hunter's attacked without hesitation. They killed with prejudice, having no remorse for the destruction they reaped." It aggravated me the way she talked about my ancestors. It wasn't exactly a lie though. The Hunters of old did attack like that, it was the way they were designed. "These two actually planned out an attack. One so cunning that I could have thought of it myself. That's not what I've come to expect from their race."

I silently praised our strategy, because it looks like it has shaken up the great Greta Everhardtht.

"They've evolved." Horatio said. "A truly frightening thought. What did they want, revenge?"

"Oh, they want revenge alright, but not on me." The way she talked, like she was a gift to the world, made me hate her even more. "These

Hunters have been under are noses for the longest time. They were living here in England with a Half-Blood Hunter family."

"Half-Blood." Horatio's face displayed the same disgust that is common with most everybody's, when the topic of Half-Blood's is brought up.

"Half Mortal, Half Hunter."

"Just lovely." Horatio mumbled.

"Apparently there are many more of them out there." Greta said.

"We need to get the group back together again. We have to find and eliminate them." This was not good. I didn't want another bloody persecution.

"There is no point. It would just be a waste of time. Like any Half-Blood, their Mortal genes protect them from Magical detection." Greta replied. "Do you remember how long it took us to find the Hunter's that escaped?"

"Yeah, we only found them through spy networks set up all over the world." Horatio said. "What do we do now?"

"Well for starters, you can tell me why with all our connections here in England. It was Jacoby Valdorn who found the Hunter's first!"

"What?"

"Valdorn had Gregor Langston send men to their home. To try and get them to join his little crusade against us."

Horatio rubbed his temples. "Bloody hell, this story is getting worse by the minute."

"Oh, it gets better. Apparently, Langston's men had managed to kill the Half Bloods when they refused to join them. But not before the young ones escaped. The house erupted in fire."

Horatio looked at Greta at the mention of the word fire. "We had a report a while back about a fire in Painswick. We didn't think anything of it, because there aren't any magical people in that area. Mortal firefighters reported that the fire engulfed the house in seconds. They couldn't stop it. After the house was gone the fire just died down. They said they never saw anything like it. It didn't spread. It just died down instantly." Horatio frowned. "They used the Immortal Flame, didn't they?" He asked.

Angelica had told me that Jacoby Valdorn had passed the knowledge of the Immortal Flame to

Gregor Langston, who then passed it on to his men. At the time of the attack, we thought it was a regular explosion. Amber and I were too preoccupied to think of anything else.

"You think? The Immortal Flame doesn't spread like a normal fire. It stays contained within its target. You of all people should know that."

"Greta. We just weren't a hundred percent sure. Reports said that a couple lived there with two foster children. They all perished in the fire. Neighbors said that they were a quiet family that never bothered anyone. There were no red flags. We never followed up on it."

"From now on, we respond to everything." Greta said angrily. "If Valdorn breaks wind. I want to know about it."

Horatio nodded. "What I don't understand is how they got there in the first place? We killed every single Hunter out there. How did we miss them?"

Greta was silent for a moment. She appeared to be contemplating something. "Do you remember the last Hunter sighting we had?"

"How can I forget? It was right..." Horatio looked around for a moment. "It happened right here. Right where we are standing."

"That's why I wanted to meet here." Greta said. "What do you remember of that fight?"

"Everything, it was the seven of us. You and Bartholomew, Valdorn, Clearwater, Killian, Shrike, and me." Jacoby Valdorn was one of the Weir responsible for the destruction of my ancestors. Why did that not surprise me? I should have realized that after Angelica told me that he possessed the knowledge of the Flame. He could have only received it from a Gypsy. Now I really wanted to get my hands on him. I made a mental note of the other names in the group. I'd get even with them also. "There were five Hunter's in total, three males and two females."

"Do you remember how the fight went?"

"It was a brutal one. We almost lost Shrike in the process."

"We killed four of them here. Do you remember the one that got away?"

Horatio nodded at the memory. "One of the females left right at the beginning. She didn't even stay to help her comrades."

"Do you remember how long it took us to track her down?"

"It took us a week. She kept changing directions like she knew we'd be following her."

"We finally caught up to her where?" This was starting to feel like twenty questions with Greta Everhardtht as the host.

"We caught up with her in Gloucestershire just outside of…" Then, his eyes widened like he just realized something huge. "Painswick." I was starting to get a funny feeling. This conversation was moving dangerously close to something personal, I just knew it.

"What do you think would drive a woman to go that far? Taking extreme precautions to get there and giving us the fight of our lives before we finally killed her."

"She was going to warn somebody." Horatio said.

"There is nothing more dangerous than a mother trying to protect her kids." Greta said.

My heart plummeted into my stomach. No, it couldn't be.

"I never forgot that Hunter's face. They're a spitting image of her, Horatio. I knew there was something familiar about them from the moment I met them. There is no other explanation. We should have searched further, then we could have avoided this entire mess."

My heart was pounding in my ears, and time seemed to slow down. I was vaguely aware of the rest of the conversation.

"We were exhausted after fighting her. We just thought that she was running away."

"She was going to warn her children. If she had made it there, we would have had to face five of them again. At least then, we could have killed them all, and we would have known about the Half-Blood's"

"There's no sense in thinking about what could've been. The question now is, what do we do about them? Valdorn knew how to track them. I can't believe he would give sacred knowledge like the Immortal Flame away like that."

"He told Langston, who in turn told his men. Jacoby should have never given that knowledge away. It was meant to stay between the seven of us." She said. "The only good that came from this, is that all of Langston's men are dead."

"How do you know that?"

"The Hunter's told me that they killed every one of them." Greta said.

"You believe them?" Horatio asked.

"The boy is very confident in himself. The expression in his eyes left me no doubt that he's telling the truth."

"You haven't answered my question yet."

Greta nodded slowly. "I told Rowan that if they were still there when I got back, that I would kill them, I meant it." She said. There was a fire in her eyes.

"I know you'll kill them, but that's not the question I was referring too. What do they want?"

"A war."

The scene began to blur, meaning that my time here was over. I was still too stunned to move. For years I've wondered what had become of my real parents. I finally knew the truth, and now, I would face the consequences of knowing it.

Chapter 22
Hindsight's

Alec
(7:00 P.M.-July 13th)

I sat on the couch, staring off into space. Not aware of anything, but the vision I'd just had. Greta Everhardtht and her team of assassins, killed my parents, my biological parents.

Growing up, I used to come up with different scenarios as to why they had left my sister and me on the doorstep of complete strangers. I'd always picture them as loyal followers of the Creator's, traveling the world in secret. When it was safe for us to be together, they would come back for us. Those were the pleasant thoughts. Then there were the not so pleasant ones, like they didn't love or care about us, Hunter's weren't supposed to have feelings like that.

As I got older, my hatred for them grew for abandoning us, and I pushed them further from my mind. Now they came flooding back in a riptide of emotion. I had stood on the ground where my father had perished, and my mother had died in Painswick. How close was she to where Amber and I had grown up?

I didn't know what to feel. I hate emotions. They just made things complicated. On one hand, my mother had cared enough to come back for us. Look what that got her, she should have stayed by my father's side. By coming to warn us, she was unknowingly leading the Weir right to our doorstep. We could have all died then.

There were just too many emotions running through my mind. I didn't know what to feel first, sad, angry, frustrated, lost. Maybe this was the reason why Hunters were never meant to have feelings.

I was so caught up in my own mind. That I didn't even notice the door opening, signaling the arrival of my sister.

"Alec are you even paying attention to me?" She asked.

"Oh. Sorry Ambs. I was just thinking about something. How did it go today?" I asked, trying to sound normal. She stared at me suspiciously. My sister and I can tell when the other is lying. I didn't want to upset Amber about the news I learned just yet. I was still trying to figure it out myself.

"I was saying that it went pretty well." She replied.

"How'd she take the news of me stealing her magic?"

Amber smiled. "Not well at first. I was expecting her to lash out like she normally does when she gets mad, but she surprisingly stayed in control. I think your training is working a little too well."

I frowned. "I was afraid of that. I don't want the Darkling to be totally suppressed. We'll have to find other ways to keep her mad."
I replied. "What else happened?"

"After that, I taught her the Rings of Solace. We spent the entire day on them."

"How'd she fare?"

"The first time I was able to breach all three rings. After that she kept me confined to the first ring."

"Good. Tomorrow get right into Hindsight's. I want her to learn of her abilities before her sixteenth birthday."

"What happens when she turns sixteen?" Amber asked.

"She becomes an adult. How that affects her powers, I don't know. Best not to take any chances."

*****

Angelica
(2:00 P.M.-July 14th)

I sat on a bench in the park. Not my park, but the local one where every Mortal in town came to. For some reason, Amber told me to meet her here. I preferred our usual spot. Here I felt exposed to everyone.

After yesterday's loss of control with my sister, I felt as if the world was watching me. I can still hear that voice in my head, egging me on to hurt someone. I should tell Amber what had happened, but I wasn't comfortable with her yet. She trained me harder than Alec. I didn't want to admit it, but I think I miss him.

"Time to get down to business." Said the familiar voice of Amber. As always, she was dressed in a nice outfit, that made you think that she was the prettiest little girl in town.

"Why did you want to meet here?" I asked.

"Because I hate being in the same place over and over again. It's so bloody boring." She said happily.

"Aren't you afraid we might be seen?" I sure was, I glanced around at the park. There were a few kids running around on the play sets, their parents talking nearby. A man was playing catch with his dog on the other side of the park. It wasn't crowded, but it was enough for me to be nervous.

"You know what the best part of being a Seer is?" she asked. I shook my head. "You get to use your magic out in the open without anyone knowing that you are. Unless you decide to get mad and blow something up, we should be good." She smiled.

I couldn't help smiling back at her. She said, that she was an in your face type of girl. She calls it as it is.

I was still worried though. "This is my life were messing around with here. If I'm exposed, my whole family is in danger."

"Yet you keep coming back for more lessons. I wonder why that is?" She said with a smile. Then she began circling around me like a lioness circling its prey. "Maybe it's because you know deep down that we're the only hope you have at discovering your true abilities. Without us, you're as good as dead Angelica and you know it."

I didn't want to admit it, but I knew she was right. "I'm sorry. I'm just really scared here."

"Don't be. Alec and I want to help you." She said. I wanted to believe her, but I didn't know what to believe anymore. Did they really want to help me, or did they just want to use me?

"Enough of this ninnying, it's starting to get really dull." She said, walking away. "Let's get to Hindsight's shall we." I followed her to the far end of the park, where she stopped and faced me. "Seeing as that you have already mastered Foresight's. This should be a breeze for you. You use the same techniques for both Foresight's and Hindsight's. Just visualize the thing you are seeing, and the vision will come naturally. The only thing different is instead of seeing what is current. You're seeing what has past." She said.

"Let's start off with something basic, like this tree here." She said, looking up at the tall pine.

"Why a tree?" I asked.

"Everything has a beginning or a birth. This tree at some point had to be born. I want you to go back and see it happen for yourself." She said. Then she stepped to the side and waited.

She said Hindsight's were like Foresight's. I visualized the great pine tree standing in front of me. It's massive height, the lushness of its pine needles, the thickness of its bark, and the strength of its roots that had to be well cemented in the earth. I sensed that this tree had to be very old, but it showed no signs of wear. The sensation this time felt very different. This time there was no vortex and I wasn't free falling. Instead the world was changing around me as I stood still. Days passed by, weeks, months, years. With each passing year the tree grew smaller. I watched the tree as it survived the harsh season changes. I watched it until it shrunk back down to nothing. Then everything was quiet. I looked around at my surroundings and saw absolutely nothing for miles. What was once Crystal Falls was now nothing, but a wide-open space of emptiness. I couldn't understand it. There had to be something here before my family created the town. Maybe I did something wrong with the Hindsight.

Then everything began to rush around me. This time we were rushing forward. The tree just emerged from the ground right in front of me. The surrounding wilderness emerged along with it. The town formed along with the park, and as soon as I knew it. I was standing back in the present.

"Well? What did you see?" Amber asked.

"I think I made a mistake." I said.

"What do you mean? You went back in time, right?" she asked.

"I did. I watched the tree as it grew smaller, which means that I was going back in time. Then it just sort of vanished along with everything else. There was nothing here, just grass for as long as I could see. As a matter a fact, there were no mountains, and no river. Nothing that's here now was around back then. When time sped forward, everything just sort of seemed to form around me."

Amber looked puzzled for a moment. Then she said. "I'll ask Alec about this later tonight. I've never heard of an environment just forming out of nowhere, but with magic you never know. Your dad is a Nurturer. Maybe he literally created Crystal Falls." I pondered that possibility. It made sense. Maybe I'd ask him, since we were telling each other everything now. "Good news is that the Hindsight was successful. You visited the past."

"Wow. It took me forever to get Foresights right."

"Hindsight's are easier. Like I said, once you know one, the other comes naturally." She said happily.

"Let's try it out on something material."

"You mean something that was made?"

"Indeed." She said. Then she reached into her jacket and pulled out a beautiful necklace. Six stars were interconnected on a long chain. The center star was the biggest. Each one was encrusted with tiny red rubies. I could sense right away that it was made from real gold, and it was magically made.

"It's beautiful." I said.

She smiled as she looked at the necklace. "The Davenport's gave it to me on my sixth birthday. It's my most prized possession. One- day curiosity got the best of me. I went back in time to see where it came from. What I saw changed my life." She said quietly. "I want you now to do the same as I did and go back in time to see this necklaces origin. I will never do it again for several reasons, and you will see why."

She carefully held the necklace up to me. As I focused on it, I soon felt myself falling. Drat! It was that stupid vortex again, or should I say timeline. When I stopped falling, I opened my eyes to a dark lit room. It was sticky warm in here. A man was hunched over a hot oven. He had long black hair that was pulled back into a ponytail. I could tell that he was a Wizard. Sweat dripped from his brow as he used his wand to remove a necklace from the heat.

The scene changed to reveal the same room with the same man. This time he was using his wand to break apart a red rock. He was very focused. He carefully inserted the ruby piece onto the golden necklace. It was clear to me that every piece he put on, was a labor of love.

The scene changed again. This time we were in a small living room. The man from before, and a woman with brown hair were standing happily together, as a small girl with brown hair like her mothers opened a package.

She was excited. Her hands fumbled opening the small parcel. Out of the package fell the necklace. "Oh papa, It's beautiful." She said. Then she rushed to hug her parents.

The dad took the necklace and placed it around his daughter's neck. "Now Emma Tomlin, you are the most beautiful little girl in town. For as long as you wear this necklace, you will be safe." The sheer joy on Emma's face was heartwarming.

The scene shifted again to the same living room. The father was arguing with a mouse faced man.

"Please Sinclair. I'll come up with the money to repay you." The father said.

"To late Tomas. I'll take my payment now." The mouse-faced man named Sinclair said.

Tomas tried to draw his wand, but he was too slow. Sinclair killed him on the spot. There was a scream from the corner of the room. Emma and her mother were huddled in the corner. Sinclair began to approach them. Quick as a flash, the mother stepped in front of her daughter, ready to defend her. Just like her husband, she was dispatched with ease. My heart raced as Sinclair approached the whimpering Emma. He raised his wand, ready to strike another killing blow. When the necklace around Emma's neck glowed brightly. There was a deafening blast, as both Sinclair and myself were knocked off our feet. When the dust cleared. Emma was gone. All that remained was the necklace. Sinclair quickly got to his feet, snatched the necklace and ran.

The scene dissolved once more, and this time we were on a busy market square in the bright morning sunlight. The mouse-faced man and a tall blond woman stood behind a stall.

"Come one come all. Come buy one of Sinclair's trinkets. We have the best magical artifacts in all of England."

"Pendant's, magic mirrors, rings, and much more." Said the woman in a screechy voice.

A bald man with a thick black beard approached the stall. "See anything you like my good gentleman?" Asked Sinclair. The bald man looked at the trinkets on the stall. Then his eyes settled on the necklace around the woman's neck. She was wearing Emma's necklace. The bald man looked at it curiously.

"That's quite the necklace." He said.

"Ah, indeed it is! It is a family heirloom. Doesn't it look stunning around my wife's neck?" Sinclair asked.

"It is stunning, isn't it?" The woman said.

"That's a lie. It is neither an heirloom or stunning around her neck." The bald man replied.

The woman gave him a spiteful look and Sinclair looked aghast.

"If there is nothing here you like, then I suggest you bugger off." Sinclair said.

"There is something here I want." He replied, pointing to the necklace.

"It's not available." Sinclair said.

"It wasn't available when you stole it from the Tomlin's house." He replied.

Sinclair looked flabbergasted. "How could you have possibly known that. It was more than 50 years ago when I took that necklace as payment."

"It wasn't yours to take." The man said calmly.

Sinclair reached for his wand. With lightning quick speed, the bald man jumped the stall, blocked the wand, and grabbed Sinclair around the throat. The woman screamed and ran from the stall. The bald man held Sinclair tight. They both glowed a bright purple, and I watched in horror as the magic was sucked out of Sinclair. His skin turned a horrible shade of black as it withered away. Then his body crumbled to nothing but dust.

The scene dissolved again to an alleyway where Sinclair's wife stumbled horribly in her high heels. She stopped short as the bald man appeared in front of her. Quickly he ripped the necklace from her neck. Sinclair's wife turned to run the way she came. When another person appeared out of nowhere and cornered her. She had soft long black hair and a gentle face. "You'll never get away with this! There were at least a dozen witnesses."

"A dozen witnesses that knew your husband was a con artist and a murderer. Nobody is going to help you." The woman said. Then she grabbed Sinclair's wife by the throat and held her high in the air. This lady was super strong. I watched again until there was nothing, but dust left too Sinclair's wife.

The scene dissolved once again. I was in another living room. This one better furnished then the Tomlin's simple room. There, the man and woman from the alleyway handed a young girl a present. She was a couple of years younger, but there was no mistaking that it was Amber. Next to her sat a younger version of Alec. He was even cuter when he was little. Amber opened the gift and she pulled out the necklace.

"It's beautiful." Amber said.

"It's a very special piece for a very precious young lady." Said the bald man. "It was given to another precious girl on her sixth birthday, like the one you're celebrating now. It's what I like to call a soul piece." The scene dissolved again, and I was back in the park. I looked at the necklace. So much death surrounded this one item.

"Now you know why that necklace is so special, and why I can never see it's past again." Amber said.

"Was that your parents?" I asked.

Amber nodded. The bald man and the woman who attacked Sinclair and his wife were the infamous Davenport's that Alec and Amber always talk about. "I can't bear to see Frank and Alice anymore. That vision was also the first time I saw what happens when a Hunter takes magic from another."

I shivered remembering their bodies crumbling to dust. "Frank called this necklace a soul piece. It took me a while to understand his meaning. I think that Emma Tomlin is still alive." Amber said holding the necklace up to the light.

"The little girl, how is that possible?" I asked. There was no way that she could be alive. I saw what happened in that room. I didn't want to remember what happened to that family.

"Her body wasn't there. Just the necklace. Her father said, that if she wore it, she would be safe." Amber replied. "I think this piece saved her life. I think that she is trapped."

"You think she is in the necklace?" I know anything is possible with magic, but that sounded a little out there.

"I know it sounds weird, but when I touch it, it almost feels alive." Curiosity got the best of me, and I reached out to touch the necklace, as soon as my hand made contact. I felt a jolt.

I was dangling from the hand of a man. I couldn't see his face. Just his well-dressed attire. "What do you think of it Sir?" We weren't alone in the room. A small boy stood facing the man holding me. A thoughtful expression on his face.

"I don't know Robert." The man's voice responded. They both had accents that I couldn't place.

"Do you think the Hunter is telling the truth about this necklace?" Robert asked.

"Like I said, I don't know. She's offering to help though. We can use all the help we can get at this point." The man responded. "I've never seen anything like this piece before."

I felt the jolt again. I was back in the park, Amber looked at me with awe. "Angelica, you just induced a Farsight."

"That was the future?" I asked. Had Amber had seen the same thing I did?

She still looked at me with wide eyes. "I've never felt a Farsight before. You are incredible." She said.

"I didn't do anything." I said, blushing.

"I've been holding this thing for years and never felt that before. You truly are special." We stared at each other for a moment.

We heard approaching footsteps. Amber and I ducked behind a tree, as Kelly Jackson and her aunt came into view. She looked disheveled and irate at something. Her eyes had bags underneath them. Her hair was messy, and her clothes were ripped and dirty. It was strange seeing Kelly this way. She was always in such a perfect state. It was also weird to see her guardian out at all. In all the years that I've known Kelly. I don't ever remember seeing her aunt out of the house, and she has the nerve calling my family weird.

"All I'm saying is that it is a mistake to put your body through that ordeal again." Her aunt said in a deep non-feminine voice.

"I did not come this far to back out now. He's counting on me to get the job done. I will not fail." Kelly said through gritted teeth.

"I think…"

"You're not here to think! Your here to support me!" Kelly shouted.

This was interesting. I've never seen Kelly this disturbed before. She was always so prim and perfect. I was about to read her mind to see what was bothering her when Amber whispered in my ear, almost startling me out of our hiding spot. "This is your next lesson. Do a Hindsight on her."

"On Kelly?" I asked.

"It's the perfect chance Angelica. Wouldn't you love to get some dirt on your enemy? There's no better way than going right to the source." She said with a smile.

Just the thought of knowing something juicy on my long-time rival was just too good to pass up.

"Do the same thing you've been doing. It should work like a charm." Amber whispered.

So, I did. I pictured Kelly in my mind. Everything about her was just so perfect. It was enough to make someone vomit. When I felt myself going back in time, I knew something was wrong immediately. The vision was so blurry that I couldn't see a thing. I did hear voices though. Of a baby crying and someone shouting, "Save Her!" The vision was spinning so fast that it was hard to pay attention to all the different voices that seemed to be shouting at the same time. I had no choice but to let go of the vision and return to the present.

Amber was gripping my arm. I felt her slowly draining power from me. I quickly jerked away from her. "What are you doing?"

"Shhhh…You were about to cause a storm." She whispered back.

I looked back to Kelly and her aunt. They both left the park, still arguing about something.

"What happened?" Amber asked.

I got up and walked back over to the bench. "I didn't see anything. Everything was all fuzzy and there were about a dozen voices all shouting. It was impossible to tell anything that was going on."

"Why do you look so upset?" Amber asked.

"I don't know. Even though I couldn't see her past, it just felt so sad." Kelly's past, whatever it might be, felt depressing. Not something I would have guessed.

"What you just described, I've felt before."

"You have? I thought that a blurry vision just meant I did something wrong."

"Maybe with Foresight's because they happen in the present. Some Hindsight's though are fractured."

"Fractured?"

"Some moments in time just cannot be visited. For instance, if you were to go back in time to see the exact moment President Kennedy was killed, the vision would be fractured and blurry. You can hear it, but not see it."

"How do they become fractured?" I asked.

"Most of the time it's from severe tragedy." She responded. I thought about that. What had been so tragic about Kelly's life, that her Hindsight was fractured?

Chapter 23
A Fury Unleashed

Alec
(July 15th-21st)

As the days past, I found ways to keep myself
occupied while Amber taught Angelica about
Hindsight's. I was literally driving myself insane.
The vision I had was still gnawing at my insides and
the articles that I received from Angelica didn't do
anything to help my state of emotions. One of them
told the history of Gregor Langston. The new leader
of the 8th Covenant. Apparently, he was nothing
more than a lowly manservant before he became the
so-called leader. The other was an article on Jacoby
Valdorn's recent activities. The article accused the
Covenant leader of ghastly things. I wondered about
this author of Weirling Truth. He or she sure knows
a lot about Weirling activity.

The articles only added anger and confusion
to my already frazzled mind. My usual calm state
was starting to become unhinged. All because of one
bloody vision. On one hand, I was angry with Greta
Everhardtht for killing my real parents. Then on the
other, I was oddly upset about their demise. I don't
know why, I never knew them.

Thinking about my parents made me think about the Davenport's. I missed them. I really needed their advice right now.

I was beginning to second-guess myself again. Was I doing the right thing coming here? Was I playing my cards the right way? Should I be training Angelica? Why was I training Angelica? That was never part of the plan. I'm enjoying this game of one ups men ship with her too much. I'm enjoying this town way too much, going to the Java Café or Logan's Diner, talking with the Krenshaw's or Ms. Monti. Lindsey and her blasted hold she has over me. It was all too much! I'm starting to care for them. The biggest mistake a Hunter can make, was becoming attached to a target.

Worst of all, I'm having visions again, at least two or three a day and they had nothing to do with one another. I should have realized that my long drought between them was a sign, and I was trained to recognize those signs. These distractions were...well. Distracting me! The visions were making me tired. My energy was draining. Soon I knew what would happen. I've been doing my best to hide it from Amber. If she knew what was happening, she would stop everything to take care of me. She needed to keep working with Angelica. We committed to this course of action. We must stick to it. I was fortunate that she came back home late. At least I could pretend to be asleep. I knew she would catch on eventually, but I would hold up for as long as I could.

*****

Alec
(9:00 A.M.- July 21st)

The morning after Angelica completed her Hindsight lessons came as a relief. I was going to tell Amber what was going on with me. She was still sleeping soundly in her bed. I was about to wake her, when the phone rang.

I groaned. The phone ringing usually meant Lindsey or her parents. I should just leave it be, but I decided to pick it up anyway. I was surprised to hear Angelica's voice on the line.

"Hey Alec. Sorry to bother you."

"Angelica. No, it's fine. Something wrong?" I asked.

"I know that Amber said I should rest today, but I really want to talk to you. Grandmother sent another article that you really need to see."

"Okay."

"Cool. Let's meet in our usual spot." She said.

"I'll be there." I said hanging up. I went to the bathroom to wash up. Staring at my reflection in the mirror, I saw that my skin was paler than usual, and there were bags under my eyes. I may have been pretending to sleep, but I was getting none. Visions haunted my every waking moment. I should just wake Amber and let nature take its course. Angelica sounded urgent on the phone though. I wondered what the article was about. I decided that a couple more hours wouldn't hurt.

I freshened myself up the best I could. I hoped Angelica wouldn't notice my appearance. If she asked, I would come up with something on the fly. I quietly opened the front door and stepped outside. It was chilly this morning. I made sure no one was around before I formed the Mist to take me to Angelica's park. It took a lot of effort to get it to form. I was even more exhausted when I arrived.

I looked around. Angelica wasn't here yet. I was about to lean on a nearby tree, when a strong forced knocked me off my feet. I crashed into the ground rather roughly. Blood poured from a split lip.

"Bloody Hell." Getting to my feet, a spell hit me dead on in the chest.

Blasted backwards, pain shot through my shoulder as I felt it pop. I swore at myself. My shoulder was out of its socket. Before I could react. Another spell grabbed hold of me and slammed me up against the tree so hard that I felt it shudder.

I searched for my invisible attacker. "How does it feel to be lured into a trap?" Said a sweet voice. Gwen Everhardtht was approaching me, a not so sweet expression on her face.

*****

Gwen
(9:33 A.M.- July 21st)

I've had enough of being afraid of these two children. It was time to stop acting weak and take a stand. I knew Angelica was sneaking out of the house to meet with the Hunter's. I should have done something sooner, but I trusted that Rowan was telling me the truth.

That hurt worse of all. Rowan knew where Angelica was going, and he's not only willingly letting her go, but he's blatantly lying to me about it. Why would he do such a thing?

I overheard the conversation that Angelica had with him last night. My blood boiled as I listened to what Angelica had been doing. It bothered me more than it should have that Angelica had confided more with Rowan than she did with me. It was selfish of me to think like that, but that's how I was feeling. I was going to charge in on them, but I realized that it wasn't my family's fault. It was the Hunter's fault. Ever since their arrival, things had gone from bad to worse. They had to be stopped.

I waited until the next morning, used a spell to disguise my voice as Angelica's and lured Alec to the park. As I waited for him. I became angrier. This place was a gift to Angelica and Merrin, and she had shared it with Alec.

When the fogged rolled in. I was a little worried. It was so thick and dense that I couldn't see anything. Then Alec appeared out of nowhere, glowing his usual shade of red. He seemed to be tired and out of breath. Good! I caught him off guard. I quickly blasted him off his feet and sent him smashing to the ground. As he got up, I smashed him again right in the chest. I heard the popping sound of his shoulder as he hit the ground. He cried out in pain, swearing in British. The third blast I sent at him, smashed him up against the tree. I sent ropes to bind him to it. "How does it feel to be lured into a trap."

He smiled at me. "I have to admit. I wasn't expecting that."

"I've had enough of you and what you've been doing to my family."

He spat blood to the ground. "Have you now?" he asked. A smug expression on his face.

"I know what you've been doing with Angelica. I know you've been teaching her about her gift of sight. That ends now!"

"Fine, if you say so." He smiled.

It was too easy. He couldn't be giving up just like that. "What did you do?"

He smiled. "It's finished. Angelica is in control of her Seeing now. Surely you've seen the difference in her."

I did see it. The last few day's Angelica was walking with more confidence. She wasn't having blackouts as she was before. She seemed to me as if she had more control. I had to admit, I was proud of her. What I wasn't proud of was the way she had gone about it.

"Aww, is mum upset that her daughter lied to her?" he asked. I stared at him. "That's rich, considering how much you've kept from her."

"I lied to protect her!" I shouted.

"Some good it did." He said calmly. "That bloody spell is going to backfire on her. At least now she has a fighting chance of staying in control."

"How would you know?" I asked.

"Oh, come off it! One moment she's Angelica, the next she's that bloody Darkling. Two personalities clashing inside one. Did you actually read that spell?"

"It was all we could do."

"You keep telling yourself that." He said with a smile.

I smiled at him. "You put on such a show, and act like you care for her, but you want the Darkling to come out! You want to control us! All so you can get your sick revenge."

He hesitated for the briefest moment. "I knew it." I said. He spat blood from his mouth again. "I appreciate you teaching Angelica how to stay in control, but now it's over. You will stay away from her, you will stay away from my family, and you will leave my town." I said sweetly.

He laughed a charming laugh. "You're good. An extremely strong Enchanter, but remember I'm a pretty good charmer as well." I tightened the rope around his shoulder and he cried out in pain.

"I said. YOU WILL LEAVE!" I poured every ounce of my magic behind my words. His will, would bend to mine. I saw the struggle in his eyes. I was winning the battle. Then he cried out, snapping the ropes. It was my turn to be blasted backwards.

My back hurt a lot as I struggled to my feet. I glanced at Alec. He drained the magic from my ropes. Placing his hand on his shoulder, I heard it pop back into place. "Bloody Hell." He swore through gritted teeth.

He looked at me and smiled. "Who's going to make me? You?" he asked.

I smiled back. "You betcha!" I shouted. Spreading my hands wide, I sent a gale force wind spiraling towards him. He dodged just in time. His speed was incredible. He raced towards me and cracked me in the chest, sending me careening through the ground, as dirt flew all around me. I got up quickly and sent curse after curse his way. He dodged them easily, but I saw that he was getting tired. Finally, I sent an explosion charm that hit its mark. He shouted as he was blasted into the air. He crashed down with such force that a normal person would have been killed.

Alec wasn't normal though. He was getting back up. I uprooted one of the smaller trees in the park. Using it like a baseball bat, I swung. HOMERUN! I hit Alec dead on and he crashed into another tree, splitting it in half. His nose was bleeding badly and there was a huge gash above his right eye. You would think a shot like that would have killed him? I flew at him, punching him in the face with both my left and right hand. Then I spin kicked him in the chest. I heard the crack of his ribs.

"I thought you were indestructible." From his knee, he punched the ground, sending projectiles flying everywhere. I was hit hard with dirt, rocks, and roots. Then he hit a close line that almost decapitated me. It felt like being hit by a semi-truck. I flipped in the air and landed on my face. Then he grabbed me from my back and threw me halfway across the park. The pain was immense. I was bleeding from several wounds, and I was sure several ribs were broken. I wasn't giving up though. My family was at stake. The good thing was that Alec looked far worse than me. He was trying to quell his nosebleed. The gash above his right eye was so bad that he probably couldn't see through it.

His clothes were torn and burnt from my explosion charm. He looked at me through his one good eye. I knew he wasn't done yet either. I screamed and flew at him. He shouted and ran towards me. We collided in the center and exchanged blow for blow. For every shot he hit. I return the favor with one of my own.

The fight seemed to last an eternity. Two immortal gladiators battling it out. I felt him tiring, he wasn't dodging as well as before. I made contact more often. Finally, a roundhouse kick brought him down. I won!

Before I could catch my breath or celebrate my victory. He took my legs out from under me, jumped, grabbed me around the throat and slammed me to the ground. The wind was completely knocked out of me as he held me down. As I stared up at him. I was shocked to see that even with all the scars and wounds that I had just given him. He was still quite the handsome young man. I watched, as specks of blood dripped from the gash above his eye.

"Now there's the Gwendolyn Fury that I heard about." He said.

I couldn't believe my ears. No one knew my Maiden name, but Greta, and Rowan. "How do you know about me?" I choked out.

"Why hide your true nature, when it is the most beautiful thing that I've ever seen."

I was taken aback at his abruptness. He let go of my throat and staggered back. Air returned to my lungs and I slowly got back up. An imprint of my body was left behind in the ground.

"You should be training Angelica, not Greta. With your husband's and your pedigree. It's no wonder Angelica turned out the way she did."

"I don't know how you know so much about me, and I really don't want to. I'm going to ask you again to stay away from her." I cried.
I had no energy left to use my Enchanter magic. Maybe I could reach him from the heart.

"I'll make a deal with you. I promise not to teach Angelica anything more, for as long as you teach her magic."

"Why would you promise that?" I asked.

"I only showed her how to use her gift of Sight. That's only part of her problem. She needs to learn how to control her Weirlind magic as well. I can't teach her magic, but you can. Nobody knows about magic more than a Fury."

"I'll agree to that. As long as you keep what you know about me a secret. Nobody can know about my past."

"I'll counter you. I'll keep that a secret for as long as you promise to be at my beck and call. Whenever I should need, you'll come without hesitation, and you will fight, when I fight." I hesitated. This is what he wanted from the get go. An alliance for a war. I weighed my options. He knew too much about me. There's no doubt that he read my mind. I needed to get him away from Angelica, no matter the risk to me. I had to keep my family safe.

"I agree.

He nodded, pulling out a piece of parchment from his pocket. He held it out to me. Our agreement was laid out and he signed it. Then he passed it to me. "Breaking this agreement results in death." He said.

I nodded and signed. He took the parchment back. I looked at him closely. "You were willing to make that deal, even before the added stipulations. You really do care about Angelica?" I asked.

He looked at me. "A Hunter's greatest weakness." He choked.

All the hatred that I had built up for him, released from my body. I didn't see a Hunter anymore. I saw a scared and tired boy, one that I had just beaten the pulp out of. My motherly instincts took over. "Are you okay?" I asked. I didn't know whether I should reach out for him.

Alec swayed on his feet. "I'm just brilliant." He walked away from me. I knew he was lying. Something was wrong with him even before the fight. I saw it when he arrived. I was just too mad to care.

"At least let me help you back."

"Help Angelica." He said, then disappeared in a cloud of fog.

Chapter 24
Moving Mountains

Angelica
(10:00 A.M.-July 22nd)

I was feeling better than ever. I had mastered Foresight's and Hindsight's. I even had a Farsight. Not even Alec or Amber could say that. I haven't had a blackout in days. That darn Darkling was quiet for once. I'm happy. I'm in control for the first time in a very long time.

Mom interrupted my moment of jubilee. "Angelica." She said softly.

I braced myself for yet another argument. It seems that's all we did now lately. Mom was surprisingly solemn though. "I want to show you something."

"What?" I asked.

"Come with me." I obediently followed her. "Put your jacket on." She said. I was curious as to her change in attitude. Normally she would be questioning my every move. Where have you been? What have you been doing?

We walked outside to the porch. "Take my hand."

"Where are we going?" For a moment, I hesitated. Where was she taking me? Was this change in attitude just a ploy? Was she going to get even with me for sneaking out of the house?

"Please." She said again. Mom would never do anything to hurt me, but she could be sneaky enough to trap me. Seeing very little options, I took her hand. Whatever was coming?
I could take it.

We teleported to the top of the mountain, it's the highest point in Crystal Falls. That's why I needed the jacket, because it's also the coldest part of town. Laid out before me was a field. There were test dummies, obstacle courses and other odd setups. If I didn't know any better, it looked like a training field.

"What on Earth…" Mom hugged me tightly.

"My dear Angie. I'm so sorry for the way I've acted. Can you ever forgive me?" I was taken aback by Mom's sincerity. It's been so long since she's hugged me, that I didn't realize how much I missed them.
For a moment. We stood there in each other's arms. Tears welled up inside me. "I'm

sorry mom, can you ever forgive me?"

Mom laughed. "Everhardtht women, too stubborn for their own good." I laughed back at her. "What's done is done. We're going to have to learn to trust each other more."

"I know." I replied. She wiped away my tears and hugged me again. "Now enough of this crying, it's time to get down to business."

"Mom, what are we doing here? What is all of this?" I said glancing around at the field.

"Something we should have done a long time ago. I'm going to teach you magic."

I looked at her. I was sure that I heard her wrong. "I thought that was grandmother's job?"

"By the time we wait for Greta. I could spin straw into gold the old-fashioned way." Mom said, and I laughed. "Look, you're my daughter, and I should be teaching you." She looked at me firmly. For a moment, I thought she knew what had been going on recently, but there was no way she could. "Besides, I know a bit of magic myself."

I smiled. For the longest time, I wanted my mom to open up to me. She was always so closed off. Now it seems, she's finally starting to come around. I didn't care anymore why she suddenly changed her mind. All I cared about was that she was going to teach me magic. I couldn't have been happier.

"Okay." I said. "It sounds great!"

She smiled at me. "This is my early birthday gift to you."

"I love you mom."

"I love you." She stroked my hair. "Now, let's start shall we." She led me over to a section of the field that contained three rocks. One was small enough to fit in my hand, the second was a medium sized rock, and the third was a gigantic boulder.

"I want you to summon the small rock to you." She said.

"Okay." That seemed simple enough. Levitating objects was rather easy. I held out my hand and pulled the rock towards me. I clasped it in my hand.

"Good. Now I want you to crush it, without using a spell." Now, that was a little bit more difficult.

"I've never done anything like that before." I've always used a spell when it came to breaking things.

"Spells can be blocked. It is much harder to block magic of the mind. Command the stone to break. Crush it with your mind."

I knew what I had to do. Mind Magic was all about concentrating on the thing you wanted the most. So as hard as a could, I thought about breaking the rock. I squeezed it in my hand. All I accomplished, was a cut. The rock was unchanged. "I can't do it."

"Your will is stronger than that pebble, remember that, and try again." She said.

I looked at the pebble. It was nothing more than a river rock. I could break it easily. I concentrated again. A puny rock wasn't stronger than me. I squeezed my hand again. This time I felt the rock crumble to dust. I laughed. "That was so cool."

"Do it again. This time to the medium rock. Don't use your hands. Use your mind." Mom said. I looked at the rock. This one was made of sandstone. I levitated it, not with my hand, but with my mind. The same way I crushed the river pebble, I could crush this sandstone. I put all my will power behind it, and sure enough. The rock split down the middle. It was now two pieces of sandstone.

"Wow." I said.

"It's an exhilarating feeling to have command over something. Not only did you break the rock in half, but also you split it perfectly. It fits together like a glove." The sandstone formed together again. "With most Weir, it's stops there. They're not strong enough to go any farther. You are a Darkling though, and you should have no trouble with this boulder."

The boulder was larger than myself. I've never attempted to work with something this big before. "It gets harder to move objects when their size increases. Before you try to break it. I want you to move it."

I focused on the boulder. It hovered not even an inch off the ground and fell back down. After it dropped I let out a long breath. Sweat was on my forehead. I didn't realize how hard I was concentrating. Then I heard her. Darkling me laughing. *"Is that the best you can do? Come on. Move it further."* She felt different this time. Usually she was fighting for control of me or egging me on to do terrible things. Now she was egging me on to try harder to improve myself.

I concentrated harder. This time the

boulder levitated off the ground. I held it for a good minute. Then dropped it back down. "Great, Angelica! Now split it like you did the other."

"You can do better than a split. Destroy it!" The voice echoed.

I willed up all the energy in my mind and sent it towards the boulder. The rock shattered into a thousand shards. Mom and I ducked for cover.

"Perhaps there's some hope for you yet." She said. Then she went quiet.

"Okay, not exactly what I meant, but that was perfect none the less."

"Sorry. I got a little carried away." I replied.

"It's okay." Mom said. "You see what I'm trying to show you?" she asked.

"No."

"Angelica, most Weir can only dream of doing what you just did. Some Weir, like our family, can do so much more. You can do so much more. By the time I'm done training you, you're going to be moving mountains." I laughed at her joke, but the expression on her face showed that she wasn't kidding.

*****

Angelica
(July 22nd-July 31st)

As the week dragged on, Mom taught me some crazy things. After learning how to break rocks with more precision, she had me crush diamonds and other gemstones. That's when you know your family is rich when you destroy priceless stones for fun. I learned that different gemstones have different magical properties after they have been turned to dust. Diamonds for instance grant someone the ability to fly for short amounts a time. Rubies leave nasty burn marks, and sapphires knock you out cold for a while. Of course, it only works if they're in the hands of a Weir. Crushing gemstones was cool. I felt like one of the seven dwarves from the TV show Once Upon A Time.

I also learned how to fly by manipulating the wind currents around me. Walking on air was the coolest, yet scariest thing that I've ever done. Mom helped me with my spells and charms. She showed me how to concentrate them more, thus, making them far stronger then I could ever imagine. Spell hands were my favorite lesson, that's where I can bewitch my hands so that when I used them in a fight, my punches would be far stronger. The biggest shocker, was learning that Mom was actually a pretty good fighter. She had a black belt for crying out loud and she never told me.

"Remember Angie, not all fights require magic to win. Sometimes a good old fashion brawl is all you'll need." I must admit. I didn't expect to hear this from an Enchanter. I always thought they were about beauty and charm. Grandma was the one who loved to fight.

Sure enough, she also showed me how to fight with grace. "Not all fight's need to be ugly, some can be very pretty. Think of it as a dance with kicks and punches." Watching mom demonstrate how to fight was mesmerizing. She made it seem like an art form. Now I know why they're called Enchanter's. They're not only beautiful themselves, but their actions were beautiful as well. You'll be so distracted by them, that you'll never see the attack coming.

Mom even came through with her promise of me moving a mountain. She wanted me to move the one we were currently standing on. I concentrated harder than I ever did before, and only managed a minor tremor, it was rather disappointing.

"It's okay. I'm not expecting you to lift the mountain off the ground. Someday you'll be powerful enough, but for now you are progressing beautifully." She hugged me, and I didn't feel so disappointed anymore.

Things couldn't have been more perfect. Mom and I weren't fighting anymore, and she was teaching me about magic. I felt myself getting stronger and stronger with every knew technique I learned. I wasn't angry, my blackouts weren't occurring. Even Darkling me wasn't so scary anymore. She talked occasionally during the lessons. She was still egging me on, but it was to get me stronger, not to do dreadful things like before.

My birthday was a night away. Mom and I just finished the lesson and were munching down on some food.

"I want to give you and early birthday gift." She said.

"I thought the lessons were an early birthday gift." I replied.

"What, a mother can't give her daughter more than one gift?" I laughed.

She pulled out a ring from her jacket pocket, it was silver with an emerald placed in the center, and gold engravings marked the sides of the ring. "It's beautiful mom." I said.

"It's an energy ring. The emerald can store reserve amounts of power, for emergency situations of course." She said.

"It's wonderful, where did you get it?" I asked, putting the ring on my finger.

She seemed lost in thought. "It's a family heirloom, forged by Irish metal makers."

"Wait a minute, I thought our family was from England?"

"The Everhardtht's are from England. My family has roots in Ireland." She said. That was the first-time mom ever said anything about her family. Any time I would ask her about them, she would just brush the questions aside.

I didn't want to press my luck any further. Just in case she clammed up again, but curiosity got the best of me. "Your Irish?"

"Well…It's more complicated than that. My family's a…mixture." She said. Then she got up and brushed herself off. Clearly the subject was closed. It was an improvement though. "Tomorrow we'll have the diner close early to celebrate your birthday. You can invite your friends, I'll even come down. What do you say?"

I didn't know what to say. I was never allowed to have a birthday party with my friends and family before. I always had to celebrate with each of them separately. "Can it be? My daughter is speechless."

I laughed and hugged her tightly. "Thanks mom."

"You're welcome. It's long overdue that I get out of the house, for a while anyway."

*****

Angelica
(5:00 P.M.- August 1st)
(A.K.A-My Birthday!!!)

We reserved the diner out for the night. Mom, Dad, and Merrin, Lindsey with her parents, Sheriff Hansen, and Grace Hansen, Brett and his parents, and much to his aggravation, his sister Blair. Logan and Violet Krenshaw catered all the food. We had everything from pork roast to sweet potato pie. I must say that Logan out did himself tonight. Everything tasted delicious.

"Well it's not every day you turn sixteen." He said with a wink.

"I've never had artichokes this tender before, you must tell me your secret." Sara Ramsey said.

"The secret is all in the cooking process." Logan replied.

"Careful Sara, you'll inflate his ego worse than it already is." Violet said with a laugh.

"Everything is quite delicious. I can't thank you enough Violet for making it possible." Mom said to Violet.

Violet turned three shades of red. "Oh it was my pleasure Mrs. Everhardtht."

"Please, it's Gwen." Mom replied.

"Gwen, it's our pleasure. Your girls frequent our humble abode quite often. They're like family." Logan responded. He was quite smitten with my mother. So was every other guy in the room. Not only was this the first time that she's showed up in town. They didn't realize just how enchanting she could be. Mom loved every minute of the attention. Sara and Grace wanted to know how she got her hair so perfectly shinny. She also gave advice to Blair and Lindsey on how to keep their skin perfectly smooth. I sighed, typical Enchanter.

Brett had trouble keeping his eyes off her all night. I really felt bad for him, not only did his sister keep tormenting him, but also Lindsey must have elbowed him at least a dozen times. He really couldn't help it. He's never been in the presence of an Enchanter before.

There was a break between courses. Ms. Monti was supplying the dessert course, I could hardly wait to see what she made.

"Hey Angie." Lindsey pulled me over to the side.

"What's up Linds?" I asked.

"Have you heard from Alec or Amber lately?" I almost forgot about them, everything was going so smoothly lately, that it hadn't occurred to me that I haven't heard a peep out of the Hunter's in a week. That couldn't be a good sign.

"Come to think of it. No, I haven't." Lindsey seemed nervous. "Why do you ask?"

"You don't think they would have left, do you?" she asked.

Not likely, I thought. "I don't know."

"I've tried calling the room numerous times, but no one's answering. They haven't been going to the café, or here either. My parents keep saying I should give them some space, but I'm starting to get worried."

"Good, maybe they did skip town." Brett said.

Lindsey gave him a dirty look. "You're so mean."

"Oh, Please Linds. Do you really think the tall and handsome Brit would just leave without saying goodbye? I don't know what you see in him, the guy practically screams arrogance and self-entitled ness."

"Don't worry Linds. It's probably just some weird British custom to not speak to anybody for periods of time." I said.

"I hope so." She responded. I made a mental note in my head, tomorrow I'd have to visit the Hunter's and see what they were up too.

Suddenly the lights in the diner dimmed. "Cake has arrived." Ms. Monti said, coming in the front door with a gigantic chocolate cake, complete with sixteen glowing candles. My family and friends joined in a chorus of Happy Birthday. "Make a wish dear." Ms. Monti said. I didn't know what to wish for. I already had everything I've always wanted right here. Both my worlds together as one. I wished that it would always be like this. Then I blew out the candles.

"This cake looks delicious Ms. Monti." I said.

"It's my latest, Chocolate Lava surprise."
She said with a wink. The cake tasted just as good as
it looked. Ms. Monti had out done herself as usual.

When it came time for presents. Mr. and
Mrs. Ramsey gave me a beautiful set of earrings.
Blair gave a brand-new makeup kit. Grace Hansen
gave me a lovely bracelet. Sheriff Hansen brought
me a baton.

"Really Dad?" Lindsey asked.

"Hey, you never know when you need to beat
some senses into a pushy boy." He responded.

"That I can agree on." Dad added. "I like this
gift."

Ms. Monti brought me my very own Java
Café mug. "Lifetime supply of free coffee refills."
She said.

The Krenshaw's gave me the complete series
of I Love Lucy and The A-Team. "We couldn't
agree on which one to get, we each decided to pay
for our own." Violet said.

"They're both classics, even though mines
better." Logan replied. Violet rolled her eyes at her
husband.

Mom and dad had gotten me a couple of brand new dresses. Merrin, a pair of gorgeous boots. "I'm sorry Ange for yelling at you the other day." She whispered in my ear.

"I'm sorry too. Tonight, when we get home. It'll be just you and me. We need to talk." I whispered back. She smiled and gave me a hug.

Lindsey bought me a beautiful heart necklace. She had one half, and the other half was for me. "Two halves of a whole." She said.

Brett's gift was perhaps the best. It was a beautiful golden locket. "Look inside it." He said.

I opened the clasp. Inside, there was a picture of the three of us. Me, Lindsey and Brett when we were eight. Engraved on the top was Best Friends Forever. "Brett this is beautiful." I said, tears welling up in my eyes.

Brett shrugged his shoulders. "It's nothing."

"These gifts are lovely. I can't thank you all enough." The rest of the night was spent talking and laughing. We were just like any other normal people, enjoying the company of friends.

Chapter 25
The Hunter's Sight

Angelica
(8:00 A.M.- August 2nd)

The next morning, I woke up early to go check on the Hunter's. I didn't like how quiet Alec and Amber have been since my seeing lessons. They had to be up to something. I teleported to the front of the B & B. Approaching their front door, I noticed that the shades on the windows were pulled down tight.

I knocked on the door. There was no response, and all was eerily quiet. I debated on whether I should open the door with magic. What if they didn't want to be disturbed? What if they were doing something bad? If they were, then I had the right to check up on them, I think.

As I was about to use a spell, the front door creaked open to reveal Amber. She looked tired, and there were bags under her eyes, like she hadn't gotten any sleep in a while.

"Hi Angelica." She said with a yawn.

"Amber, you look terrible."

"Well thanks for the compliment." She replied. "What's up?"

"I was wondering where you guys have been the past week?" I asked.

"Right here."

"I can see that. Amber what's wrong? You look like you haven't gotten any sleep in days."

"Ten days' to be precise." She yawned.

"You haven't slept in two weeks?" Was this a weird Hunter ritual?

"Where's Alec than?" I asked.

Amber hesitated for a moment. I could tell she was debating on whether to tell me something. "Come in, I'll show you."

I stepped into the room. Their bedroom area was always gloomy, but now it was extra spooky without any light coming in from the windows. The only light in the room came from Alec's dim red aura. He was laid out on the bed. Upon first glance, he appeared to be sleeping, but once I got closer, I could tell that wasn't the case.

Something was wrong with him. He was paler than usual. His eyes seemed sunken. His hair was matted down by sweat and he was twitching uncontrollably. "What's wrong with him?" I asked, concerned.

"It's called the Hunter's Sight." Amber replied.

"Is that like a Hunter's illness?" I asked.

Amber frowned. "Alec would kill me for telling you this. Oh well, he's going to be blooming mad with me anyway that I showed you him like this."

Amber yawned again. "You see, the reason why Hunter's in the past could find gifted people so quickly, was not only because of our incredible sense of smell."

"Okay, I gather it has something to do with this Sight thing." I said.

"It was another deadly gift that was bestowed upon our race. The Hunter Sight is when we are forced to see visions of the gifted people of the world."

A revelation dawned on me. "That's how you knew where to find us?" I said.

Amber nodded. "Partly, yes."

I shook my head. Yet another secret revealed about these two. "Unbelievable."

"They're a curse." Amber said firmly. "We have no control over the visions. They happen one right after the another. We can't sleep, eat, or do anything else. We're entirely vulnerable until they're finished. They can completely drain us of our energy."

"The same way I am after a vision." I said.

"Same concept." She replied.

"How long do they last?"

"It varies. He's been like this for two weeks."

"How is that possible?"

"There's a lot of magical people in the world." Amber replied.

"Is there any way to help him?" I asked.

"What do you think I've been doing? I'm sharing the visions with him. It doesn't drain him as much that way. Back home it was easier, the

Davenport's were an immense help. We would take turns sharing the visions. Now it's just the two of us."

"How often do they happen?"

"Every couple of months." She replied.

I looked at Alec. He looked so uncomfortable. "Is there anything I can do?"

"Thanks, but I got him. I think he's reaching the end of them anyway. The visions are getting shorter."

"Do you necessarily have to be a Hunter to share the visions? Can another Seer share them?" An idea came to mind.

Amber frowned. "I know what you're asking. He'll kill me."

"C'mon Amber, you're exhausted, I can do it. Just show me how." I asked. I could tell by her reaction that she really wanted to lay down and rest. I was offering her that chance. Of course, I had other reasons for wanting to help. I was curious to see what Alec saw when he had visions. Were they the same as mine?

She still seemed unsure. "You said he was going to be mad at you anyway."

"Fine, but only for a little bit. Then I'll take over again. All you have to do is take his hand. You'll feel the difference immediately. If you need me, I'll be over here. I'm just going to lay down for a minute." She curled up on her bed and was silent.

I looked at Alec. Amber must have been lying next to him, I wasn't quite comfortable with that idea. I looked around for a chair. I grabbed the one from the desk and sat down next to him. I took a deep breath. What was I doing? What was I about to see? Carefully I reached out for his hand.

As soon as I made contact with him, I felt the usual sensation of a vision in my mind. I appeared instantaneously on a wide-open desert plain. At least two dozen Weirlind were traveling on camelback across the Gobi Desert. The scene changed, I was in a cold and leaky wine cellar in Romania. An extremely tall vampire was admiring his bottled wine collection. I wondered if the liquid inside was really wine. Then I was on the lawn of a huge estate in Australia, two gigantic wolves were racing one another. Then I was on a street in Sydney, where a man was talking to a young boy. The man was clearly a werewolf, the boy a mortal. I feared for his life.

The scenes just kept coming. One right after another. I saw visions of Vampires, Werewolves, Shape Shifters, and Weir. Then there were others that I had no idea what they were. I saw men, women, children, and animals. Some were old, some were young. Some lived in small towns, others in big cities. No matter where we seemed to land, I knew the exact location. Boston Harbor, Washington D.C., The Amazon Rainforest, The Arctic Circle, those were just some of the places I saw.

No vision was like the last. Who knew that there were so many gifted people in the world? I even caught a glimpse of Hiram Garratty, he was having a discussion with some Mortal men in suits.

The visions continued. Now I understood what Amber meant about the Hunter's Sight draining you of energy. I was literally exhausted. How long have I been holding Alec's hand? I've lost total track of time.

It didn't deter me, I held tight to his hand and bared the visions with him.

Then, out of nowhere the visions stopped. I was sitting in the chair next to his bed again. Breathing heavily, I glanced at the clock, it read 4:00. Have I really been gone that long?

"Angelica?" Alec said weakly.

"Hey, how are you feeling?" I asked.

"How much did Amber tell you?" He asked.

"About the Hunter's Sight." I replied. "Everything."

Alec closed his eyes.

"Don't be mad at her. She was tired, and I wanted to help." I said.

"She still shouldn't have told you."

I frowned. "The least you could do is be grateful."

He smiled. "Thank you." He said quietly.

"What's that, I couldn't hear you." I replied.

"Don't push it."

I laughed. "Was that so hard to do?"

He laughed back. "Help me up." He tried sitting up in the bed.

"You really need to lie down." I said.

"I've had enough of lying down. I'm starving. I'll rest after I get something to eat." He said.

"What you really need is a shower." I said. Helping him to sit up. Truthfully, he didn't really smell that bad. He was still as alluring as ever. "How do you have any energy left?"

He held up our connected hands. I blushed. I didn't realize that I was still holding his. It just seemed so natural to hold his hand. "Your energy flowing through me helped a great deal during that last stretch." He said.

"My pleasure." I responded. For the longest moment, I just stared into his eyes, lost in his endless sea of red.

"Fine. Shower first, then food." He said. I helped him to the bathroom, then left to wait for him in the bedroom. Amber was snoring peacefully on her bed. She really was exhausted. I put my head back on the chair to rest just a moment.

Alec gently prodded me awake. "What part of bloody starving don't you get?" he asked.

"Sorry. Dozed off." I replied.

Alec and I walked over to the diner. I couldn't believe how much time had passed during the Hunter's sight. It only felt like a couple of minutes. Alec swayed a little as we walked. On those occasions, he would lean on me. "Sorry, don't want to give any of the townsfolk something to talk about."

"It's okay. They'll talk no matter what." I replied.

Once we got to the diner. Alec ate like it was his last meal. He polished off two orders of pancakes, one classic cheeseburger, one pastrami on rye, and two milk shakes.

"Well everybody's staring at us now." I said.

"Sorry. Starving, remember. I'm afraid I made quite the pig of myself." He said with a smile. I laughed at him.

"What?" he asked.

"You have milkshake on your lip." I said giggling.

After paying for the meal, Alec and I walked passed the park and sat down on one of the benches. "You sure you don't want to go home. You're probably exhausted."

"Oh, trust me. I'm going to sleep good tonight." Alec glanced around at the quiet park.

"How do you feel about the Hunter's Sight?" he asked.

"I'm starting to get used to the big revelations with you, Alec." I replied. It was the truth. There always seemed to be something else that would surprise me about him.

He sighed. "What day is it?"

"Sunday, August 2nd." I replied.

"Bloody Hell. I guess I'm a little late with this." He pulled a small wrapped package from his pocket. "Happy Birthday."

I was stunned that he got me a gift. I took the package from him and unwrapped it. Inside the small box was a pendant. "Alec is…"

"I know I know. I wasn't supposed to touch them, but I had good intentions." The pendant was one of the crystals from the lake. When did he take this, I watched him the whole time we were there. "Don't be mad at me."

"Why should I not be mad at you?" I asked.

"Well for one thing, I'm giving it back to you. Secondly, I've put it to beneficial use, it's better than sitting at the bottom of a stream." He replied.

"What did you do?"

"Remember how I said they were vessels, that they could be practically anything."

"Yeah."

"I manipulated a bit of your Weir Wall magic and placed it inside." He said.

"You took magic from the wall again?" I asked incredulously.

He held up his hands in defense. "Only a tiny bit. I caused no harm to its structure."

"Why would you do that?"

"I found a way to keep your magical storms from causing destruction." He replied.

I looked at him closely. "How?"

"It's sort of like the wall I placed around our room. So instead of keeping magic out, it keeps magic in. It'll create a sort of a haven around you, keeping the damage within. I'm afraid it's the best I can do. We might not be able to ever stop the storms completely."

"That's alright." I replied. "I haven't had a vision since your lessons anyway. Best of all my mom has been teaching me magic, I feel so much stronger."

He smiled. "You look it. If I would have told you what I just did a few weeks ago, you would have flown off the handle and destroyed something."

"I know. Alec, I still feel my Darkling every now and then, but she's not trying to control me anymore." Alec thought about that for a moment.

"Angelica are you telling me that you can feel your Darkling half?" he sounded quite stunned.

"She talks to me in my head." I replied. "You're the only one I've told this too."

"How long has she been communicating with you?"

"If I'm being honest, she's always been there. My blackouts were her controlling me. She only started talking to me a couple of weeks ago. I must admit she scared the living daylights out of me. I felt like I was possessed. She would talk to me at nights, saying how she should be the one in control, she was always egging me on to do terrible things." It felt good talking to someone about the voice in my head.

"Now though, she's mostly quiet. When she does talk, it's always to egg me on to do better. To improve myself."

"That's brilliant! You're creating a harmony between your halves." He smiled brightly. He seemed genuinely pleased with my news. "What does she sound like?"

"Like a creepier version of me." He laughed, and I followed suit. "Thanks for this Alec." I said holding up the necklace.

"Would you like me to put it on you?" he asked.

I smiled. "That would be great." I pushed my hair out of the way as he placed the necklace around my neck.

"How do I know if it works?"

"Well I guess you won't until you have a vision." He replied.

"I hope that's not for a long while."

Chapter 26
The Riders of Arcaine

Angelica
(6:00 A.M.- August 3rd)

Unfortunately for me, a Foresight came that very night. Maybe I shouldn't have jinxed myself. Everything was going so smoothly, that I didn't want it to end. I should have known that it wouldn't last forever.

My *Yani* tugged away from my body and went soaring out my bedroom window. Thankfully I've been leaving my bedroom window open at nights, just in case I did have a vision. I don't want to go smashing through it in the dead of night.

I thought that maybe the Foresight was taking place in town again. I immediately thought that Alec and Amber might be up to something, I wanted to think there was some hope for him. He's been on his best behavior lately. Even though, it was because he was stuck in the Hunter Sight for two weeks. He did get me a thoughtful gift, even if he did steal it from me in the first place. I sighed. He could be so infuriating.

The vision wasn't taking me to the town. I went straight through the Weir Wall and soared over the endless fields of trees beyond. Now this was cool! I always wanted to see what lay beyond our borders. We really were in the middle of nowhere. The hills and trees seemed to go on forever.

Just when I thought the tree line would never end, twinkling lights gleamed in the distance. I was approaching a small city. As I got closer, the sounds changed, gone were the chirping crickets and the squawking birds. They were replaced with cars zooming up and down the streets, and car horns echoing off the surrounding buildings. I've never been to a city before, unless you count that fateful back alley vision. I wasn't used to all the noise that came with living in one. How do people sleep here?

I landed outside of a bar called Hooligans. With a name like that, I had the feeling this was going to be an interesting vision. The bar was situated off the beaten path from the rest of the city. It also appeared to be slightly rundown. No respectful customer would ever come to a place like this. I could tell Hooligans was for the unsavory group of customers. There were at least three-dozen motorcycles parked outside. If you just happened to be a Mortal walking by, the motorcycles would appear to be just like any other. For a Witch, I could tell these weren't your average bikes. They were all magicked with some sort of power.

Before I could go investigate them further. The sound of a teleporting Weir grabbed my attention. It was Jacoby Valdorn. I knew this vision was going to be trouble. Panic began to set in. What was he doing in Minnesota? Why was he so close to Crystal Falls? What was he up too? What on Earth is he wearing?

Instead of wearing his usual Wizard robes. He had on a tight black leather jacket and jeans. Were those cowboy boots he had on?

Jacoby made his way to the front door, and I followed him. My parents would kill me if they knew I was walking into a bar. The inside smelled of old beer and cigarettes. Thankfully, I've had the good sense to sleep with slippers on my feet, just in case of a vision. I was getting tired of stepping on things with my bare feet. The floor of Hooligans is so sticky that my slippers squeaked every time I moved. Rock music blasted from a nearby stereo player. There were scattered mismatched tables around the bar. Along with a well-worn out pool table. The place was alive with loud chatter. The owners of the motorcycles were noisily shouting at each other, playing pool, drinking who knows what, and being generally annoying. This placed reeked of Weirling, these bikers are all Wizards.

Jacoby glanced around the room, smirked, then made his way over to the table furthest from the bar. Several of the bikers took notice of the newcomer. Some of them were even sizing him up. Jacoby walked with a purpose. He knew how to handle himself. A pudgy Wizard with a long gray ponytail covered by a bandana, and an equally long beard sat with two other bikers. Why did bikers always wear so much leather? Looking at their logo on the back of their jackets. It read; The Riders of Arcaine.

"Karl Strenthon?" Jacoby asked in his deep voice.

"Who's asking?" The pudgy man responded.

"The Red Dragon." Jacoby replied.

The pudgy Wizard motioned to the other Wizards sitting with him, they immediately left the table. Jacoby took one of their empty seats.
"So, you're the famous Jacoby Valdorn?"

"Here, you will call me Dragon, and nothing else." Jacoby responded firmly.

The Wizard laughed. "Whatever you say Mr. Dragon."

Jacoby sneered back. From reading his thoughts, I could tell that he thought this man to be nothing more than the scum under his boot. "Do we have a deal?"

"You better give me some good incentive, this plan of yours is crazy."

"Really Karl? You're the leader of the Riders of Arcaine. You and your boys fear nothing. Surely going up against a family of Weirlind is a piece of cake for you?"

"You're talking about the Everhardtht's. They're not your average Weirlind Family."

"True." Jacoby agreed. "Maybe this will help." Jacoby placed a small brown sack on the table. Karl opened the bag and let out a whistle. "There's more where that came from, after the job is complete of course."

Karl pulled out a shiny gold coin and held it up to the light. He smiled, placed the coin back in the bag, and placed it in his jacket. "I'm listening."

"Crystal Falls is North of here. You'll take your boys straight to their doorstep. They'll sense you coming immediately and will intercept you. Give them a fight. Maybe lose a few of your boys in the process." Jacoby said.

"Just like that?" Karl asked.

"A few casualties will make it look better. Surely, you're not sentimental, Mr. Strenthon?"

Karl slammed his hands down on the table. "My boys are loyal followers, they'll die for the cause."

"Good, be sure that they do." Jacoby responded. "Don't interact with them for too long, just long enough for them to attack."

"You forget Mr. Dragon, that the Riders are not part of any Covenant."

"That's why you'll be carrying this." Jacoby pulled out a sealed scroll from his pocket and tossed it to Karl. "That's a sealed document from my Covenant to the Everhardtht's, seeking a meeting of peace. You and your boys are my honorary messengers. Of course, they won't know about the scroll until it is too late. We'll be at war." Jacoby sneered. This was Jacoby's plan, send these bikers after my family to start a war. Too bad for him, that I'm going to warn my family.

"You're so sure we'll get to Crystal Falls without any trouble?" Karl asked.

"The pathway's been cleared for you. You should have no trouble getting there."

Karl smiled. "You're telling me you have an inside man?"

Jacoby grinned. "A deep-seated spy. The Everhardtht's will never see it coming." I felt like I was just punched in the gut. A spy, in Crystal Falls? How was that possible? Who was it? Surely by now we would have known if there was a spy in our town? Especially a deep-seated one?

Karl laughed. "Bartender! A round for everyone!" The bikers shouted hoots and hollers. "Riders of Arcaine. We have our course." They shouted their excitement. Jacoby just sat still, his mission accomplished. I stood there in shock as the vision pulled me back towards my bedroom.

*****

Angelica
(9:00 A.M.- August 3rd)

I awoke with a start. I glanced around my room, everything was the same as it was the night before. My shirt was a little damp, but for the most part I felt fine. I didn't have time to celebrate Alec's pendant working. I quickly ran from the room. I had to find Mom and Dad.

They were in the living room with

Merrin. They were talking loudly. I recognized the spiky white hair before she turned. Grandma was back.

"Grandma! Your back." I said.

"Rise and shine sleepy head." Merrin said to me, we were talking to one another again. After my birthday party, we stayed up until the crack of dawn, talking about everything.

"Oh no! I know that look. What did you see?" Grandma asked.

"Jacoby Valdorn. He's sending Wizards after us." I said. Mom exchanged a worried glance with dad.

"Are you sure?" Mom asked.

"Yeah I'm sure." I quickly launched into my story. Nobody interrupted me.

After I finished, grandma looked disgusted. "A spy!" The lamp shattered on the table.

"How is that even possible?" Dad asked.

"We've become too lax. That's why! All our enchantments and spells were removed, that's how those Hunter's got through unscathed." Grandma said through gritted teeth. "I made sure I placed them back up before I left."

"It appears this spy has removed them again." Dad responded.

"Which makes no sense, we would have felt someone leaving the Weir Wall." Mom added.

"What about these bikers? Who are they?" Merrin asked.

"Imbecile Wizards on motorcycles." Grandma shook her head. "Arcaine was a 18th Century Lord who was obsessed with turning Mortals into Wizards. His followers were said to be just as insane as he was."

"And they're coming here?" Mom asked. I could tell she was worried.

"What if we don't confront them?" I asked.

"They'll still cause some sort of mayhem that will alert the townsfolk." Grandma responded. She was still aggravated that she allowed a spy to go under her radar.

"Maybe we could grab that document there carrying somehow." Mom said.

"We would still have to get close enough to them for that." Dad responded.

"Then maybe we should fight!" Merrin said. Everyone got quiet. "Aren't you always telling us Grandma that we should stick up for ourselves. Never to let the government control you. We're Everhardtht's! We shouldn't be ruled by this Valdorn scum." Merrin's stare was intense. In that moment, I saw the Combatant Witch.

"Fighting will give Jacoby exactly what he wants, a war." Mom responded. The room was silent, all of us lost in our own thoughts.

A female voice broke the silence. "Sounds like you're in quite the jam." I turned to see Amber's smiling face. Before I could react, she seized hold of my magic. Mom, dad, and grandma were grabbed too.

Merrin popped from the room before she could be caught. She reappeared just inches from Amber. She lunged at her but was stopped in mid-air.

"Nice try." Alec appeared in the room, he tossed Merrin aside like a rag doll.

"How?" Was all I managed to say. This was impossible. How did he get up here?

"That's not important." He responded with a grin.

"I thought I told you to take care of these two." Grandma said to dad. She was clearly infuriated.

"I was going to tell you about that before we were interrupted." He responded.

"A lot has happened since you left Greta, let me catch you up." Alec said.

Merrin shouted again. She appeared right in front of Alec. She landed a few punches before he grabbed her around the throat and lifted her off the ground. She gasped for air as she dangled from his hand. She was so small compared to him. Alec held her like she was nothing more than a toothpick.

"You're a feisty one today, I like it." Alec said to Merrin.

"You're going to pay." She choked out.

Alec laughed merrily. "Just like your grandmother."

"Please don't hurt her." Dad said.

"Oh, I'm not going to hurt her. I need that fire that she has boiled up in there. However, she does need to be restrained, can't have any more distractions." Ropes appeared out of nowhere and wrapped around Merrin. "You have her Amber?"

"I have her." She responded. Merrin hovered in mid-air. Amber was concentrating hard. She was holding all five of us. I wondered if I could use mind magic to knock her off balanced.

"Oh, and just in case any of you get any ideas." Alec flicked his hand. A knife flew out of nowhere and pressed up against Merrin's throat. "I just love a house with magical artifacts lying around."

"I don't know how you two got up here, but I'm going to kill you." Grandma said firmly.

"You're not going to do anything Greta." Alec responded.

"Why's that?" she asked.

"Because I have the undying support of your family." He responded.

Grandma looked confused. Alec smiled. "Let me show you." Alec waved his hand, and three parchment agreements hovered in the air. One of them was mine, the other was dad and Merrin's, and the third one was mom's. I was stunned again. When did he get her?

"What is this rubbish?" Grandma asked.

"This rubbish as you say, are agreements. Signed by each of your family members, promising me their support whenever I should need it. If I fight, they'll fight with me. That means if I decide that I want to fight you. They'll have no choice, but to join me, or risk breaking the agreement and dying themselves."

My heart clenched in my chest. I knew that agreement would come back to haunt me somehow. I didn't think it would be in such a cruel way though. "Just when I thought there was some good in you." I said. I didn't want to show him how hurt I was by his actions.

"Remember what I said before I started teaching you?" Alec asked.

I thought back. "Never trust you."

"Correct."

"What does he mean by teaching you?" Grandma asked.

"You see, I had to promise some things in return for these agreements to work. I promised not to kill Merrin if Rowan signed. Then I promised not to kill Rowan, if Merrin signed. I promised to teach Angelica about Seeing, because we all know you weren't going to. Then I promised Gwen that I wouldn't teach Angelica anymore."

Dad turned to mom. "When were you going to tell me about this?" he asked.

"Excuse me? When were you going to tell me?" she retorted.

"I didn't want to worry you." He responded.

"So instead you lied to me, all three of you. You didn't think I'd find out what you and Angelica were secretly talking about?"

Dad closed his eyes. "I overheard your conversation. I had had enough. I lured Alec to the park and did something about it." Mom said.

"Oh, by the way. I want a rematch. I wasn't at my full strength that day. You had me at a bit of a disadvantage." Said Alec. "Even though I did win."

"Let me go, and I'll give you what you want." She responded.

Alec smiled. "Tempting, but no."

"I'm sorry for lying dear." Said dad.

"Me to." I added.

"I know, you were just trying to protect me." She responded.

"Well this is all very touching, but you have more pressing issues at hand." Alec said.

Alec folded the agreements back up and placed them in his jacket. "You have visitors coming."

"So what?" Grandma asked.

"You're in quite the jam. Fight and start a war. Don't fight and risk revealing yourselves to the townsfolk."

"You're enjoying yourself?" she said. "You won't be in control forever."

"That may be true, but for now I am. I have a proposition for you. A way to avoid this whole big mess."

"What would that be?" Dad asked.

"What could you offer us?" Grandma added.

"I told you from the get go. I wanted you as allies. Why do you think I went through so much trouble with these agreements?"

"We will never align ourselves with you." Grandma sneered back.

"It's a little late for that, I have them already. I really don't need you." Alec responded.

"You'd have my own family members kill me, how pathetic."

"If it came down to it, but I really don't want to." Alec paced around the room, he was enjoying being in control, just like grandma said. "Whether this war starts today, like Valdorn wants, or whether it's on our terms. You're going to want us as your allies."

"And why's that?" Grandma asked.

"Remember how I said that the Davenport's were scholars?" he asked.

"That's how you know so much." Dad answered.

"Well, I lied." No surprise there, I thought. "They were actually spies." The room went silent. Alec smiled. "Leaders of a spy ring of Half-Blood Hunter's across the globe.

Grandma looked like her worst fears had come true. "No."

"Yes, you can't detect Half-Bloods, but they can detect you. They're all over the place, watching, and waiting for a command to attack."

"Attack what?" I asked.

"Everything." He said simply. "You see the original plan was to attack, with the support of the Half-Bloods. Target every major magical group, kill every major player. We were going to make a statement that would change the course of history." Alec smiled. Just listening to him talk, gave me goose bumps. "Then the Weirling threw a monkey wrench into the plan. They not only took away our family, but they took away our leaders. You should thank them, Crystal Falls was one of the attack sites."

"That's how you know so much. Your spies fed you all the information, and you knew exactly where to place them because of your Hunter's Sight." I spat at him.

He smiled. "It has its advantages." I hated that smug expression on his face. I hated how he still seemed so alluring after all that he's done. I hated him. "So here we are now, between a rock and a hard place."

"What is this proposition you have?" I asked.

"Let me an Amber face these riders. Let us handle them, let us exact some revenge on the Weirling." I didn't expect that response.

"Why would you want to do that?" I asked.

"Weren't you listening Angelica? REVENGE! That is why! Let us show you that were serious allies!" He responded with force.

"There's more to it than that." Mom said. All eyes turned to her.

"What are you talking about Gwen?" Dad asked.

"He has other reasons for wanting to help us." Mom looked directly at Alec. He avoided her gaze. "He doesn't want to admit that under his hard exterior, there's a heart that cares."

"Rubbish, their hearts are black." Grandma responded.

"That's what he wants you to think. In truth, he cares more than he'll admit." Alec still avoided her glare.

"Is this true?" Dad asked.

Alec was breathing heavily. Amber who's been quiet the whole time was staring at her brother. "In the beginning, you were just a mark. A target and nothing more. Than we came here and met you. And…" he shook his head. "We never intended to…" he stopped again.

"What Alec?" I asked.

"We never intended to grow attached, to this place, and to the people who lived here. They made us feel welcome. They made us feel at home. Something that I'd never thought I feel again after losing the Davenport's."

"You're going to tell me that you feel bad for us now?" Greta asked.

"I don't give a bloody hoot about you!" he shouted. Then he stared directly at me. His eyes were so tense that I couldn't look away.

"Yes! I had evil intentions. I wanted to make you stronger. To use you as a weapon, but the more time I spent with you, the more I started to care about what happened to you, to Lindsey, and even Brett, Ms. Monti and the Krenshaw's. The Davenport's told us that our greatest weakness would be emotion. They were right. The way we felt about them, and the way we feel about you guys."

"How do I know this is true?" I asked. "I'm tired of you lying to me."

"He's telling the truth." Mom said.

"We're just supposed to trust that!" Grandma said.

Amber let go of her hold on my magic. Dad and Mom were free too. "A show of good fate." She said finally. "We're not lying."

"Attack them now!" Grandma shouted.

I couldn't move. I was still staring intently at Alec. After all his bravado, he seemed put out. "I think they're telling the truth mother."

"You're bewitched Rowan, snap out of it!"

The knife pressed against Merrin's throat fell to the floor, as did the ropes binding her. She coughed as she was gently lowered back down.

Mom went to attend to her. "I don't trust them, but they have a point." She said.

"What do you mean Merrin?" Mom asked.

"If they confront the riders. We wouldn't be starting a war. Jacoby has no idea that they're here. We have the advantage."

"Merrin's right." Amber replied. Merrin gave her a scathing look. As far as she was concerned, she was never trusting Amber again.

"If you're doing this because you genuinely care about our town. Then prove it to us. Destroy those contracts. Take away our binds. If you do that, then I'll believe you, and I'll agree to side with you no matter what." Dad said.

Alec looked at my dad. I could tell there was an inner battle raging within him. Alec looked at me. For the longest time, we just stared at each other, not at all awkward. He pulled out the agreements. While in the palm of his hand, he set them on fire.

Dad nodded. "Okay then. Let my mother go."

"How can we be sure she won't attack us?" Amber asked.

Dad turned to Grandma. "Mom, they showed us good fate by burning the contracts. Return the favor, please."

I could tell that Grandma wasn't convinced. "Fine." Amber released her hold on her. "I can't believe I'm agreeing to this. I'm watching you though, one wrong move, and you're both finished."

"Fair enough." Dad said. "What's your plan?"

"Alec and I will meet the riders at the wall. We'll take them all out." Amber said.

"What about this spy?" I asked. I was worried that whoever it was could mess things up.

"The spy is the least of our worries. If any of the townsfolk find out, we'll be in deep trouble." Grandma said. "Don't kill them all. Bring me the leader. Maybe will get some information out of him."

"None of you guys should be near the fight." Amber responded.

"Then how will we know what's going on?" Grandma asked.

"With Gwen's permission. I would like to teach Angelica one more lesson." Alec said softly. It was the first thing he said in a while.

Mom nodded her head. "What do you want to show me?" I asked.

"The last thing I can teach you about your gift, Sight Sharing." He said.

Chapter 27
A Spy Revealed

Angelica
(2:00 P.M.- August 3rd)

The plan seemed simple enough. I would be able to see everything that Amber was seeing. Then I could report it back to my family, like a play by play announcer. Alec called this Sight Sharing, where one Seer can look through another's mind.

Amber had allowed me access to her mind. When I reach out for her, I could find her without a problem. They said that they did this all the time, so that they can keep track of one another, and to know what the other was feeling and seeing.

Now I'm going to be able to see and feel everything that Amber did. A part of me was disappointed that I wasn't sharing with Alec. Now more than ever, I really wanted to know what he was feeling.

"We're sure this is going to work?" Grandma asked. She was sitting across from me on the couch. Mom and Merrin were sitting next to me, Dad was pacing around. He had suggested using his animals to watch from the forest, but Alec shot down the idea. The less involvement we had, the better.

"All I have to do is reach out for her." I said. Of course, I've never reached out for someone's mind at this much of a distance before, but how hard could it be. I closed my eyes and focused on Amber. She told me where she was going to be. So that made it a little easier. I remembered the feeling of being inside her mind. Everybody's mind feels different. Amber's felt fun and exhilarating. I searched for her, and sure enough, I felt her presence.

I opened my eyes. Instead of seeing my grandmother sitting on the couch. I saw the endless open road before me. This is so surreal, I thought. Amber must have been feeling cold, because I felt her body shiver. She glanced around. They're was very little sounds. Not even the crickets seemed to be out. All was quiet. I turned to look at Alec standing next to me. His gaze was intense.

"You okay." I asked. Or rather, Amber did. She was concerned that her brother's head wasn't in the game.

"I'm fine." He responded. "I sense them coming."

"Bloody Hell, even if they didn't have magic. I could smell them from miles away." She responded.

"Is she watching?" Alec asked.

"I feel her." Amber responded. *"How does it feel Angelica?"*

"Strange." I responded.

"Well what do you see? Is it working?" Grandma's voice was right next to me.

"I'm in her mind. They're standing at the bridge. They're coming." This was so weird. I was looking through Amber's eyes, yet I was still able to talk to my family and Amber at the same time.

Then I heard approaching motorcycles, from across the open plain. The first rider came into view. It was Karl Strenthon.

"The one up front is the leader. Karl Strenthon." I said to Amber. Coming into view behind him were the rest of the Riders. There appeared to be more than the ones I saw at the bar. They seemed uglier and menacing as well.

Amber tensed up. I felt the excitement pulsing through her mind. She was ready for a fight. Strenthon stopped. Karl held up a hand to the others and they followed obediently. "What is this nonsense?" said the rider closest to Karl. His hair was in a long black Mohawk, piercing's all over his face, and at least a dozen tattoos that I could see. "They're not the Everhardtht's."

"Who are you?" Karl shouted at Alec and Amber.

"You're not welcome here. Turn back now, and you get to live." Alec responded.

There was a resounding cry of laughter from the riders. "Do you know who we are boy?" Karl asked.

"Yeah. The Riders of Arcaine. A bunch of ugly gorillas on motorcycles." Alec replied.

Karl's face paled. The others gave outbursts of contempt. "How dare you insult us. You're nothing more than a child."

"And your nothing more than an overweight bum on a bike." Alec replied.

"Watch your tongue boy! Do you know who we worship?" Mohawk guy shouted.

Alec laughed. "Lord Arcaine, a bloody lunatic."

"Enough of this! Sasha, Boris. Show these two children we mean business." Mohawk guy ordered.

Two members detached themselves from the group, circled around once, then charged straight for Alec and Amber. Both drew their wands and pointed. Amber didn't even flinch. A dense fog rolled in, covering up the field. When it cleared, both Sasha and Boris were gone.

"What was that? Where did they go?" shouted Karl.

"If they kept driving, then they're currently in the Bering Sea right now. If they stopped, then I'm afraid there lost." Alec responded.

"Nothing but parlor tricks." Mohawk man spat. He wasn't scared of Alec and Amber, but Karl was starting to panic. Amber was reading their minds. "Where are the Everhardtht's? Too scared to face us?"

"I thought you were the leader Mr. Strenthon. Is this guy your mouthpiece? He doesn't shut up." Karl paled, shocked that Amber knew his name.

"This is nonsense Karl. Let's get them." Mohawk man said.

"This guy is starting to annoy me." Amber said to Alec.

"Let's make an example of him." Alec replied. They both reached their hands forward. Mohawk man lost control of his bike and it sped towards Alec and Amber. Flung from his seat, he landed in front of Alec. The bike came to a halt in front of Amber. Alec grabbed the biker from the back and forced him to look at Amber.

"What are you doing to me?" he asked. "My magic."

"Watch." Alec whispered.

Amber grabbed hold of the bike handle. Instantly it began to glow, as did Amber. I felt the power from the motorcycle flowing through Amber's body. The magic felt good. Soon the bike was nothing more than a pile of rust. "My bike!" The man shouted.

"If you thought that was good, wait to you feel this." Alec said. Mohawk man began to scream as Alec sucked the magic from his body. Amber watched with delight as the man's skin shriveled up until there was nothing left but dust. Cries of rage were heard from the other bikers.

"Devils!"

"Heathens!"

"Kill them!"

"Death be upon them!"

"Sound the charge!"

"Angelica! Any kind of update would be nice." Grandma said. My body jumped. I almost forgot that she was there.

"They just took out three of their men, it's looking volatile." I responded.

"Spectacular. How many are there?"

"At least three-dozen." I replied. "Maybe more."

"Now the fun begins." Amber said to me. *"Try not to ninny out. Remember, I can feel your thoughts too."*

"Please be careful." She didn't seem to hear me, or she just didn't care. Her mind was focused on one thing. Her prey is there before her. She was on the hunt.

Karl looked mortified. He wanted to retreat, he didn't sign up for this. He would rather deal with

Jacoby's wrath, than face the two monsters before him. His men were hungry though. They wanted revenge. Nobody picks a fight with the Riders of Arcaine and gets away with it. He couldn't show weakness in front of his boys.

"GET THEM!" He shouted. Motorcycles stormed to life. Screams of battle echoed across the open field. Alec and Amber charged. Amber came out at an exhilarating pace. I realized that she's faster than Alec. Two bikers had charged to the front of the pack. As she neared the first biker, the world turned upside down. She somersaulted over the first rider. While still in mid-air, she barreled down on the second one, killing him instantly. Amber turned to see that Alec disposed of the first rider. She grinned with delight. The others were coming. Spells were shot at her as she threw the fallen riders bike into the oncoming mass, taking at least two other members down.

"They're fighting." I said. "It's total chaos."

Amber charged in an out of oncoming motorcycles. She dodged spells left and right, sending magic of her own back at them. She jumped on the nearest rider's back and snapped his neck with ease. Absorbing the bikes magic. She charged at the next rider, kicking him off the bike and blasting him straight in the chest. Alec was no longer in sight, but Amber knew from the cries of the riders, that he was nearby causing destruction. A rider charged at her. Swiping her hand at him, he lost control of the bike and fell off. Quickly getting to his feet, he sent a spell at Amber. She dodged and broke his arm. He gave out of wail of pain before she sucked him dry.

Everything was progressing smoothly. They had the advantage. Then, sirens were heard in the distance, coming from the bridge. "Oh no. That can't be good." I said.

"What is it Angie?" Mom asked.

"The sheriff is coming to investigate."

"What! That's not possible." Grandma said, but I wasn't listening. As Sheriff Hansen's cruiser came over the bridge, a rogue spell hit the front tire, causing a massive explosion. The cruiser flipped over on its side.

"The sheriff's car just crashed." I said. It looked bad. Amber was feeling the same way I did. Please make him be alright.

"Amber!" Alec shouted. She turned to face Alec, who was wrestling with a particularly large Wizard. His aura was brighter than I've ever seen it. "Go help him."

Amber raced towards the overturned cruiser. With ease she jumped on top and ripped the driver's side door open. Coughing, Sheriff Hansen pulled himself out of the car. He was bleeding from his cheek, but he seemed to be alright. "Amber. What in blue blazes." Then he looked up at her. Whatever he saw, he was horrified. Oncoming spells forced Amber to toss him to the ground, getting him out of the line of fire.

A moan came from the car. Lindsey was in the passenger seat. "Lindsey's with him." I cried. "She's hurt."

"Oh dear." Mom said.

"They must have been on their way home from work, when they heard or spotted the commotion." I added.

My best friend was laid out in the seat. Her head had smashed up against the window and she was crushed underneath the dashboard.
The gash on her head looked bad. "Lindsey!" The sheriff shouted.

"Stay down there." Amber ordered. He obeyed her, he was terrified. "Alec! I need help! It's Lindsey."

Quick as a flash, Alec appeared. He ripped the top off the cruiser and removed the destroyed dashboard with ease. He sped around to the other side with Lindsey. "Her leg's badly injured." Now I saw what the sheriff did when he looked at Amber. Alec's red aura radiated pure fear. His eyes were glowing red, and he was covered in blood. He looked like a devil.

"What's going on? What are you two?" Sheriff Hansen asked.

"Amber get them out of here. I'll take care of the rest of them." Spells shot off the car, sending up sparks.

"I'm not leaving you." Alec didn't abandon her when she needed him. She wasn't going to do that to him. Two Wizards appeared close behind them. One of them was Karl Strenthon. Both fired spells at Alec. He knocked the wands from their hands and kicked Strenthon in the chest. The other Wizard was fast, he kept teleporting out of the way. Finally, Alec grabbed hold of him and snapped his neck. He began to drain him.

"Alec?" Lindsey moaned. She was watching him. "Alec. What are you doing?" He wasn't listening. "ALEC STOP!" Alec turned his eyes to Lindsey. They were back to his normal shade of red, his aura dimmed. He looked like he just saw a ghost. Than a spell blasted him off his feet.

"Alec!" Amber shouted. Strenthon fired a shot directly at her. I lost the connection.

*****

Alec
(3:33P.M.- August 3rd)

"ALEC STOP!" Lindsey's voiced pulled me from my rage. I had only halfway drained the Wizard of his powers. I looked at Lindsey. She stopped me. Her voice pulled me from the hunt. That wasn't possible. Nobody can stop a Hunter when they were in that phase. Somehow though, Lindsey's voice brought me back to reality.

Unfortunately, it also distracted me long enough for a spell to hit me in the back. Knocked to the ground, I heard Amber shout before she crashed into the destroyed police cruiser. The fat leader just fired a spell at her. I got up quickly and punched him in the face, knocking him out cold. I rushed over to Amber's side.

"You okay?"

"Yeah." She moaned. "I lost the connection."

"Doesn't matter now. You need to get them out of here." I said, glancing at Lindsey and her dad. Their arrival was not part of the plan. I didn't want them to get hurt, and they've already seen too much.

"Are you sure?" Amber asked.

I glanced at the field. Carnage was everywhere. Bodies laid in broken heaps. Motorcycles were on fire or destroyed. There were only about five Wizards still standing, three of which were wounded. I could take them with ease. "Yeah. I've got the rest. Get them to safety." Amber looked unsure. "I'll be fine Ambs." She nodded and formed the Mist. She went to sheriff Hansen side.

"Wait! What are you doing? Don't touch me!" Before he could protest further, Amber picked him up with ease and sped off into the Mist.

"Dad!" Lindsey shouted. "Where did she take him? What's going on? What are you?" I avoided looking at her. She did something to me before. She stopped me dead in my tracks, she controlled me. That was truly scary.

Amber reappeared just as quickly, picked up Lindsey and sped off again. Lindsey let out a scream as they went.

I was worried for her. They both saw us at our worst phase. Nothing is more terrifying than a Hunter on the hunt. For most people, it's the last thing they ever see. I took a deep breath. I'll handle them later. Time to finish off the Riders of Arcaine.

*****

Angelica
(3:33 P.M.- August 3rd)

"What do you mean you lost the connection?" Grandma asked.

"Amber got hit with a spell. Alec's down too." I replied.

It all happened so fast. The sheriff's car exploding, and Lindsey being hurt. It was just too much to process. My heart was beating on overdrive. It felt like it was coming out of my chest.

"Get the connection back." Grandma said.

I closed my eyes and tried to reach out for Amber, but I couldn't feel her. "I can't find her anymore."

"Does that mean she's…dead?" Merrin asked.

"That's it! I'm going down there." Dad said.

As if on cue, the front door slammed open, and Amber carried in sheriff Hansen. She deposited him on the floor and sped back out the door.

"Oh crud!" Dad mumbled. Kyle Hansen just stared at us. He looked completely bewildered.

Amber returned. This time with Lindsey in her arms. She laid her down on the sofa and sped off once more. "Lindsey." I ran over to my friend.

"Angelica." She cried. "What's going on? What are they? What…"

"I know." I said. "Just relax and let me help you first. Your leg looks really bad."

She winced in pain as I felt her leg. "Is it broken?" Her dad asked.

Lindsey looked at me. Confusion filled her eyes. "Angelica…"

"Just relax Lindsey dear." Mom said soothingly. She stroked her cheek. "All will be explained in due time." Lindsey relaxed, though she was still confused about what was going on.

"We should knock them out." Merrin said.

"Whoa! You're not touching us with your sorcery." Kyle Hansen replied.

"We will Merrin, but not yet. Mr. Hansen here has some explaining to do." Grandma stared at the sheriff. He avoided her gaze. He didn't seem confused like Lindsey. He's scared, but he understood what was going on. Something's fishy here. He just mentioned sorcery.

Minutes later, Alec and Amber arrived back in the room. They were both covered in blood and dirt, but they didn't appear to be hurt. "It is done." Alec threw the large body of Karl Strenthon to the floor. He landed with a thud.

I breathed a sigh of relief. It's over, the danger is gone.

"There's a huge mess down there." Amber said.

"Gwen and I will handle the clean-up." Dad said. He turned to Grandma. "Mother can you handle things here?" A silent understanding past between them. It was too fast for me to catch.

"Oh, I'll handle them alright." Grandma said.

"I'll come with you guys." Amber said.

"You should rest dear." Mom said.

"My adrenaline is too high. Besides, it's the least I can do after making it." Amber replied.

Mom and dad teleported from the room, and Amber sped off out the door. Grandma seemed to be in a daze. She stared at Karl on the floor. Then she stared at Kyle and Lindsey Hansen. She didn't know which one to handle first. Finally, she settled on Karl.

She revived the biker from his sleep. After realizing where he was, he swore under his breath. "Hands off me Witch." He cried. "Now you show yourself, after your heathen attack dogs destroyed my men."

She punched him in the face. "Shut up. You'll speak when spoken too." Grandma replied. She hauled him off the floor and threw him on the sofa. "Jacoby Valdorn sent you here to attack my family. I guess he's going to be sorely disappointed that you failed." Karl was surprised that Grandma knew who sent him. "Who's his spy?"

Karl laughed. "Haven't a clue." He spat.

"Wrong answer." She touched his shoulder. Karl let out an ear-splitting yell. "Who's the spy?" She asked again.

"I said I don't know, Witch." Karl screamed again.

"I can do this all day. WHO?" Grandma shouted.

"I DON'T KNOW!" Karl cried. Grandma shocked him again for good measure, and he crumpled in the chair.

"What did she do to him?" Lindsey asked me. "He called her a Witch." Then she looked at me. "Angelica. Are you a…" I didn't need to respond, she saw the answer in my eyes.

Grandma turned to face us. "Move away from her Angelica." She said.

"Wait. Why?" I didn't understand why she looked as mad as she did. Lindsey did nothing wrong.

"I said step aside!" I obeyed her. Grandma never spoke like that to me unless there was danger. She approached Lindsey. Sheriff Hansen stepped in front of her, his gun drawn.

"Don't move." He said. "You stay away from my daughter." His hands shook as he pointed the gun. "I know what you are, all of you. I won't let you go anywhere near my daughter."

"Sheriff Hansen…" I tried to talk to him. Something was not right.

"I said stay back." He pointed the gun at me. I froze dead in my tracks, Lindsey looked terrified. She looked at her father, to me, to Alec, and then at my Grandmother. She had no idea what to think.

"You're going to allow us to leave." Sheriff Hansen said.

"I don't think so. You seem to know what's happening here. I want to know how?" Grandma asked. He pointed the gun back at her. "Who are you? How were you able to get through the wall?" she asked.

"What wall?" he asked. He's playing dumb, he knew exactly what she was talking about.

"It was pretty convenient of you showing up like you did. Makes me wonder. Are you the spy?" Grandma asked.

"What are you talking about?" Kyle asked. I didn't want to believe that my best friends dad was a spy, but it wasn't looking good. He's acting guilty

"Grandma, relax." Merrin said.

"Yeah, let's just calm down." I added.

This situation wasn't going to get resolved with tempers flying.

"No! You both don't understand. He went through the Weir Wall. They both should be dead. The only reason I could think of for that not being the case, is that they're not who they say they are."

I had to calm this situation down fast, for Lindsey's sake. "Grandma, just relax."

"You're out of your mind lady." Kyle said. "I have no idea what you're talking about."

"Liar!" She reached out to him. He fired. Merrin, Lindsey, and I screamed.

Grandma stopped the bullet mid-flight. It hovered in the air in front of her for a moment then fell to the floor. "I'm going to ask one more time. Are you the spy?"

Before sheriff Hansen could answer. A small red rock landed at my feet. "Look out!" Alec knocked me down to the floor.

BANG! Time seemed to slow down. A horrible ringing sound screeched in my ear. I couldn't see a thing. The room was blanketed in a layer of smoke and dust. As it began to clear, I noticed Alec laid out, not too far from me. He wasn't moving.

Where did that *Zeft* come from? I tried getting to my feet. I was so dizzy that I almost fell back down. Holding on to the couch for support, I grabbed my ears. The ringing was still painfully loud. The room was a disaster. Red *Zeft's* were like little EMP'S.

Merrin was out cold. The blast must have smashed her up against the far wall. Sheriff Hansen had dragged Lindsey away from the couch. They were both awake. Grandma was trying to shake the cobwebs from her head.

As the ringing slowly receded. I heard a voice behind me. A cold sneer, that I knew all too well. I turned to find none other than Kelly Jackson smiling at me. What was going on here today? How did she get up here?

"What…" I stuttered badly.

"Don't stutter Angelica. It's horribly unattractive." She smiled. She was wearing a tight black outfit with gigantic combat boots. She looked ready for war.

"How did you get up here?" Then I

noticed the numerous *Zeft's* attached to her belt. No way! It couldn't be! Reality came crashing down around me again. "You're the spy?"

"Guilty as charged." She smiled.

Anger surged through my body. I didn't care how, or why. Kelly had tormented me forever. At least now I could hurt her without worrying about being discovered. Before I could launch an attack. I froze dead to the spot. At first, I thought it was Alec, but he was still knocked out. Kelly held up an orange *Zeft*.

"I've gotten really good at using these. So, don't try anything." She said happily.

"It was you? Your Jacoby's spy." I asked.

"Daddy's little girl."

How many times was I going to be completely floored today? "You're Jacoby's daughter? Your Mortal though." She had no magical qualities besides the twenty or so *Zeft's* she was wearing.

Kelly's smiled darkened. "Not all of us our born with a pedigree like yours. What a disappointment you must think I am. A Mortal being born from one of the most powerful Wizards of all time."

"Powerful Wizard of all time. What a farce." Grandma launched a spell at her. Kelly quickly used a *Zeft* to put up a shield. Then quickly changed to another, shocking Grandma to her knees. She did it all with one hand, while still holding me down with the other.

"I told you I was good with these. Just because I don't have magic of my own, doesn't mean I still can't use it." She said angrily. "Now stay down! Or the next one of these is placed on Angelica." She held up another red *Zeft*. "Don't try any of that mind magic stuff either. I'm shielded from all attacks." She held up a turquoise stone, she came prepared. Kelly approached me and placed the orange stone in my shirt pocket.

"There, that should hold you down."

"You can break out of this Angelica. You can break through the shield she has. Concentrate! Kill her!" Darkling me cried. It was a tempting thought. I shook my head.

"How long?" I asked. For as far back as I could remember, Kelly had spent her entire life in Crystal Falls. I knew her since pre-school.

Kelly smiled. "Technically I've only been here since I was thirteen. However, I use a rare *Zeft* that manipulates a person's mind. You only think that you've known me your whole lives." She smiled. "I just love *Zeft's*, there so hard to track."

"How did you get to Crystal Falls?" Grandma asked.

"Oooh. That's a good story, but I'm afraid we don't have the time for it. You see, Daddy's waiting for a report back. That buffoon over there." She motioned to Karl, who was still out cold? "Messed everything up. Now I must eliminate him and clean up the mess he left. Speaking of messes. Those pajamas are horribly in poor taste Angelica." I hadn't realized that I was still in nightclothes. With everything going on, I'd forgotten to change. Leave it to Kelly to point out a fashion flaw while giving a villain speech.

"I bet being a spy was all you were good for." Kelly looked at Grandma. "I know Jacoby. I bet he was really disappointed with you?" Grandma asked.

Kelly's face darkened. I recalled the day in the park, when I couldn't read her mind. Something happened to her, that fractured her memories. I wondered if it was because of Jacoby.

Kelly shocked Grandma again. "Do you know what I have sacrificed for my father? All that I've done for him! I successfully infiltrated your impenetrable fortress! I successfully established myself in the community! I removed all the spells protecting this town! Do you know how long it took, a year and a half. All the pain I suffered to remove those spells, then when I finally get everything complete. He shows up!" Kelly pointed to Alec, who was finally on his feet.

Kelly stared daggers at Alec. "You show up and everything changes. Greta realizes the spells had been removed, and she places them back up again. I was back at square one!" Kelly was frazzled that day in the park. Now I knew why. The "he" she was referring to, was Jacoby, her father.

"Sorry, I didn't do it intentionally if it makes any difference." Alec replied. He was still disoriented, because by now he would have made a play for her *Zeft's*. When he pushed me out of the way, he took the brunt of the blast. He got it the worst.

"You're so ridiculously handsome. Everybody's always fretting over you. I knew you were a gifted person. I just couldn't figure it out. Then I saw that show you put on down there." Kelly licked her lips. "A Hunter. Daddy's going to be so happy that I found you." Kelly smiled. "You did me a favor by knocking your girlfriend out of the way. You worry me the most."

"This girl needs to die!"

"You do realize Angelica is a Darkling?" Grandma asked.

"Yeah, Daddy told me. I have to say, I'm not impressed."

"Do it Angelica!" I needed to break this hold. If I concentrated enough, I could break free. I didn't want to kill Kelly, maybe I could just knock her out.

"I'm going to shake this off eventually. When I do, you're going to be in a world of trouble." Alec said.

"Really? Well we can't have that." Kelly said. "Come in Auntie." In walked Kelly's aunt. I should have guessed she was involved in this as well.

The old woman stared around the room. I didn't like that look in her eyes. They looked hungry.

"You see auntie here, is not really related to me. She's a companion, that daddy gave me. She's a Weirboar." The old woman huffed like a boar would. I didn't know a lot about Weir Creatures, but I knew enough to know we were in trouble. "You know what I love about Weir Creatures Alec?"

"What?" he replied.

"While in Mortal form, you can't detect them or control their magic, yet they can still retain the properties of the animal they are." The woman huffed again. She circled Alec like prey.
"Take care of him." The woman charged.

"Bloody Hell." He mumbled as they both went crashing through the front window.

Kelly laughed. "That should keep him occupied for a while." She was so giddy that I thought she would start dancing. "I'm having so much fun that I don't want to leave yet. Oh well, I'm afraid that all good things must come to an end."

"You're sick." Kelly looked at Lindsey. She was still huddled in the corner with her father. He still had his gun drawn.

"Lindsey! I forgot you were here." Kelly smiled at her. "How are you feeling? Oh Wait! Don't tell me. You're probably feeling scared? Betrayed maybe?"

"I don't even know if this is real right now, or if it's some sick dream I'm having, but I always knew you were disturbed." She replied.

"You're pathetic." Kelly laughed. "The only good that you ever served was finding a way to this

house for me. Thanks for being my test dummy."
Kelly did purposely send Lindsey into the forest. It
wasn't her being mean like I thought. It was to
figure out how to get up to my home.

"I've had enough!" I shouted. I was done
being bullied by this girl. I broke the hold that Kelly
had on me and attacked her with her own freezing
Zeft. Kelly froze stiff. She wasn't expecting me to
break free. Using a spell hand like mom taught me,
I prepared to deliver a killing blow. I saw the fear in
her eyes as I prepared to strike. Wait! What was I
doing?

"Do it Angelica. She has to die." No. This
wasn't me. I lowered my hand, and Kelly broke free,
shocking me so hard that I smashed backwards into
the wall. Grandma saw an opportunity and attacked.
She kicked her straight in the chest. Then fired off
curses at her. Kelly blocked and pivoted. Sending
her own shocks back at her. Their exchange was fast
and furious. I couldn't believe how fast Kelly was
blocking Grandma's attack.

From behind, Grandma was hit by a spell.
Karl Strenthon had awoken and pulled a hidden
wand from his shoe. Grandma turned her attention
to him. The two exchanged a volley of spells. I got
up and attacked Kelly again. This time as myself. I
put all my strength behind my spell. Kelly put up
her shield to block.

"Not strong enough! Let me do it!"

I held the spell for as long as I could, but my energy was draining. Kelly sidestepped my weakening spell and shocked me for the second time. I flipped over and landed on my face. My body stung with pain so bad that I couldn't move. *"You're going to have to do better than that."* Darkling me shouted.

"Leave me alone." I moaned.

"Talking to yourself Angelica? Weirdo?" She shocked me again. I screamed loudly. It felt like my insides were being set on fire.

"Some Darkling." Kelly said. I prepared for another blow.

Just then, Alec came careening through the wall, throwing Kelly off balance. He was a mess, cuts and bruises all over his face. His clothes were torn and mangled. The Weirboar charged in after him. They locked up in a wrestling grapple. Grandma and Karl's duel had carried over into the kitchen. I heard breaking glass. This was chaos!

"We need to get out of here?" Sheriff Hansen tried getting Lindsey to her feet.

"Going somewhere? You wouldn't want to miss all the fun." Kelly sneered.

Kyle Hansen drew his gun and fired. Kelly didn't react in time. The bullet grazed her shoulder. Furious, Kelly launched him into the curio cabinet. Which collapsed on top of him. "Dad!" Lindsey shouted.

"This is a brand-new outfit!" Kelly fingered her shoulder, concerned more about the torn fabric than the bullet graze. "I'm going to make him pay for that." Lindsey was dragging herself to her dad. I thought she was going for him, but she was reaching for his gun.

"Lindsey No!" I shouted.

My shout drew Kelly's attention to her. "Enough of this nonsense." She beat her to the gun and grabbed her by the hair. She pulled out a purple *Zeft*. She was going to teleport! Ignoring the pain coursing through my body. I leapt at Kelly and missed. Kelly and Lindsey were gone!

My world stopped. Darkling me was screaming inside my head. Blaming me for being weak. She was right.

Everything else passed by in a blur. Sheriff Hansen eventually got back to his feet and unloaded his gun into the Weirboar, causing her to transform and nearly gore him to death. Now in her magical state, Alec could latch hold of her and drain her magic. The Weirboar squealed and turned to dust, just as Karl Strenthon was tossed from the kitchen.

Everything stood still. It was quiet except for Darkling me who was calling me several unsavory names, all of which I deserved. Alec looked exhausted. Grandma seemed angrier than before. "Where's Lindsey?" Kyle asked, holding his leg. It was bleeding badly from the Weirboar tusk.

I was too stunned to speak. My best friend was gone. "Where did she take her?" he cried again.

Mom and Dad teleported into the room. They looked beside themselves. "What happened? We couldn't get through to the house?" Dad asked.

Amber sped in after them. "A *Zeft* was blocking our path." She looked around at the room. "Bloody Hell." She noticed Sheriff Hansen's leg and went to help him. He was too stunned and tired to protest.

Mom ran to Merrin, who was still out cold. "Kelly Jackson's the spy. Her, and her Weirboar aunt, got the drop on us." Grandma responded.

"Where's my daughter?" Kyle Hansen asked again. He was beside himself now. He winced as Amber laid a hand on his wound. It healed instantly.

"Wasn't she with you guys?" Dad asked.

"Kelly escaped. She took Lindsey with her." I cried. "I should have stopped her." Tears stung my eyes. I had the chance to stop her and I didn't. I should have let Darkling me kill her. Lindsey would still be here then. "I was weak! Throughout the whole fight I could have done so much more."

"I'm sure you did your best Angie." Mom said.

"I'm a Darkling! I should have easily defeated her!" I cried. "Lindsey was innocent in all of this. She's gone because of me. I failed my best friend." I've never hurt as bad as I did now. I couldn't stop crying.

"What will she do to her?" Kyle asked.

"Probably kill her." Grandma responded. I didn't want to imagine what Kelly would do to her.

The room was silent except for my sobs. Karl moaned. Grandma grabbed him and pushed him up against the wall. "You're going to give me some answers." She demanded.

"He doesn't know anything, I read his mind before." I said.

"Then he's useless." Grandma snarled. With one swift motion, she slashed his chest. Karl coughed out blood. Then crumpled to the floor.

"Not completely." Alec approached Karl's now lifeless body. Out of his jacket flew the sealed document. "This passed from Valdorn's hand to his." Alec smelled the document. "I can trace this document back to its source. I'm willing to bet that's where we'll find Jacoby, and wherever he is, Kelly is."

"And Lindsey." I added. A shimmer of hope flared inside me.

"I'll find her and bring her back. I promise." Alec said.

"I'll go with you Alec." Amber said.

"No, I need you to stay here. Once Jacoby finds out his plan failed, he'll send more attackers. You need to protect them Amber." He replied.

"At least take one of us with you." Dad responded.

"I'm faster on my own. I'll be fine." He replied. "Besides, there's too much to do here. He's obviously not telling us something." He said looking at the sheriff.

"That's for sure." Grandma said.

"I'm coming with you." Dad responded. "It's not a request."

"Rowan…" Mom looked like she was about to protest.

"I'll be fine. You and mother can handle anything that happens here. Besides, if Alec is as fast as he says he is, then we will be back before you know it."

Grandma looked at him and nodded. She saw the determined look in his eyes. There was no talking him out of going. "Be careful, of that one especially." She said, looking at Alec.

"If you're sure you want to come, then who am I to stop you." Alec said. He looked at me. His expression grim. Then, he darted over to my father's side. "Hold on." He said with a smile on his face. Before anybody could say another word. They vanished from the room.

Coming Soon

The Guild Chronicles
Witches & Warlocks
A Coven of Gypsies

Red Knight

Lindsey
(Date-??? Time-???)

They left me alone, with nothing to drink and nothing to eat. My hands were shackled above my head, and I ached from head to foot. It was cold and damp. It caused my already mangled leg to hurt ten times worse. I could tell that I was in some sort of dungeon. There were cells along every wall, and the place also gave off the vibe of being underground. That notion frightened me. I was petrified of being underground.

What day was it? How long have I been here? I've lost all track of time. I replayed events over in my head. The shiny lights and noises that caused my dad to go investigate beyond the bridge. The car flipping on its side, causing the damage to my leg. The cold malice in Alec's eyes as he killed a man. The revelation that my best friend and her entire family were Witches. The battle in the living room. Reaching for my dad's gun, then having the wind knocked out of me as Kelly and I disappeared.

Everything was a blur. I couldn't believe this really happening? I must be dreaming. I kept telling myself that I would open my eyes, and this would all be one horrible nightmare. I knew that wasn't the case though.

The door to the dungeon creaked open. The small man with the green robes was back. Kelly Jackson was with him this time. A third man, in pure black robes was behind her, he had long black hair and a beard.

The small man had been peppering me with questions for who knows how long. He was more annoying than scary. Kelly made my blood boil. I promised myself that I would get my hands on her if I ever got out of here. The third man frightened me. I've never seen him before, but he screamed evil.

"Has she said anything useful?" The man had an accent like Alec's.

"Not much Sir. Most of what she did say, we already knew." The small man replied in his Irish brogue.

"Then she's of no use." The tall man replied.

"She may be a bargaining chip daddy." Kelly said. This must be Kelly's father. The evil dude everyone was talking about.

"If she was of any value, the Everhardtht's would have responded by now." He replied.

Why hasn't anybody come for me, I thought. Dad? Angelica? Alec? Wasn't I worth something?

"She's a nobody." The man said finally.

"What should I do with her Jacoby?" The small man asked.

Jacoby turned his cold eyes on me. I saw death in his eyes. "Kill her."

www.ingramcontent.com/pod-product-compliance
Lightning Source LLC
Chambersburg PA
CBHW061022030726
47504CB00002B/225